THE DRAGON KINGS

BOXSET TWO (BOOKS 6-10)

KIMBERLY LOTH

Copyright © 2021 by Kimberly Loth

All rights reserved. No part of this book may be reproduced, transmitted, downloaded, distributed, stored in or introduced in any information storage and retrieval system, in any form or by any means, whether electronic or mechanical without express permission of the author, except by a reviewer who may quote brief passages for review purposes.

This is a work of fiction. The characters, incidents, and dialogues, in this book are of the author's imagination and are not to be construed as real. Any resemblance to actual events or persons, living or dead is completely coincidental.

PROLOGUE

The fog rolled in on the streets of Belfast. Donahue walked quickly, looking over his shoulder at the slightest sound. It was eerily quiet, and the air smelled wet. It was only a matter of time before he faced certain death. He just hoped it wouldn't be tonight.

He'd made a mistake and talked in a public place, an old pub where the American was waiting. He pulled his dark brown coat around him. Mist coated his hands and face. He wished, once again, he could simply take his dragon form so he wouldn't be cold.

He snorted. Some dragon. He had not stretched his wings in over a thousand years. None of the dragons he knew had. They'd all been cursed.

Donahue had taken a risky gamble, but he couldn't help it. He'd seen on the news that the American dragons had liberated themselves. Obsidian, their king, had defeated the white witch. And now they lived openly among the humans.

For twenty years, he'd known this. For twenty years, he'd wanted to hop on a plane, find the American king, and beg Obsidian to liberate him as well. But he was a coward and feared the unknown consequences, and so he didn't.

But Donahue couldn't live that way anymore. Couldn't hide in the little hovel of a house, terrified of his own shadow. He'd been part of the rebellion movement, but just before the American liberation, he had retired because it was too taxing. When the American came, asking questions about where all the European dragons went, Donahue decided to take a chance.

And now, he would pay the price.

He slipped down the alley that led to his home, two-story buildings on both sides. Clouds covered the moon, and the alley was dark with no streetlamps. A man stepped out in front of him.

Dragon's Teeth!

Donahue jumped back, holding his heart. It was a habit he'd picked up from his human friends.

The man pushed Donahue against the wall, the wet stone hard against his back.

"We've heard you've been talking about the queen," the man growled in his face.

"Says who?" Donahue studied the man, hoping to find some clue as to who he was. Donahue should be scared. He knew the queen would send people after him, but he found he was strangely calm.

"Does it matter?" The man's breath was thick with garlic. His eyes were a steely green and his short beard white.

Recognition dawned, and Donahue nearly pissed his pants. He'd seen this man once before. This was one of the twelve, the Beheader. Donahue didn't realize he'd warranted such a personal response. Normally, the queen sent one of her many minions, her army of dragons who watched over everybody, the ones who made sure they lived and died under her command. The twelve, though, they were closest to her, and the Beheader was known to be fierce and deadly.

"You spoke evil of the queen," said the Beheader.

Donahue was going to die. He knew that now.

"I did no such thing," he replied, trying to keep his voice from trembling.

The Beheader squeezed Donahue's neck. "You spoke evil of the queen, and you shall die."

"Where's your proof?" Donahue spluttered. This was a lost cause, but he couldn't help but try to save himself.

"Proof? Who needs proof?" The beheader gave Donahue a nasty grin. "But, I like a chase...so run."

Donahue raced off. He had not run in years. He stumbled along the cobblestone streets, past the thatched roof houses, waiting for a chase that never came. No footsteps followed him. In fact, the street was deathly quiet save for his fumbling thumps. He finally made it to his front door, panting and out of breath, wondering how he had been so lucky.

Though, it was only a matter of time. They knew where he lived. He was a dead man, but perhaps he bought himself a few days to get his affairs in order.

He could see it now. The Beheader would come to his door, whip out two gleaming, silver swords, and take his head off before he could even register what had happened.

He grappled for his key, unlocked the door, and lurched over the threshold. The lights were on, and fire blazed in the hearth. Sitting in a chair at the well-worn kitchen table was the last person Donahue wanted to see. She was his daughter, his beautiful Lilly, whom he hadn't seen in years. The one he had distanced himself from so she would stay safe. She never knew of the rebellion, and she didn't know of his treachery. She obeyed the queen's every command.

And yet, there she sat at his table waiting for him even though he told her he never wanted to see her again. It took him a second to register that both her hands and feet were bound.

The Beheader stepped out of the shadows and grinned at the terror on the old man's face. Without warning, he whipped out his two signature swords.

"Daddy, help," Lilly cried. Tears from her cheeks streamed into pools on the table. Donahue couldn't believe the Beheader brought her here to witness his death. She'd be scarred forever.

"Please," Donahue begged. "Just take me away. Don't do this in front of her." He couldn't even look at her.

The Beheader cackled, his bald head gleaming in the harsh light. "In front of her?" His wicked smile stretched farther across his face. Donahue's heart stopped beating in his chest. "She's my target." The Beheader spun around, his two swords slicing through the humid air, and took off the head of Donahue's beautiful girl.

"No," Donahue cried and fell to his knees.

The beheader crouched down and gripped Donahue's chin. "You will live for two weeks," said the Beheader.

Donahue's breathing came out in rasps as he focused on his daughter's vacant green eyes. The image of her head falling to the ground burned in his memory.

"With the time you have left, warn your people to never betray the queen again."

CHAPTER 1

*I*sa's sword sunk deep into the emerald green flesh, and the cloying smell of blood assaulted her. No matter how many times she'd done this, she'd never get used to the smell.

Blood pooled around the sword, and the great beast swung its snout around and knocked her off her feet. *Dammit.* She'd missed the heart, and now the sword was stuck in its flank.

Again.

She should be better at this by now.

She stood, shaking out her arms. She was blinded for a second from the sunlight streaming through the windows four stories above her in the circular room. The room was cold, but since she was chasing a dragon, she was roasting, the heat pouring off him like a bonfire.

The dragon roared, his bright green flames nearly singeing her hair. That was close. Sweat formed on her forehead, and she ran behind the dragon so he couldn't see her.

She had to get her sword back or she didn't stand a chance. The dragon moved his head, his jaws snapping at the weapon. She focused on the sword as she ran, her slippered feet soft on the hard stone. She hid behind his tail, waiting for him to swing his snout around.

Instead, he swept his tail back, knocking her off her feet. Dragon's Teeth! She hit the floor hard, her head cracking on the stone. She blinked the stars out of her eyes and jumped back up, but the dragon seemed to have forgotten about her altogether. The tail must've been an accident.

He was focused solely on the sword in his flank, trying desperately to reach and pull it out. He snapped at it again and missed. If he wasn't careful, he would bite himself and do her job for her. She watched for a moment as he struggled.

Hands really were beautiful things.

He roared, letting loose flames, and flung his head back up. She leapt over his tail and gripped the hilt of the sword. It was slippery with blood, but she managed to hold tight and tear it out.

The dragon bellowed in pain. While it was distracted, she stabbed three inches to the right, and the dragon collapsed. Bingo. She'd hit the heart.

Finally.

The dragon shriveled, turning into a fair-skinned, dark-haired young man with blood seeping from the two stab wounds on his chest. She waited until the transformation was complete and then touched his forehead, reviving him. The wounds healed right up, but the blood on his shirt remained.

Jude blinked open his forest-green eyes and grinned. "I almost got you."

"But you didn't." Isa held out her hand. He took it, and she hoisted him up. The training room in the castle felt larger without dragons. Sound echoed around the walls, and a chill fell on her.

He rubbed at his chest. "It hurts when you miss."

"Maybe you shouldn't have moved so much," she teased.

He took the sword from her, concern etched on his beautiful features. "I have to keep things exciting. If anything ever happened to us, you'd have to protect yourself."

Isa rolled her eyes. She'd heard it so many times. She'd never even been away from the castle grounds. She knew the stakes. She was queen, and the rebels wanted her dead.

So she had to stay inside. Thank the gods she could revive dragons or she would never be able to train properly for the day the rebels came for her.

Because someday, they would.

It was imperative she stayed alive. Her grandmother taught her that before she died. She wished she'd be able to fly, and then she'd be able to fight better, but she wasn't allowed to take her dragon form. Ever.

Isa held the magic within her that protected her dragons from the prying eyes of humans. In America, dragons flew openly in the skies, always in fear for their lives from the humans hunting them.

But in Europe, dragons were invisible, and so they were protected.

By her.

The humans in Europe believed the dragons had all perished or gone over to the new world thousands of years ago. They had been hunted nearly to extinction, and so Isa's great-great-great-grandmother created a spell that would allow them to live openly but unseen. She saved the dragons, and the daughters after her continued to protect them.

But that spell had dire consequences for the queen.

Isa was a dragon, but she'd never see her wings because she was forced to live her days as a human. Even as a child, she was not allowed to take her natural form.

She left Jude in the arena and skipped up the stairs to her tower. It was her private place, the only room in the castle that had a window she could open. Her guardians weren't allowed in there—no one was except her. Her grandmother had taken her up here a few days before she died. It was where the magic lived. Well, really, it lived inside Isa, but this was where her grandmother passed the spell on to her.

She'd created herself a sanctuary up here with squashy chairs and couches. Blankets covered every surface, but the fireplace was never lit. There was no point because she always opened the window. Isa grabbed her thick fur cloak from the closet and made sure it was tied up tight before she flung open the shutters and let the icy air in.

The snow-covered mountains of the island in the Arctic Ocean surrounded her, and tips of evergreens dotted the mountainside. Below her was a snowy valley, and trees went on for miles. The view never changed, and she still loved it. She'd come up here as often as she could and stand at the window until her cheeks burned with the cold.

Her favorite days were when soft snow fell, but today, the sun shone brightly. A flicker of green caught her eye. It was far enough away that she knew she'd be okay for at least another ten minutes. She often watched her guards fly in, and most of the time, it was cloudy and snowy, but they were glorious in the sunlight. They didn't like it when she watched because she'd be in danger if it wasn't one of them.

She wasn't sure who was flying toward her at the moment. At any given time, four of her guards were out in the kingdom, listening for news of assassination plans from the rebels or gathering things she needed.

They were her ears. She made her decisions based on their information. She was queen, and she ruled well and fairly even though she was young, only seventeen. Her grandmother taught her how to reign. Isa spent most of her days discussing plans for the kingdom. She longed to go out and talk to her dragons, face-to-face, but she understood that it was impossible.

Her people were only safe if she remained captive behind the castle walls.

CHAPTER 2

Sid grabbed the two cups of coffee from Damon, Ella's son, and set them down on the counter at the Purple Dragon. Ella still owned the coffee shop, but she basically retired a few years ago. Her husband, Freddie, loved to travel, and she wanted to go with him. She also didn't need the money anymore since Freddie's software on dragon tracking had made them multi-millionaires. But she still made Damon work, something he complained about frequently.

"You going to watch Liam fight tonight?" Damon asked, excitement pouring off of him. He looked exactly like his mother with dark eyes and hair. He didn't have her penchant for dying it a thousand different colors though.

Sid flinched. He hated the way they talked about it. It wasn't really fighting, but his son had taken up with the dragon warriors and was often found fighting in the training fields.

"I don't know. Maybe. You?" Sid never went.

Damon gave a smile that reminded Sid of Ella. "I never miss one."

"Well, make sure he doesn't get hurt." He knew Liam wouldn't really get hurt. He never did. Well, not seriously anyway.

Damon chuckled. "You know I can't do that. It's a good thing you and Aspen can heal him."

Damon wasn't kidding. After every fight, Liam came home with cuts and bruises, but he loved it, so Sid didn't stop him. He'd just turned eighteen, and Sid wasn't sure he could stop his son even if he wanted to.

Well, he was king, so he could, but he'd never been a dictator even to his own son.

Liam was something they never thought was possible, and they'd been surprised when Aspen got pregnant. A king rarely had offspring. He wasn't sure what was different between him and Aspen, but they'd had a child. He'd expected it to just be human, but at two, they'd walked into his room and discovered a small dragon instead of a screaming toddler. Some of Skye and Val's kids were the same. As dragons, they would have matured slowly, not coming to age until about fifty, but their children matured as humans. So even though to him, it felt like Liam was still a little boy, he was already a man.

Sid joined Aspen at a small table. The Purple Dragon

was crowded, but she'd still managed to find a place to sit. Though, she had Sugar and Spice up on the table.

"I'm not setting these down until the cats are on a chair or the floor."

Aspen scratched Sugar behind the ear and then pulled her into her lap. Spice jumped down.

Two tables over, a wide-eyed ten-year-old boy stared at him. Sid winked, and the kid ducked his head. He was used to being watched and had learned to ignore it.

Aspen took her coffee and inhaled. She was still gorgeous all these years later. He couldn't believe twenty-two years had passed. She wore her hair short, had laugh lines around her eyes, and moved slower than she once had. But she was still a daredevil and went to all of Liam's fights, cheering him on.

"Why didn't you tell me about Liam's fight tonight?" Sid asked, taking a sip of his latte.

She shrugged. "You don't like to go."

"True." He didn't like watching them even though the fights were necessary. The dragons had to keep up their skills in the event of another war. The last war had wiped out several dragon races, and they couldn't risk anything like that again. But he hated the spectacle of the matches. Everything with his kingdom was a spectacle these days.

"Besides, I thought you had a council meeting tonight to discuss the search for hidden dragons."

Sid sighed. There had been stories of dragons hiding out in various places. The biggest rumor was about a few surviving arctic dragons planning revenge, but he and the council had sent out a few scouts all over the world, looking for hidden dragons or unhatched eggs. All had returned with no information, but they were still waiting for the one who went to Northern Europe. This council meeting would be pointless.

He hated meetings. Even the useful ones. He still didn't get along with his council.

Although he didn't want to find any arctic dragons, he wished they would've discovered some others they thought had gone extinct. He longed for the day when the sky would be graced with a rainbow of colors again, but they'd only managed to find the red fire eggs along with the green and purple ones. No white arctic or orange canyon eggs. And they had the eggs of the surviving races—the silver and gold royal, the yellow river, the blue sea, and the brown underground. They hatched regularly.

Green and purple were the colors that, when combined, made up the woodland dragons. Sid knew very little about them other than they originally came from Europe. Though a few of the hatched were now near twenty themselves, they still acted like children. And they would for the next thirty years or so.

The kid was staring at him again.

"Whatcha looking at?" Aspen asked and swiveled around.

The kid ducked, but this time, his parents noticed. They grinned.

"We should go say hi," Aspen said.

Sid nodded. He loved kids, but he and Aspen had only had the one. Val and Hazel had three, and Skye and Rowan had ten with another one on the way. Rowan said he wanted to make it an even dozen. It was a madhouse at their home.

Sid and Aspen got up and stopped at the table. He crouched down next to the boy. As a royal dragon, Sid could feel the emotions of those around him, and this boy was extremely nervous. "What's your name?"

"Eli."

"Do you like dragons?" Sid asked.

Eli nodded vigorously.

"Well, if it's okay with your parents, how would you like a ride?"

Eli's mouth fell open, and he bounced in his seat, his nerves turning to pure excitement. Sid thought about blocking the kid's feelings because they were so intense, but he liked the thrill.

"Sure, you can go," his dad said.

Sid followed Eli and his family outside. This was one of Sid's favorite things to do.

Life was good even if it was a spectacle.

CHAPTER 3

*L*iam hunched down in the forest, his eyes on the lookout for the dragon he was hunting, his gold scales glinting in the sunlight—a dead giveaway. He wished he could camouflage himself like his buddy Baden, but he was not an underground dragon, so camouflage eluded him.

The sharp scent of pine pricked his nose, and a spring breeze ruffled the needles above him. A few black bears stood still several yards away. They always liked watching the dragons.

So far, Liam's tracking skills were failing him. He'd tried using all of his senses, and he'd caught Felix's scent once, but it disappeared quickly. He'd scoured the forest floor for spots of glittering gold. He'd even sent Baden out to look.

But nothing.

Felix could be anywhere.

Though, this was why he loved training with Felix so much. Felix knew how to stump him, and Liam had been searching for over an hour. This wasn't good.

Baden landed softly on Liam's head. The tiny river-underground dragon had been with Liam since he was a child and demanded to join him when he started training as an assassin. Baden's skills had served Liam on more than one occasion, and he couldn't ask for a better partner.

No sign of him, Your Highness.

I didn't think there would be, but thanks for looking.

Liam thought for a moment. Felix might be hiding out in a cave somewhere, but he didn't think so. The message Felix sent to school specifically said the forests. Which should have been an easy hunt, but this was proving to be more difficult than he'd anticipated. Liam had used all of the training he'd been given so far, but none of his tricks had worked. He supposed he shouldn't be too disappointed. He'd only been training for a few months, but still, he didn't like losing.

Liam pictured himself sneaking up on Felix and smirking at the old dragon. He'd only succeeded once, and he was fairly certain Felix was being lazy on purpose that time.

Out of nowhere, claws sunk into his back, and he collapsed onto the ground. The claws didn't draw blood, but they still hurt. Felix growled in his ear.

You forgot one important lesson. Liam struggled underneath the dragon but couldn't get his footing. His face was pressed into the dirt and pine needles. *What lesson?*

To remember that when I'm hunting, I'm also being hunted.

Very good.

Felix climbed off Liam's back, and Liam shook out his wings, sending dead leaves on the ground fluttering around them.

I failed. Again.

It's not meant to be easy. You've only been training with me for six months. Give me another five years before you start moaning about failure.

Liam sighed. He'd actually started his training two years ago, but his dad, Sid, had put a stop to it fast. It took a year and a half for him and his mom to convince his dad he'd be safe. Liam had wanted to be an assassin, like Felix, for as long as he could remember. Not that much assassinating went on anymore though. In fact, it'd probably been ten years since Felix assassinated anyone. It was more like advanced tracking, but wars often came out of nowhere, and Liam wanted to be on the front lines when that time came. Felix knew what that was like, so Liam wanted to train under him. Plus, he was the best.

Felix had fought in the war against the white witch and afterward became a tracker assassin. Liam's grandpa had trained Felix, but he died in the war. Sid still spoke of him often, and he was the primary reason Sid didn't want Liam training to be an assassin.

Come, let's go do some more combat training.

I'd rather do more stealth training.

But it's what I want, not you, that matters. Besides, don't you have a fight tonight? You want to win.

Liam grumbled a bit on the way to the training fields. He liked his one-on-one training, and combat usually involved multiple dragons plus a crowd of onlookers. In the twenty-two years since the white witch was defeated, the dragons had become a normal part of human life. In Yellowstone, people frequently sought out opportunities to watch the dragons. The training fields always had a crowd because it was one of the few places where they could watch dragons fight. The big fights, like tonight, would bring in a few thousand people. Considerable money was bet on who would win.

The dragons didn't fight for the crowds' benefit though, despite what the humans believed. They fought because they did not want to be caught off guard if another war broke out. Sid made sure all the royal dragons were trained in combat.

Stealth and assassinry was another story altogether.

When the next war started, because there would be a next one, Liam would be a hero.

CHAPTER 4

Missy danced next to Isa as she laced up her boots and tugged on her coat.

"I know it's been way too long. Almost a week." Isa reached down to pet Missy's soft white fur. "Let's go for a walk."

Missy yelped and bounced up and down. Isa rescued the arctic fox when she was just a few weeks old, and she loved that creature more than anyone else in the walls. She'd do anything for Missy.

They trounced down the spiral stairs, and Isa tugged on her gloves. She loved walks in the woods, but in the last few weeks, her guardians had increased her training schedule, so she'd barely had time to think.

She walked down the wide drafty hall lined with tapestries and scenes of dragons and castles. It was a past

Isa missed even though she'd never witnessed it. She was trapped here in this castle, but she longed for the days when the dragons flew in the open and she could explore the world.

But that had never been her life and never would be. Not if she wished to protect her people. If she left, the magic that lived both inside her and on the island would fail, and the humans would kill the exposed dragons.

It'd only been in the last couple of years that she'd been allowed to rule at all. She was only twelve when her grandmother had died, and the twelve guardians ruled in her stead. Technically, Isa wouldn't be fully in charge for another two months when she came of age, but Pierre had been teaching her the ways of being a queen and had been letting her make some decisions.

She rounded the corner and made for a side door, Missy at her heels.

She unlocked the door and gripped the handle. A hand grabbed hers, and she met Jude's stormy green eyes. "You can't go outside," he said.

She pouted. "Why not? I go outside all the time."

He leaned against the door, crossed his arms, and bit his lip. He looked adorable when he did that. "I'm not supposed to tell you."

She placed a hand on his chest and stood up on her tiptoes, bringing her face as close to his as she dared. She knew what effect she had on him. "Come on, Jude. I'm the queen. You have to tell me everything."

He chuckled and extracted himself from her. He shivered and rubbed his hands together. He was only wearing a short-sleeve shirt and trousers—which was fine when you were in the inner halls and rooms, but this close to the door, forget it. The lack of warm clothes meant he wasn't guarding the door. He was guarding her.

She was getting too old for this, and once she came of age, she would come and go as she pleased.

"You and I both know that's not true. But there's been an increased threat. Apparently, the Americans want you dead now, too."

Isa couldn't help but appreciate Jude's body. He was definitely the favorite of her guardians. Well, maybe Pierre, but he was an old man, and Isa would never kiss him. Jude, *yes*. There were a few other guardians with whom she liked to flirt with as well, but Jude kept her attention the longest. She'd never seal herself to him, of course, but she enjoyed his company. And his kisses. She was so distracted by his looks that it took her a minute to process what he said.

"Why?" she asked, now needing answers more than kisses. Though, what she really wanted was to go outside, and she'd give Jude anything for that. He was too used to her kisses by now though to be persuaded by them.

"Probably rebels. They're spreading lies about you again. We can't risk you going outside. It's too dangerous."

She resisted the urge to stomp her foot like a toddler. She'd go mad if she couldn't get outside. "I just want to go for a walk and get some fresh air. Why don't you come with me?"

He shook his head, and she knew she'd lost. Not only that, but he'd dog her steps for the rest of the day.

"Fine. Then change your clothes. We're going to dance."

Jude hated dancing.

CHAPTER 5

Liam took in the crowds surrounding the training field. Every seat was filled. Beyond the stands, the pine trees rose high around them. It'd been a natural arena before, but when people started coming to watch, the park service put in the stands to protect the trees and ground. They charged additional entry to this part of the park, which also limited the number of people who could be there.

Liam's parents had played a big role in ways to implement the changes to control the crowds. Sometimes his mom would reminisce about the days when the parks were empty because everyone was afraid of the dragons. Now, people from all over the world came to see them.

The fight would start in about fifteen minutes. He'd been practicing with Felix all afternoon, and he felt pretty good about his chances. His opponent was an older dragon named Arum, who had fought in the dragon wars. While he was fierce, Liam knew his weaknesses and would exploit them.

Liam changed into a human and walked over to Damon, who was leaning on the fence, staring into the stands. Damon was his best friend and had been since they were toddlers. Damon wasn't a dragon, but he might as well have been. He was always with them.

The night air was cold. Spring had come, but it would be some time before it warmed up.

Liam nudged Damon. "What are you looking at?"

He jumped. "Dude, don't scare me like that." He jerked his head back to the crowds. Liam followed his eye line and spotted a very pretty girl. Liam felt Damon's nerves. As a royal dragon, Liam could always feel the emotions of people around him, but he wasn't very good at it, so he didn't even notice it most of the time anymore unless it was a very strong emotion.

"Emma Frost. Nice choice. I take it you're getting over Tess."

Tess lived up in Bozeman and came down for the dragon fights. Damon was smitten with her, and they went on a few dates, but then she ghosted him. Poor guy wouldn't leave his house for a week. Liam didn't understand it because he never fell very hard for girls. He liked them, but he liked dating a lot of them, not just one.

Damon tugged on the strings of his Pearl Jam hoodie he

probably inherited from his mom. Emma waved at them, and they both waved back.

"She's probably looking at you." Damon dropped his shoulders and sulked.

"Emma? Nah. She likes you." Liam tried not to think about the way girls threw themselves at him. He knew it was the fame. But he could always throw that fame around to help a friend.

"They all like you, Liam. You're a dragon prince. I'm a human." He wasn't being pouty about it, just matter of fact.

Liam shrugged. He'd never admit to Damon that he was right. It didn't matter though because now that he knew Damon liked her, he'd do what he could for him. "Bet Emma will still go out with you."

Damon looked back to the stands. "You know, it's not fair that you get all the girls because of your parents."

"No. I get girls because I win fights." He tried to give Damon a grin to show he was joking, but Damon only had eyes for the stands.

"Whatever, man."

Damon was his best friend, and Liam was pretty sure he'd give his left arm to be a dragon. He was good at hiding his jealousy though. Most of the time. Liam always brought him along to anything dragon-related, and Damon was one of the few humans who were welcomed into the dragon community without question.

The announcer walked onto the field, and Liam patted Damon on the shoulder. "Time to go. See you in a few."

"Win this one, will you? I've got a hundred bucks on it."

Liam shook his head. "I always do. It's not really fair to those who bet against you."

Liam changed into a dragon, and the cold air raced past his face as he soared over the stands, the crowd cheering and yelling his name. He loved the exhilaration their emotion gave him. He looked to the opposite side of the training field.

Arum flew straight for him, and Liam swooped up in the air away from the crowds. He had to get away from the stands, or the fight would start there, and he didn't want to risk hurting innocent bystanders. They also had to be careful how they fought so they wouldn't unintentionally really hurt one another. Aspen could heal his wounds, but if they accidentally struck a death blow, there was no coming back.

Aspen usually took care of his injuries before he got home so Sid wouldn't get mad. He didn't like Liam fighting.

Liam met Arum in the air, and they clawed and scratched at one another. Arum was definitely a good fighter. They tumbled through the sky, and Arum flew underneath him, biting his leg. Liam roared and let out a jet of gold flames.

That hurt.

And he was losing.

Liam watched for an opening and, finding one, flew quickly over Arum and grabbed him by the joints of his wings, one of Liam's signature moves. Arum struggled, but he couldn't get out of it, and Liam drove him straight into the packed earth.

The crowds erupted with cheers and applause.

Arum lay on the earth, stunned but not hurt.

Damon jogged out onto the field, and Liam turned back into a human, clutching his side and glancing down at his bleeding leg. His mom wouldn't be happy about this one.

"How'd I do?" Liam asked.

"Good, but you let him hit you a couple of times." Damon creased his eyebrows in concern.

"Tell me about it." Blood was seeping through his shirt, one of his favorites that he would now have to throw away.

The crowds descended into the field, the sounds of the metal stands rumbling with their feet. They always came onto the field after a fight. Usually, Liam turned into a dragon before they did and flew away, but today, he waited because a certain blonde-haired beauty was heading their way.

"Hey, Liam," Emma said, resting a hand on his shoulder.

"Hey," he said and winked at Damon. "I gotta go."

He turned into a dragon and raced across the night sky, leaving Damon on the field with the girl he was crushing on—his good deed done for the day.

CHAPTER 6

A pounding sounded on the door, interrupting movie night with Sid's family. They always watched movies after fights. Tonight, Liam had come home bleeding, and it took all of Aspen's persuasions for Sid not to hunt down Arum and give him a piece of his mind.

"I've got it," Liam yelled. Most of the time, human visitors were Liam's friends, and Sid doubted today would be any different. They could have more guests, but after the dragons became public, Sid put in a gate and a guard. Liam's friends knew the guards. When it was anyone else though, the gate guard called him first before letting them in.

"Dad, Dad, come quick," Liam yelled from the front hall. Even though Liam was in another room, Sid could feel his fear.

Sid set down his popcorn bowl and raced for the door, his feet pounding on the tiled floor. He came around the corner and found Liam holding an old man with a long beard. Another young man stood behind them.

"I must see the king," the old man rasped. Liam crumpled to the ground, the man still in his arms. Sid fell to his knees next to them and blocked all the crazy emotions around him. The entryway was large and airy, but with the four of them standing there, it suddenly felt tight.

"I'm here. What's the matter?" Sid held the man's face and looked into his bright green eyes.

"The queen, you must kill her." The old man had a thick accent Sid couldn't place.

"What queen?" The only queen he knew was Aspen.

"The queen," the man coughed. "The queen, you fool. The one who has us enslaved. You must do away with her and save us all." The man went limp, and Liam's blue eyes widened. He slowly set the man on the floor and scooted away, his long blonde hair falling across his face. It was rare to see his son scared.

Sid took the man's wrist and felt for a pulse. Nothing.

Sid didn't move for a moment until he stood and faced the second man on the other side of the threshold. The tall man with white-blonde hair and light green eyes stepped over the dead man on the floor.

He held out a hand. "I'm Jens, and my associate is Donahue. I do hope you'll hear what I have to say, Your Majesty." He had a different thick accent than his fallen brother. The man gave a quick bow but did not drop his hand. Sid shook it but remained wary.

"How did you get in? We have a guard."

"We flew, Your Majesty."

Dragons were allowed in at any time. It was the humans he kept out of his yard.

Sid could at least hear what he had to say. "Come in. I will find someone to help your friend. Perhaps we can ship his body back home to his family."

"That won't be necessary. He is a dragon, so once I deliver the message, I will take care of his stone and ensure it is returned."

"I thought I knew all the royal dragons, but I don't recognize you."

"That is because we are not royal dragons." The man regarded Sid with skepticism, which was a little rich considering he had just invaded Sid's home.

"But you have a human form." Only royal dragons had the ability to take human form, and between the accents and the dead man on his floor, Sid was entering uncharted waters.

"Ah, yes, of course, you do not know us. We are from Europe. My associate is from Ireland, and I am from Denmark. We are part of a group of rebels who wish to bring down the queen."

This couldn't be right. The European dragons all came over to the United States when they were being hunted thousands of years ago. They didn't exist in their purest form—as green or purple dragons—because they had interbred once they arrived. As far as Sid knew, they had not left any of their kind back in Europe.

The scout he sent to Europe had never returned. Sid just assumed he was still hunting for information, but now he wondered if perhaps his safety had been compromised.

"There are no dragons in Europe," Sid said tentatively.

Jens cocked his head. "Dragon's Teeth! You had no idea? There are thousands; though our numbers are diminishing."

Sid stepped back, gripped Liam's arm, and whispered fiercely into his ear, "Go get your mother, and tell her to meet me in the kitchen. Send Baden to find a few dragons to take care of that body."

Liam's face was white as he rushed off toward the theatre room.

"Come and sit. Can I get you something to drink?"

"Water is fine, thank you."

Sid grabbed a couple of bottles of water, and he and Jens sat at the weathered table. "Please, tell me about the European dragons."

Jens picked up the bottle and took a sip. Before he could speak, Aspen flew into the room, popcorn bowl clutched in her hand.

"What's this about European dragons?" Her hair was wild, and her eyes bright with excitement.

Sid pulled her into the chair next to him. "Jens was just about to tell us."

Jens barely seemed to notice Aspen's presence. "The dragons in Europe went into hiding when the wizards and knights tried to annihilate us thousands of years ago. In addition, the dragon wars were starting, and we didn't want to be a part of it. So our queen found a way to hide us out in the open. I'm not entirely certain how the magic works, but we avoided being dragged into that ridiculous war. We lived free without fear of persecution because we are not visible to humans. Or at least, we used to be free."

Jens wrung his hands. "Over the years, our queen has grown increasingly bold and tyrannical. Most of us have had our flight privileges stripped, and we are forced to live out our days as humans."

"This queen has the power to take away your ability to fly?" Aspen questioned.

"Yes, we are also not allowed to take our dragon form on pain of death. But there are other rules as well. We are not allowed to procreate. If we do, our children are taken from us and killed. Our eggs have been confiscated and are presumably in the queen's care. We are not allowed to talk about dragons with outsiders, or the queen's minions will kill us."

"How many of you are left?" Sid had never heard of this queen, and his heart broke a little for these people. He had to help them.

Jens stroked his chin. "That's hard to say. The queen has a couple hundred dragons who do her bidding. They are able to fly without being seen by the humans. The rebels have about three hundred, but we used to have over a thousand. She's killed them all. As for the rest of the dragons, probably a few thousand. It's hard to say for sure because they are all hidden. They are spread out across Europe.

Sid sat back and took in his words. Thousands of dragons that they were not aware of. How was this possible?

"Why are you coming forward now?"

"Because you have gained complete freedom. It has given renewed strength to our band of rebels. We've even had more join us in the last few years."

"What happened to your friend?" Sid glanced toward the door, wondering if the body was still in his entryway.

Jens frowned. "Oh, that is a tragic story. He was caught sharing the story with a few Americans in a pub. The queen's men killed his daughter and then put a curse on him to die two weeks later. I told him to die peacefully at home, but he wanted to be the one to deliver the message."

At least there was nothing Sid could've done to prevent his death. This queen sounded powerful if she could do spells like that.

"How can we help you?"

Jens snorted. "Isn't it obvious? You can help us kill her so we will be free. Didn't you kill the Arctic witch?"

The last thing Sid wanted was to be thrown into another war for people he didn't even know existed until fifteen minutes ago. He had just hoped to offer them refuge in America. He had *his* dragons to think about. They had just attained peace themselves.

But he couldn't sit around and do nothing. This queen was oppressing her people.

"You've had a long journey. Why don't you shower and rest, and I will meet with my council. Then, we will see how we can best help you. Where is the queen located?"

"On an island in the Arctic Ocean." Another ice witch. Lovely.

Baden flew back into the room, currently a bright blue and orange. Sometimes, he reminded Sid so much of Runa that it still hurt. Even though she'd been gone for over twenty years. "The dragon has been taken care of, Your Majesty."

"Thank you. Would you show Jens to a room please and make sure he has a change of clothes?"

Baden rolled his eyes and changed direction. Jens stood and gave a small bow. "Thank you, Your Majesty. This means the world to me."

He followed Baden out of the room. Sid wasn't sure what to think of this new development. Since the war, he never wanted anything but a boring life.

But life never gave him boring.

CHAPTER 7

Isa loved the traditions of being queen. The dancing and the fancy dresses. The bowing and being called Your Majesty. The pampering and breakfast in bed. Without them, what was she?

Just a girl trapped in a tower.

Never to be able to spread her wings.

The frivolity made her look shallow and conceited, but it wasn't that. Though, she'd be the first to admit she might be a tad on the vain side. She didn't know how else to cope with her prison—because it was a prison. She had to indulge sometimes, or she might find it in herself to run away, and she owed it to her people to stay put.

So she did. And she did everything she could to make it seem like she was a normal queen. Which involved a lady's maid who did her hair, long baths, and men who came when she called.

Dinners were probably her favorite.

Everyone at the castle dined with her. Even the cook and the servers because there were only about twenty people who lived here, and they never had visitors. The staff sat on the edges of the table, though, so that if they had to help with something, they could.

It took Grace an hour to dress Isa every night before dinner, and Isa reveled in it. Tonight, she wore a deep red dress with a plunging neckline and wide skirt. Her red slippers matched. She had a platinum necklace with a giant diamond that rested on her cleavage. Grace pulled Isa's dark hair up so that it revealed her milky white neck, and she spent a good deal of time on Isa's eyes, leaving smoldering lids. She finished it off with ruby lips.

Isa examined herself in the mirror. Beautiful, as usual. Without the magic Grace worked, Isa thought she looked a little plain.

"Anything else, Your Majesty?" Grace asked.

Isa swiveled around in her seat to look at her lady, who was prettier than Isa, her hair and eyes much lighter. "Lady Grace, You should dress to match. I want you on my right side tonight."

"Of course. I will see you at dinner." Grace bowed and escaped through the bedroom door. Grace was her best friend, but she kept her distance emotionally when Isa decided to be formal. When Isa wasn't being formal, they lay on her bed and giggled about boys. Grace was excellent at reading her.

Isa sat by her window and watched the snow fall. Missy nudged her hand, and she stroked the soft fur. She longed to go out there and stretch her wings. Just once, she'd like to be a real dragon instead of pretending. She'd give up all of this just for her wings.

But she couldn't. She had to remain queen. So she indulged herself.

A knock sounded on her door.

"Come in," she called and stood, smoothing her skirt. Pierre entered, wearing a suit. He looked dashing as usual with his salt and pepper beard. She had hoped Jude would escort her to dinner, but Pierre was a good second choice.

Over the years, he'd become a father figure to her. She'd never known her father or even her grandfather. Her parents had been killed by rebels when she was a baby. Twelve years later, they murdered her grandmother too. Her fate might be the same someday, or she might miraculously live to die a natural death. She hoped so, but she knew better than to expect it—even with the careful eye her guardians kept on her. Her grandmother had the same protections but was still killed.

But Isa was better trained than her grandmother, and she wouldn't go down without a fight.

Isa slipped her hand into the crook of Pierre's elbow, and they descended the spiral stairs.

"Jude tells me you tried to go outside today." He kept his voice neutral, but she detected a hint of disapproval.

"Yes. I wanted to take a walk. Is that too much to ask? I've done it loads of times before." She loved the smell of the forest after a fresh snowfall.

"Always with an escort. You didn't talk to anyone, just tried to go outside by yourself. It's too dangerous. You cannot risk your life. You know this." His voice shifted into a harder tone. It was a tone he used often with her.

"So come with me on the walk. I cannot stay cooped up. I'll go mad."

He patted her hand. "As soon as this risk has passed, I will personally take you out for a walk. I promise."

Everyone stood when they entered the dining room. Jude's eyes lingered a little too long on her cleavage, and she gave him a grin. Let him look. Then, maybe he'd take her outside.

The dining room was meant for much larger parties. The table could be extended to sit a hundred, but currently, it was the perfect length for the twenty of them. The room felt empty with its twenty-foot ceilings and unfilled space on the other side of the table. The pictures and tapestries on the walls helped, but Isa longed for a massive party to fill the space.

According to her guardians, that wasn't possible. It was too dangerous to bring in outsiders because the rebels hid among the masses.

Grace sat on her right and Pierre on her left. The

servers delivered the food. Once everyone had their food, they stared at her.

She picked up her plate and stood, moving to the other side of the room. She took Olga's plate and placed hers in front of Olga, the cook. Then, she took her new plate and sat back down.

"Eat," she commanded, and everyone dug in except for Isa. She watched for a few moments while her people devoured the herb chicken breast and new potatoes. They buttered steaming white rolls and took bites of the bright green asparagus. Once she saw that everyone was eating, only then did she eat herself.

She'd been trained well by her guardians. It was the only way to protect herself from possible poisoning. Too many people wanted her dead, so she chose a different person to swap plates with every evening.

She could never be too careful.

CHAPTER 8

Grace had lived in the castle her entire life. She was as trapped as Isa, but she didn't mind. She had no desire to go anywhere else. Her father had raised her here and died a few years ago. Now, Grace had to take up his cause. She and Isa grew up together, and when she was old enough, she fell into the role of Isa's lady-in-waiting easily.

Isa was gallivanting around the castle somewhere, and it was time to prep her chambers for the evening. Grace slipped quietly into Isa's room and let her eyes adjust to the semi-darkness. She snapped her fingers, and the candles ignited.

Grace picked up Isa's dressing gown from the floor—that girl never put anything back where it belonged—and froze. Lounging on the bed was Missy.

"I trust you not to say anything about the magic." She studied the Arctic fox.

Of course, Missy couldn't say anything, but Grace had heard rumors that animals could talk to dragons. Isa was a dragon, but she'd never seen her wings, so maybe she didn't have the other powers either. Grace couldn't let Isa know about the magic, and she really should be more careful to not use spells for frivolous things like lighting all the candles.

Isa's room was easily the largest bedroom in the castle and kept warm with two fireplaces and walls covered in thick tapestries. There was a window, but it couldn't be opened. A few couches and chairs were spread across the room so Isa could sit and contemplate her life.

Though sitting was not something Isa did well. She was constantly on the move or planning something. And since she was trapped in the castle ninety-nine percent of the time, the burden of executing her plans and schemes fell on the small servant staff. Grace didn't mind—she generally enjoyed Isa's adventures—but the others thought it was too much work because nearly all of Isa's ideas involved copious amounts of food and decorations.

Grace folded down the sheets, and Missy pressed her cold nose on Grace's cheek. She giggled and pushed her away.

The door flung open, and Isa entered with a flourish. "Dinner was lovely, wasn't it?"

"It was. Thank you for allowing me to sit next to you."

Isa turned around so Grace could unlace the elaborate dress. "I wish you could sit next to me every night. But I have to be diplomatic. We should have a dance. Don't you think? Jude and I were practicing this afternoon, and it was delightful."

"That would be lovely, but I'm not sure the guardians would approve, what with the raised concerns for your safety. I can ask though. When do you want to have it?"

"Tomorrow."

Grace rolled her eyes. "Your Majesty…"

Isa giggled. "I'm going so stir crazy! Please, Grace. Who cares what those fuddy-duddies say. You know what? We won't even ask. Just get Olga and Marissa on it." Marissa served many roles in the castle, but her main job was to clean and serve meals. She'd arrived after the old queen died and was a few years older than Grace.

Olga and Marissa wouldn't be happy about this impromptu dance. Plus, Grace hated going against the guardians. They scared her a little. Not individually—well, maybe some older ones—but as a whole, they were formidable. And they had warned the staff about the threat and the need to keep a closer eye on Isa.

Isa pulled off her earrings and stepped out of the dress. Grace helped her into her white silk nightgown and washed the makeup off her face. Then, Isa slipped into bed, beneath the down comforters and slick sheets—both bright red because that was Isa's favorite color.

She flicked her eyes up to Grace. "Who do you want to dance with? I saw Benjamin eyeing you at dinner."

Grace shuddered. Benjamin was the cook's son, and he'd liked her for years. In the last few months, he'd become even worse, blushing and fumbling over his words. She just wanted to be his friend. Sometimes, he was chatty and easy with her, and other times, he wasn't. Grace hung up the dress and cleaned the makeup stand.

"I'd rather not dance with Benjamin."

"Why ever not? He's a nice boy."

If Grace danced with him, she'd give him the wrong idea, and she'd be even further away from being his friend.

Grace sighed and put down Isa's hairbrush. She perched on the side of Isa's bed, sinking onto the squishy bedding. "Come on, Isa, you and I both know that he's not boyfriend material." He always seemed so young to her even though they were the same age. Plus, she always looked at him more like a brother.

Isa giggled. "I know. But I saw him drooling over you. Just like Jude, who couldn't keep his eyes off my cleavage."

Grace's chest constricted. She didn't like the way Isa toyed with Jude. "He did seem to be enjoying that quite a bit. Must you tease him so much?"

"It's not teasing if I enjoy it just as much as he does."

"Oh, so you'd be willing to let him see the rest?" She said it lightly but was actually fishing for information. She didn't know how serious Isa's relationship with Jude had gotten.

"He has."

Grace blushed. She thought perhaps Isa and Jude had been intimate, but now it had been confirmed. She didn't like thinking about them together.

Isa leaned forward and gripped Grace's hand. "It's time for you to get a boy. Who do you want? Perhaps one of my guardians. Drew is quite talented, and he's nice to look at as well."

Graced swallowed. She couldn't tell Isa the truth about who she really wanted. Drew had never interested her before, but she could play along for Isa's sake.

"Maybe, but he's never really looked at me before. I like dark, and he's fair."

"Then maybe Seamus."

"Hmm. Maybe." Seamus's eyes always lingered too long on any woman who passed him. Grace didn't know why it was different than the way Jude looked at Isa, but it was.

"I'll tell you what. I'll make sure you dance with each of them a few times tomorrow, and you can see which one you like better. Then, I'll let a hint drop that you're available to whoever you like. You'll be kissed before you know it."

Grace brought her fingers to her lips. She'd imagined her first kiss many times, but never with Benjamin, Drew, or Seamus.

"Thanks, Isa. I'd like that." She didn't want to disappoint or argue with Isa.

Isa crawled out from under the covers and settled on

her knees next to Grace. She grabbed both of Grace's hands, her wild black hair framing her face. She looked a bit deranged. "But you have to promise me one thing."

"What's that?"

"You have to give me all the details afterward. I want to know when and where and how."

Graced leaned her forehead on Isa's. "Of course. I tell you everything. You know that."

Isa cocked her head. "Everything? Doubtful. But I know you love me."

And she did. She loved Isa like a sister.

Grace climbed off the bed. "I should go. It's been a long day, and I'm tired." She wasn't actually tired, but she'd grown uncomfortable with the way the conversation had gone, and she feared if she stayed any longer, Isa would talk her into doing something she didn't want to do.

"Can you do me one more favor?" Isa asked.

Grace picked up a pillow that fell on the floor. "Sure, anything."

"Will you stop by Jude's room and send him up here?"

Grace swallowed and bit back her scream. "Do you want me to give him any other sort of message?"

Isa winked. "No. He'll know what I want."

CHAPTER 9

Sid flew past the sapphire gem halls and into the enormous cavern where the council met and landed hard on the rock floor. He was the first one there. It had taken him all day to hear back from the council, but they agreed to meet late that night, and so he'd had all day to worry about this.

He didn't want to have to do this again. Not after the annihilation of four dragon races twenty-two years earlier. He did not want his entire reign to be marred by war. But he couldn't let those dragons suffer.

Currently, he was revered as the king who brought together the humans and dragons, but the cost was so great. During the war, the canyon and arctic dragons went extinct, and only one member of the fire and woodlands survived. He'd give up that reverence to have the dragon races back. But life didn't work like that.

Now, this.

No matter what happened with the council today, he would get more information before he made any final decisions. War would not be declared lightly. He couldn't make this decision rashly and didn't want to risk any more lives.

The council arrived one by one. Kairi the bright blue sea dragon, Xanthous the yellow little river dragon, Pearl, Sid's sister, and Nedra, the tiny underground dragon.

They'd hatched the red fire eggs and the green and purple ones from Europe, but those dragons were too young to hold a position on the council. Eventually though, there would be a place for them. As would the canyon, arctic, and woodlands if they ever found their eggs. He'd debated putting Murdoch, a mixed canyon dragon, and Sequoia, the lone woodlands dragon on the council, but they would rather raise the babies.

You don't call meetings very often, Pearl said. *What's wrong?*

It was true. Usually, it was a council member who called the meetings, and he always attended rather reluctantly.

Sid changed into his human form. He thought better when he could pace. He explained about Jens and Donahue as he walked back and forth in front of them. Then, he waited, meeting each one eye to eye as they contemplated his predicament—their predicament.

This is unheard of, Pearl said. *We thought they were extinct. Now, what are we going to do?*

"That is why I am here with you now. I need your council." Never before had he needed them as much as he did today.

"But are they under our jurisdiction? They have a queen? Why is it our responsibility to do anything at all?" Xanthous asked. He was the only dragon who could speak out loud because he was a river dragon.

Sid would never be that heartless. Though his heart got him in trouble a time or two. "Of course we have to do something. She's not allowing them to be dragons and is killing them and their children."

He did understand where Xanthous was coming from, and he didn't want a war either.

Pearl shuffled next to him, and Xanthous cocked his head. "Actually, it sounds like she's protecting them. They've been able to live for years undetected. We didn't even know they existed."

Xanthous is right. We need a diplomatic solution, not one where we go in with guns blazing, Pearl said. *We don't even know if Jens is telling the truth.*

But Jens made it seem like the queen was butchering them. If that was the case, no diplomatic solutions would work. "What do you propose?" Sid asked Pearl.

Send a delegation of ten or twelve dragons to talk to her. Find out what she is like and do some recon.

Kairi snorted, and Pearl glared at her. *Do you have a better idea?*

If she's really as brutal as these dragons make her seem, then we could be sending our people into a massacre. We should send an army over there but not engage. Feel her out. If she's as evil as they say, we'll attack, and if she's not, we'll back down.

"I appreciate your opinions. Thank you," Sid stated. "Kairi, I'm not sure I agree with yours." Sid was a little irritated that she jumped straight to war. "If we do that, she'd feel threatened, and even if she is a good queen, she might attack us. We know she has magical powers because she is able to hide them from human eyes. She might be able to take out an entire army. She sounds suspiciously like the white witch."

Then what should we do? Kiari was exasperated with him. *Fine. Let her be.* He wasn't going to war over one man's testimony.

"I have no idea."

Once again, Sid was thrust into a role he never wanted and didn't know how to handle.

"Let's keep thinking," he suggested, hoping he'd know a good idea when they came up with it. He didn't want more dragon blood on his hands, and he wasn't acting until he had a good plan.

CHAPTER 10

Grace shut the door to Isa's room quietly and leaned against it. Isa was her best friend, and she couldn't tell her the truth.

She wanted Jude.

From the moment he showed up at the castle, she'd fallen hard. She loved his pretty green eyes and thick black hair that he let grow to his shoulders. He was who she dreamed about at night.

Not dumb Benjamin. And she'd never even really talked to Drew or Seamus. But Jude...

Her heart fluttered at the thought of him.

Now she had to send him to her best friend's bedroom. Ugh. This was impossible. She knew they liked each other, but Isa had flirted pretty hard with Drew and Seamus as well too. The three men showed up after Isa's grandmother died. It was the first time they'd had young dragons among them. She and Isa spent a lot of time expounding their virtues late at night, but Grace hadn't realized Isa had settled on Jude until tonight.

Grace trudged down the stairs and into the guardian's hall. She stopped in front of Jude's door. She'd imagined coming to this door many times, but not in this manner. She'd had hopes that he'd call for her.

Grace hesitated at the door. This was highly inappropriate. However, Isa was the queen, so Grace couldn't get in trouble. Yet, she didn't know how this would go.

She knocked.

A crash sounded from the other side, followed by a curse. Jude must've been asleep already. He cracked the door open and rubbed his eyes. He had no shirt on, and his black pants hung low on his hips.

Grace sucked in a breath.

"My lady, is everything okay?" Jude beckoned her in. She slipped inside and shut the door behind her. She couldn't think straight, staring at his bare chest and abs. So she forced herself to look at his face. This wasn't much better.

"Isa would like you to go to her room."

He raised an eyebrow. "Why?"

Grace's cheeks burned, and she clasped her hands in front of her. "I think you know why."

He licked his lips. Oh gosh, she was making a fool of

herself. Of course, that was probably all in her head, but she still felt like an idiot standing there.

"I see. Should I put a shirt on or go like this?"

Grace met his eyes. He had a grin that melted her heart.

"I suppose that is up to you."

"But I'd like your opinion, knowing what she's asking for. If I were to come to your chambers, would you rather have me with a shirt on or off?"

Grace's blush deepened, and she dropped her eyes. "I'm not the queen, so I don't know. But honestly, Jude, if it were me, I'd come to you, not the other way around. So think of what you would want."

Jude chuckled. "Well, Lady Grace, I would very much like to see you show up at my door topless, so I guess that answers my question."

He said her name. Never mind everything that came after it. He'd never addressed her directly before, at least not using her name. None of the guardians really did except Pierre. They mostly overlooked her or simply called her Lady.

And he said he'd like to see her topless. Maybe she did have a chance after this whole thing with Isa blew over.

Because it would blow over.

At least, she hoped it would.

No. She was being silly. He was just being friendly.

But he said her name.

CHAPTER 11

Grace wasn't sure the blush had completely worn off when she got to the kitchens. She pushed open the door, and Olga frowned at her. "What are you doing back so late?"

Benjamin gave her a small smile from the other side of the room. Marissa and a few of the other servants sat at the table in conversation.

"Isa was chatty tonight. You know how she gets."

"Yes, we know how she gets. Did you see her take my plate tonight? Like she wanted me to be poisoned." Olga slammed the dish on the counter that she'd been washing. At least it didn't break. Which had happened more often than it should.

Olga didn't like Isa much because Isa was always changing the dinner plans at the last minute or requesting food she found in a book that Olga couldn't get or didn't know how to make. Isa didn't do it on purpose, but it happened more often than it should.

"You know she has to vary whose plate she takes. It's nothing personal."

"Look at you standing up for her. You know she'd betray you faster than you can say boo."

Sometimes Olga was too dramatic. Isa would never hurt Grace.

"Olga, I love Isa, and she loves me. We're best friends."

"Keep telling yourself that, sweetie." The sarcasm in her voice was evident.

Olga was one of the few who didn't always keep her mouth shut, but the rest of the servants did. Grace, though, figured they'd likely agree with Olga, but she didn't care. She knew the truth.

She grabbed a couple of cookies off the shelf and poured herself a glass of milk. She hated it when they badmouthed Isa. She supposed if Isa had tried to befriend them, they might not think so poorly of her, but Isa kept her circle tight to protect herself—allowing only Grace and a few of the guardians in.

Benjamin was pulling eggs out of a basket and putting them into a carton. One slipped from his grip. Grace watched it fall with fascination, and at the last second, she slowed it down so it landed softly on the floor without breaking. She dropped her eyes immediately so no one would suspect her. She wondered how many people saw the egg fall.

That was foolish. She knew better than to display magic in front of anyone, but she'd been flustered, not only by the shirtless Jude but by Olga harassing her about Isa.

She barely even thought about what she was doing. She just didn't want the egg to break. Grace was a wizard, and everyone knew the wizards went extinct thousands of years ago.

Except they didn't.

Grace's father had been the last of his kind, and now Grace was. If she died without heirs, then they really would go extinct.

And if Isa were to find out Grace was one, she might cut off Grace's head.

Of course, she might not, but Grace wasn't taking any chances. The wizards' sole goal in life was to annihilate the dragons.

Benjamin stared at the unbroken egg and then checked the room furtively, but she busied herself with her cookies. He picked up the egg cautiously and shook it. Grace wished she knew what he was thinking.

He tossed the egg in the trashcan. So much for saving the egg. Benjamin put the rest of the eggs away and didn't drop another one. Grace was staring, but she didn't care tonight.

Benjamin caught her eye and grabbed his own plate of cookies and milk. He sat across from her.

"How was your evening?" His face flamed. He was always so formal now. Not easy like Isa and Jude.

"It was nice. I like it when Isa is chatty." She and Isa had a complicated relationship. On the one hand, she was Isa's servant, and she had to behave as such. On the other, she and Isa grew up together and were best friends. Those nights when Isa was chatty and let her guard down were Grace's favorites.

He frowned but didn't say anything else.

"How was yours?" Grace needed to be more polite.

He fidgeted with a napkin and wouldn't meet her eyes. "Uneventful. I helped Mother clean up from dinner, and then I gathered the eggs from the chickens and fed the cows and pigs."

Grace hated the barns. They were near a heated pool, so they stayed warm enough, but they smelled something awful. And the smell lingered on Benjamin, one of the many reasons she would probably never like him.

"Isa wants a dance," she said. She was looking forward to it now. It'd been a long time since they'd had a dance.

Olga snapped her head up. "What? When?"

"Tomorrow night."

"Dragon's Teeth! What will that girl ask for next?" Alfred asked. He was the maintenance guy around the castle, and every time Isa had a party, he had to move a bunch of stuff around.

Olga muttered a bunch of words in a language Grace didn't understand, and Benjamin rolled his eyes.

"Why does she always spring these ridiculous events on us with no warning?" he asked.

"You get to dance too."

"Yes, but only after I help Mother make a gazillion desserts that won't get eaten and help Frederick clean the ballroom. Dances are the worst."

Grace stood, tired of all the people whining about Isa. It'd been a long day, but she wanted Benjamin to feel better.

"I'll save you a dance." But just one. She didn't want to give him the wrong idea.

Benjamin's cheeks reddened again, and Grace knew she wasn't the only one who would be having pleasant dreams tonight.

CHAPTER 12

Most of the guardians hated meetings. Isa loved them. She'd only been attending them for two years, and for the first year, she had to sit and listen without contributing. Now, she could ask questions and even make a few decisions. Next year, she'd be the one conducting the meetings and making all the decisions.

She couldn't wait.

She entered the meeting room, and the guardians stood. She swept past them in a gorgeous sapphire day dress and took her chair at the round table. It was just big enough for thirteen of them to sit. There was a fourteenth chair that she was told would be for her husband when she married, but she didn't want to think about that because she was too young.

She would have to eventually marry because she would

need an heir to continue holding the magic after she died. Though, she hated thinking about cursing another person to be trapped within these walls.

Thankfully, she didn't have to marry until she fell in love and sealed herself to someone. She planned on waiting for a long time. For now, she enjoyed her dalliances with Jude.

The room was small with a roaring fireplace and sunlight streaming in through the high windows. The fire made it far too warm, and she shrugged off her cloak. Jude gave her a grin, and she returned it.

On either side of him sat Seamus and Drew. They arrived at the castle to replace the three guardians who died protecting her grandmother. Unfortunately, that day, her grandmother had died too. They were younger, just boys really, and they'd been the only source of crushes since the rest of the guardians were old enough to be her grandfathers.

The guardians always had twelve dragons. Pierre was in charge, and when he wasn't around, Bartlby or Giovanni filled that role. They were easier to deceive than Pierre, but she wasn't as close to them. The other six, Felipe, Mateo, Tavish, Diego, Tad, and Otis were generally quiet during meetings and rarely addressed her directly. But they would protect her if it came down to it.

Pierre gave her a nod, and she smiled. This was her favorite part. She loved hearing about the kingdom.

"Giovanni, tell us about the rebellion movement in Ireland," Pierre said.

Giovanni faced Isa. "We were able to eliminate five dragons involved, but we still aren't certain when or how the American dragons will attack."

Pierre continued around the table, and Isa listened intently to all of the issues concerning various countries. The guardians visited their territories a few times over the month before they held their meetings. Most of the issues were minor and easily addressed. The American dragons bothered her though.

After they finished, she cleared her throat. "Why can't we send a dragon directly to the Americas to see what is going on?"

Pierre jerked his eyes to Tavish and then back to Isa. "We could, but it's highly dangerous. They don't even know we exist."

Isa sighed. She was so over not being completely in charge. She wanted to try something. "Tavish, you are the best spy in my kingdom, correct? Or is my intel wrong?"

His eyes widened. "I do believe your intel is correct, Your Majesty."

"Very well. You will leave this moment and go find out what the Americans are doing. When you return, you will report immediately to Pierre so he can take appropriate action, and then you will tell me what you learned."

She glared at Pierre and dared him to contradict her. To her surprise, he didn't.

"That is an excellent idea, Your Majesty. Tavish, we will see you when you return."

Tavish pushed his chair back and left the room. Isa was excited to speak to him when he returned. She wondered how long it would take. She'd read plenty of books about the Americas, but she'd never met anyone who had been there. She wanted to hear about the people and the landscape. She knew it was silly. Tavish was going on official business, but she would still ask him all the questions.

They discussed the rest of the issues. Isa chewed on her lip as the meeting drew to a close. She'd planned on demanding to be let outside, but she didn't want to appear childish again. It was prudent for her to remain in the castle until the threat passed, but she wasn't giving up. She just wouldn't bring it up now.

"Anything else you'd like to discuss?" Pierre asked.

"Oh yes, there is one more thing. Tonight after dinner, there will be a dance."

A collective groan echoed from everyone, but Isa smirked, stood, and sailed out of the room.

CHAPTER 13

The next day, Sid slumped at the table and sipped his coffee. He had no idea what to do about the European dragons. Gray clouds floating in the sky matched his mood, and his kitchen seemed unusually empty this morning.

"You okay?" Aspen sat down next to him.

He shook his head. "The council was no help. We still don't know how to handle the situation with Jens."

Aspen blew on her coffee before taking a drink. "Seems pretty straightforward to me. We have to help them."

"Do we? We don't even know if he's telling the truth." There was the crux of Sid's problem. He was flying blind into a situation he didn't understand, and all of the avenues leading to him acquiring the information put someone at risk.

Aspen glared at him. "What do you mean? You saw the dead dragon in the living room." Her bleeding heart would get her into trouble someday.

Sid ran a hand through his hair. "We have two dragons. That's it. I don't want to start a war with just that. Maybe she's protecting them. Have you ever thought about that? What if two of the arctic dragons had gone to her and said the same thing about me during the dragon wars, and she'd worried we were the bad guys? We have to consider all possibilities. She could be their protector or their captor. We have to verify."

"But if she is doing what they say..." Aspen stared down into her coffee.

"Then we absolutely need to intervene." He rubbed his eyes. Sleep had not come easily last night.

Aspen gripped his hand. "I wish I could be more help. What did the council say?"

He shrugged. "They were absolutely useless."

If he could choose his own council, he'd keep his sister...but the others, he'd replace. Sometimes he felt like they argued with him for the sake of arguing. Plus, they often thought of only how things would affect their own tribes, not necessarily the good of all the dragons.

"Why don't we get out of here for a while? Clear your head and think," Aspen said.

"Where do you want to go?"

She stood up and grinned. "Where do I always want to go? Yosemite."

ASPEN LOVED VISITING THE BABIES. Technically, they weren't babies anymore, but Sid would always think of them that way. They were twenty, but they had the mentality of the human equivalent of an eight-year-old. At least they wouldn't accidentally incinerate her now. Sid had only let her come visit them starting a few years ago, and they adored her as well.

The babies were still too young to see what gifts they manifested, but Sid was curious to know what kinds of abilities these new dragons had.

Sid landed in a sea of green and purple. As soon as Aspen slid off his back, the kids swarmed her. A few were as tall as Aspen now, but most came to her shoulders or waist. The cave they lived in was large and wide with several gaps in the ceiling for light. Snow fell through the gaps, but only lightly. A few of the dragons were waiting for it to fall on their heads, and another one was blowing fire at the flakes, creating a puddle at his feet.

Sid greeted a few of the kids and then headed for where Sequoia, Pearl, and Murdoch were talking.

Pearl told us about the European dragons. Sequoia shifted from foot to foot. *Are they going to take away our children?*

Sid mouthed a quick thank you to Pearl and faced the other two. *Of course not. They don't even know about you. But I don't know what to do about this supposed evil queen they have.*

I don't want to send an army. But I also don't know if I feel comfortable sending a delegation.

Pearl stretched her wings. *I've been thinking since the meeting, and I have an idea. You should send a spy. Someone to scope it out. Then, they can report to you, and you can go from there.*

Sid gaped at Pearl. He was an idiot.

A spy.

He should've thought of that himself.

CHAPTER 14

Isa thought the dance would make her feel less antsy, but it didn't. She still felt like she wanted to crawl out of her skin. Bartlby, who ran the old record player, was putting the records back into a box. It was over, and everyone would be heading to bed soon.

The room looked amazing. Once again, Olga, Marissa, and Grace had outdone themselves. Tables were strewn across the room with elaborate sculptures, some made of ice and others of chocolate. Additional tables held enormous flower decorations.

The dessert table was a sheer work of art with chocolate fountains and cakes made into dragon shapes. She would extend her thanks tomorrow so they knew how much she appreciated everything they'd done.

She spotted Grace chatting with Seamus in the corner. He stood extremely close to her. They made a cute couple, and Isa grinned. She would definitely be asking Grace about that tomorrow.

She could tonight, but she was restless even after having danced with every man in the castle at least once. She had to get out. She shouldn't feel claustrophobic in this big castle, but she did. She'd never gone this long without going outside before.

She sighed. Her dance was over, and all it had done was to remind her that life inside the castle was not normal.

Pierre stopped and gave a small bow. "May I escort you back to your room?"

She held out her arm. "Of course you can."

He patted her hand as they walked down the drafty hallways. "Are you okay? You seem distracted."

She brushed a hair out of her eyes. "Yes. I'm just restless. You know me. I thought the dance would help, but I'm still itching to go outside. Do you think tomorrow you could take me onto the grounds? It doesn't have to be long. Please?"

He didn't say anything as they ascended to her room. He pushed open her door. "I would love to give you that. I know how much you want it, but it's not possible. The risks are too great. I'm sorry. As soon as this is over, you can. I promise."

Isa watched him descend the stairs. This wasn't fair. She

would go mad if she didn't get out of here soon. She tried doing this diplomatically, but now it was time for drastic measures.

CHAPTER 15

Aspen sat in a side cavern, surrounded by several dragon kids, who stared at her, enraptured. The shadows from the cave gave her a somewhat eerie look, and she gestured animatedly in the middle of the group of children, her face full of excitement. Sid turned into his human form and sat down next to her.

A green dragon rested his head in Sid's lap.

"And then the evil white dragon came for me. I lifted my sword, and it got her in the neck." Aspen mocked stabbing someone.

The dragons gasped as Aspen thrust her hand into the air. "And that is how I became queen." She waved her hand and bowed to them all.

Another story, one of the purple dragons shouted.

Sid put an arm around Aspen. "I need to steal Aspen away."

No. She's telling us stories, the purple one whined. She bounced on her feet, and several other dragons joined the complaining.

"I'll bring her back in a bit, I promise," Sid said.

Aspen stood, and Sid scrambled up. He took her hand and led her away from the squawking dragons. A few tried to follow, but as Sid and Aspen left the cave, Sequoia called the kids back.

"What's up?" Aspen asked once they were quite a ways away from the kids. They walked down a path surrounded by giant trees. Purple flowers poked up through the remaining snow on the ground.

"Pearl suggested we send a spy."

"That's a good idea. I'm surprised no one thought of it before."

Sid nodded, still embarrassed by that. "Who should we send?" He had some ideas of his own, but he wanted Aspen's take. She often thought of things that he didn't.

Aspen stopped and plucked up a few of the flowers. "Well, it should be a royal dragon. We don't know the situation, so they should definitely be able to become human. It should also be someone who is well-traveled and can blend in. So, one of your trackers. The thing is, they'll know he's from here because he'll be gold and not green or purple."

Those were all good points. Sid bit his lip. "I was thinking of sending Pearl."

Aspen was quiet for a few moments. "I don't know. The little dragons look up to her even though she isn't here all the time. She's like their grandma. This is a potentially dangerous situation, and if something happened to her, they'd be devastated. Plus, she doesn't really have the skills to defend herself. You need a warrior if things go bad. Maybe Jeremiah?"

"He's doing his human experience." Sid thought. Jeremiah was good, but Sid didn't like interrupting the human experiences unless it was an emergency. Which this was, but he had a better idea. "Felix," Sid suggested. "He's a skilled tracker."

"He's perfect. And if the queen does end up being evil, he's your best shot at killing her without any fanfare. He'll be long gone before anyone even knows she's dead."

"Do we trust him to decide whether she lives or dies without consulting us?" Sid asked. Felix had been his most trusted tracker after his father died, but he always considered himself an assassin first and spy second.

"I think so. He's very levelheaded. It's why I trust him to train Liam, who will be very upset his mentor is gone. He trains with Felix almost every day."

Sid grumbled. "Liam needs to stop growing up so fast. I don't know why he thinks he has to be an assassin. They have too high a mortality rate."

"Well, considering you're the king, you don't ever have

to send him out on any dangerous jobs—even once his training is complete. Felix or another tracker can do those."

Sid rubbed his face. His son would be the death of him at some point. He chuckled. Once upon a time, he thought that of Aspen. He loved that Liam was like her, but he wished his kid would be more cautious.

"Felix is good for the job. Come on, let's get him on his way. Maybe this problem will be over before it turns into another war."

Aspen squeezed his hand. "I know. That's the last thing we need."

Sid hoped this would work. Then, he could return to his peace and quiet where his biggest worry was that Liam would crash his Ferrari.

CHAPTER 16

*L*iam liked his lessons on the private training fields loads better than the ones on the public. It was isolated, high in the mountains. This was where he learned the good stuff.

He and Felix had just gotten started when he saw his dad flying in from above with his mom on his back.

This wasn't good. Not now when Sid had way too much going on with the European dragons. If he was here, that meant trouble.

Sid landed hard on the snow-packed earth next to them and changed into a human. Out of respect, Liam and Felix did as well. Liam immediately started shivering since he was not dressed for this weather. He tightened the strings on his hoodie, but the wind still chaffed his cheeks.

Felix bowed. "Obsidian, how can I help you?"

Sid flicked his eyes to Liam but didn't say anything. Liam assumed his dad thought he wouldn't notice that, but Felix trained him to notice things. This was definitely bad news if he didn't want Liam around.

Aspen looped her arm through Liam's and rested her head on his shoulder. She wasn't terribly affectionate unless something was wrong, but he appreciated the warmth she gave off anyway. He hoped no one had died.

"Felix, we need you to go to Europe," Sid said with a grave voice.

Liam's stomach lurched. He could still feel the dead man in his arms. He'd never actually seen a dead body before, and he was lucky he hadn't lost his lunch. As it was, he wasn't sure he'd ever forget that moment. He just hoped he would stop having nightmares over it.

"Who is the target?" Felix asked, stroking his short beard.

Sid ran a hand through his hair. "It's dangerous. You might not make it out alive. There is a queen in Europe who has single-handedly enslaved the entire race of dragons there. Or at least that's what I've been told. It might not be true. I thought instead of starting a war, we'd send you in to spy on her and assassinate her if you find that the rumors are true."

Felix's eyes lit up. "I haven't had a job like this in years. And never overseas. I'd be honored."

"I'm going with," Liam said though he wasn't quite sure

why, other than a need to prove himself. Also, an opportunity to learn like this might never come again.

"Absolutely not," both of his parents said at the same time.

"Why not? I want to go. This is what I'm training for, and this will be a much harder job than Felix has done in a long time. I can go with him and help."

Sid rounded on him. "Son, let me make this very clear. You are not going to Europe. I will not put you in danger like that. This queen is a threat like we haven't seen in years, and she may even be worse than the white witch. That is no place for a novice."

Liam shrugged out of his mom's arms. "Why let me train if you won't let me fight? What's the point?" He wasn't a child anymore. He hated that they treated him like one.

"You're seventeen years old." Sid pointed a finger at him. "You aren't going. End of story. Felix, when can you leave?"

"First thing in the morning. She'll be dead in a week if she is what they say she is. Where is she located?"

"On an island in the Arctic Ocean. Just north of Svalbard."

They chatted for a few more minutes, but all Liam could think about was that there was no way in hell he would miss this.

Not long after, his parents flew away.

"Let me come with," Liam said.

Felix chuckled. "And directly disobey an order from the king? I don't think so." His face grew serious. "I will tell you about it when I get back. You're not ready for something like this."

Liam tried to think of an argument, but none came. If both his parents and Felix thought he couldn't handle it, then there was no point in trying to convince them otherwise.

He just wouldn't ask permission.

CHAPTER 17

Grace didn't bother to change out of her ball gown before heading up to Isa's room. She had fun at the dance, and Jude was nice to her, but he really couldn't take his eyes off of Isa. Grace's heart hurt, but she'd survive.

She trudged up the stairs, and a white blur raced past her. At the top, Grace met Missy, who wagged her tail and stared up with knowing eyes.

"You still keeping my secret?" she whispered.

Missy clawed at the door, and Grace pushed it open and found Isa sitting at her dressing table, staring off into space.

"Sorry, I didn't see you leave the dance." Grace stepped into the room. "I was helping Olga with the cake."

Isa jerked her head around. "It's okay. Please, be sure to

give my thanks to Olga for all she did tonight. It was amazing."

Isa stood, and Grace unlaced her dress. Isa seemed distracted, and so it was a good time to bring up Missy because then she wouldn't remember the conversation later. Grace wanted to make sure Missy wasn't telling Isa her secrets.

"I heard a rumor that dragons can talk to animals and they talk back. Can you talk to Missy?"

"What?" Isa asked.

"Missy, does she speak to you?"

Isa stepped out of the dress. "Oh, no. She never has although I've tried. I asked Pierre about it once, and he tried talking to Missy, but she didn't talk to him either. So, either she can't do it, or I can't talk to animals. I don't know which one it is."

"Have you ever tried with other animals out in the wild?" Grace was now curious about the extent of Isa's dragon powers.

"Only after I got Missy. It's never worked."

Missy whined, and Isa dropped a hand to her head, rubbing her behind the ears. "Thank you, Grace, for helping me tonight and being a good friend."

"Always, Isa." Inside, her knots untied. Her secrets were safe with Missy. She helped Isa into bed and scratched Missy under her chin. "Is there anything else?"

"Yes. Send Jude up, will you?"

And just like that, the knots were back.

Jude was still dressed when Grace knocked on his door, and he didn't tease her this time. In fact, he barely said anything to her at all. And she returned to her room.

Grace shut and locked her door. Then, she waved her hand so that it was magically locked as well. This was the one place where she felt relatively safe from the rest of the world. She could practice her magic here without anyone noticing.

She looked around her small, tidy room. It had a bed just big enough for her, a dresser, a fireplace, and a tiny dressing table.

She undid her long braid. The night had been nice even if Seamus seemed to take more notice of her than she'd like. Drew was fun to dance with though. When Isa asked, she'd tell her that she liked Drew.

Grace took off her stifling dress and nearly collapsed onto her bed. But she had things to do before she slept.

She went to her dresser and opened the bottom drawer. She muttered a few words, and the contents changed from underwear and socks to several boxes and other magical trinkets. There was her box with marbles that would paralyze a dragon, the bag of powder that would darken a room, and a few potions that would render men unconscious. Her favorite item though was the sword. She carefully lifted the box out of the drawer and placed it on her bed. She ran her hand along the polished wood. This was her favorite time of night.

She opened the box and stared at the sword that lay within. It sparkled even under the dim candlelight. This sword never dulled or broke, and it was forged by magic years and years ago by her great-great-great-grandfather. The sword had many names but was most commonly known as a dragon slayer.

Grace came from a long line of wizards. Her ancestors were the ones who defeated the dragons of old, and they led the charge to eradicate them and nearly did. When the dragons went into hiding, so did the wizards, for the humans feared them as well and had begun hunting them.

One by one, they had died until Grace's family was the only one left.

Her family ended up with the queen though Grace wasn't sure how that happened. Grace was privileged to know her grandfather, and he taught her the magical arts but made her promise to keep them secret. When he died, her father continued her training. Now, she had to learn on her own.

She picked up the sword and gave it a swish. It sang through the air. She danced around the room, thrusting and swiping. She practiced every night, and the dance rarely changed. Her moves would be weak against a dragon, but still, she kept up with the things her grandfather and father taught her. Just in case.

The sword blurred in her vision as she spun in circles.

She loved the way it moved. She wondered if she'd feel this same exhilaration in Jude's arms.

Maybe.

Maybe not.

She finished her dance and sat down on her bed. She held the sword carefully to her face and stared at it. She kissed it gently and then placed it back in its box.

The box went into the drawer, and she waved her hand. Socks and underwear appeared in its place. She closed the drawer quietly and leaned her head on the dresser.

"Father, someday, I promise to use that sword and avenge your death."

Grace climbed into bed, pulled the blanket up over her chest, and fell into dreams of Jude and swords.

CHAPTER 18

Liam looked around his room. He debated packing a bag but thought better of it. What would he do with it? If he was going to help Felix take out the evil queen, he had to put into play all he'd learned so far. He had to be stealthy.

He slept for a few hours, knowing he wouldn't get much sleep after this. At three a.m., his alarm went off. Baden hit him on the nose with his wing. "Why are we getting up so early?"

"You're not. I am. Wish me luck." He was finally going on a real mission. His blood buzzed with excitement.

Liam stood and stretched. He put on a black, long-sleeve t-shirt and black slacks. He pulled on a sweatshirt and his winter gear, including a warm hat, gloves, and boots. He'd overheard his mom and dad talking about how cold it was where the queen was rumored to be living. It wouldn't matter as long as he stayed a dragon, but if he had to turn into a human for any reason, he didn't want to freeze. That was a lesson Felix taught him. Always be prepared to do your dirty work as a human.

Felix always hid a slew of weapons on himself when he went out on any job. Liam didn't have any weapons, but Felix would share when he showed up.

"Where are you going?" Baden asked. Liam jumped. Baden had turned a dark blue, the color of Liam's sheets, and completely blended in. His bright purple eyes blinked up at Liam. Baden was a complication he hadn't thought about because Baden nearly always joined Liam when he planned shenanigans. Liam wasn't stupid though. Baden only went along with things so he could stop Liam if things got out of hand. This was one of those times.

"When Mom and Dad wake up, tell them I've gone to help Felix."

Baden raised an eyebrow. "And you expect me to stay behind? No way. I'm going with you."

"It's dangerous."

Baden had been his near-constant companion since childhood, but he was often meddlesome and prevented Liam from doing things he wanted to. Taking Baden along on this adventure could put him in unnecessary danger.

"You're going, aren't you? Then so am I."

Liam debated for a moment. If he forced Baden to stay

here, he'd risk him spilling the beans too soon, and Liam would never make it out of the country. He would let him tag along as far as Felix's cave but ditch him there.

He glanced down at his phone. "Fine. But we have to go now."

Liam opened his third-story window and glanced down. There wasn't a soul in sight.

He jumped out the window and was a dragon before he'd dropped ten feet. He flew off toward Felix's cave, and Baden hurried to catch up.

He was going on his first-ever real job. He would finally manage to prove to his parents that, not only was he good at this but this was what he was meant to do.

Liam landed softly on the edge of Felix's cave. If he came in noisily, he'd be dead before he knew what hit him. Felix attacked first and asked questions later. Baden rode on his head as they crawled through the entrance, and once they got close enough, Liam declared his presence.

It's just me. Don't kill us.

Liam expected an obnoxious response back from Felix, but none came. Liam continued his slow crawl into the cave, declaring his presence every few feet, but he never once got a response.

He rounded the corner to Felix's living quarters. The light from the bright flames lit up the space. The weapons cabinet was on the far wall with the door slightly ajar.

Liam quickly turned into a human and rushed for it.

The cabinet was normally filled with all sorts of

weapons, but today, there were a few key missing ones. Namely, the dragon slayer that hung proudly above the rest of the swords. The one Felix had gotten from Rowan after the war.

Felix was already gone.

CHAPTER 19

As soon as Grace left, Isa jumped out of bed. She flung off her nightgown and threw open her wardrobe. She pulled on a long sleeve t-shirt, a thick sweater, leggings, and a pair of fleece-lined pants. Then, she laced her boots, buttoned her coat, and dug a hat and gloves out of the cupboard.

The knock came a few minutes later. She opened the door, but instead of letting Jude in, she shoved him against the far wall and planted her lips on his. He pulled her close and deepened the kiss, his tongue teasing hers.

Isa had to time this right. Jude pushed her toward her room, and she knew this was the moment she needed to pounce. She pulled away.

"Take me outside." She stared at him, hoping he could

see the desperation in her eyes. She couldn't stay in the castle for another minute.

Jude's breathing slowed, and he looked her up and down, his messy hair framing his gorgeous face. He furrowed his eyebrows and frowned. "Isa, you know I can't."

She pouted and stroked his cheek. "Yes, you can. Just for a few minutes. Then, you can do whatever you want with me." She slid her other hand up his shirt, and he hissed. He pulled her close to him again and dropped his lips to her ears.

"Whatever I want? You promise?" His breath tickled her ear.

Isa giggled. "I promise." She knew the kinds of things Jude wanted, and all of them were worth a walk outside.

He sighed. "Okay, but you can't tell Pierre. He'll kill me. I have to change first. Meet me by the door you were trying to escape through a couple of days ago. I swear you are more cunning than a wizard."

Isa let the wizard insult slide. He gave her another quick kiss and jogged down the stairs. Isa felt a smidge guilty for using him this way. She didn't love him, and she wasn't entirely sure how he felt about her. She hoped he wasn't falling too hard.

She craved that feeling. Love. She thought, once upon a time, she was in love with him when he moved here. He'd been the first young man she'd ever laid eyes on. But the feeling quickly faded.

She did like kissing him though.

"Come on, Missy. Let's go."

Missy wove her way around her ankles and pranced down the stairs. Isa froze when she heard voices.

"What are you doing up at this hour?" Pierre asked, his voice carrying down the long halls.

Isa poked her head around the corner. She could see the back of Pierre's head and Jude standing there, gloves in his hand. His face didn't betray anything. This was why she liked him more than the others. He knew how to play it cool. It's how they managed to sneak around long before anyone else knew something was going on between the two of them. It'd only been recently that Isa decided she didn't care what people thought about her romantic endeavors.

"I thought I heard something and decided to do a quick patrol."

"But there are guards out there already." Pierre sounded a bit irritated. Isa hated it when he used that voice on her.

"Which is why I'm doing it as a human and not a dragon. I heard voices, and it's possible the threat to Isa's life will come from someone on the ground, not the air."

Pierre shifted his feet. "Perhaps I should go with you."

"That would be silly. I'm much stealthier than you. Go back to bed. I'll report my findings in the morning. If I need help, I'll alert Mateo and Drew."

Pierre gripped Jude's arm. "Be safe."

Jude nodded. "I will."

Pierre trudged away, and Isa watched until he turned the corner. Then, she met Jude's eye. He grinned at her and waved her toward him. They slipped down the hall and out the door.

She inhaled the icy air and let it out. This was heaven. She felt more alive outside than she ever did inside. If she could have her wings, she'd probably never go back indoors again.

"We can't go far. It's snowing, so our footprints will be covered up, but if we go out into the woods, we risk the patrol finding us."

Isa sighed. "I know. We can stick to the castle. I just wanted to be out here."

Snow landed on her cheeks and eyelashes, and she blinked it away. Jude led her to a bench, and they sat.

She reveled in the fresh and clean air. She loved the snow, and it was always snowing here. She'd read books of places that didn't have snow, where the air was so warm they could go outside without a coat and gloves, and she wondered what that would be like. Someday, she hoped the rebels would be neutralized so she'd be able to go to a place where the sun was hot, where she could slip into an ocean and not freeze to death.

"What are you thinking about?" Jude asked.

She'd been quiet for too long. "Just what life is like in the rest of the world."

"It's not all the books make it seem to be. It's harder

because there are so many people, and you don't know who to trust and who might kill you. It's dangerous."

"But warm. I'm tired of being locked up in the castle."

Jude sighed. "I know. I wish I could help, but I can't."

They sat in silence for several more moments, and then Jude stood. "Come on, we can't stay out here much longer. Besides, it's time for you to give me whatever I want." He gave her a cheeky grin.

She slipped her hand into his. "Okay. Thank you for taking me outside." She leaned up and kissed him on the cheek.

They walked back to the castle, hand in hand. Just before they turned the corner, Jude froze. He brought a finger to his mouth and looked around, putting his lips to her ear. "Wait here."

Isa didn't hear anything, and she didn't know what he was going on about. He snuck around the corner, and Isa turned around to find out if she could see anything, but there was nothing there.

A hand covered her mouth, and an arm gripped her waist, pulling her into a hard body. Dragon's Teeth! How on earth was she going to get out of this?

"Do you see how easy it would be for someone to kill you?" Jude asked, and Isa relaxed, but he didn't release his grip. "If I had been sent to kill you, your throat would be slashed right now. Don't ask me to take you outside anymore. The only thing I want from you is your safety, and you're not safe outside."

CHAPTER 20

*L*iam grabbed another sword and a handful of daggers.

"Those are useless against dragons." Baden perched on top of the weapons chest and watched. Liam tried not to think about what he was about to do. Felix was gone, and Liam had to track him. But Felix was a pro at hiding himself.

"I know. But our enemies could just as easily be humans. Felix taught me to always be prepared. Especially in a situation like this."

Baden bobbed his now silver head up and down. "How exactly do you expect to find Felix?"

"My tracking skills are the best." This was a lie, and Baden knew it.

Baden chuckled. "And that's why you didn't even notice

that Felix was gone. Or that you've only managed to successfully track Felix once."

Liam pointed one of the daggers at Baden, but Baden didn't even flinch. He knew Liam would never hurt him.

"I took the liberty of getting to know Jens, the European dragon a bit. I asked him everything he knew about this queen we're going after."

Baden snorted. "And he wasn't suspicious at all?"

"He seemed to like talking about it. Let's go. I'll tell you about it on the way." If Jens was right about even half the stuff he told Liam, Felix would need another person to help him. Liam couldn't stay behind.

Liam surveyed the weapons cupboard one more time. He grabbed another dagger and shut the doors. He turned back into a dragon and flew out into the cool air.

He'd be flying for a long time and would need his energy. He didn't like eating as a dragon, but desperate times…

He flew low over the valley and spotted a deer. He dived for it, and its bones crunched in his jaw. He glanced over. Baden grabbed a rabbit.

It was time to go.

CHAPTER 21

Sid blinked his eyes open just as Aspen threw on a robe.

"I'm waking up Liam. I think he shut off his alarm," she said, tying the robe tight across her body.

"Good luck. He'll be salty today because he didn't get to go with Felix. He'd rather be helping with that instead of going to school." Sid stretched and collapsed back into bed. He wasn't really a morning person. No one in his family was.

Aspen snorted. "Did he really think we'd let him go into what could potentially be the most dangerous situation on earth?"

"He's too much like you." Sid climbed out of bed.

Aspen shoved him on the shoulder. "Probably. But still. If she's as bad as Jens says, Felix won't survive."

"Felix has a good head on his shoulders. He'll survive. Liam wouldn't though. He's too reckless." Liam came home with a speeding ticket at least once a month, and he always fought aggressively in the dragon fights.

"That he is. You want to come wake him with me? We can see which one of us can irritate him more."

Sid nodded and pulled on a pair of pants. Poor kid had parents who liked to tease him. "Tell me. Why does a seventeen-year-old need his mother to wake him up? Doesn't his phone have an alarm?"

"Sure. But he sleeps through them. Especially on days he'd rather be doing something else. Besides, I like waking him up."

Sid pulled Aspen close to him. Even after all these years, he still loved being near her. "Maybe we can wait a few minutes." He dropped his lips to her neck.

Aspen giggled. "That will take more than a few minutes. We can come back to bed after we wake him if you want."

Sid held her tighter, loving the feel of her against him. "Yes, I would like that. Maybe we can stay in bed all day and not see Jens at all. He will probably be upset that we didn't send an army."

"I see how it is. You don't really want me. You just want to use me as an excuse."

Sid nodded. "Maybe. But it's a good excuse, don't you think?"

Aspen leaned up and pecked him on the lips. "The best.

But we still have to wake up our son, or he'll be late for school."

Sid loved this time of the morning when the house was quiet and peaceful. He preferred his life that way too, but peace was quickly coming to an end. Either he had an evil queen to defeat or a rebellion to help quash. He wasn't sure which one was worse.

Aspen threw open the door to Liam's room. "Rise and shine," she yelled in a voice that was far too chipper for this early in the morning. He couldn't wait to hear Liam's grumbling.

Sid flicked on the light.

It took him a second to register the scene. Clothes were strewn everywhere, but that was normal. The bed was mussed, but no boy slept there. And the window was wide open.

Liam was gone.

CHAPTER 22

*I*sa skipped down the hallway on the hunt for Pierre. She wanted to go outside. For real this time, not just the stolen minutes Jude had given her the night before. It wasn't very nice of him to trick her like that, but she supposed he was trying to prove a point. Last night had not been nearly long enough. She would make Pierre listen to her.

She found all the guardians except Tavish congregating in the entrance hall. He still hadn't returned from the Americas.

The hall was wide and drafty, large enough that a few dozen dragons could congregate comfortably. But right now, it felt too big with all of them in their human forms. The doors were twenty feet wide and thirty feet tall.

"What's going on?" she asked.

As one, they turned and bowed to her. She wished they wouldn't be quite so formal. Jude, Drew, and Seamus weren't always, but if Pierre was around, they would be.

Pierre approached her, and she pouted at him. "How come you get to go outside, and I don't?"

Pierre chuckled. "We're not all going, but we found the threat. He's camped out in a cave on the edge of the island."

Isa let out a breath of relief. "That's excellent. What are you doing about it?"

"Jude, Drew, Seamus, and Tad will hunt him down and take care of him. It should be easy. He's a dragon, not a wizard."

Isa didn't like the idea of anyone being killed, but if this dragon was here to assassinate her, then it had to be done. This was her life. A series of threats and people constantly seeking her head.

"If they get him, then can I go outside? Please. I've been trapped inside for weeks now."

It was a bit of an exaggeration, but she didn't care.

"Yes, of course. I'll take you out myself once we get this guy," Pierre assured her.

Jude, Seamus, Drew, and Tad approached her, decked out in winter armor with furs and plates. They all had two swords strapped to their backs and carried spears. They would likely fight as dragons, but if they needed to fight as humans, they had to be prepared.

"Come and kneel," she commanded them all. She didn't often get to see them off. They usually went without her knowledge. The four knelt before her, and she kissed them on their foreheads for good luck. Except for Jude.

Jude she kissed on the lips, and he gave her a cheeky grin.

Pierre cleared his throat. "Your Majesty, they should be going now."

"Of course." She backed away, and a few other guardians pried open the massive front door.

They stood in front of Pierre for a moment.

"Bring me his head," Pierre said with a growl.

Isa gulped. She didn't want to see any heads of dragons unless they were alive and attached to a body. She really wished they could imprison the traitors instead, but Pierre explained that imprisoning a dragon is near impossible. Plus, he didn't want to risk bringing the enemy into the castle.

The wind blew the snow in, and they made their way out. Isa crossed her arms against the cold but stayed put. Watching them change filled her with awe. As soon as they cleared the door, the four men became four massive, glittering green dragons. They looked like the emerald she wore on her neck.

They spread their wings and took off in the bright sunlight.

Isa inhaled. She loved the smell of snow. She couldn't wait to get back out into it.

CHAPTER 23

Sid rushed into the bedroom and flicked on the light in the en suite bathroom. Liam wasn't in there either, and there was zero evidence he had been. The shower was dry, and so was the sink.

"Where is he?" Aspen's voice had risen a few notches. Sid felt his own panic setting in. Liam snuck out now and then, but Baden always kept them apprised of where Liam was going. The fact that Baden had not kept Sid in the loop did not bode well.

"Maybe he had to get to school early for a project or something." In his heart, Sid knew this wasn't true.

Aspen snorted. "He doesn't go in early."

Sid rubbed his eyes. He didn't want to think about the worst-case scenario here. "Okay. Maybe he has a new girlfriend or something and he snuck out to see her."

"That is definitely a more realistic possibility. But he also knows he doesn't need to sneak." Her voice shook, betraying her fear. He could feel her terror in his bones. He thought about shutting it off but wanted that connection with her.

Sid shrugged. "But the girl might. Let's check the garage. If one of the cars is gone, then we'll breathe easier."

"Sid, what if he…" Aspen's voice caught. He knew what she was about to say.

"Don't think about that. Even he wouldn't be that foolish, and if he was, Felix would never let him go."

But Liam had been itching to prove himself for the last couple of years. Sid and Aspen were insanely proud of him, and they told him all the time, but he never seemed to be happy with his achievements.

When he chose to train with Felix, Aspen had been all over it, but Sid wasn't convinced it was the best place for him. Assassins were always in danger.

He pushed open the door to the garage and turned on the lights. Three Jeeps, two motorcycles, a Land Rover, a Mercedes, and two Ferraris.

Aspen brought a hand to her throat. "Sid…"

He gripped both of her hands. "We still don't know where he went. He might be at a friend's or a girl's house. He could've just as easily flown there. Let's go back inside and make some phone calls."

Aspen gave a stiff nod. He couldn't let her see his own worry.

They spent a good hour on the phone, calling everyone they knew. Most of the kids were at school, so they didn't answer, but texts came in from everyone.

Liam wasn't at school, Damon hadn't heard from him, and Ella hadn't seen him at the Purple Dragon.

Sid sent out eagles to search for him, but he knew that would be pointless.

Aspen called Liam's phone and eventually found it under his pillow with all of Aspen's calls and a few dozen text messages from friends warning him that his parents were looking for him.

This was absolutely the worst-case scenario.

"I don't know who else to call," Aspen said.

"Me neither." His stomach was in knots.

An eagle landed on the windowsill, and Sid flung it open. "Please tell me you have good news."

Late last night, Liam was seen flying into Felix's cave with Baden. He flew north after that.

Sid met Aspen's eyes.

Their only son was in mortal danger.

CHAPTER 24

Why does she kill her own people? Baden asked. The air was quite a bit colder near the North Pole. They hadn't seen civilization in hours. Baden rode on Liam's back as he was too small to keep up. His little wings were no match for Liam's wide wingspan.

Because they don't listen to her. She refuses to accept any sort of dissidence. Even if they are harmless. She rules with an iron fist. I expect she thinks she's doing the right thing. Those are the most dangerous kinds of rulers. The ones who believe they know best and will do anything to stop someone who gets in their way.

But you said that no one has seen her in years. How does she manage that?

Liam watched the beautiful bobbing ice in the teal water. *She has a group of dragons who are loyal to her and do her bidding. They've killed hundreds of rebels in the last few years. She has to be stopped.*

But why us? Why can't the rebels do it on their own?

Because they don't have the manpower. From what Mom and Dad said, we're basically going in there to make sure Jens was telling the truth.

Land came into view, and Liam dropped low, not wanting to be seen by other dragons who might be in the area. He knew what Felix would do, and he searched for an opening in the cliff face. He spotted a trail of smoke coming from one.

He's in there.

How do you know?

Because I can smell him.

Liam landed on the hard-packed snow above the cave.

Aren't we going in?

No. We'll wait and follow him. If we reveal ourselves now, he'll make us leave.

Baden shook his head. *You're going to get yourself killed.*

Liam hid in the trees and waited for Felix to come out while Baden explored the area. *Not much here but polar bears and whales. It's pretty, though.*

The scene was beautiful in a strange way. White as far as the eye could see with occasional flashes of blue and green. His mom would love it. She'd probably try to befriend a polar bear and get eaten, but she'd still have fun.

Later in the day, Liam heard movement in the cave below. Most dragons wouldn't notice the sound, but Liam wasn't most dragons. Sure enough, Felix sailed out and over the trees above them. Liam waited a few moments longer and then rushed out after him. He wouldn't be able to keep his identity secret for long—not if he wanted to keep his head—but he'd try. Because the longer he waited, the better chance he had of Felix not sending him home. And his goal was to stay and help.

Baden flew silently next to him, nerves pouring off his little body.

What are you scared about? Liam asked.

Felix might let you live out of respect for your father, but he'll kill me for letting you come.

Ah, you'll be fine. I won't let him hurt you.

Though, Baden had a point. If Felix was going to hurt either one of them, it would be Baden. Liam would protect him though. They were all here on the same mission. He'd make Felix see sense.

Felix was far ahead of them, a gold dot on the horizon. Suddenly, that gold dot spun around and flew straight for them. Showtime. Liam raced through the arguments in his head about why he should be here.

We've been noticed, he warned Baden.

Liam floated in place, waiting for Felix. This wouldn't be a pretty meeting.

WHAT THE HELL ARE YOU THINKING?

Liam had definitely been yelled at worse, but this was probably only the beginning.

I want to be the best tracker and assassin I can. I can't do that unless I do real jobs. Seeing as they are few and far between, I have to take advantage of them all.

Felix flew in circles around them, smoke escaping his nostrils. *Go home. This is not a training mission. I will likely be killed, and so will you.*

I'm not going anywhere except that mountain over there where this evil queen lives. You need my help. I have information you can use.

Felix spun around, his eyes searching the sky. Liam used the time to regroup and think of other things he could say, but then, without warning, Felix dove into the trees, and Liam had the good sense to follow. Felix turned into a human as soon as he hit the ground, and so did Liam.

Liam felt the iciness of the air. He'd noticed it as a dragon, but he could stay warm in dragon form. This was as cold as any mountain top in Yellowstone. Baden landed next to him.

Felix pulled Liam close, his eyes blazing. He put his mouth to Liam's ear. "We've been spotted."

Liam looked to the sky.

High about the trees flew a half-dozen green dragons.

To Be Continued...

Copyright © 2021 by Kimberly Loth

All rights reserved. No part of this book may be reproduced, transmitted, downloaded, distributed, stored in or introduced in any information storage and retrieval system, in any form or by any means, whether electronic or mechanical without express permission of the author, except by a reviewer who may quote brief passages for review purposes.

This is a work of fiction. The characters, incidents, and dialogues, in this book are of the author's imagination and are not to be construed as real. Any resemblance to actual events or persons, living or dead is completely coincidental.

CHAPTER 1

"Call the council and Valentine," Sid told the eagle perched on his bedroom windowsill. He needed all of his available resources at the moment. He tried to ignore the knot in his stomach.

His son was gone.

Chasing after an unknown enemy.

One that could kill him.

The eagle bowed and flew away. Aspen paced in front of him. "Why would he do this?" Their bedroom, which was one of Sid's favorite rooms in the house, felt small and claustrophobic. The heat was on because the temps had dropped below freezing again overnight, and it made the room stuffy. He wanted to fly out into the morning like the eagle.

Sid gave Aspen a tight grin. "Because he's like you."

And Liam had been. From the moment he could walk, he was fearless and adventurous. But Sid never thought that would someday put his life in serious danger. Well, he'd known it would, but not to this extent. He figured Liam would get stuck in an avalanche or wreck his car. Not go chasing after a murderous queen.

Aspen glowered. "Don't you dare blame this on me."

Sid sighed and reached for her hand. He didn't want to blame her. "I'm not. I'm just stating a fact. He has no fear bone. Neither do you."

"I do now," she shrieked and jerked her hand out of his. "He could die out there."

Sid grabbed for her again, refusing to let go. It was rare to see Aspen frazzled or upset. "Yes, he could. But he could also survive, so let's not write him off yet. Why don't you take a shower while I make breakfast? We need to eat so we can think properly." He'd learned that in the last war. Food and sleep were essential to strategizing.

She gave a stiff nod and escaped into the bathroom. Sid would never tell Aspen this, but if the queen was even half as evil as Jens said, Liam didn't stand a chance. Though if he was with Felix, then he might survive.

Why would Felix let him go?

He wouldn't. Which was Sid's worry. If Liam was out there on his own, he could be in real danger.

Sid dug out the eggs and bacon from the fridge, but

before he could even so much as crack an egg, Pearl crushed him in a hug.

"Liam is going to be okay." Her voice was thick with emotion.

He ignored her anxiety that poured into him. He had enough of his own to deal with.

"You got here fast."

"I was actually on my way over to see if everything went okay with Felix. The eagle found me midflight. I didn't expect Liam to hijack his trip." She searched Sid's face and extracted the egg carton from his hand. "Now, you let me take care of this." She shooed him into the dining area. He wanted to make the eggs so he could distract himself, but Pearl was trying to be helpful, so he let her.

Sid sat at the table and stared out the window. He was glad he'd had Aspen shower. She'd cry and get all of her anxieties out. Then, she'd come down.

Jens walked into the room, and Pearl jerked her head around. "Who are you?"

"He's the dragon that came over from Europe and asked for help," Sid said.

"Thanks a lot. Now my nephew is in mortal danger." She went back to attacking her eggs. Jens didn't respond, just poured himself a cup of coffee and sat next to Sid.

"What happened?"

"Liam followed our assassin that was going to take out your queen."

Jens whistled. "That woman is right. He is in mortal danger."

"Oh, I'm sorry. That's my sister, Pearl."

Pearl slammed a plate down on the table. "And if anything happens to him, I'm holding you responsible."

Jens stood. "I understand. I will leave you two alone. If you need anything Obsidian, you know where to find me." He turned and left the room.

Pearl visibly relaxed after Jens left. Sid thought about scolding her concerning her behavior toward him but didn't have the energy to do so. Breakfast was tense and quiet. Pearl tried to keep it light, but after her third story about the babies' antics, she stopped talking as well.

The side door banged open, and Valentine and Hazel rushed in. "What can we do?" Val asked.

Sid shook his head. "I don't know yet. The council will be here soon. Help yourself to some breakfast."

SID WELCOMED the council to his home, and Aspen stood at his side, studying the small band of dragons as he talked. After he finished his story, no one said anything for a good minute. Sid was disappointed that nobody had any ideas, and he could feel the collective dread in the group.

The early morning air was cool, but not cold. Liam would be freezing because it was much colder where he was headed. Sid swallowed the lump in his throat. He couldn't think about where Liam was right now.

Finally, Pearl spoke up. *Why don't we send a small group of warriors to collect him?*

That's a great idea, Kairi responded.

"Yes, that is a good idea." He looked up at his sister. She always was wise and made good decisions. It's why he chose her as the council member who oversaw the babies. "We'll send only the best. And I will go with them."

"Sid, no," Aspen said. She crossed her arms and let out a breath.

"Why not? This is my son. I'm going on the rescue mission to save him."

Aspen's right. You shouldn't go. Pearl stood tall, her silver scales reflecting in the sun.

That was a bunch of bull. He had every right to go rescue Liam, and they couldn't tell him no. He was just as good as his warriors, he hadn't let himself go soft.

"Why the hell not?" Sid clenched his fists. They would not convince him to stay behind.

"Because you're the king, and we need you alive," Skye said. "If this queen is truly evil, she could capture you and use you as leverage to enslave not just Europe but America as well. You can't go."

But he knew Liam like no one else did. He would find him and save him. He could not risk someone else going after him. They didn't love him like Sid did. They wouldn't risk everything for him.

Pearl nodded. And then, so did Xanthous, Kairi, and Nedra. His eyes met Aspen's.

"They're right," she said.

His jaw clenched. They couldn't tell him no. He would put himself on the front lines to protect his son. What was the point of being king if you couldn't even save your own family?

He would not be left behind.

CHAPTER 2

Felix shoved Liam into the shadows, and he stumbled back. "You hide in the trees, and I'm going to fight."

Cold bit at Liam's face, but he barely felt it. A fight was coming, and he was not about to be left out. Baden perched on his shoulder, claws digging into Liam's skin.

Liam stepped forward, his feet sinking to his knees in the snow. "No way. I'm fighting with you." He fought loads of times and was ready for some real-world action. He knew Felix could handle this on his own, but he could at least do something.

Felix grabbed Liam by his jacket and pulled him close. "Our purpose here is to find the queen. We've been spotted by other dragons, and we don't know their purpose. If I am captured, then you will need to carry on by foot. With any luck, they don't know about you, and this can be used to our advantage." He shoved a sword into Liam's gloved hand. "If I die, kill her. Under no circumstances will you come to my aid. The mission comes first."

Liam didn't like it, but he understood. Information was gold in these situations, and the fighting would have to wait. If the queen thought only one dragon was coming after her, she'd be caught off guard by two.

He glanced at his hand and saw that he held the dragon slayer. Felix had never let him wield that weapon before. Liam attached it to his belt and retreated into the trees while Felix turned into a dragon.

Liam wanted nothing more than to turn into a dragon himself, but he would not let Felix down. Felix could handle this. He'd told Liam stories of times when he'd faced up to twenty enemy dragons on his own. Felix was the best at what he did. Once he defeated these dragons, maybe he'd trust Liam to help with the queen. But he'd only do that if Liam listened to him now. The first rule in war was to listen to your general. So he followed the directions even though his instincts were screaming at him to fight.

He spotted the wave of emerald green dragons up above. He'd never seen dragons that color. Sure, they had the green babies, but they were tiny and darker in color. He thought back to his history lessons, but he couldn't recall learning about the green dragons. He was never a great student unless the lesson involved swords or battles.

The approaching dragons were bigger than the royal dragons, but not like the arctic dragons—which his mom had said were as big as houses.

The dragons rose high above the trees and out of Liam's sight. The area reminded him of the mountains in Yellowstone. All snow and tall pines. He tugged his coat tighter and pulled his hat farther down over his ears. This was colder than most winters on the ground at home, and he wouldn't last long as a human out here. He stepped out into the clearing, just a few inches, but he couldn't see anything.

Baden, can you go watch?

Yes, Your Highness.

Stay below the canopy. Don't let them see you. If Baden was spotted, Liam risked Felix's task. Silence and invisibility were key.

Yes, of course.

Baden flew into the trees, turning green and brown. His camouflage was handy like that. When Liam was a kid, Baden would sneak into the kitchen for him and get snacks in the middle of the night. As he got older, Baden was instrumental in helping him sneak out of the house. He'd also been a great partner as Liam started training to be an assassin.

Liam followed the sounds of slashing and the occasional flashes of fire. The snow was hard to navigate, but most of it was packed down. Snowshoes would be handy right about now.

Some of the fire was green, but he saw his fair share of gold as well. Felix was holding his own as Liam knew he would. This would be a fight they'd be talking about for a long time, and Liam wished he could see it and learn from it. He'd never fought more than one dragon at a time.

The trees above him suddenly rained pine needles, and Liam crouched down as a green tail swished above him. He retreated farther into the trees, but the fight rose high in the sky again, and Liam still had no idea what was going on.

Baden, talk to me. What do you see?

The green dragons are fierce. It's four against one. Felix is doing good though.

Liam's stomach soured. Four against one. Sure, Felix could handle it, but Liam wanted to be a part of this. He could do this. He could make sure that Felix won.

I'm coming up there. He projected his thoughts to both Felix and Baden.

NO. DON'T YOU DARE, Felix roared in his head.

Liam clenched and unclenched his fists. This was so frustrating. He didn't want to just be a tag along. Well, he'd deal. When this was over, they would have a fire, eat some fish, and Felix could relive the whole fight.

Maybe then Liam will have felt like he was there. He wondered what scars Felix would have. Felix had scars from all of his fights, and he always said the scars told the story of his life.

Out of nowhere, Baden rushed at him, pushing him

farther into the trees. Claws dug into Liam's chest, and tree branches scratched his cheek. He fell, hitting the snow-packed earth. Wet cold seeped into his neck as branches above them snapped and fell. Pine needles and snow showered down.

A loud thump hit the ground where he'd been standing, and Liam scrambled up. A great gold headless body lay in front of them. It took Liam a second to register the scene.

No.

This couldn't be happening.

Liam rushed forward, ignoring all the blood, toward the scarred and lifeless body sprawled out in the snow,

Felix was the best-trained tracker and assassin his father had. He'd fought in countless battles. He'd hunted down evil and vile dragons. He'd known how to handle it all.

But not this.

Felix was dead.

CHAPTER 3

The dance the night before had been fun, but Grace didn't dance with Jude at all.

There were only three men close to her age in the castle, Jude, Drew, and Seamus. She had no idea how old they were as they were dragons, but they appeared—and acted—like they were in their late teens or early twenties.

Grace stopped in the hallway to straighten a few vases that had been knocked askew on a shelf. No doubt the work of drunken guardians. Or perhaps Missy had been playing here.

She stepped back to survey her work. Much better. She wasn't a maid, but she'd grown up with her mother being the head maid, and so she liked things tidy. She was pleasantly surprised to find very little dust on the shelf. Her mother would've been proud of the way the castle was maintained.

A hand slid around her waist, and she was pulled tight against a hard body.

"Imagine finding Lady Grace alone in a dark hallway," Seamus whispered, his lips brushing the tip of her ear. Dragon's Teeth! She didn't move, unsure of what to do. He slid his other hand down the side of her thigh. Bile rose in her throat. "I did so enjoy our dances last night, didn't you?"

Grace remained silent. She didn't want to say yes and encourage him or say no and make him angry. This was something she'd never dealt with before, and she wasn't sure what to do.

"I thought you were out hunting the threat to Isa's life."

"I had to bring a report to Pierre. I'm going back out, but I saw you and thought I'd talk to you first."

This was hardly talking.

Footsteps came around the corner, and Seamus let go. She let out a breath. Thank the gods.

"There you are. Pierre will see you now. Come on," Bartlby said. Grace threw him a grateful look even though there was no way he would understand why. He gave her a small smile.

"I'll be right there," Seamus said. Grace hoped Bartlby would wait for him, but he didn't. He was already around the corner. Seamus turned to her and stroked her cheek, sending shivers down her spine.

"You are stunning. Not as gorgeous as the queen, of course, but a very close second. We will definitely have to finish this. Perhaps you could come to my room later." His voice had dropped to a near whisper.

"I have to attend to the queen." Grace tried to hide the tremble in her voice. Now, she wished they'd never danced at all. Or that she had just danced with the old guys and Benjamin.

"All night?" His eyes glinted with questions.

"Sometimes." She forced the confidence and took a step back, hoping he'd get the hint.

He gave her a creepy grin. "Well, isn't that an interesting development? Another time, then. Another dark hallway."

He turned and sauntered away.

"No, wait. That's not what I meant." Oh, he was going to have all kinds of bad ideas about her.

But he was already gone.

Grace ran a shaky hand through her hair and gripped the shelf with the vases. The guardians had always been incredibly respectful of her, but Isa had put her in a gown last night that made her look like a lady instead of a servant. She'd gone to the dances before but always just in her normal clothes. Perhaps they'd never looked at her in that way until now. She'd wanted to be noticed, but not like this.

And she didn't want to be scared that Seamus would be down every dark hallway. What on earth was she going to do?

She let out a breath, took one last glance at the vases, and made for brighter hallways.

CHAPTER 4

*L*iam raced for the body and collapsed next to it. "No, no, no, no, no…" The cold snow seeped into his knees. His chest felt hollow and his mind blank.

Felix was invincible. Untouchable. He couldn't be dead. Tears pricked at Liam's eyes. He'd never known anyone who had died before. The wars had happened long before he was born, and the possibility of Felix dying had not even occurred to him. Not even when Felix shoved the sword in his hand and told him to finish the job if he was captured. He thought Felix was being dramatic.

Felix's body was still warm. Blood oozed from several spots and gushed from his neck, melting the snow around them. Liam had a hard time even processing what he was seeing.

Felix was dead.

Not coming back.

Liam focused on the body in front of him and swallowed down the sick that threatened to come up. He raked his eyes up and down the war-torn scales. "Baden, find his head," he choked out.

Baden leaned his little body next to Liam, his warmth a welcome relief against the cold.

"They took it with them," his voice cracked.

Liam had to bite down the scream that formed in his throat. If they heard him, they would come back and finish him and Baden off, and Felix's sacrifice would be in vain. Now, Felix's plan made so much more sense to Liam. He couldn't believe he didn't see it before. Felix never stood a chance against them. He sacrificed himself so Liam would survive. Liam always knew Felix was tough and brave, but he never realized he was the type to sacrifice himself for his friends. Liam wiped at his eyes.

"Follow them. See where they go, and come straight back here. Don't let yourself be seen."

"Yes, Your Highness, I'll be back in no time."

As soon as Baden was above the trees, Liam slumped next to Felix. The warmth of the body protected him from the cold, and he sobbed. Felix was his mentor, his closest friend aside from Damon. Felix believed in him when even his parents did not. Over the last several months, they'd spent hours together training, and even though Felix was hard on him, Liam knew he was the only one Felix had trained for more than a few weeks. Felix knew Liam would be able to one day be as good as him.

And now he was dead.

Liam wiped away the freezing tears and took three deep breaths. He could allow himself no more time to grieve. Felix taught him that. Grief was not a productive emotion, and on the battlefield, it caused warriors to fall who would otherwise have lived. And he had to live.

For Felix.

He had to think about his next moves. He would avenge Felix—that much was sure—but he had to be careful. This was so much more complicated than anything he had ever dealt with or trained for. There had been at least four dragons fighting Felix.

Liam suddenly realized how blind they had been. They had no idea what kind of army this queen had or how many dragons they'd be facing. They didn't know anything about her or her powers. This was dumb.

Liam was grateful he came though because, otherwise, Felix would've died, and no one would know. Felix's body grew cold, and Liam turned into a dragon as much for his own sake as Felix. He would freeze to death as a human.

He stared at the body and then let out a long gold flame, turning Felix's body into a golden gemstone. It was a shame that the head wasn't there, but he still had to honor his friend and make sure the stone made it to the halls of heroes.

Baden arrived a few moments later. He landed in front of Liam, shaking off snow. "About five miles east of here is a fortress bigger than I've ever seen carved into the mountain. The spires of the castle reach high into the sky, and it's protected by more than just a few dragons. I could feel the magic radiating off of it."

Did you see the queen?

"No. The only things I saw were the dragons who fought Felix entering a cavern. The one in the back had Felix's head in his claws. I'm guessing he'll deliver it to the queen."

The queen was responsible for the death of Felix. She would pay. And then he'd personally tear the heads off all of the dragons who helped her. Liam tried not to give in to the anger in his chest. Anger would cause him to do something careless.

We don't know what we're dealing with here. I want you to take Felix's stone back to my dad, and I'm going to sneak into the castle.

"That is not a good idea. You should return with me and let your dad decide what to do next." Baden's eyes widened.

Baden, I'm not asking permission. I'm commanding you to go back and leave me here. I promised Felix I would finish the job. I'll be fine. Trust me.

Baden's whole body shook. "No. You won't. I saw what those dragons did to Felix. They'll kill you, and then your parents will kill me for leaving you here."

Give me a little credit. I'm not going in there as a dragon. I'll do so as a human. Take the stone back. This is not up for discussion.

CHAPTER 5

Ruby sat in a window seat overlooking the ocean, her massive headphones covering her ears. The sight of three sea dragons flying close distracted her. She knew them, of course, but wasn't ready to see them. They would interrupt her.

She glanced at her lap. She had only about thirty pages left in the book but would never finish it now. However, she could try. Sometimes her siblings left her alone when she was reading, but that was never something she could count on.

Her dad, Rowan, sat at the table reading his own book. He never bothered her while she read. They were the same like that though she looked nothing like him. She inherited most of her physical looks from her mom, Skye, but she was a lot more like her dad; except in the one way she wanted to be.

Her dad was human.

Ruby was a dragon.

And she didn't want to be one. She rarely took on her dragon form. Only when she wanted to fly to Everett's old cave where all the books were stored. Which was nearly every day, but still. Some of her siblings only became human when Mom made them come into the house.

Ruby didn't know how her dad could concentrate without headphones. Their house was always a cacophony of noise and chaos. She wondered what it would be like to be an only child like her cousin, Liam. Probably lonely.

But blessedly quiet.

Today, her Grandma Jewel had taken the three youngest with her to visit her cousins in the ocean, but Trinity and Gabe were making a racket in the kitchen. They inherited their love of cooking from Mom, but they argued loudly every time they made something. Opal, Sapphire, and Jasper watched some cartoons on the TV and had turned the volume way up because of Trinity and Gabe.

Hughie sat on the other side of the window seat from Ruby. He was definitely the favorite of her nine siblings. Only six years old and not a dragon at all, he had somehow managed to inherit magical abilities. Mom didn't know how since neither she nor Dad had them.

When Hughie had first exhibited magic, Ruby set herself on the task of researching it, but their family was a rarity in all of history. No dragon had ever had babies with a human before. Even the kings who had had human wives never procreated, which kept the peace so that when the king died, anyone could inherit the throne, and the dragons would be loyal to them.

Her mom, Skye, was a dragon but could no longer take a dragon form since the white witch took it from her before Ruby was born. Her dad was human. Seven of the ten kids they had could take on dragon forms, and three could not. She had cousins in the same situation.

Val and Hazel only had three kids though, all way younger than Ruby. Two of them were dragons. Aspen and Sid only had one, Liam, and he was the most arrogant dragon Ruby had ever met.

Ruby thanked her lucky stars every day that she didn't have to live in Yellowstone with Liam.

Something hard hit the side of Ruby's face. She ripped off her headphones and got ready to yell at Gabe and Trinity for throwing food, which happened on a regular basis, but it didn't reach this far that often.

"Sorry, sorry, sorry," Hughie said, scrambling over to her and snatching the marble that hit her cheek.

She rubbed the spot that was surely a bright red and stared at the terrified eyes of her little brother. She gave him a fake smile. She could never be mad at him. "It's okay. What happened?"

He gathered a few more marbles and scooted closer to her. "Watch."

He held them in his palms, and one by one, the marbles floated above his hands and looped in circles. His magic was getting better. "One got away a second ago."

"That's really cool." She was so proud of him.

Hughie smiled. He didn't practice magic very often because it scared some of the other siblings, but Ruby appreciated it and encouraged him. Someday, that might be a skill he needed.

The door crashed open, and the marbles fell to the seat. Hughie gathered them up, stuck them in his pocket, and went to join the others watching TV.

Loud chatter filled the room, and Ruby stuck a bookmark in her book. There would be no more reading today.

CHAPTER 6

Grace flung open the curtains and let the bright afternoon sun filter through Isa's window. The side windows were made of a rose patterned stained glass, and red and green light danced off the white quilt on Isa's bed. Isa was up in her tower.

Missy blinked up at her from the bed again, her favorite napping spot.

"You are one lazy fox."

Missy stretched and yawned. She stood and jumped off the bed, winding her way around Grace's ankles like a cat. She slunk off to her bucket of toys in the corner, dug out a ball, and left it at Grace's feet.

Grace tossed the ball across the room. Missy bounded after it, and she chuckled as she watched the fox. "You know, that's not in my job description."

Missy dropped the ball where she stood and ran around in circles, jumping on the bed and the dressers. Grace raced for the dresser just as Missy hit a statue of an eagle, one of Isa's favorites. Grace caught it before it hit the ground. Phew.

Missy brought the ball back to Grace.

"Okay, point proven. You are not a lazy fox." She was curious about this animal who understood way too much English but didn't speak with her dragon master.

Grace threw the ball again and wondered if she'd get any work done. She moved to the armoire and flipped through Isa's dresses. Her mind flashed to the dark hallway and Seamus. She could pretend like it didn't happen, but it did, and she might not be so lucky next time.

She could tell Isa, but Isa might not see it as a problem. She might think the whole thing was good since she wanted Grace to hook up with one of the men. And Isa had never been harassed, so she didn't understand what it felt like. The guardians were too afraid of her to pressure her, as well they should be. One wrong move, and she'd have them executed. Not that she'd ever done that before, but she could.

Isa's grandmother executed a few people in the castle in her day, but Grace didn't know if Isa had it in her. No one had openly defied her, so it was hard to tell how she would react.

Even so, Grace didn't think Isa would understand her problem. She had been trying to set Grace up with Seamus or one of the others, in the first place. Missy nipped at her foot, and Grace glanced down. The ball sat next to her.

She threw it absentmindedly, and Missy pranced after it. She wished her only problems were how to get work done with a pesky fox around. She could still feel Seamus's grimy hand on her thigh. She shivered.

Grace's hand settled on a blue dress with woven pink flowers, one of Isa's favorites that she hadn't worn in quite some time. She pulled it out and set it on the bed. Missy jumped up, ball in mouth, and lay on top of the dress, getting white fur everywhere.

"Missy. Get off." She pushed at the fox, but Missy hopped back up.

"Ugh. Give me the ball."

Missy gave it up, and Grace grabbed the slobbery thing. She threw it as far as she could so she had time to brush the fox fur off the dress.

A crash came from the far side of the room. Missy stood on the dresser, ball in mouth, while the eagle lay in a thousand pieces on the floor.

"Dragon's Teeth! You dumb fox. Now I have to clean another mess. Out you go."

She picked up Missy, and Missy snapped at her all the way to the door. Then, she went back for the ball and tossed it down the stairs. Missy ran after it.

Grace shut the door and sighed. Today was not her day.

CHAPTER 7

"I don't know how much help we can be," Val said. He threw a rock and watched it splash in the ocean. As one of the three dragon kings, Val had been a huge help during the previous wars. Sid wished both Val and Skye were still dragons. But that had all changed at the end of the war when the white witch spelled them to be human and then died before they could switch back into dragons. They'd been stuck as humans ever since. If they had retained their dragon forms, then they could rule together as kings and queens, and Sid wouldn't have to make decisions on his own.

Then he could rescue Liam without the council freaking out.

Sid sighed and handed Skye's toddler, Odin, a seashell that the kid promptly put in his mouth. Skye snatched it away and picked him up, propping him on her hip. She was a natural mother who never seemed frazzled or bothered by her kids.

"Val's right. Maybe when we were dragons, we could've helped, but we're useless like this." Skye bounced Odin up and down, and he giggled.

Sid inhaled the cold, wet sea air. He had no idea why Skye chose to settle on the Oregon coast, but Sid didn't like it here. The sun never shone. He tried to read their emotions, but neither one was feeling particularly strong. They were mostly indifferent but worried.

"Except, you're not useless. You two were my biggest support during the last war, and I could use your expertise. You are the ones I trust. I tried to tag along with the rescue group, but they wouldn't let me. They told me it was too dangerous. But I'm going after him, and I don't want to do this alone. Will one of you please come with me?"

Skye laid a hand on his arm. "There's just not much we can do as humans. And besides, I don't think it's a good idea for you to go after him. But you aren't alone. You have a competent council, and Aspen is always by your side. We will be better help doing what we do best."

"What's that?" Sid sank onto the sand. He needed them with him, and he thought they'd be on board with rescuing Liam together. If it were Skye's daughter Ruby or Ember, Val's son, they would want to be on the rescue squad themselves. Fear and dread poured off both of them. Or maybe those were his own emotions. He couldn't even tell anymore.

Skye set Odin down, and he changed into a tiny blue dragon and then back into a toddler again.

"We have to think bigger than just rescuing Liam," Skye said. "I have a feeling the dragons you sent to get him will be back in a few days with a sheepish Liam in hand. You have some of the best warriors we've had in centuries. They won't fail. But this problem with the queen will last longer. Val and Hazel should still work with the human liaison office. If another war breaks out, they'll need that office. Rowan and I can do research in Everett's library and see if we can find any information on this queen. I had no idea the dragons still existed in Europe."

Skye made good points, but he wanted them by his side in case all hell broke loose. "Research can be done in Yellowstone. I want to have you two with me every step of the way. Will you please at least come back for a little while? Just until this clears up." He didn't want to say, "To help me when my son dies and I fall apart." He needed these two. Besides, he still hadn't ruled out flying to the island himself.

Odin picked up a clump of sand and threw it at Val, but the wind caught it, and it flew into Odin's face. He let out a wail. Maybe Aspen was right to stop at one.

Skye picked him up and wiped the sand off him. She and Val shared a look. Meanwhile, Odin continued to cry. He shifted into a dragon, and Skye set him on the ground and faced him toward the ocean. Sid remembered those days with Liam. He never knew what form Liam would be in, and he set three cribs on fire.

"Okay, we'll come, but I have to bring my whole family. I'm not leaving them behind."

Sid wanted to kiss her. "Of course you're bringing your whole family. You'll stay with us. We have plenty of room. We can enroll your kids in school with ours. Liam and Damon will be thrilled to show Ruby the ropes." His voice caught in his throat. Liam wouldn't be there to welcome her. But if the rescue party succeeded, then he would be able to help Ruby at school on Monday.

If Liam hadn't returned in two days, then Sid would fly out there himself and personally bring Liam home.

CHAPTER 8

*R*uby fumed in the cave of books, not far from her house. There was no way in hades she was moving to Yellowstone.

She sat on a bench and stared at all the books. She couldn't stay here forever. Eventually, her mom and dad would find her, but she would make them search. It took longer for them to get here anyway unless they got Trinity and Gabe to give them a ride. Which they probably would.

Ruby paced the cave. They couldn't make her go. She was seventeen and would be eighteen in a couple of months. That was old enough to live on her own, right? She'd get more reading done anyway. Maybe she'd figure out what to do about Hughie's magic if she had more peace and quiet. She always wanted alone time, and this was the perfect opportunity to prove to her parents that she was responsible. She'd just stay home.

Yeah, that's what she'd do.

She stared at the massive stacks and shelves of books. She could spend a thousand years in here and probably still not finish them all. She would try though. She'd already read six hundred and forty-seven of them. This cave had been her refuge when she came home from school in third grade and tried to escape the words of her teacher and classmates.

Beast.

Brute.

Dumb.

Before she moved to Oregon, she'd been a straight-A student, but when she got here, she was suddenly getting Ds and Fs on her assignments. She hid them from her parents, and when they found out, they figured it was because of stress from the move. She didn't correct them. She was too ashamed.

She'd hoped for a different teacher the next year, but Mrs. Jenkins moved from third to fourth grade and then from fourth to fifth grade. The school was small with only two teachers per grade, and she'd been unlucky enough to get Mrs. Jenkins three years in a row.

Her grades improved in middle school, but her reputation preceded her. It didn't help that in fifth grade, they had the birds and the bees talk, and Mrs. Jenkins basically told the students that if they dated a dragon, it would be bestiality and was no different than dating a bear or dog. She'd cried herself to sleep for weeks after that.

That rumor flew through the whole middle school the next year, and she was considered un-datable. She felt that way too. Unworthy of love.

She'd hated her dragon self ever since. In her logical mind, she understood that it was irrational. She even understood Mrs. Jenkins' prejudices. But she couldn't tell her emotional self that. Every time she tried, her shame stepped in.

She just wanted to be a normal human. Then she could love herself.

She couldn't go to Yellowstone. They *loved* dragons there, and Liam was the worst kind. Cocky and full of himself. He thought dragons were somehow better than humans, and that wasn't true. She avoided visiting whenever she could, and when she did, she hid from Liam and Damon because they wanted her to be a dragon and hang like they did when they were kids.

And she didn't want to.

A clattering came from the other side of the cave. She'd been found. She rehearsed her arguments in her head about why she would not go to Yellowstone.

She waited, facing away from the entrance, with her arms crossed. She would not make this easy on them. Let them rant first.

"Dear, stop being ridiculous."

Ruby spun and glowered at her mom. "Ridiculous. You

know how much I hate it there. Plus, I don't want to go to school with Liam and Damon."

Mom sighed and took a few steps toward her. "You didn't even let us finish telling you why we are going. Liam is missing. We have to go help Sid and Aspen."

"What do you mean missing?" She looked between Mom and Dad, who had just walked in.

This was news. Liam was invincible. Or at least he thought himself so.

"He went after some evil dragon in Europe and hasn't been seen since. We have to go help them."

Ruby snorted. He would be fine. He'd come back either flush with victory or with his tail between his legs. He was way overconfident, and she wasn't surprised he'd go missing and ruin her life.

"I'm staying here. I'm old enough to take care of myself."

"No. You're not. You're coming with us whether you like it or not. I need your help, and you need ours."

Ruby threw her arms into the air. "Of course you need my help. Maybe if you'd stopped before ten kids. Oh wait, you're pregnant again, aren't you? I'm sorry, eleven kids."

Mom brought her hands to her already swelling belly, hurt crossing her features. Ruby had gone too far. But she really, really didn't want to go to Yellowstone and be reminded of all the parts of herself that she hated.

Her father glared at her and put his arm around her mom. "You don't mean that. If we'd stopped at three, Hughie wouldn't be here. Now, I know you don't want to go, but Sid needs our help, and so we'll go. You'll finish school there."

"It's two months left of my senior year. I can hardly start over."

"We've already spoken with both schools, and they are going to make the transition easy. You're coming with."

Ruby clutched at her hair, her fingers digging into her scalp. "What if I don't?"

Dad stopped and thought for a moment. That was never good. When her dad thought about things, he usually came up with unarguable responses. The huge cave suddenly felt much smaller. She could already feel herself losing this fight.

"Well, I guess it might be easier if we don't take the kids. We'll have more time to focus. If you feel like you're responsible enough to live here by yourself, then you can watch the kids too."

The kids would never listen to her, and she wouldn't get a second of peace and quiet.

"What? No. I'm only seventeen. You can't do that to me."

"Then you can't stay here." He crossed his arms.

Ruby stomped out of the cave and flung herself off the edge, her wings catching her before she fell.

Sometimes, she did not like her dad.

CHAPTER 9

"And I really hope I got all the glass pieces, or the queen will get one lodged in her toe," Grace said with a sigh. She sank onto a rough bench next to Olga's worktable. The whole place smelled like yeast, one of her favorite smells. If she didn't have to attend to Isa, she'd be in the kitchens all the time.

Olga laughed. She always appreciated Grace's stories.

"I know. I shouldn't find it funny, but I do. Here, knead this." Olga passed her a chunk of bread dough for tomorrow's breakfast.

"It is a little funny. Usually Missy doesn't want anyone but Isa playing with her. I just wanted to get her dress ready." Which took her another good thirty minutes to brush after she cleaned the glass. She'd locked Missy out and had to listen to her whine and scratch at the door the whole time.

After dinner, Isa had wanted a bath, and she liked to be alone down there, so Grace had a little bit of time before helping her get ready for bed.

The kitchen was quiet tonight. Just her and Olga. This was unusual. Normally, there were a few other servants in here. Alfred spent all his free time here since he was sweet on Olga.

The cook had been like a mother to her since her own had died many years ago, and she trusted Olga. Maybe she could help with the dark hallways problem.

"Olga, can I talk to you about something?"

"What's on your mind?"

Grace folded the dough over and beat it for a second. "Well, um, have you ever had any of the guardians come on to you?"

Olga waved a hand down her ample body. "Good lord, have you seen me? No, I haven't. But you have?" Her face was full of concern.

Grace's face flushed, and she stared at her dough. "Just recently. Seamus."

Olga shivered. "Ooh, that boy gives me the willies. Have you talked to Isa?"

Grace shook her head. "I don't think she'd understand. She likes the attention they give her, and they would never do anything inappropriate to her."

It felt good getting this out. Grace beat at the dough as she talked, grateful she had Olga.

Olga dusted her hands off on her apron and opened a cupboard. She came back with something. "When I was a young girl, skinny and pretty like you, my father gave me this."

She held out a knife in a sheath with a leather belt and handed it over. It was odd to think of Olga as a young girl. She hadn't always lived in the castle.

"You tie that around your leg with the knife on the outside of your thigh. You use it if you have to. The queen will understand."

Would she though? Grace hoped she could trust that Isa would take her side, but she didn't know for sure.

"Thank you." The knife felt heavy in her hands, and she hated that it had come to this, but she'd feel safer with it.

"Put it on now. There's no one here."

Grace hiked up her skirt and fastened the weapon on her thigh. It was a tad uncomfortable but would be a good reminder that it was there. She reached for Olga and gave her a big hug. "Thank you."

Olga returned the hug. "Anytime, dear. I might send Benjamin after you from time to time to make sure you're safe. If anything else happens, I want you to tell me."

"I will." But she wasn't sure she would. She trusted Olga, but if the situation escalated, Olga might take things into her own hands, and Grace didn't want her getting into trouble.

She was torn between two worlds. Isa was like a sister to her, but her real family was in the kitchens. Well, as real as non-blood family could get.

As she left, she pressed her hand against the knife. At least she could protect herself now if she had to.

CHAPTER 10

Grace was halfway up the stairs to prepare Isa's bed when she heard footsteps behind her. She spun, her heart racing.

Four guardians raced toward her, Jude in the lead and Seamus in the rear. They were decked out in their winter gear and breathing hard.

"Lady Grace, where's Isa?" Jude asked.

"In the baths."

"We need to talk to her."

"You know she hates being interrupted." Isa had been spending more time there than usual lately, and that was the one place she demanded to be left alone.

"Yes, but this is important. She'll want to hear it," Jude said. His face was dirty and tired looking, but he still made her heart melt.

She hesitated. Isa didn't have many hard and fast rules. Most of the time, just about anybody could interrupt her, and she'd be gracious about it. Her baths were a different story. She usually told Grace what time to get her, and Grace never came earlier. A couple of times, Grace had returned on time to find a very grumpy Isa thinking she was early. She'd be likely to take off Grace's head the next time they sparred.

She wrung her hands. "Why don't I go first and see what she wants to do."

Jude shook his head. "No. We'll come with you. We'd go ourselves, but since she's in the baths, we don't want to accidentally find her naked."

She expected a smirk or something from him, but he was being serious. Something big was happening.

This was still a bad idea, but she couldn't let them go there by themselves. Even if Isa was fully dressed.

They turned, and she followed them down the hall. Jude held the door to the stairway to the baths open for her. She held tight to the slippery rail and made her way down first.

"Funny meeting you in yet another dark hallway. I like this." Seamus placed a hand on her back, and she stiffened.

"Leave me alone."

"Perhaps you will join the queen in the baths, and we can watch."

Grace hurried away from him and hoped against hope that she didn't fall. Seamus kept his distance, thank goodness. She spun around before the door to the baths. Four shadowy figures stood there, Seamus in the front. She looked past him to Drew instead.

"Wait here. I'll let you know if she'll see you." Grace took a few deep breaths. She'd never interrupted Isa in her baths, and she'd seen Isa's temper before. Isa wasn't cruel, and she didn't yell, but she did effectively use the silent treatment for days if she was upset.

Grace pushed open the door and then shut it behind her and took a couple of deep breaths. She wasn't sure who she was more scared of at the moment, Seamus or Isa.

The baths were in a large cavern with hot springs. The whole room was humid and warm and glowed red. Grace was sweating before she even made it four steps.

She kept her steps light as she crossed the cave floor. Ahead of her, she could see the ruby lights and steam from the baths. She reached the edge of the pool, but the queen was nowhere to be seen.

The cavern was vast, and the pool seemed to go on forever. The floor was slick, smooth rock, and the air hot and humid.

"Isa, are you here?"

Splashes came from the other side. "What did I tell you about interrupting my baths?" Isa swam over and glowered at her.

Grace crouched down. "I know, Your Majesty, but a few of your guardians came to me and insisted they see you. I thought it would be best if I asked you first. I'm sorry."

Isa gripped the rock edge by Grace. "Did they say what they needed?"

"No, only that it was important. They would've come themselves if I hadn't insisted on seeing you first. Would you like to get dressed?"

Isa wrung out her hair. It was difficult to see her body in the water. The guardians could come in and not see anything Isa didn't want them to.

"No, I'll be fine here. Send them in. But let them know that if I don't deem it important, I will be very displeased they interrupted my baths. No one interrupts my baths."

"I know, Your Majesty. I will be right back."

She opened the door, and all four men stood there waiting in the cramped space. "She said this better be important."

"It is," Jude said and pushed past her, the others following. Seamus's gaze lingered on Grace.

She shut the door behind them. She didn't want to be that close to Seamus, but she felt like she had to supervise in case Isa needed her. She secretly hoped it wouldn't be important though because then maybe Seamus would be punished for something.

CHAPTER 11

Isa floated in the warm pool of water and waited for the four guardians. She hoped they brought good news. If they didn't get the dragon, then they wouldn't let her out of their sights until they did. And she wanted some of her freedom back. She knew her limits and always abided by them, but occasionally, when a specific threat came in, the guardians were a lot more protective.

Footsteps approached, but she didn't acknowledge them. Let them wait for a moment. Her baths were sacred, her only time to be alone, and she reveled in it. But there were other reasons.

A few years ago, she found several American books on being a good leader in her library. They were old but still valuable. One story stood out to her about a band that demanded they have a bowl of M&M's in their dressing room. But all the brown M&M's had to be removed. They didn't do it to be obnoxious. They did it because their concert had many moving and dangerous parts, and they knew that a crew who wouldn't bother to remove the brown M&M's might take shortcuts in other areas as well, putting themselves and their people in danger.

The baths were Isa's brown M&M's. If her people couldn't respect her decision here, they wouldn't respect it when it counted. So far, she hadn't had to test the theory.

Seemed today it would happen. She hated doing it, but she would have to put her foot down.

After what she felt was a good amount of silence, she swam to the edge.

Jude crouched next to the water with his eyes sparkling. That was good news. Hopefully, she was about to get her freedom back.

"So. Did you get him?" Isa asked. She glanced up and noticed the other guardians standing quite a distance away with Grace. They were chatting amongst themselves, so they couldn't hear this conversation.

"Yes, we did, Your Majesty. His head is in the front hallway if you would like to see it."

She flinched. She hated the thought of a dead dragon. Death was the one thing she couldn't stand. She was grateful for her gift to bring things back to life, but the one time she needed it, she wasn't there. "No, I would not. In fact, please make sure it is no longer there when we go outside tomorrow."

Jude nodded. "Yes, Your Majesty."

She waited for him to tell her more, but he just stared at her. She thought about this poor dead dragon. He came here hunting for her. Probably because he was with the rebels, and while she knew that they were generally trying to usurp her powers, she'd never actually interrogated one.

She knew the rebels had been around for a long time. They wanted to destroy her and allow the dragons to fly free in Europe once more. But they didn't understand how dangerous that was. If even one wizard remained, it could kill them all.

"Why did he want me dead?"

"We asked no questions." Jude chuckled.

Isa gripped the edge of the stone. In the past, when there had been threats, she'd been too young to know the details, but she expected more than kill-first-ask-questions-later. "Then, how do you know he wanted me dead?"

"Because everyone knows they are not allowed on the island on pain of death." Jude practically glowed with the flush of victory.

She knew that, but still. Maybe the dragon was seeking help or something. The rule was in place to protect her, but she didn't like it.

"Was he a mountain or forest dragon?" The deep violet mountain dragons hadn't been seen in centuries, but Isa was always hopeful they would show up, even though she'd been taught that they were all killed by wizards.

Jude's eyebrows creased. "Neither."

"What do you mean?"

He hesitated for a moment. "He was gold."

"Gold? But those dragons are from America. What was he doing here?"

"A mercenary perhaps. Hired by the rebels to kill you."

"But why would the American dragons listen to him? If someone came to me, I would double-check what was going on. They can't be that ignorant." She swallowed her anger. They should have questioned the dragon before they killed him or, at least, tried.

"We don't know why, but we will make sure the Americans know not to send any more assassins our way."

"I want to know why. Perhaps the American dragons aren't even aware the rebels are recruiting them. Is Tavish back?"

"Not yet. But I'll let Pierre know."

"Anything else?"

"Can I join you?" Jude's eyes danced.

She splashed him. "No. This is my bath, and I'm not rewarding you for interrupting me. In fact, I've decided on your punishment." She swallowed. Brown M&M's. She could do this. If they understood how important her rules were, they would've waited. Interrupting her baths could only happen in an emergency, and this was not one.

Jude looked at her in mock horror. "Punishment? But we've given you good news."

"And that news could've waited until I was in my room. Plus, you took too long, so I couldn't go outside today." She played it light, but she was being strategic.

"Fine, then. What's the punishment?"

"Tomorrow, I'm hunting four dragons with arrows."

Jude cringed. He'd told her before that the arrows hurt. Which was why she didn't do it very often, but she had to keep her skills up. Especially if the American dragons were out to get her too. She needed to practice with arrows soon anyway, but let him think it's because they interrupted her baths.

Pierre kept her in the dark on a lot of things—mostly because he didn't want her to worry, but she was old enough now that she should be made aware of what was going on in her kingdom. She would have a long conversation with him about who they could kill and when. No more of this nonsensical killing without questions.

That could wait until tomorrow after she went hunting.

She glanced over to Grace. Her baths were ruined, so she might as well get out now, as soon as they left.

She was a little happy though.

Tomorrow she got to go outside again.

CHAPTER 12

"Lady Grace, come here, please," Isa called. Grace scurried over, leaving the others by the door. She'd wanted to eavesdrop on Isa and Jude's conversation, but she thought that would've been a bit obvious.

Grace hurried to the side of the pool, and wet dripped down her back from the humid air of the baths. Usually, she helped Isa dress and undress, but she never lingered, and now she remembered why.

She wiped her damp forehead and stood as close to the pool as she dared. "Yes, Your Majesty?"

"Please see the guardians all the way out and then come back with my robe. I'm done."

"Of course." Grace straightened and adjusted her skirt, looking at Jude and avoiding Seamus's eye.

Grace pointed to the door. "The queen would like you to leave now."

Jude let his eyes linger on Isa for a moment longer, and Isa winked at him. At least she wasn't in a bad mood from having her baths interrupted.

Grace followed the men to make sure they made it up the stairs. That's what Isa meant about all the way out.

Seamus held the door for the rest of the guardians, and Grace hung back, hoping to take the door from him, but he motioned her through. She didn't know how to politely decline, and she didn't want to make a scene. So she went through and hurried up the stairs as quickly as she could, but he was faster. Before she knew it, he pinned her against the wall. The other guardians were already up the stairs and out the door. She wished she'd kept a sword on her. She knew how to fight with those. But only the guardians carried them outside of the sparring rooms.

"Why do you keep trying to get away from me?" His breath was hot on her face, and her chest constricted.

She squirmed underneath him and flailed. "Let me go."

He grabbed both of her hands and held them above her head. "I don't think I will."

Now she couldn't even reach for the knife. How she wanted to stab him in the heart. She swallowed the fear that was creeping up her throat. She sent a silent prayer to the gods. She didn't know how she would get out of this.

Seamus slid a grimy hand down her body and along her thigh. He paused at the weapon. "What do we have here?"

He reached under her skirt and found the knife. He unsheathed it and brought it to her neck.

"Was this for my benefit? That backfired on you now, didn't it? I think I'll keep this as a souvenir of our rendezvous." His voice was hard but quiet.

Grace shook uncontrollably underneath him, her back plastered against the cold, wet stone. She had to get away from him.

He dropped his head to her ear. "Now, what shall we do first?"

"Seamus, come on, man," Jude yelled from the top of the stairs.

Seamus gave a creepy grin. "Guess we'll have to wait. But now I know your tricks." He pressed his lips against hers and stuck his tongue into her mouth. Then, he let her go and raced up the stairs. She gagged and spit on the floor. She had to stop this. She couldn't let it go any further.

Her arms and legs shook as she made her way into the baths. The knife hadn't helped at all. She had to tell Isa.

But would Isa be helpful or dismissive? She hoped the first.

Because if not, Grace was screwed.

CHAPTER 13

Ruby dumped her stuff in her new room and escaped to the library. It wasn't as good as Everett's library in Oregon, but it was the last place in the world Damon would search for her, so she'd take it. He was sure to come over the second he found out she was in town and concoct some plan to go rescue Liam.

And she still wasn't convinced he needed rescuing.

Plus, it would be quiet, which was a rarity for Ruby. Sid's house was so big that she could hide out easily there. She grabbed a few random books off the shelf and dropped into an armchair.

She cracked open the spine of one and began to read though the words slipped right out of her mind. She couldn't believe she was here. It was three-quarters of the way through the school year, and she had to start all over. She wasn't concerned about friends and stuff. She didn't have many of those at home due to the rumors and Mrs. Jenkins, but she liked her studies, and she'd have to learn a whole new system. Which meant she might look dumb. And she didn't want that.

Why couldn't Liam have waited one more year? Then she'd be at college somewhere and not in this nightmare. Her parents could've moved here without her.

She'd tried again last night to beg her parents to let her go home or at least homeschool here, but they'd said no. Now she had to go to school with Damon, who was the exact opposite of Mrs. Jenkins. He worshipped the dragons.

The door cracked open, and she peeked up.

Speak of the devil. She avoided his eyes, hoping he'd take the hint, but of course, he didn't.

Damon threw himself into the chair across from her. Such a boy. They took up so much space. She peeked over her book. She hadn't seen him in at least three years. Liam had come to Oregon with his parents a couple of times, but they never brought Damon with.

His t-shirt revealed a muscular chest and arms. He probably wore it tight like that to get girls' attention, which Ruby was certain he had with those dark eyes and his devastating grin. If he had been anyone else, Ruby would've found him incredibly handsome.

"Well, the elusive princess has come home at last," Damon said with a smirk.

Ruby leaned forward. "Don't call me that." When she was a kid, before she moved to Oregon, she and Liam were proud of their prince and princess titles. Though, technically, her mom wasn't a queen anymore. She couldn't be because she could no longer take on her dragon form.

"Why not? You are, aren't you? Embrace it. I can't wait to introduce you to everyone at school. It's been so long since we've had a chance to hang out."

Oh, he was going to make this difficult, wasn't he?

Ruby pinched the bridge of her nose. "Listen. We will not hang out at school, and you will tell no one who I am. I don't want to be here, and I plan on keeping myself quiet. I don't want people to know I'm a dragon."

Damon creased his eyebrows. "Why?"

"Because I like being human, okay. Plus, I don't like attention. People won't remember who I am, and I want to keep it that way. It's only two months."

He leaned forward, his eyes bright. "But I was so excited. We need a girl to round out our posse."

"We? I thought the whole reason we are here is because Liam is missing."

Damon rolled his eyes. "You know as well as I do that he'll be back in a few days. I can't believe you'll be in school with us. You're going to love it."

Ruby looked back to her book, still not reading the words.

Damon chuckled. "Gotta run. I have to work tonight. But you'll change your tune once school starts."

Damon would eat those words.

Ruby would see to it.

CHAPTER 14

Grace's hand still shook as she helped Isa dry off and get into a robe. She managed to escape an attack, but she wasn't sure how much longer she had before Seamus took things all the way.

"You know, they could've waited until after I was done with my baths," Isa said, irritation crossing her features.

Grace tried to ignore the sweat pooling under her arms. "Did you tell Jude that?"

Isa nodded. "Yes. But he thought they were doing the right thing. The good news is that I can go back outside now. The threat is gone, and so tomorrow, I'm going hunting."

Grace followed her to the door and up the stairs, trying not to think about what just happened. She realized she hadn't responded to Isa and tried to clear her mind.

"What are you hunting?"

Isa wasn't a big hunter. The guardians hunted polar bears occasionally but always as dragons, never humans.

"Dragons." Isa laughed. "That will be their punishment. They have to let me shoot them with arrows."

Grace should've known that's what she was talking about. They wanted Isa to practice her skills so that she could defend herself if attacked, which meant she spent hours training with the guardians, trying to kill them. Isa could bring anything back to life, so she never actually killed anybody, permanently, when hunting or training.

Isa chattered until they reached her room, but Grace only half-listened, her mind still on the attack in the stairwell. Once the door was closed, Isa spun on her.

"What's wrong? You've been quiet."

"Oh, um." She had to tell Isa. She was the only one who could do anything. Grace had expended her options and didn't know how to fix this. "Well, Seamus kissed me."

Isa's eyes lit up. "No way. Tell me everything. No, wait. Let me get dressed first. Then, we'll lay in bed, and you can relive it for me."

"No, Isa, it's not like that." But Isa was already stripping off her robe and searching for her pajamas. Missy was sound asleep in bed.

Isa held out her nightgown, and Grace slipped it over her head. Then, Isa grabbed Grace's hand and pulled her onto the bed, shoving Missy out of the way. Missy yawned and moved to the foot of the bed. Grace lay amongst the mass of pillows and stared at Isa's excited face. She didn't know how to tell her this. She didn't want her to be all disappointed, but she couldn't let this go on anymore.

"So. When did he kiss you?" Isa asked, her eyes wide.

"Isa, you don't understand. I don't like him, and he gives me the creeps. I didn't want it."

Isa paused for a moment, drawing her eyebrows together. "Then, tell him you don't like him."

"I did, but he didn't listen. He trapped me and…"

"That stinks that you wasted your first kiss on a guy you don't even like. We should definitely make sure to find someone better. Maybe Drew?"

Isa didn't get it, and Grace didn't know how to explain it to her. She would have to find another way to ward off Seamus's advances. Grace sighed. "I like him a lot more than I like Seamus. That's for sure."

"Well, we'll have to see what we can do about that."

Drew was okay, but she had other things on her mind. Namely, how she would keep Seamus from doing worse things to her.

She'd never felt so helpless in her life. She wished her dad were still alive. He'd have some magical solution that no one would ever suspect.

She stopped listening to Isa, realization dawning. She didn't need her dad. She could do her own magic to stop Seamus. Why hadn't she thought of that before?

Suddenly, she couldn't wait to get out of there.

CHAPTER 15

Isa chattered on for way too long. Grace tried to keep it light and did not let on that she was itching to leave her room. She did a pretty good job too as Isa never once asked Grace if she was upset.

As soon as Isa fell asleep, Grace jumped out of bed and rushed for the door. Missy got tangled under her feet though, and she nearly fell flat on her face. Someday, that fox would be the death of her.

"Stay out of my way," Grace muttered, but Missy followed her out anyway. She didn't know what the fox wanted with her, but unless she raised her voice, Missy wouldn't leave her alone, and she didn't want to wake Isa.

Grace silently slipped down the stairs and prayed she wouldn't run into Seamus. As long as she made it to her room, she could create a spell that would ward him off for good. She rounded the corner, and Missy growled.

Grace jerked her head around and heard voices coming down the hall. They sounded like drunk guardians. Missy's hackles rose, and Grace moved around her. She opened the door to the stairway to her room, and Missy sat next to the door staring down the hall.

She didn't know what was going on, but it was almost as if Missy were protecting her. Maybe Missy was a better judge of her problems than Isa. After this, she wouldn't be cursing Missy again, that was for sure.

"Thank you," Grace said. But Missy didn't even look back. Grace shut the door and quickly made her way to her room and locked her door, both with the latch and magic.

She opened the drawer with her sword and pulled out a book, ignoring all of her other goodies. She didn't think any of them would work against Seamus. Well, the marbles would, but then someone would know there was a wizard in the castle.

Her magic was ancestral through her father, so she didn't normally need spells. However, occasionally, in a situation like this, she would utilize one. This was longer-term and very specific.

Grace didn't like casting spells. They were too easy to trace, unlike the magic she usually used. Not that anyone in the castle knew how to trace magic. But she couldn't take any chances.

Because there was always the possibility that someone was doing magic in secret like her.

But she couldn't risk herself with Seamus, so she'd take a chance this time. Dragons and wizards were enemies. Even when her father lived here, no one knew he was a wizard. They wouldn't even think that. Everyone thought the wizards were dead. Isa would kick her out or kill her if she found out because Grace would be a threat she couldn't control.

Grace ran a hand over the cover of the book. It had the wizard mark. A sword wrapped in a ribbon. The wizards of old had the mark on their wrist, but the ceremony that gave them the mark was long forgotten. Now they found it only on wizard books and places where magic resided.

Grace cracked open the book. At the very beginning was the prophecy given long, long ago, but it haunted Grace every day.

In the end, when wizards are a thing of fairytales and dragons are no longer seen, an orphan wizard will rise up and avenge her father.

She will be betrayed by those she trusts.

She will kill those she loves.

She will succeed when others fail.

She will wield the dragon killer and usher in a new world.

Grace knew the prophecy by heart, and so she flipped through the book, past the spells involving dragons—which was most of the book—and slowed down once she saw ones involving humans. Sure enough, the book had a spell to ward off unwanted advances. She hoped this worked. Spells like this sometimes went awry for her.

She dug out her casting bowl and lit a green flame, her least favorite color flame. She preferred purple.

"Calling all my ancestors young and old who wish to protect my innocence." The flames grew brighter, and faces appeared in the flames. She wanted to look for her father, but that would be wasting time. "Protect me from the man called Seamus, who walks these halls and haunts my steps. Allow him to touch me no more, and if he deigns to speak to me, close his lips."

She spit into the fire, and it went out. Spell cast. Now she just had to wait and see if it worked.

She hit the pillow and had a thought before drifting into dreamland.

Seamus was no man.

He was a dragon.

CHAPTER 16

Something had been bothering Isa all morning, but she couldn't put her finger on it. She was still in her rooms, finishing her breakfast, and Grace was flitting around, gathering her linens and dresses.

Grace was in a better mood than yesterday, but she was still twitchy. Isa had a feeling she was keeping a secret from her, but they never kept secrets from one another, and she didn't know why they would start now. It was obvious Grace was upset by something. Isa would figure it out eventually.

Today, she got to go outside, and she would take advantage of every minute of it. Though, realistically, she couldn't stay out for more than a few hours because of the cold. The walk should make her ecstatic, but she wasn't because she worried about Grace.

"Grace, do you want to go out with me?"

Grace shook her head. "You know I don't like the cold."

Isa sighed. "Yes, I know. But I wanted to invite you anyway. I'm planning on going out after lunch. Will you make sure you're here to dress me? I want to stay out for as long as I can, so please prepare my warmest things."

Grace nodded. "Anything else you need this morning?"

Isa grabbed Grace's hands. "Are you okay?"

Grace wouldn't meet her eyes. "I'm fine, Isa."

That was a good sign, at least Grace wasn't calling her "Your Majesty." Isa would give her a couple more days and then declare a sleepover and make her spill the beans. She didn't want to push Grace too much, or she'd be liable to clam right up.

Isa stood and examined herself in the mirror. She looked fierce. "Okay, I'm off to find my victims and let them know what time they will die."

A smile played at the edge of Grace's lips. "Try not to hurt them too badly. Well, maybe Seamus."

"I'll make sure I get him in the gut. Those hurt the worst." Isa skipped down the stairs, and it hit her why Grace had been acting so weird. She would never suggest that someone be hurt worse. Ever. That went against everything Grace stood for. She hated it when Isa had to fight the dragons because she was always afraid someone would get hurt. Mostly, she worried about Isa, but she expressed concern for the guardians as well.

Isa thought over their conversation last night. The one

where Grace told her that Seamus had kissed her. It was not the conversation she had imagined with Grace about her first kiss.

He gives me the creeps.

I didn't want it.

Oh, Isa was an idiot, and Seamus was an ass. This she could take care of. She couldn't believe she didn't see it last night. No wonder Grace was acting weird.

She found the guardians in the study. It was a masculine room with several tables and stiff chairs. They stood and bowed, only because Pierre was in the room. He always demanded formality from his guardians, but when he wasn't around, Isa told them to not be so stuffy.

She approached Pierre and kissed him on the cheek, and then she settled in the chair next to him. The rest of the guardians resumed their activities. Most were reading, but a few were playing cards or chess.

Pierre had been old even when she was a young child, but he never seemed to age. He'd been in the castle for longer than all of them. In fact, she was fairly certain he knew her great-grandmother though he never talked about it.

"The threat has been neutralized, right?" she asked.

He nodded, keeping an eye on his guardians.

"So, I'm going hunting this afternoon."

"Sure. Who are you hunting?" He seemed distracted. Which wasn't unusual for Pierre, but usually it meant that something was going on. Something he didn't want to tell her.

She expected an argument from him since hunting involved going outside, but none came.

"Jude, Seamus, Tad, and Drew."

"Yes, Your Majesty." He flicked his eyes to the boys playing cards.

"Then I'm going for a walk. By myself. Well, I'll bring Missy with me." This he would certainly argue, but she just wanted some peace and quiet in the woods.

Pierre got very quiet.

"Okay. But the four guardians you hunt will remain outside in case you need them."

She squealed, jumped up, and gave him a hug. "Thank you."

That was easier than it should've been. Perhaps he was tired of her complaining about being cooped up.

"You're welcome."

She bounced over to the other side of the room where the four youngest guardians sat at a table playing cards.

"I swear by the way you're winning you must be a wizard," Drew accused Seamus.

Seamus stood and sent his chair flying. "You take that back."

Isa tutted. Boys were so sensitive. Especially where wizards were concerned. Isa decided to put a stop to the fight before it began.

"Gentlemen. Be ready after lunch. We're going hunting." She hadn't been out with the bow and arrow in a while. She was looking forward to seeing if she still had the touch.

Seamus sank back down into his chair.

"Who?" Drew asked.

"You four."

A collective groan sounded around the table, and Jude didn't look up from his cards. Apparently, Jude didn't fill them in on their conversation last night. Figures.

She had one more thing to take care of, and then she'd leave them be. "Seamus, can I speak to you alone, please?"

"Ooh, somebody is in trouble," Jude said. He wiggled his eyebrows at Isa.

She rolled her eyes. They could be such children sometimes. But he wasn't wrong.

Seamus followed her out into the hall, and she led him far enough away that no one could eavesdrop. She stood tall, but he still towered over her. "Is it true that you kissed Lady Grace?"

He swallowed and looked at his boots. "Yes, Your Majesty."

"And is it true that she didn't want you to kiss her?"

She hoped he gave the right answer, or she'd kick him out of the guardians. And she wouldn't hesitate. No one messed with Grace.

He chewed on his bottom lip for a moment before responding. "I may have misread the signals."

"That is not how I understood it." She took another step

closer and forced him to look her in the eyes. "Listen to me. You will not so much as look Lady Grace's way ever again, or I will personally behead you, and I will not put it back. Do you understand?" This was a threat she'd happily follow through on.

He hung his head. "Yes."

"And no harassing any of the other staff either. If you are looking for a girlfriend, you'll need to find her outside these walls."

"Yes, Your Majesty."

"You may go."

Isa wasn't sure if she handled this right or not. Maybe she should've just kicked him out anyway.

CHAPTER 17

Damon sat on a table in the courtyard at school. The weather was nice today, so everyone was outside. The usual entourage was there, and Damon had been asked at least four times where Liam was. He wasn't allowed to share, and so he sent Liam another text. He'd only sent him about a billion since he left. Liam would have to check his phone eventually even if he was in Europe, chasing down some crazy dragon. Damon had to just play dumb in front of his friends and say that he didn't have a clue where Liam was.

Dude. I'm tired of this. The masses await your presence.

Still no response.

Emma crossed the courtyard, and his heart rate sped up. Today, she wore tight jeans and a t-shirt that dipped low on her chest. He'd had crushes before, but this one was different. It started freshman year when she sat in front of him in English, and the scent of her raspberry-mint shampoo drove him crazy. But she didn't run with his crowd back then.

Last summer, she'd ditched her glasses, dyed her hair blonde, and lost the braces. She was pretty before, but she was an absolute knock out now. Though, he liked her better with her auburn hair.

She sat next to him at the table, that fruity shampoo scent hitting him like a ton of bricks. She'd probably smack him if he leaned over to smell it. He wasn't a creeper, so he didn't, but he wanted to.

"Where's Liam?" she asked.

He rolled his eyes. "I don't know. Everyone has been asking about him. Why do you care?"

She bit her bottom lip and blinked her long lashes. His stomach fell out. Careful there, buddy, or you might seal yourself to her. Oh, wait, no. He couldn't do that because he wasn't a dragon. He'd been spending too much time with them.

"Can you keep a secret?" she whispered.

"Yeah, of course." Anything for her.

She leaned closer to him, and her hair fell between them. He nearly tumbled off the table. How did she pull that off?

"I have a major crush on him, and I'm hoping he'll ask me to prom."

All of his muscles immediately tensed. This was the

worst possible thing. He'd been trying to get her to notice him for three years, and now she wanted Liam. He leaned back and lowered his shoulders. He should've known Liam would ruin this one for him.

Damon contemplated telling her Liam already had a date, but that would be a lie. Liam always waited until the day before any dance to ask a girl out. They always said yes, even if they had another date. Liam didn't do it on purpose. He just never planned ahead.

"You won't tell him, will you?" She fidgeted with a strap on her purse.

Damon shook his head. Liam might go overboard in trying to talk Damon up, and he didn't want that either.

She let out a breath. "Okay. Thanks. Do you think I have a shot?"

He wanted to tell her no. That she should go with him instead, but he couldn't do it. "Yeah, of course you do. Tell you what, I'll feel him out and see if I can get him to ask you. You know he always waits until the last minute, right?"

She nodded. "That would be a dream come true. I've liked him since middle school. I actually died my hair blonde because I noticed that the last three girls he asked out were blonde."

Damon clenched his fists. Why did they all like Liam? Even the girls who dated him always like Liam first. "You shouldn't have to change to get noticed."

She giggled. "I know, but it's Liam, you know? I'd be

anything he wanted just to be with him. Most of the girls at school would."

Damon groaned on the inside. "I didn't know that." He did, but he hadn't wanted to admit it.

Zach sat across from them and grunted at Damon. Emma flushed and averted her eyes, looking anywhere else but at Zach. They'd gone out for a bit before spring break. Damon didn't know what happened, but Zach had a reputation for dating a girl until she slept with him and then ditching them. If he found out that Zach did something to Emma, he'd beat the crap out of him.

"Oh, who's the new girl?" Emma pointed over at Ruby.

"That's Ruby."

"How do you know her?"

"She's Liam's cousin. Skye and Rowan's daughter." He'd been surprised to find her in Sid's library, looking prettier than he'd remembered.

Emma's eyes widened. "She's a dragon?"

Damon nodded, still distracted by the fact that most of the girls in school would do anything for Liam. He wondered if Liam knew that.

"I'm gonna go say hi." Emma slipped off the table and sashayed over to Ruby. Damon couldn't keep his eyes off her as she talked animatedly to Ruby, who listened politely. The first bell rang, and people started gathering their things and moving. Emma waved goodbye to Ruby, and Damon lost her in the crowd heading inside.

Someone punched him hard in the arm, and he jerked back.

"Thanks a lot," Ruby said, her voice a few pitches higher than normal.

Damon rubbed his arm. She punched hard. For a girl. He supposed with that many siblings, she learned to defend herself.

"For what?"

"You were supposed to keep my identity a secret. Now, I'll never get any peace." She glared at him with her nostrils flared.

"What are you talking about?" He did not understand this at all. Everyone loved the dragons, so he just made her instantly popular.

She pinched the bridge of her nose and closed her eyes. She gritted her teeth. "You don't remember the conversation in the library? The one where I told you to not tell anyone who I was."

"Oh, that. Yeah, I thought you weren't being serious." He didn't understand this at all. If he were a dragon, he'd never hide it.

Ruby hugged her books to her chest. "Of course you did."

Then she turned on her heel and stormed away.

Women.

He didn't understand them at all.

CHAPTER 18

Ruby sat in the front row of homeroom, fuming. She couldn't believe Damon had outed her. All he had to do was keep his big mouth shut, and she would've been able to fly under the radar and maybe make a couple of good friends who wouldn't care if she was a dragon or not.

But no.

Now, everyone would know and want to be her friend just because she had wings. They'd be asking her to show off her flames at parties, and heaven forbid they found out Skye was her mom. She'd never have any peace. She didn't want to be worshipped for being a dragon.

Plus, her teachers might give her good grades because of who she was instead of her skills. Which would do her no good if she planned on being successful in college next year.

She listened to the teacher drone on about things that were happening this week and looked at her schedule. She had calculus next and then A.P. Bio. At least Damon wouldn't be in those classes. He liked school about as much as Liam.

The school was small, and she easily found her way to calculus. She planted herself in the front row and waited. She still had six minutes until the bell rang. Students slowly trickled into class, but she kept her head down, studying her book. She didn't want to talk to anyone or answer any more questions about Liam. That Emma girl was nice enough, but it was painfully obvious she was angling for a friend to get close to him.

Someone sat in the seat next to her. "Well, well, well, if it isn't the dragon girl."

Ruby spun around and found a guy smirking at her. His neck was too thick and his ears too small, and he oozed confidence. Ruby hated guys like him. They always thought they were God's gift to women.

Kind of like her cousin.

And Damon.

She dropped her gaze to her book and ignored him. She would not be reminded of her dragonish self any more than she had to be.

He moved closer to her. "Why so shy?"

"I don't like people," she snapped at him.

"Aw, really?" He ran a finger down her arm. "I bet you'd like me."

She jerked her arm away. "Don't touch me."

He leaned back and spread his long legs in front of him. "Come on, you wanna give me a ride, don't you?"

Oh, the nerve. Being an outcast in Oregon was bad, but this was worse.

"I'm not a horse, thank you very much, and even if I was into that sort of thing, you'd be the last one I'd give a ride to."

He frowned at her. "Why?"

Oh, he knew why. He just wanted to keep her talking.

"Because you're a prick. If you want a ride, go find Liam. I'm sure he'd love to help you out."

A girl behind her snorted. "Fat chance of that. Liam hates him."

Ruby gave the boy a sugary smile. "Well, then, for once, Liam and I agree on something." She didn't even want to know why Liam hated the kid.

The bell rang, and the teacher walked in. Ruby hoped the rest of her day went better, but most likely, it wouldn't. If that boy had heard about her, then others had as well, and now she had zero chances of making real friends.

She turned to the girl behind her. Maybe she'd be friendly.

"I'm Ruby."

The girl looked down her nose. "I know. And, just so

you know, I'm not friends with dragons, so don't waste your time."

The words stung, but Ruby understood. Most of the kids at her old school felt the same way.

If Damon had kept his mouth shut, she wouldn't be in this mess.

CHAPTER 19

"Psst. Your Majesty. Wake up."

Sid bolted upright in bed, and Aspen groaned. "Go back to sleep."

They'd taken a couple of sleeping pills so they would be able to think clearly in the morning for whatever came, but sleeping pills left him groggy and disoriented if woken in the middle of the night.

But the voice wasn't a dream. Someone had spoken. Sid looked around wildly and found a little yellow dragon perched on the headboard.

"Baden?" Sid asked, rubbing his eyes. He almost said Runa but caught himself. She'd been dead twenty years. And yet, he still expected her to pop up out of nowhere.

Aspen threw off the sheets, her eyes and hair wild. She looked deranged. "Baden? Where?"

Sid grabbed her hand. "He's right here. Baden, please tell me you have good news."

Baden hung his head. Shame poured off of him. "I'm afraid not." He fluttered to Sid's side table and nudged the golden stone that sat there. It took another minute for Sid to register what the stone meant.

Aspen gasped and covered her mouth, and then Sid's stomach dropped out. A stone only meant one thing. "That's not…"

"It's not Liam."

Aspen relaxed, and Sid took the stone in his hand. It was cold and heavy. "Felix?"

"Yes, Your Majesty." Baden's voice cracked.

A knot formed in Sid's stomach. He'd known this was potentially a dangerous situation, but Felix was the best tracker and assassin they had. Even better than Sid's own father, who'd been murdered during the last wars.

This was likely only the first of many deaths they would face. He hated to think how they were being thrust into another war, but it was obvious now. At least Baden brought Liam back, and he wouldn't be on the frontline. Sid would lock him up until this was over. Because if Felix was dead, Liam would want revenge.

"How is Liam doing? Where is he anyway?" Sid would give Liam some time to grieve, but the boy was in a world of trouble for leaving like that, and he, Aspen, and Liam needed to have a long talk.

Baden shuffled back and forth on the small table. "I

didn't bring him back. He refused." It took a moment for Sid to process that information. His best assassin was dead and Liam…

Sid jumped out of bed and grabbed the little dragon, holding him high in the air. "You left him there after she killed Felix? How could you do that?" He couldn't believe Baden had been that careless. He'd been Liam's guard since Liam was a baby. He'd always protected Liam.

Baden breathed heavily and trembled. "Your Majesty, the queen didn't kill Felix. Her guards did. And Liam refused to come home. He is planning to sneak into the castle as a human, and he commanded me to return. I had no choice."

"I can't believe you left him there," Aspen shrieked and jumped out of bed. All color had drained out of her face.

Sid dropped Baden and drew Aspen into a fierce hug. He needed her close. He couldn't believe Liam would be so reckless. Baden landed on the side table again and cowered behind Felix's stone. Liam was still alive but in grave danger. If the queen didn't kill him on sight, she'd take him prisoner once she found out he was Sid's son.

Baden flew up and out of reach, changing color to match the white ceiling. "I had no choice." He repeated. "Liam gave me a command." Baden's voice had gone shaky.

Liam was playing it smart. Going as a human might provide him a cover that a dragon would not. Perhaps he wouldn't be in as much danger. Baden shouldn't have left him there, but Sid had to think of what would be best now.

"Go back. Find the band of warriors on their way and warn them about what happened. Tell them their human forms will be safer. Then, you find a way into the castle, find Liam, and bring him home. That is my command, and he cannot override it. Do you understand? Knock him out and carry him home if necessary."

Baden bowed. "Yes, Your Majesty."

"Wait," Aspen said, stepping forward.

"What?" Sid asked.

"Come downstairs with me, Baden. You need food and rest."

"Aspen, time is of the essence." Sid couldn't believe she'd be this foolish when their son's life was on the line.

Aspen glared at him. "And if Baden passes out on the way from lack of food, it will do nobody any good. Let me feed him first, and then we'll send him back."

Baden gave a nod. "I promise, Your Majesty, I'll do everything I can to bring him back safely.

Sid watched Aspen and Baden leave the room and then stared at the golden stone. It was the first of what would probably be many casualties. After the last war, Sid never wanted to see another one of these in his lifetime.

He didn't get his wish.

He just hoped that the next stone wouldn't be Liam's.

CHAPTER 20

*L*iam had been gone two days now, and Damon hadn't heard a word from him. He was starting to get worried. Not to mention that the kids at school were constantly asking where Liam was.

Damon spotted Ruby sitting under a tree at lunchtime, reading a book. So typical of her. He settled next to her, and she barely glanced at him.

"What do you think Liam is up to?" he asked, just to make conversation. He didn't know why she was so cold to him. He'd never done anything to her. He hated when people just ignored him for no reason like they were better than him or something.

"Don't know, don't care." Her voice was cool but calm, and she flipped a page in her book.

"Seriously. I haven't heard anything else, but he should

be back by now." Damon wasn't really all that worried, just a little irritated that Liam didn't fill him in before leaving.

Ruby finally took her gaze off her book and rolled her eyes at him. He'd forgotten how enchanting those eyes could be.

"Unlikely. He probably didn't even go to find some evil dragon. He just made that up to prevent Sid and Aspen from looking for him. He probably got drunk with some girl, passed out, and hasn't woken up. He'll come around, and then he can apologize to everyone who has been looking for him. Which he won't. He'll be pleased everyone was so worried."

Damon couldn't believe her nerve. She had no right to talk about Liam like that. "You know, just once, it would be nice for you to at least pretend to care about us."

She looked down and flipped another page. "But I don't. So why pretend?"

This was useless. He got up and brushed the grass off his pants. He couldn't figure her out. When they were kids, they were all friends. They played hide-and-seek at Sid's house, flew over the mud pots in Yellowstone, and begged his mom to give them coffee instead of hot chocolate at the Purple Dragon. He'd always flown on her because Liam didn't like giving rides.

Then after she moved, she stopped talking to them. It was so sudden. He and Liam tried a few times to get her to hang with them when she visited, but she never did. As the years went on, her visits became farther and farther apart. Skye and Rowan still came a lot, but she didn't.

After a while, he didn't even bother to talk to her. But he was excited when he found out she'd be going to school here. He'd missed her, and he hoped that meant they could be friends again.

But obviously not. He wished he knew why she was so bitchy.

Emma waved to him across the way, and his heart flip-flopped. He walked over to her, hoping he looked cool and not like a dork, and she gave him a smile and patted the seat next to her.

"So, I heard Liam is missing. Any idea where he might be?" Her face was full of worry.

Damon shook his head, disappointed that the first thing she brought up was Liam. He should've known.

"You don't think he's with a girl, do you?" She looked down at her hands and picked at her nails.

"No. But I guess it's possible. Liam can be reckless, but he's never gone missing before. I'm actually pretty worried." Yeah, he was playing the sympathy card. He'd seen it work for Liam before. But maybe he was a little concerned. Liam didn't usually disappear like this.

Emma put a hand on his shoulder. "Oh, I didn't think about how this might be affecting you. I'm sorry."

He hid his smile. Liam would be so proud.

Actually, if the truth be told, her hand was affecting him

way more than any worries for Liam. He was sure his best friend would be fine. Liam was always fine.

"It's okay."

"Maybe I can help you search for him this afternoon." She bounced in her seat and grinned.

"Yeah, that would be great. We can check out places he normally goes. We can even fly if you want. I know a few dragons."

Her eyes lit up. "That would be awesome. Yeah. Let's go find Liam after school."

He swallowed. Sure, she liked Liam right now, but if they spent time together, maybe she would change her tune.

CHAPTER 21

The lunch table filled with others who were worried about Liam, and Damon lost Emma's attention to Brooke, the school gossip. At least they'd get to spend some time together this afternoon. Alone. His palms sweated at the thought of it.

He hoped to have a good story when Liam got back. His stomach fell. It wasn't like Liam to be gone this long without a word.

The weather was nice today, and so everyone was outside. Even the breeze was warm.

Damon ate his lunch: cold pizza and Cheetos, and listened to the chatter around him. He'd always run in this group, and they hung out with him strictly because of Liam. But he didn't care. Liam was his best friend.

Damon was well-liked, but to be honest, anyone who

ran in the popular group didn't really like the other people with them. They were just there because it made them look cool. Damon would rather hang with people like Emma or Ruby if he were being completely honest. Though Emma was now a part of this group, and her attitude was changing.

Brooke leaned over and tapped his arm. "Come on, you have to know where Liam is."

"I'm telling you. I don't."

Technically, he did, but he wasn't allowed to share that Liam was in Europe. Damon hoped he was okay, but Damon also hoped Liam hadn't left him behind if he was doing something fun. Damon didn't think Liam was shutting him out, but stranger things had happened.

"Maybe his cousin knows." Brooke pointed across the courtyard, but Damon looked over at Emma instead. He couldn't keep his eyes off her. He'd barely even heard what Brooke said.

"Who?"

"Ruby. The new girl. She's his cousin, right?" Yep, a cousin who didn't care what happened to Liam.

Damon snorted. "She hates him. Why would she know?"

Brooke's eyes widened. "She hates him? Why? Liam's awesome."

Now, everyone was staring at him. Oh man, he should've just kept his mouth shut. "I have no idea. Why don't you ask her?"

A few of the boys went quiet, listening intently.

"But you know her better than we do," Brooke continued. "You were talking to her earlier."

Damon avoided Brooke's intense stare. "Yeah. That's because my mom told me to be nice to her since she's new and all. You know our parents are friends. But, and don't repeat this, she's a real bitch. Like she doesn't even care Liam is missing."

"Um, Damon, buddy…" Zach said from across the table.

"What?"

An ice-cold Coke poured over the top of his head, and he spluttered and turned around. Ruby stood there, her eyes full of hurt and anger instead of the cool indifference she always exuded.

"Just proving your point," she said and raced away.

Zach handed him a napkin, and he wiped his face. Emma sat there for a moment, her expression hard.

"That wasn't a very nice thing to say. I'm going to make sure she's okay." Emma got up and rushed from the table, Brooke on her heels.

Zach frowned. "Maybe you should apologize."

"What do I have to apologize for?" He knew what, but he had to keep his pride.

"Well, she is Liam's cousin."

That's right. She was a dragon, and that made her invincible. Sometimes, he hated the fact that he wasn't a dragon. If he was, they'd never say that to him.

"She poured Coke on me."

"Because you called her a bitch." Zach glared at him.

"Whatever, I'm going to clean myself off."

He ran to the bathroom, his hair sopping. But he didn't really care about that. Now, Emma thought he was a prick and would probably think even worse after she talked with Ruby. Damon had no chance with her now.

So much for getting her alone. There was no way she'd go searching for Liam with him now. Let alone prom.

CHAPTER 22

Missy jumped into the snowbanks ahead, but Isa kept her eyes on the sky and the bow in her hands. The cold bit at her face, but the rest of her was toasty warm because she had fur-lined everything.

She should've seen one of her dragons by now, but she hadn't had any luck. It'd been too long, and she'd lost her touch. Not for the first time had she wished she'd been up there flying with them instead of down here, hunting.

She didn't hunt with arrows very often because she didn't like hurting her guardians. Or anything else for that matter. At least, when she stabbed them in the hearts, they didn't feel it.

All at once, the four dragons flew over the trees, sending snow cascading down. Oh, those sneaky bastards.

They were coming after her as one. Well, she could do this. She'd done it before, but it was more difficult.

Jude was in the front, and she nocked her arrow. She watched him for a few seconds to judge his trajectory and the wind. Then, she let the arrow fly. It got him right in the heart, and he fell into the snow, blood trailing behind him. Without missing a beat, she hit both Drew and Tad. She had not lost her touch even though she hadn't done this in months. They were all dead in seconds. If they had been enemy dragons, she would've been able to protect herself.

Seamus flew quickly toward the castle. She aimed differently for him. She didn't plan on taking him down with one arrow but maybe three, maybe four. The first one stuck in his wing. He faltered but didn't fall. Good. That hurt like mad. She hit the other wing as well.

He dropped a few feet but kept flying. She let two arrows fly at once and hit him in the gut. He fell, but he wasn't dead yet.

She stomped over to him. His breathing was labored, and she was certain he was in pain. Good. He hurt Grace, and she intended to make sure he never did that again. Her threat earlier might not have been strong enough.

She unsheathed her sword. "I meant what I said. Don't you even think of hurting Lady Grace or any other girl for that matter." Then she stabbed him in the heart. His eyes went glassy. She'd let him be dead a little longer than the other guardians.

She raced across the snow to the bodies that had shriveled down into humans. She tapped them one by one on the forehead, and they came to.

Jude sat up. "Good aim. That didn't even hurt."

"I'm glad. I don't like hurting you." She wished there was another way to make sure there were no more attacks, but her guardians insisted this was the best way to train.

She helped him up, and he looked around.

"Where's Seamus?" he asked.

She pointed across the field. "Maybe I should just let him be dead."

Jude creased his eyebrows. "What'd he do to you?"

She shook her head. "Nothing. I'll go take care of him."

Tad and Drew waited in the field, but Jude followed her. "Dragon's teeth! You did a number on him."

"I know."

"I don't know what he did to you, but make sure I don't do the same."

Seamus had turned into a human, and she tapped him on the forehead. He blinked his eyes open, and she gave him a look that dared him to complain.

He didn't.

She knew one thing for sure. He wouldn't be harassing Grace anymore.

CHAPTER 23

Ruby didn't even know where the best hiding places were at this new school, but she wasn't about to stay in public where she could be pitied. She hated being the new girl. Hated Damon and his hurtful words. Hated that she couldn't even find a stinking bathroom.

She turned the corner and spotted the door to the library and slipped in there. A few kids sat at tables and on beanbag chairs, reading, and another handful sat at the ancient computers with headphones on. She headed to the nonfiction section. No one was ever there.

Once she found a corner, she sank down, tried to slow her breathing, and rested her shaking hands on her knees. At least she wasn't crying. She'd been made fun of before at school, and she'd learned real fast that tears made things worse. She had hoped this new school could be a fresh start, but Damon had ruined that. He didn't understand anything about her.

She jerked her head around at footsteps, and the girl who was sitting with Damon turned the corner.

The girl sat next to Ruby and didn't say anything for a moment. "The library, huh?"

"I couldn't find the bathroom." Ruby sniffed. She really, really hadn't wanted to be found.

The girl chuckled. "Well, at least you're in the right section."

She motioned to the shelf in front of them, and Ruby looked up.

How to Win Friends and Influence People. Maybe I Should Talk to Someone. Dealing with People You Can't Stand. People I Want to Punch in the Throat. Girl, Stop Apologizing.

Ruby couldn't help herself, and she laughed. "I could probably use all of those."

The girl pointed to *People I Want to Punch in the Throat.* "That one, I think. I'm Emma, by the way."

"Ruby."

"I know. Being the new girl sucks, huh? Even for a dragon?" Emma nudged her and gave her a smile.

"Especially for a dragon. What he said about me not caring…it's not true. I just don't like Liam very much. Besides, I'm sure he's fine." She didn't want to get into details about her relationship with her cousin.

Emma cocked her head. "Why don't you like him?"

"He's so cocky and full of himself. Damon too. I don't

like people like that. Well, I don't like people much anyway. I prefer books." Ruby looked at her hands again, taking calming breaths. They always seemed to help.

Emma pulled her bag in front of her and dug around inside it. "I guess I can understand that. I'm not that way, but my mom is, so I get it." She handed Ruby a Snickers. "Here. Chocolate helps."

Oh, wow. This girl was way sweeter than most girls who hung with the popular crowd.

Ruby took the candy bar. "Thanks. It really does. Why were you hanging out with Damon anyway? You're too nice." A thought occurred to her, and she quickly backtracked. "Wait, you're not his girlfriend, are you?" She might've just put a big foot in her mouth. With the first person who had been nice to her, too. She had to start thinking before she spoke.

Emma sighed. "No. I like Liam, and Damon is his best friend, so…"

Ruby narrowed her eyes. "You're being nice to me because I'm Liam's cousin?" So much for finding a friend. She should've known it was too good to be true.

"No, not at all. I actually didn't even think about that when I came after you. I don't like seeing girls being picked on. Plus, I knew the second you poured the Coke over Damon that we had to be friends. That was a ballsy move, and I loved it."

Ruby thought about that for a moment. She hadn't even

realized what she was doing, and she might have to answer for her actions at some point.

The bell rang. "We should go to class. Thanks for checking on me. It means a lot."

Emma stood and held out her hand. "No problem. Let's sit together at lunch tomorrow."

Ruby took her hand. At least she'd have one friend in this hellhole.

CHAPTER 24

Snow fell lightly on Isa's face. This was her favorite weather. It was cold but not too windy. She looked longingly into the woods. That was where she wanted to go. When the snow fell, it looked so pretty in the trees.

"So, we are supposed to wait while you take a walk," Jude said, dropping his eyes. Drew, Seamus, and Tad stood behind him, all breathing hard. The training had taken its toll on them.

Isa sighed. She had to make this good if she was going to get away from them. They knew how much she loved being outside, and they'd be suspicious if she suddenly decided to not go for a walk.

"It's been a while since I've been outside, and I'm beat. I'll walk tomorrow."

"Oh good, cause I'm famished," Jude said.

She followed them back to the castle, Missy trotting behind her. They went through the side door, and she looked around frantically.

"My sword. I left it out in the field."

Jude gave her a look, and Tad groaned. Seamus and Drew were already halfway down the hall.

"I'll go get it." Jude shivered and rubbed his hands together. He wasn't dressed well for a long stay outside.

Isa waved him off. "No, it's okay. I'll get it. It will take me all of two minutes. You guys go on."

"Are you sure? I should go."

"I'm positive. I know you're cold and tired. Get something to drink. It's the least I can do after making you take arrows."

Jude gave her a nod and continued down the hall with the others, and she turned and escaped out the door.

"Missy, I can't believe they fell for that." Oh, sweet freedom. It'd been way too long.

Missy yelped and ran across the field. She liked being outside as much as Isa did.

Isa pulled her sword out of the snow and cleaned it off with her glove. The snow had gotten most of the blood off it. She sheathed it and then scooped up some snow and threw it for Missy, who flew after it.

Isa took one last look at the castle. No sneaky guardians watched her. They would definitely get in trouble for this. She'd have to put in a good word for them when she got back so Pierre wouldn't go too hard on them. But really, she'd done this walk thousands of times and a few times alone. She was fine.

"Come on, Missy, let's go for a walk."

CHAPTER 25

Grace hadn't seen Seamus all day, and for that, she was exceedingly grateful. She wasn't sure if her spell had worked, and she wasn't ready to see if it failed. She was still nervous that because he was a dragon, the spell wouldn't work. She sat in the kitchens again, frosting chocolate cupcakes for Olga. Benjamin sat across from her, frosting the strawberry ones.

They kept the conversation light, but Benjamin blushed a lot. At least, he wasn't fumbling over his words anymore. She wished he'd get over liking her so they could just be friends again. She had no friends as it was, and Isa was queen, so she couldn't really be her friend even though it felt like it at times. She sometimes wished Marissa liked her, but Marissa had been standoffish from the day she showed up at the castle. She was only a few years older than Grace, but she rarely talked to her.

Olga burst through the door. She didn't say anything as she bustled along and grabbed drinks and goblets off the shelves. She looked up. "Where is Marissa?"

"She's sick, remember, Ma?" Benjamin said, setting down a strawberry cupcake.

"Oh, good lord, I forgot. You two will have to do this instead. The guardians are back from their walk with Isa, and they want drinks and dessert. Benjamin, put the cupcakes on the tray, save a few for the queen, and, Grace, can you serve them drinks?"

Grace nodded, the nerves in her belly dancing. This would be the true test of whether her spell worked. At least, it would be in a room full of people, so if it failed, Seamus couldn't do more than say something nasty and pinch her butt when nobody was looking.

Grace followed Benjamin out of the kitchens and into the guardians' dining room. She didn't come in here often. This was Marissa's domain. But Benjamin seemed right at home, and a few of the guardians greeted him warmly. No one really said anything to her.

Coats and boots were flung around the room, and they all spoke jovially with one another. Seamus sat next to Drew, and she didn't want to meet his eye.

She served Pierre and the older guardians first and saved Seamus for last. She poured a drink, but he wouldn't even look at her.

"Can I get you anything else?" she asked, just to be sure.

He shook his head and kept his eyes focused on the plate by him.

Jude tapped her hand. "Can you fetch me another of the chocolate cupcakes?" He had frosting on his upper lip, and it looked adorable.

"Sure."

Benjamin was on the other side of the room with the tray, and Grace snatched a couple of chocolate ones and set them in front of Jude.

She felt fantastic. No more worries about Seamus. Maybe she should use magic to get out of all her problems.

"Can I get you anything before I head to the kitchens?" she asked.

Drew shook his head. "I don't think so. Would you like to take a walk with me later though? I've been dying to talk to you since the dance."

This smelled like it had Isa written all over it. Plus, she wasn't ready to trade in one guardian problem for another. Not that Drew would be a problem, but she didn't want to take any chances.

"Can it wait? It's been a long day. Maybe next week." She kept her voice cool on purpose. She didn't want to give him the wrong idea.

She glanced at Seamus. So far, not a single leering look or anything from him. The spell was meant for humans, but apparently, it worked on dragons as well. This was the first big spell she'd performed, and it had gone off smashingly.

Now, if she could figure out a spell to make Jude fall in love with her, all would be well in the world.

CHAPTER 26

*L*iam found a cave to hide out in overnight. He had to rest and figure out his next move. Plus, he needed time to grieve his friend. The next morning, he set out on foot. He couldn't turn back into a dragon. That would be a death sentence for sure. But it was so cold here. Colder than he'd ever been before. He tugged his hat around his ears and trudged forward. The snow was packed, but that didn't make the walk any easier. His feet still slid into the snow occasionally, sneaking into his boots, and falling snow made it hard to see where he was going. It wasn't blowing or anything, but it was definitely coming down.

After a few miles, Liam came across a distinct stand of trees and found one with a hollow opening in the bottom.

He shoved the dragon slayer in there as well as most of his weapons but kept a dagger on him.

Once he reached the castle, they would capture and question him. This was his plan. He wanted to be seen as a lost human and hopefully do some recon while he was there. Once he had the information he needed, he would kill the queen if he could, but if he couldn't, he would fly home and tell his dad everything. He thought about just going home now, but he promised Felix and owed it to him.

He and Felix had discussed this technique before—willingly surrendering for a greater cause—but he didn't like it. He felt vulnerable and weak, but he didn't have much choice. He could fly home now with no answers or press forward and achieve something.

And he wanted to achieve something.

The sun blinded him but didn't give any warmth. The ice-cold air bit at his nose and cheeks, and he wasn't even sure if he was heading in the right direction anymore. Snow fell, and the wind blew, making it hard to see anything.

He had no idea how far he'd walked or how much farther he had to go. This was a dumb plan. He should turn around and fly home, but this close to the castle, he risked being seen and attacked as a dragon. He'd gone too far to turn back now.

He took another step and sank waist-deep into the snow. He stood there for a moment, debating what to do.

Next to him was a tree, and he grabbed the trunk and hoisted himself out of the snow. He lay down and watched the snow float above him.

His limbs were cold, and his fingers numb.

He needed to rest. Just for a moment.

His eyelids fluttered shut, and he was lost to the cold oblivion.

CHAPTER 27

Isa ducked below the trees, tromping through the snow in her snowshoes. She loved the woods, the birds, and the peace. It was so quiet. The light filtered through the branches and shimmered on all the snow. Snow fell from the sky, but it was soft with massive flakes.

Missy ran circles around her, and she threw another snowball, but her aim was off, and she hit a tree instead. Isa laughed. Oh, it felt good to be outside. If it wasn't so cold out here, she'd never go back inside. If she had her dragon form, she wouldn't have to.

She tried to throw another snowball and hit yet another tree. Missy gave her a look that said, "Real nice. Try another one."

And so she did. This one went between the trees, disappearing into the shadows.

Missy raced into the dark, searching for her snowball. A few minutes later, she came back carrying something, but it wasn't a snowball.

Isa crouched in front of her fox. "What do you have there, girl?"

Missy dropped it, and Isa picked it up. A glove. But not one like she'd ever seen before. It was black with a strange lining and had a tag on the bottom that read REI.

"Where did you find this?" All the gloves she and her dragons had were custom made and never had any tags. This glove was also thinner and had no fur anywhere. It wasn't warm enough for this climate.

Missy jumped up and down, her legs sinking into the snow when she landed.

Isa hoisted her out of the bank. "Show me where you got this."

Missy took off, and Isa had to jog to keep up with her, which was hard in her snowshoes, but she'd run in them before. Missy went around a band of trees, and Isa froze. Lying on the ground was a man. Fear crawled across her stomach. This was not a man she recognized. She turned to run, but Missy rushed for the man.

"No," Isa called.

But Missy laid her snout across his chest, and Isa didn't know what to do. She'd never met anyone who didn't live in the castle. Surely, if Missy thought he wasn't a threat, then Isa would be safe.

Plus, she was only at risk from dragons. This was a human. A nearly frozen human. She hoped he wasn't dead.

What was he doing in her woods?

Missy barked.

"Okay, I'm coming."

Isa fell to her knees next to the man. His eyes were closed, and his face was red and chapped. She brought her ear to his nose and mouth. A light breath blew across her cheek.

He was still alive. She shook him, but he didn't stir. He couldn't have been out here that long, or he'd be dead. But how did he get here?

"Missy, go get help. Now."

Missy took off, and Isa studied the man. She took off her cloak and draped it over him. He wasn't dressed right for this weather and obviously wasn't from around here.

A nagging feeling told her she was in danger, but she couldn't figure out why. This was just one man.

She shook him again, but still, he didn't stir.

Well, she'd have to wait until he was well to find out what he was doing here.

A thrill raced up her spine.

A stranger.

She'd never met a stranger before.

To Be Continued...

Copyright © 2021 by Kimberly Loth

All rights reserved. No part of this book may be reproduced, transmitted, downloaded, distributed, stored in or introduced in any information storage and retrieval system, in any form or by any means, whether electronic or mechanical without express permission of the author, except by a reviewer who may quote brief passages for review purposes.

This is a work of fiction. The characters, incidents, and dialogues, in this book are of the author's imagination and are not to be construed as real. Any resemblance to actual events or persons, living or dead is completely coincidental.

CHAPTER 1

Isa stared at the man on the ground. She tried poking his face and tugging on his arms, but he wouldn't wake up. This wasn't good. Isa shivered, rubbed her arms, and then blew into her hands, warming her face. Maybe she shouldn't have given him her cloak. But he might die.

She stared out through the trees. Missy needed to run faster.

Isa stood and lifted the man's feet. She pulled on him but couldn't move him more than a few inches. Isa was highly skilled in many things, but brute strength was not one of them. It would take her too long to get to the castle. She hoped Missy brought at least two or three men with her. Otherwise, they'd never get him back alive.

The snow began to fall harder, and the wind started up.

Isa paced in circles around the man, trying to keep herself warm. He was so exotic looking. His skin was not as pale as most of the guardians and his hair a golden blonde, though he wore it long like Jude. His dark lashes rested on his smooth skin. He was beyond handsome.

His clothes were like none she'd ever seen, and although they were winter clothes, they weren't sturdy enough for the extreme cold. She wondered for a second if he was a dragon.

That's stupid. Dragons would fly in, not freeze to death in the woods. How did he get here and manage to stay alive so far? She had so many questions, but if he died, she would never get those answers.

A motion came from the trees, and Isa stared through the snow. Finally. Missy bounded toward her, Grace following.

Isa's heart sank. Grace wouldn't be able to help at all. She wasn't any stronger than Isa.

"Dragon's Teeth! What's this?" Grace asked, her eyes wide. She'd hastily thrown on a cloak and gloves, but she wasn't dressed for a long time outside either.

"A man I've never seen before, but there is no way you and I will get him to the castle. I need you to bring me guardians, three or four of them at least."

Missy growled, and Isa dropped her eyes to the man, but he still hadn't stirred. Missy stared at her but didn't growl again. She'd never understood that fox.

Grace looked once more at the man and raced toward

the castle though it wasn't easy because she hadn't put on snowshoes. Grace took far longer than Isa would've liked. He would freeze to death before people got here to help him.

Missy lay across the man's chest and nuzzled his cheek, her white fur bright against his chapped face.

"You like him too?" Isa couldn't explain her attraction to him, but she wanted him to live.

Missy swished her tail back and forth.

Isa knelt on the ground and studied the man some more. She'd never had an outsider in the castle before, and she was so excited to learn more about him.

That is if he survived.

"What are you doing here?" she muttered to him.

Missy yelped, and the man flinched. Isa shook him. "Are you awake? You have to get up."

He wouldn't die out here after all.

He groaned, and Missy yelped again, pushing against his cheek with her nose.

Isa grabbed his shoulders. "Come on, wake up."

His eyelids fluttered open, and Isa stared into the bluest eyes she'd ever seen.

CHAPTER 2

*L*iam had to be careful. Even in his frozen delirium, he knew he was in enemy territory, but he was distracted by the black-haired beauty who stood over him. She couldn't be that much older than he was. He had to keep his wits about him, or he'd be dead. Course, the weather about did him in already. His limbs were numb.

"Oh, you're awake, thank the gods. Can you stand?" She spoke English but with a lilting accent that was quite beautiful. It was hard to tell what she looked like as she was completely bundled up with a red hooded jacket over thick black pants. A grown-up Red-Riding Hood. Her bright white cloak lay over him.

He was able to move his arms a little, and he tried to wiggle his feet, but he couldn't tell if they actually did anything. "I'm not sure."

She jumped when he spoke but didn't say anything more. His voice had come out weak. What was he thinking, trying to freeze to death out here? Felix would be so disappointed with him. A pang in his chest reminded him that Felix was dead, and someone was responsible for his death.

"Well, try, will you?" she asked. Her wide blue eyes were mesmerizing, but he could be hallucinating because of the cold. He tried to focus on the trees behind her, but they blurred together, so he watched her again.

She rubbed her hands together, took her cloak back, and buttoned it up. Then, she offered him her hand. He took it but could barely feel anything. He certainly couldn't feel his legs and hoped he wouldn't be losing any limbs. The woman tugged on his hand and managed to help him stand, but his knees buckled.

She looped his arm around her shoulder and laced her arm around his waist. "We've got to get you to the castle as soon as possible."

The castle. Right. Where there was an evil queen who would kill him on sight. Maybe not. Maybe they wouldn't ask too many questions since he was coming in nearly frozen to death.

Maybe this girl was a servant or something. This was looking better and better. Though he had to be careful what he said because his mind was foggy and had trouble focusing. He'd be liable to say something he shouldn't.

She led the way, and he stumbled on next to her.

She grunted and continued on. "Sorry I can't be more help, but this is better than waiting. I sent Missy to get help, but she came back with Lady Grace. Can you believe it? So I sent Grace to fetch a few guardians, but they'll take too long. What's your name?"

He thought for a moment and saw no reason to lie. "Liam."

"I'm Isa."

That was a pretty name. And she was dressed well, so probably not a cook or a maid. Though maybe everyone dressed that way in the freezing cold weather. Liam had a story all worked out about why he was here, but right now, he couldn't put the details together because his mind was fuzzy. He hoped they'd let him sleep and heal before they started asking questions because he wasn't ready to answer them.

They came out of the woods, and a monstrous castle rose up the side of the mountain.

"Wow," he said. It was a deep gray stone with multiple spires. It looked just like a lair of an evil snow queen.

"My castle is pretty magnificent, isn't it?" Isa asked.

He wasn't sure he heard her right. Maybe she just meant her home. Because the castle belonged to the queen, and this kind, beautiful woman couldn't be the evil queen who had Felix killed.

They walked farther, and the castle loomed high above them. It was hard to tell where it ended and where the mountain began. Liam had never seen such a place before.

He thought his house was big, but this was gigantic, a place where dragons and humans could all live. He wondered why they didn't do that at home. It'd be easier than putting the dragons in the garage when they had to stay. He shook his head. He couldn't lose track of why he was here. He needed information, and then he needed to fly home.

"What do you mean by *my* castle?" Liam asked though he wasn't sure he wanted the answer. Because if she meant what he thought she did, then he should kill her before they got any farther. He had a dagger, and he could, well maybe could. He wasn't sure in this state.

Besides, this innocent girl helping him out of the woods could not be the same person terrorizing all of Europe. She couldn't be responsible for Felix's death.

His knees gave way again, and they both dropped but recovered.

"I'm the queen. Welcome to my home."

CHAPTER 3

The front door of the castle flung open, and Drew and Jude rushed out.

"Oh, thank goodness. Help me with him, will you?" Isa asked. Her shoulder was killing her. With every step, the man's arm got heavier, and his feet moved slower. She ground her teeth. If they'd let her spread her wings, she could've easily carried him back.

They took Liam from her and trudged inside. Pierre rushed at Liam with a knife while the rest of her guardians closed in around her. The wide hall suddenly seemed much smaller.

"What the devil are you doing here?" Pierre held the knife to Liam's throat. His voice echoed around them.

"Pierre, stop. He's hurt. Let him go." Isa struggled to make her way through the guardians, but they formed a wall. She could barely see Pierre and Liam. Missy wiggled through and stood by Liam.

He slumped, his head rolling forward, and Pierre moved back a few feet. Isa thrust her way through them and grabbed the knife from Pierre.

"He's not going to hurt me."

Pierre put a hand across her chest and pushed her back. "We don't know that."

Isa pointed to him. "He passed out." She yanked Pierre's arm down and stalked up to Jude and Drew. "Put him down. He's just a human." Isa worried that might be the wrong thing to say. Humans and dragons were natural enemies. Before the dragons were hidden, they were hunted ruthlessly both by humans and wizards. Though the humans were quite useless without the wizards. He couldn't possibly be a wizard. They'd died out years ago.

They dropped Liam, and he collapsed to the ground. She glared at Jude but then examined the man. He was alive but not conscious. Her power only worked on dead people or dragons. She couldn't make someone wake up. She discovered that one day when she and Drew were sparring, and she had knocked him out. She just had to wait for him to wake up. Missy curled up on Liam's chest.

Grace rushed to her side. "Your Majesty, maybe we should let them take care of him."

Isa shook her head. "No. Look at what they've done. Prepare a room for him."

Grace looked up and met Jude's eyes, but Isa didn't care

what they thought. If this man wanted her dead, he would've killed her already. She didn't know why he was here, but it wasn't to hurt her.

"That's not a good idea," Pierre said. "He's likely working with the dragon we killed yesterday."

"Put him in a room. Get him warmed up, fed, and then we can talk to him. There are many of you. Surely you can guard him."

Pierre didn't look convinced, but he nodded anyway.

Grace placed a hand on Isa's arm. "I'll get the room ready across from the dining hall."

"Thank you, Lady Grace."

Pierre spun on Isa. "You shouldn't have been outside alone." His voice was low and angry.

"I was walking. I've done it loads of times before." She stood tall to show she wasn't afraid.

He towered over her. "You could've died."

"I could've. But I didn't. Besides, you said the threat was neutralized."

His nostrils flared. "Why did they leave you out there alone?" His eyes flicked up to Jude and the others.

This was ridiculous. She was tired of being treated like a child, and it was time she stepped up and took control. She was queen here, not Pierre. Before the boys could answer, she did.

"Because I ordered them to. My command overrides yours, does it not? I am queen, and I'm tired of you treating me like I'm not. If I want to go outside by myself, I will, and if you have a problem with that, then I no longer need you as a guardian."

He clenched his fists. "Our job is to make sure you are safe."

"And I am. You have trained me well. Even if Liam had been a threat, I could've easily killed him myself."

Footsteps rushed down the hall behind them. "The room is ready," Grace said.

"Good. Jude, Drew, will you help Liam to his room?" Isa asked. She didn't look at Pierre. This was the first time she'd ever stood up to him like that, and she didn't want to see the consequences.

Jude and Drew hoisted him up, and Isa followed them to the guest room in the middle of the castle with a towering four-poster bed and navy blankets. Since she'd been alive, they rarely used the guest rooms.

They dumped Liam on the bed, ruining the pretty picture of pillows and comforter. She wished they'd be gentler with him, but she supposed they were angry.

Grace removed his odd boots, and Isa helped get him under the covers. He looked like he was sleeping. Hopefully, he'd wake soon so they could talk. She wasn't leaving his side until she was able to get some answers out of him as to why he was here.

Isa sat with him for a couple of hours, various guardians hovering around her. She even took her dinner in the room, and soon it was late evening. Her eyes would barely stay open, and her head drooped forward.

Grace touched her shoulder. "Come on, Isa, let's go to bed. He'll be here in the morning."

Isa nodded. She'd be no good if she was sleep deprived.

"If he wakes up, you send someone to me right away," she instructed a grumpy Seamus. She hoped her threat from earlier would ensure they'd listen to her.

"Of course, Your Majesty."

CHAPTER 4

"Where did you put him?" Isa marched into the guardian's lounge, a room she rarely entered. Dragon's Teeth, she was mad. The room had been designed for the men with rich dark wood and deep green furnishings and curtains. She clenched her fists tight and glared at Pierre.

He sighed and set down his fork. She'd interrupted his breakfast, but she didn't care. He'd moved Liam without her permission, and she wanted answers. He had no right.

He stood and led Isa to a side table, on which sat a lone dagger. Out of the corner of her eye, she saw Missy jump into Pierre's abandoned chair.

Pierre waved his hand over the weapons. "You see these? After you went to bed, I had the guardians search the man."

Isa swallowed. She'd thought he was a good guy. But Pierre was overreacting. "It's just a dagger."

Missy snatched a sausage off of Pierre's plate and slunk to the floor, but Pierre didn't notice.

"It's more than enough to kill you. He is still unconscious, but we intend to find out why he is here when he wakes." Pierre picked up the dagger.

Isa chewed her lip and looked at the glittering dagger. Missy was chowing down on Pierre's eggs now and didn't even bother to jump down when caught. Pierre was probably right, but she wanted to believe that Liam wasn't here to hurt her.

Pierre adjusted the dagger in his hand and offered her the hilt. "This dagger is yours now. If the increased activity to our castle has shown me anything, it's that you might need that. I don't know what's going on, but I intend to find out."

"How?"

"We moved that man to the dungeon. He will be fed and kept alive. He will tell us why he is here and who sent him. Then we will kill him." Pierre clenched his jaw.

"Must you kill him? Maybe you take him back where he came from."

Pierre chuckled. "My queen, your soft heart will be the death of you. If we let him go, he will just come back. He has to die, but I will spare you the details."

Pierre was right, but she didn't want him to be. She also

was angry with herself. The one time she chose to stand up to Pierre, and she was wrong.

"Please, let me know what he says. I wish to know why he came." She wanted to go with them to question him. She was inexplicably drawn to the young man though she couldn't figure out why. She knew that would be foolish though. If he was here to kill her, that would give him an opportunity to do so. Perhaps he didn't before because he was too weak with the cold.

Pierre nodded. "Also, you should always arm yourself at this point. If the rebels managed to get a man inside the castle, it is not safe."

She hated fearing for her life in her own home, but such was her lot. She would always be threatened by someone. She couldn't believe her naivety. She'd brought him into her home, and he was here to kill her. She was lucky he couldn't brave the weather, or she'd be dead.

Pierre turned back to the table. Missy jumped off the chair and raced out of the room. He looked at his plate and then at Isa.

She gave him a half-smile. "You know you can't leave a plate full of food alone when she's in the room."

He rolled his eyes, snatched up the plate, and headed for the kitchens.

Isa wanted to laugh, to pretend like this was all she had to worry about, but a sinking feeling settled in her stomach.

She'd always known the rebels sought her life, but now it was real, and they'd sent someone right into her castle. She had to get answers out of him. But keeping him starved and cold was not the way to go about it.

CHAPTER 5

Grace found Isa and Pierre arguing in front of the door to the dungeons. This was a new situation, and she didn't know how Isa would react. She never reacted well to being told what to do. But she'd also never been threatened in her own home.

Pierre was listening to Isa, but his eyes were on Missy, who wound her way in and out of Isa's ankles.

Isa reached out and grabbed Grace's hand and pulled her closer. "Lady Grace will bring food and blankets to him and make sure he's comfortable."

Grace nearly shook her head. She had hoped to find Isa on her own and see how everything was going, but now she might have to attend to this dangerous prisoner when Isa could have the guardians do it.

Isa's face might have revealed nothing to Pierre, but

Grace could see the worry lining her eyes and the slight downturn of her lips that usually came when she was confused. She was obviously concerned about the prisoner but unsure of his motives.

Pierre sighed. "That's not necessary, Your Majesty. We can take care of him. Or Benjamin. The dungeons are no place for a lady."

Isa gripped Grace's hand harder. "I insist. Men often misjudge the needs of a person, and Lady Grace will ensure he is well enough. I also will trust her reports that he is being cared for. I know you mean well, Pierre, but you took him away in the middle of the night against my wishes. I will have Lady Grace down there unless you want me to personally deliver his food myself."

Pierre gave a slight bow. "Whatever you wish, Your Majesty."

Grace didn't like this. Not one bit. But she had to do it, or Isa would do it herself, and if Isa did it herself, she could die. Grace certainly didn't want to die either, but she knew that would be her fate one day. She was raised to kill someone. She figured that someone was probably Isa, but until she understood her place, she wouldn't jump to conclusions, and she would keep Isa safe. The prophecy foretold of her killing someone she loved, but that someone might not be Isa.

Pierre walked away to talk with Jude, and Isa hissed into her ear. "I want to know everything that is going on down there. Find excuses to bring him things. Blankets, pillows, snacks, whatever. Listen to their conversations. I don't think they are telling me everything, and I want to know why Liam is here."

Isa straightened up and spoke in a slightly louder voice. "It's breakfast time. Lady Grace, you'll bring food to our prisoner?"

Grace gave a curtsey. "Right away, Your Majesty."

She hustled away from Isa, her mind racing. She didn't want to go into that dungeon. She'd never been there before.

Grace went to the kitchens and grabbed a plate from the shelf, glad Olga hadn't cleaned up. She dished up hash browns, eggs, and sausages and found a few other things. Then she took a deep breath. She could do this.

Halfway down the hall, footsteps rushed behind her. She stopped and turned. Pierre caught up to her, out of breath. "Lady, I wanted to catch you before you returned."

Grace groaned inwardly. She'd never really liked Pierre. He always looked past her like she wasn't there. "How can I help you?" she asked.

"You wish for the queen to be safe, yes?"

Grace nodded.

"Then you must, uh, bend the truth a little about the prisoner. Our primary goal is to make sure the queen is safe, and that man is dangerous. We need answers out of him, and if he is comfortable, he will never give us those answers. Just tell the queen all is well no matter what you find. Keep your time there short and be cautious and wary. Whatever you do, don't speak to him."

Grace jerked her head up. That was a strange request.

"Why not?"

He gave her a hard glare. "Because I told you not to. Don't question me. Do you understand?"

Grace clenched her fingers tighter on the plate. "Yes, sir."

She'd never been one to rebel, but she certainly wouldn't listen to him over her queen. What exactly was Pierre afraid she'd find out?

CHAPTER 6

Sid picked up his phone and looked at the date. It'd been three days since Liam disappeared. Three days that he was in constant danger. Sid didn't want that three days to turn into forever.

Aspen slid a hand down Sid's chest and brought her lips to his ear. He shivered and set down his phone. They had a houseful of people sitting in the kitchen. She should know better, but then again, she never let it stop her before.

"I want to go see the babies," she said.

That was not what he expected to come out of her mouth.

He grabbed her hand. "We can't. We need to stay here in case word comes on Liam."

She slumped in the chair next to him and pouted.

"Please. I need something to take my mind off all this. I can't stop thinking about the danger he's in."

"Play with Skye's kids." He nodded to the window. Yesterday, he had a massive playground installed so they would stop tearing up his house. Six of the ten were out there playing. Though he wasn't sure how long it would last with two of them constantly turning into dragons and fighting. As soon as one let out a flame, the playground would be toast.

"Do you think he's okay?" Aspen asked, dropping her eyes. Sid could feel the worry pouring off of her. Or maybe that was his own. It was hard to tell.

"Of course Liam's okay. We'd know if something bad happened." They wouldn't, but he wanted to say those words. He didn't know what he would do if something happened to his son.

"I just want him to come home." She folded in on herself a little.

They'd had this exact same conversation at least forty times in the last few days, but he'd keep reassuring her even if he wasn't sure himself.

"He'll be home before you know it, crowing about his accomplishments." Sid was so proud of the man his son had become, even if he was a little cocky sometimes. He just prayed he was right this time.

Aspen gave a small grin. "I hope so." She stood and paced in front of the windows. "But we need to do something. Go somewhere."

Sid wrapped his arms around her from behind, and she laid her head on his chest.

"We can't. We have to stay here and wait for news."

"Ugh, I hate waiting. You know, the last time I was this worried, Rowan was missing."

"And look at how that turned out." Liam was more resourceful than Rowan was at that age. He'd make it. He had to.

Aspen chuckled and spun around. It was good to see her smile. "If he comes home with a beautiful bride, we're in more trouble than we thought."

"Ten grandkids would be nice though." He couldn't believe he was having those thoughts. His son was eighteen for crying out loud. He supposed with the possibility of losing him forever, he suddenly thought far into the future.

Aspen turned back to the window and watched two small blue dragons squabbling in the air. "Are you sure? Didn't you tell me you had that thing built to keep them outside?"

"Truth." Sid chuckled.

He enjoyed this lighthearted banter with her. This was what life was normally like, but it had taken a dark tinge the moment Liam disappeared. His heart clenched. Sid wanted to believe he'd be okay.

But he knew that was not how this would likely play out.

Jens entered the kitchen and gave him a stiff nod. He poured himself a cup of coffee. Sid hadn't talked with him much, but that was mainly because he'd been so preoccupied with Liam. Aspen slipped away from Sid and stood next to Jens. They chatted about something, but Sid couldn't hear the conversation. Aspen was always better with guests than he was.

The door burst open, and a gust of cool spring air rushed in. Trinity and Gabe stomped inside, arguing. Skye raced into the room and intervened. It actually made things louder.

Sid ignored them and thought about the problem at hand. All the reports he'd had from Jens said that the queen killed first and asked questions later. He needed more information about her. Once Liam was rescued, they would have to take action.

But what would be the appropriate course?

He chewed on his bottom lip. Jens spoke of villages of dragons in Europe. He wanted to visit one and talk to the people, but he couldn't leave now. He had to stay here and wait for word of Liam.

But he could send someone else. Someone less threatening who people would open up to.

"Hey, Skye, how would you like to go to Europe?" He grinned at her. She was always up for a trip anywhere.

CHAPTER 7

*L*iam blinked his eyes open. Every part of his body hurt, but he didn't know why. His teeth chattered, and he sat up, and his eyes adjusted to the dim light. The room was tiny and cold with damp stone walls and bars. He'd managed to land himself in prison. A few torches were all that lit the area. Had this place never heard of electricity?

And to think that he was starting to doubt that the queen was evil. He stood and stretched. His body was a little sore, but otherwise, he felt fine. He wore strange clothes and soft leather boots.

He cracked his neck. He had to escape and go home and tell his dad everything he'd learned. Which wasn't much. He'd met the queen and a few of her guards. It would be enough to call this mission a success. Well, not really, but he couldn't stay here.

He briefly remembered being awakened in the night and dragged down here. They'd asked him all kinds of questions, but he refused to answer any of them. If he was going to stay alive, he had to keep his mouth shut.

He walked the length of the cell. It was about ten feet long and twelve feet deep. He rubbed his hands together and blew on them, but it didn't do any good. They still had little to no feeling.

He gripped the icy bars. They weren't going anywhere.

Think, Liam, think.

Felix had taught him well, but he'd never taught him what to do if he landed in prison and had his weapons stripped. Though, Felix probably never landed himself in prison.

No. Felix was dead. Killed by these bastards.

Liam paced back and forth, if for nothing else but to try and get warm. He studied the bars. He wasn't sure what they were made of, but he could probably melt them as a dragon. The question was: would he fit?

Only one way to find out.

He stood in the middle of the cell and concentrated on his dragon form.

Nothing. His hands were still human and shaking.

He'd never not been able to shift before. It had always been second nature to him. Did the queen have magic?

Well, of course she did, but could she take away his ability to shift?

Ugh. This was impossible. He'd never get out of here. He sank down onto the bench. He should've listened to his parents. If he ever saw them again, he would tell them he was sorry and that they were right.

He grinned. His mom would never let him live that down.

He shivered and wondered if he would freeze to death down here. He suddenly missed his pampered life. He knew that most people didn't live in fancy houses and drive sports cars. He'd never had to fight for anything, and now he was fighting for his very life.

He'd have to talk his way out of this. So far, he'd basically been semi-conscious when he'd seen people. He didn't remember talking at all, but maybe he'd had some half-delirious conversations.

He shook out his hands. He could play this in so many ways. He thought about all his training with Felix. He could pretend to be terrified, and when they let their guard down, attack and escape. But he didn't know the castle or where he was.

He could be overly confident. It was always a risky move, but it usually worked with captures that involved multiple people because, eventually, his confidence would convince someone in the group to betray the others and help him escape. In a place where he didn't know the lay of the land, this was the best option.

He shook out his hands.

At least, being cocky was something he'd mastered.

CHAPTER 8

Grace stood outside the dungeon's doors with a steaming plate of potatoes, sausage, and eggs for the prisoner. She had a fork in her pocket. Nerves danced in her belly. She wasn't sure how this would go.

Jude stood guard at the door. Of course, it would be him.

"I'm supposed to take this to the prisoner," she said, not meeting his eyes. Instead, she stared at his black boots.

"Pierre said no one was allowed down there. I'll take it myself." Even his voice stirred the butterflies in her stomach. She could not let him distract her.

He held out his hands, and Grace took a step back. "I was told to bring it myself. The queen insisted."

Jude dipped his head toward her. "Come on, Grace, you won't want to go down there. It's not a place for a lady."

Grace ignored the shiver down her spine. Those were the exact words Pierre used. She tightened her grip on the plate.

"His food will get cold. I have orders from the queen, so unless you want to explain yourself to her, then you must let me go."

Jude rolled his eyes. "Fine, but I'm coming with you."

That wasn't exactly what Isa wanted, but after they got used to Grace visiting the man, they'd let her go alone, and she could get the information Isa wanted.

Jude held the door open, and she slipped past him, trying not to notice how close he was to her. He smelled like the forest.

The stairs were slick, and she had to take care to not slip and drop the plate.

Jude pointed down a long hall. "He's there."

"Why so far?"

"Less chance of escape."

The dungeons smelled like dead rats and piss. Grace had no idea there were places like this in the castle. She'd never ventured down here. They walked side by side, passing all the empty cells, Jude lighting the way with a torch.

Grace's hands shook with the cold. It was freezing down here.

Jude stopped in front of the metal bars. The prisoner

lay on a stone bench with nothing but a thin blanket. Well, listening to Isa wouldn't be a problem. Grace would find lots of excuses to bring him things.

"You can put the food there." Jude pointed to a cutout in the stone next to the metal bars. Grace dug out the fork and set it on the plate. Jude snatched it up. "You can't give him any weapons."

The man stood and sauntered over to the bars. "What am I going to do? Stab you with it? It's a fork."

Grace agreed, but she didn't want to argue with Jude in front of him. Jude didn't react at all. In fact, he barely acknowledged the prisoner.

The man stared at the food in Grace's hands and licked his lips. She shoved the food in the stone cubby.

He took the plate and picked up a sausage with his fingers. Grace watched him with fascination. In spite of not having any utensils, he managed to not make a mess of himself. Where did he come from? Why was he here? What was his life like back home? She supposed he was good looking in a foreign sort of way. His skin was darker than theirs, but only just.

"I'll make sure to bring you more finger-friendly foods next time." She placed her hands on the cold bars.

He rolled his eyes. "Or you can give me a fork."

Jude gave a sharp shake of his head. "No forks. No knives. No spoons."

This was ridiculous. This man couldn't hurt anyone while in a cell. They didn't even know that he was a bad guy yet. He deserved a little dignity. "What about a pillow or warmer blankets. Think he'll hurt you with those as well?"

The prisoner chuckled and flashed a smile. "I like this girl. She thinks logically, unlike you imbeciles who left me here to freeze to death. A warmer blanket would be nice."

She gave him a slight nod. "I'll bring you one in a bit."

"Thank you."

"That won't be necessary." Jude's fingers tightened on the pommel of his sword. "We can take care of him."

Grace spun on him. "Obviously not." Isa would be furious when she found out the state they were keeping him in.

The prisoner stuck his hand out of the bars, and both Jude and Grace jumped.

"I'm Liam."

Grace didn't take his hand but met his bright blue eyes. "I'm Grace."

She stared at him for a few moments and then hustled away. She followed Jude out and up the stairs, wondering what this adventure would bring. Because it was an adventure. The first real one she'd ever had.

CHAPTER 9

Ruby looked at the quaint inn with a thatched roof and bright white exterior. She was thrilled when her mom asked her to accompany her on a quick trip to Scotland. She'd never been here before. And here they were in the small village of Buidseach.

The air was damp and heavy, but not any colder than Yellowstone or her home in Oregon. Everything was green, and flowers bloomed in window boxes.

Spread out behind the tiny village were fields as far as the eye could see. A few farmhouses had barns with cows and sheep, but mostly crops covered the fields.

As soon as they dropped their stuff in their room, they went to dinner. A girl Ruby's age brought them their food. On her plate were two large pieces of fried fish and giant fries.

Skye looked up at the girl. "I would like to talk to your mother."

The girl's eyes widened. "If the food isn't what you like, I can bring you something else."

"The food is fine, but I have a message from a friend of hers."

The girl gave a stiff nod and escaped behind a door. "She seemed scared," Ruby said.

Her mom nodded. "But teens sometimes are intimidated by adults. Especially foreign ones. I'm glad you're not like that."

Ruby grinned as she munched on her fries. Her mom probably wished she was more like that sometimes in spite of what she said. Ruby argued with her mom and other adults all the time.

The innkeeper came out, rubbing floured hands on her apron. She had a warm grin on her face. "How can I help you?"

"I was told by Jens that you might have some information for me."

She glared at Skye. "I don't know the name." Her voice had gone cold.

Skye gave her a dazzling smile, which worked on most people. Ruby's mom was capable of getting about anything she wanted. Mostly because she was beautiful but also because she was always so sincere. "He said you might say that. But I know you're a dragon, and I know you're being oppressed by the queen."

The woman snorted. "Dragon. You're barking mad. The only queen I recognize is the Queen of England, and she hasn't done anything oppressive in years. Now, if you'll excuse me, I have bread to finish."

She escaped to the kitchen, and Mom sighed. "Well, I knew it wouldn't be easy, but I didn't expect downright denial."

"Did Jens give you other people to talk to?" Ruby was excited to see what they would find. She'd never been on a mission before. It seemed so exciting.

"He did. Let's finish eating, and we'll check out the town."

It was dark by the time they got back to the inn. Not a single person would admit to being a dragon, but there was evidence everywhere. Dragon paintings on the walls. The pub was called the Drunken Dragon, and every single eye averted at the name Jens.

Something odd was definitely going on, but Ruby wasn't sure if they would be able to find it.

CHAPTER 10

The guardians never let Grace visit Liam on her own. She brought him all the things he needed, so at least, he wouldn't freeze anymore. In the evenings, she brought a pitcher of hot water so he could wash.

She always waited while he ate, an impatient guardian at her side, but never in the evenings. She wanted him to have his privacy. She wasn't able to give Isa any useful information though as the guardians always hovered. Isa was angry about the conditions he was being kept in, but so far, she'd been unable to convince Pierre to let him out.

Grace carried her steaming pitcher of water and stopped when she came around the corner. Seamus stood by the dungeon door. He'd not bothered her since she cast the spell, but she'd never put herself in any situation where they were alone. And he'd never been on guard before.

She took a few deep breaths and continued on. She could do this.

She paused in front of him. "I need to take this to Liam." She nodded toward the pitcher in her hands.

He opened the door, and she slipped past him, but he didn't follow. Relief flooded her lungs. Her spell must've worked better than she thought. Not only that, but now she could talk to Liam freely. Hopefully, Seamus would be on guard more often.

Liam waited by the bars as she approached. "Where's your guard?" he asked.

"He let me come alone."

"They realized I can't hurt you from here, huh?" He seemed so cavalier for being locked up.

Grace shrugged and shoved the pitcher in the cubby. He retrieved it. "I'd give anything for a shower."

"What's a shower?"

He chuckled. "You don't have showers? It's like a bath, but the water pours over you from above."

Grace had never heard of such a thing. "Like a waterfall?"

"Sort of."

Grace glanced down the hall and worried she'd see Seamus coming to get her. She didn't know if she'd have the opportunity to talk to Liam again. "Why are you here?"

He raised his eyebrows. "I see why they let you come alone. They couldn't get answers out of me, so they got you to do their dirty work."

Her cheeks flushed. "It's not like that. I just wanted to know."

Liam took the small towel she'd brought and dipped it into the water. "Well, you tell the queen that if she wants answers, she has to come get them herself."

He scrubbed at his face. Grace didn't want to intrude on his bath, and he obviously wouldn't tell her anything useful.

"I'll let you have your privacy. I'll see you tomorrow."

"Thank you for taking care of me. I appreciate it. Your kindness won't be forgotten." His voice had gone quiet, and he gave her a small smile.

She blushed and rushed from the cell, ashamed that she enjoyed their conversation.

GRACE BRUSHED out Isa's hair. "I'm sorry. I don't know what else to do, but I'll continue to see if I can get him to talk. He was insistent he wanted to talk to you."

Isa huffed. "I wish I knew what his motive was. If he's here to hurt me, then obviously I can't go down there, but if he's here for some other reason, I have to know."

"He doesn't seem like a bad guy. In fact, he's quite charming."

Isa spun on her. "Are you sweet on him?"

Grace tried not to let her emotions show. "No. I'm just stating that he's nice."

"The guardians won't allow me down there."

"Jude might."

Isa went quiet for a moment. "Is he on duty tonight?"

"No. It's Seamus." Grace thought quickly. She wanted Isa to visit Liam so they could find out why he was here. She could fix Seamus using magic for Isa. "But between you and me, Seamus can't stay awake all night."

Isa leveled her a look but didn't say another word.

Grace helped Isa into bed, which was more complicated than normal because Missy was in the mood to play. She kept pouncing on the covers every time Grace moved them, and Isa thought it was funny, so she encouraged her.

After finally getting both of them in bed, Grace slipped down the hall and downstairs. Then, she took a detour past the pathway to the dungeons. She didn't have to be that close, but once she could see Seamus, she muttered a few words ensuring he would soon fall asleep and wouldn't wake until the early morning.

CHAPTER 11

Isa poked her head out of her door. She wouldn't put it past her guardians to post someone there to protect her.

It was two a.m., and she couldn't sleep, Grace's words echoing in her mind. She hoped Grace was right about Seamus. Missy nudged her ankle.

"We're going to get some answers."

She wanted to know why Liam had come. Grace didn't have any information, and her guardians hadn't been able to get any answers out of him either, so Isa had to go to the source.

Liam would be behind bars, so he couldn't hurt her. She tried a couple of times to go during the day, but Pierre put a hard stop to that. So, she resorted to the middle of the night. It was his fault, really.

She crept down the dark halls. No one was awake. Torches lit the hallways, and Missy kept pace with her.

She made it to the dungeon door and found Seamus sitting next to it, sound asleep. Grace's knowledge was solid.

Isa suppressed a giggle and softly pushed the door open. She grabbed a torch from the sidewall and lit it. She hadn't been here in years. Grace told her Liam was being kept near the end of the hall in a small cell with bars instead of a door. They weren't sure if he was a dragon or human, so they put him in the cell where he couldn't change.

He was awake, sitting on the sorry excuse for a bed, and he cocked his head at her.

"Your Majesty. You are the last person I expected to see. Did your friend send you here?" He seemed genuinely pleased to see her, but he could be faking.

"Yes. But I've been trying to come anyway. I wanted to see you myself, but my guardians are overprotective."

He snorted and stood. He was tall, but not as tall as her guardians. She tried to not appreciate the way he moved.

"You are queen. You can do what you want."

She clasped her hands in front of her. She was still given a short leash with control. Someday she would though. "I wish."

Liam approached, and Isa backed up, but Missy stuck her nose through the bars. He crouched down, and she clenched her fists. If he hurt Missy, she would personally see that he was killed.

He reached through the bars and scratched her behind the ears. "She's very beautiful."

"Thank you, I've had her since she was a baby."

He gave her a grin. "I was talking to the fox."

It took Isa a second to process what he said. She blushed. He was just trying to flatter her, catch her off guard. Oh, he was good. She stood straighter. "Why are you here?"

He glanced up. "Because I want to help you."

How could he help her? He was here to hurt her, wasn't he?

"I don't understand."

"I know." He stood up, and Missy whined. "Look, I'm from America. A few days ago, the rebels came to our king and asked for help defeating you. They told him a sob story about how you ruled with an iron fist, and they needed help ending your reign so they could live freely. I didn't believe them, but the king did. I wanted to warn you of their treachery and possible invasion. But you're so threatened by us that you didn't even ask questions. You killed my friend without cause." He gritted his teeth.

She wished he wasn't so logical about everything. He was right. They shouldn't have just killed that dragon without questioning him. But she couldn't very well tell this man she doubted her own people.

"So you're a dragon?"

"Yes. But after my friend was killed, I thought I'd have

an easier time warning you as a human. And I was right. Why did you kill him?"

"He was a threat. We thought he was here to kill me."

"Well, I'm glad I decided to use my human form."

She took a deep breath, trying to make sense of his story. All the evidence pointed to him coming to kill her. "You had weapons on you. Lots of them."

He pushed his face into the bars. "I had a dagger. Would you go anywhere without one?" Of course she wouldn't. She totally understood that. If a dagger was all he had.

"But the guardians found a stash of weapons in a tree."

"I brought a dagger with me. That's it. I swear." He held his hands up like he had nothing to hide.

"I'm not here to hurt you. If I was with that group of rebels, I would've killed you the second I saw you. That is their goal. I'm not with them. I'm with you."

Isa stared at him for a long moment before turning and racing down the hall.

She had no idea if he was telling the truth or lying.

And that terrified her.

CHAPTER 12

A few days later, Seamus was on duty again when Grace brought lunch, a hot roast beef sandwich, cold carrot sticks, and a chocolate chip cookie.

She hadn't been alone with Liam since that night she brought him the water. Isa had managed to sneak down here once, but she was cryptic about her thoughts on the whole thing.

Grace always wore a cloak when she went down because it was freezing. She didn't know how Liam was managing.

He jerked his head up from the book he was reading when Grace approached. Over the last several days, she'd found various excuses to bring him things. He had multiple pillows and blankets, a few books, and a couple of changes of clothes. Her task from Isa was to take care of him, and she would not fail.

"You're alone again," Liam said in that funny accent he had.

She set his food in the cubby. "I am."

"Would you stay and talk? It's awfully lonely down here."

She nodded, and he shoved a pillow through the bars. She set the pillow on the damp stones and sat, pulling her arms inside her cloak to stay warm. The last time he'd clammed up, but today she would avoid serious things. Maybe he was like Isa.

He settled on his own pillow, food in lap, and smiled at her. He was attractive, but he didn't make her belly dance like Jude did.

"Where did you come from?" she asked. She'd been insanely curious about him.

"America."

She figured that.

"I've read about America. What part are you from?"

"Have you heard of Yellowstone?"

She'd read a book about American national parks. Reading was the only thing that kept her from getting bored in the castle. "I've seen pictures. It's very beautiful."

"Yes, it is." His face lit up.

"Are you a dragon?" She figured he was, but no one had confirmed that with her.

"I am. Are you?"

She shook her head. She'd never tell him what she really was. He took a bite of his sandwich. "This is so good. Did you make it?"

"I put it together, but our cook Olga made the food."

"Well, please give my compliments to her. All the food you've brought me has been fantastic."

"Are there a lot of dragons in America?"

He nodded. "But not as many as there used to be. Several years ago, a war wiped out the canyon, fire, woodland, and arctic dragons."

"There are different kinds of dragons?" Grace tried to wrap her head around that.

"Sure. Don't you have that here?"

"No, we only have one kind."

"Only the green ones?"

"What do you mean? All dragons are green. The purple mountain dragons were all killed by the wizards." She could barely say the word. It had been so forbidden to her.

He chuckled. "No. They come in all different colors. I'm gold."

"Really?"

He told her about the different dragon races, and her mind spun. The pictures of Yellowstone didn't have any dragons in them. In fact, none of the pictures she'd seen of America showed any dragons.

"But what happened to them all? Why did you have a war?"

"That's a long story." He nibbled at the cookie she'd brought him.

"I have time." As long as he was willing to talk, she was willing to listen.

He sighed. "Well, I suppose it all started the day my…I mean, the king and queen were bonded. One of the arctic dragons didn't like my…the chosen queen and tried to kill her. The queen, in America, is always human. Anyway, she had a dragon slayer in her hands, and she cut off the arctic dragon's head."

He continued his story full of battles and excitement, but Grace's mind drifted back to the dragon slayer he spoke of. She had one in her room. She thought it was the only one.

In the old days, there had definitely been more, belonging to the wizards, but each had been handed down from parent to child. Her father had told her the rest of the wizards were killed and that she was the sole survivor. Had he lied to her, or had they just gone over to America and let everyone think they were dead?

She had more questions than she could stand, but she couldn't ask. As much as she liked Liam, she couldn't trust him. And this American queen. Was she like Grace? A wizard?

Maybe she could help Grace fulfill her mission or at least help her make sense of what she was supposed to do. The prophecy haunted her all the time. She knew it spoke of her and Isa. She loved Isa, and someday she might have to kill her.

She waited for Liam to finish his story.

"Tell me more about your queen."

"My…you mean, Aspen? Oh, she's amazing…"

CHAPTER 13

A slamming door startled Liam awake. After the queen had visited him in the middle of the night, he'd been staying up late, hoping she'd come back, but she never did. Her maid did though, and he felt like he was making some progress there. But she only came during the day.

Isa was his best bet at getting out of here alive. He wasn't sure what to make of her yet. She had Felix killed, but she had thought he was a threat.

If he could get her to trust him enough to let him out, he'd try to get close to her and find out what she was really up to. If he discovered she was evil, he could still kill her, and if she wasn't, he'd be able to give his dad the information he needed. But as of yet, he didn't have anything.

His cell door banged open, and he looked up. Two of

the guards rushed at him. Rough hands grabbed him and dragged him out of the cell. He didn't know where he was going, but he hoped it wasn't to die. They brought him to a room on the other side of the dungeon and dumped him onto a chair. The two men secured his hands behind his back, and he looked around. A small fire burned in the grate to the side.

Various weapons hung on the walls. He recognized some of them, but not all. Realization hit him the second an old man sat down in front of him with a set of small knives.

"Why are you here?" the man asked. Liam steeled himself. So far, he'd ignored their questions, but he wouldn't be able to anymore. But at least now, he had a good story to feed them.

He told the same story he had for the queen.

"Liar," the man spat. He took one of the knives and pressed it against Liam's throat. "Let's try this again. Why are you here?"

"I already told you." Liam doubted the man would kill him. At least, not yet. But he couldn't underestimate these guys who'd killed Felix without a second thought.

"Wrong answer. Jude, bring the brand."

Jude carried over a long metal stick from the fire. Liam squirmed, fear slicing through his insides. If he told the truth, they'd kill him, so he had to stick to his story.

Jude handed the stick to the old man, who held the red-hot end close to Liam's face. "Care to change your answer?"

"It's the truth." Sweat formed on his brow. This was it. He was going to die.

The burning tip pressed against Liam's forehead. Pain burst from his head, and he screamed. The stick was removed, and Liam took deep breaths, his forehead searing. The man gave the stick to Jude, who stuck it back into the fire for a few moments and returned again.

The old man leaned on the table in front of Liam. "Who is the leader of the rebels, and where can I find him?"

Liam swallowed. He didn't have these answers. "I don't know. I told you I'm not with the rebels. I just came to warn you about their plot with the American dragons."

"Wrong answer. Again." The man grinned. He pressed the stick down on the back of Liam's hand.

The pain was worse than anything he'd ever felt before.

CHAPTER 14

*G*race found an empty room that hadn't been cleaned in a while. She wasn't a maid, but she had to clear her head, and nothing did that better than a pail of hot soapy water and a filthy floor.

She cleaned the floor, but her mind kept drifting to her conversations with Liam about Aspen, their queen.

Liam spoke as if he knew her quite well. Either that, or she was just that well-loved in their world, and everyone knew her story. What Grace couldn't figure out was that if Aspen was a wizard, then why did she marry the dragon king?

Sure, they kept themselves close to the dragons; otherwise, their magic would fade, but their sole purpose was to protect the humans from dragons. Aspen couldn't do that if she was a queen.

Grace shook her head. Actually, that made sense. If she married the dragon king, she could protect the humans. If the king ever breathed a word about hurting them, then Aspen would be in the right place to kill him.

Sort of like Grace and Isa.

Grace scrubbed at the floor harder. She never thought she'd find another person like her. She wasn't a hundred percent sure that Aspen was a wizard, and Liam hadn't said anything about magical powers. But if Aspen was in hiding like Grace, she wouldn't reveal her powers either, so maybe the dragons didn't know she was a wizard. But Aspen had a dragon slayer, and Liam knew about it. And only wizards had those.

Grace wanted to meet Aspen, but that would be impossible because she couldn't leave the castle.

Unless.

No. She couldn't think about that. She would never betray Isa.

The door to the room banged open. "There you are."

Benjamin bounded over to her with Marissa in tow.

"I never get to talk to you anymore because you are either with Isa or the prisoner," Benjamin whined. He wouldn't look at her. She was so tired of this.

Marissa flung herself into a chair, and Benjamin grabbed another towel and kneeled next to her. This was typical. He'd work so he could talk to her without having to look her in the face.

"I'm sorry. I've been busy." She understood that

Benjamin might want to see her, but she didn't understand why Marissa was here. Most days, she hardly gave Grace a second glance.

Benjamin looked around. "Pretty sure we don't need this room." His eyes widened, and he looked at her for the first time. "Unless they are moving the prisoner here. Are they?"

"I needed to clear my head."

They were right though. She couldn't remember the last time she'd set foot in here. Covered chairs and couches were flung around the room, and it had a wide fireplace. It'd make a nice sitting room. But they already had three of those they used.

"Well, clear it with us instead," Marissa said. Grace was skeptical of her intentions. Marissa usually reserved her comments toward Grace as short commands. "We want to know everything about the prisoner. You've been spending an awful lot of time in the dungeon. I heard he's gorgeous."

"Where did you hear that from?" Grace was certain she and Isa were the only girls who had laid eyes on him. But now she understood Marissa's motives. She probably had to talk Benjamin into hunting her down.

"One of the guardians mentioned they were worried Isa would fall for his charms."

"He is nice looking, but no more so than the younger guardians."

"I wish I could see him." Marissa waved a hand in front of her face, and Grace hid her grimace. This was the most

Marissa had ever spoken to her. The snoop must really want information on Liam, and then she'd go right back to ignoring Grace after this.

Benjamin worked as he spoke. "What's he like?"

"He's nice." She scrubbed harder at the floor. She hated all these questions. She wasn't even sure what she should think about Liam at the moment.

Marissa grabbed a towel and started dusting off a dresser. "Oh, come on, you can give us more than that. If you had to clear your head, something is bothering you."

"I guess I don't understand why he's locked up. He doesn't seem to be a threat at all."

"He must have you under a spell if he's got you thinking he's not dangerous. Don't you know the ones that seem the least likely to be dangerous are the ones you can't trust at all?" Marissa whistled softly.

Grace dropped her soapy rag. "Don't be ridiculous. He's very polite and smart, and he's here to help Isa, not hurt her." Her voice raised a few notches, but she couldn't help herself.

"Oh my, someone's defensive. Tell us more."

Grace sighed. She'd never clear her head now.

CHAPTER 15

𝒜 loud crash, followed by a scream woke Ruby from a dead sleep. Mom bolted out of bed, and Ruby followed her, rubbing her eyes. She slipped on her shoes and trailed her mom outside.

The lamplight cast an eerie glow around them, the streets in chaos. The villagers were outside in their pajamas, holding bags or wooden crates. Everyone seemed terrified. A group of a half-dozen tall men dressed in heavy winter gear wandered around them. But the thing that stood out the most was the swords that hung at their hips like they were in some medieval movie.

A couple of men stopped at the house next to the inn.

"This is it? Surely you have more potatoes," a man huffed.

"I…I…don't. You weren't supposed to be here for another week. That's all I have."

The man hovered over him. "And the queen has guests, so we need more food. I don't believe you. Seamus, go check his cupboard."

The one called Seamus, who was far younger than the others, shoved past the man and through the door.

"No, please," begged the villager. "I won't be able to feed my family. Please. I only kept back enough so we wouldn't starve."

A young woman put her arms around him. "It's okay, Dad. We'll figure it out."

Skye rushed for the man and his daughter, and Ruby wasn't about to be left behind.

"Excuse me," Skye said.

"What?" the man snarled.

"If you need food, I have money. You don't have to take it from them. If you give me a moment, I'll run to my room and get it."

The man gave a laugh. "Who are you?"

She stood tall. "My name is Skye."

"Well, Skye, your money is no good to me. I need food." He glowered at her.

"Very well, then I will give this gentleman money to replenish the food you took."

The man took a step forward, hovered over Skye, and put a hand on the hilt of his sword. Ruby swallowed. If this man ran her mother through with a sword, she didn't know what she would do.

Seamus came out of the house carrying another bag full of what Ruby assumed was potatoes. He set the bag at the villager's feet. Then he grabbed the sobbing young woman and yanked her into the house.

The girl didn't even scream or protest, but Ruby was certain she knew what was about to happen.

"You're American?" the evil man seemed to rise up in front of Skye.

Skye nodded.

"What are you doing here?" He crossed his arms and studied Skye with narrowed eyes.

"Just visiting."

He flicked his gaze to the inn. "Cora, what is the meaning of this?" he yelled.

The innkeeper ran toward them, her face white "We didn't think you were coming until next week. There won't be any guests then."

He moved away from Skye to Cora. "Your inn-keeping days are done. Do you understand? Those rooms are only for us."

She gave a stiff nod.

"As for your guests, I suggest you take them to their room and lock them in until we leave. Unless you'd like to see your pretty daughter lose her head." He pointed to the girl who had served them dinner.

Skye looked back. "We'll go."

"Good. And, Cora, this conversation isn't over. We'll be back later tonight."

Skye grabbed Ruby's arm and dragged her inside the inn. Ruby had no idea what was going on, but she knew one thing for sure. She didn't want to stay here another night.

CHAPTER 16

The next day, Marissa and Benjamin wouldn't leave her alone, and Grace was grateful when it was finally time to bring Liam dinner. She rushed down the hall, the plate of roast chicken and green beans hot in her hands.

Seamus grunted at her as she slipped through the door. She didn't know what else she would say to Liam today. If she kept asking questions about Aspen, he might get suspicious.

He laid on the stone bench under a threadbare blanket. All the things she'd brought him the last several days were gone.

"Liam, are you okay?"

He didn't respond, and she set down the plate and banged on the bars. "Liam."

Still no response.

She looked at the lock, and without thinking, she opened it with her mind. She rushed into the cell and found Liam unconscious. Dragon's Teeth! He was covered in bruises, cuts, and burns. What had they done to him?

He blinked his eyes open. "Help me," he croaked.

She sat on the edge of his stone bed and gripped his hand. She knew how to heal him, but if she did, he would know her secret. And everyone would want to know how he healed so fast.

He groaned in pain, and she lifted the blanket. Deep purple bruises covered his bare stomach. He dropped back into unconsciousness, and his breathing slowed. She didn't know the extent of his wounds, but if she didn't do something, he could die. She couldn't let him suffer. This wasn't right. None of it was.

She closed her eyes, concentrated, and healed his injuries. It took less than thirty seconds.

She opened her eyes and found him sitting upright, staring at her. His chest and stomach now free of bruises and his face clear of the burns.

"You healed me. How did you do that?" He looked at himself, wonder on his face.

She shook her head, scared now. She'd never displayed her magic in front of anyone. She stood and paced the cell in front of him.

"You can't tell anyone. Please."

"I…I…won't. But what are you? You said you weren't a

dragon. The only person I've ever seen heal that wasn't a dragon was Aspen."

Grace very nearly faltered at the mention of the queen, but all she could think about was how she'd shown her secret to a near stranger.

His eyes flicked to the open cell door, and she rushed for it, locking it behind her. She nearly tripped over the food but picked it up and slid it into the cubby.

"Why would Isa do this to me?" He slumped against the wall, studying his hand.

She stopped for just a second. "Isa wouldn't. And if she ever finds out that you were tortured, she won't rest until they are killed. But please, you can't tell her either because then she'd want to know how you were healed. Oh, this is impossible. I've made a mess of things."

She turned her back to him. That was so stupid. She'd gone and ruined everything. She raced away, not sure what to do now. Her slippered feet slid on the stone stairs, and she gripped the handrail. If she wasn't careful, she'd end up flat on the floor with her own concussion.

Everyone would find out about her magic, and she'd be banished or killed.

Oh, she was a fool. Marissa and Benjamin warned her, but she didn't listen. She'd let herself get too close. Too attached.

She cared too much. If she didn't, she would've just left the food and gone on her merry way, never even knowing he was hurt.

But she had cared, so she'd gone to him, and healed him. Whoever discovered Liam would know she did it because she was the only one who came down here.

She was in a world of trouble.

CHAPTER 17

*L*iam woke in the middle of the night. After Grace healed him, he had lain down and was out before he had time to even think.

He examined his arms again. Every single burn was gone. He stretched. Nothing hurt. It was as if he'd never been tortured. He found a set of clothes in the corner and pulled the shirt over his head and tugged the pants up. They weren't as warm as the clothes Grace had brought him, but they would have to do. He wrapped the thin blanket around himself and took out the plate of roast chicken and rolls Grace had left him. The food was cold now but still tasted good.

He thought about the things Grace told him. He would have to keep her secret, but also, she said the queen had no idea of what was happening down here. Did that mean that the queen was innocent in all of this?

Maybe. Maybe Grace was misinformed.

He hated not having all the information. But that was why he was here. Wasn't it? To figure out what was going on.

So if Isa wasn't in charge, who was? The old man? Or did he take his orders from someone else? The thought made Liam's head spin. This was so much more complicated than anything he'd trained for.

Light flickered from the hall, and his muscles tightened. He didn't know if he'd be able to handle another torture session. But a white nose stuck itself through the bars.

You're back, Liam said.

Yes, my mistress wanted to see you. The fox had chatted with him before, but he'd been more focused on Isa.

Why?

To talk to you. I know you think she's evil. She's not.

Then who is?

I don't know. But I don't like her guardians. They are hiding something from her.

Can you talk to her like this?

No. She does not hear me.

That was interesting.

Quiet footsteps padded down the hall, and Isa came into view. She smiled at him and stood closer than last time. He let her take him in, but she didn't seem surprised at his good health. Grace could've lied to him. Isa might be behind the torture session yesterday, but he didn't think so. His instincts had always been good. It was why Felix agreed to take him on.

"Your Majesty," he said.

She grinned. "You told me last time that you are a dragon."

"Yes."

"What color are you? I've heard there is a rainbow in the United States, but I've never seen any dragons but my emerald green ones."

"I'm gold."

She sucked in a breath, and her blue eyes flashed. "You're a royal dragon. Like me."

"Yes. So you are silver?"

She dropped her shoulders. "I've never spread my wings, so I don't know. I just know for a fact that I'm not a forest dragon." She took a few steps closer.

"Why?" This was not what he expected from her. She wasn't some bold, fierce woman. She was a scared girl.

"Because I don't have green eyes."

"No, I mean why can't you spread your wings?"

"It's part of my burden as queen. I'm not allowed to be a dragon."

He wanted to know more, but as long as she was here and talking, he had to plead his case even though everything he was telling her was a lie.

"Isa, you're in danger from the American dragons, and

no one knows them like I do. Let me out, and I promise I won't hurt you. I can't help you from in here."

"I…I…can't."

Liam let out a breath of frustration. "Aren't you the queen?"

She stood a little taller. "I am."

"So what's stopping you?"

"Fear that I might be wrong. You could kill me."

She was close enough to his cell that he could reach out and grab her if he wanted. He could kill her if that was his plan. But he wasn't sure if that should be his plan or not. He needed more information first, and he couldn't get that locked up in a cell.

He reached for her hand, and she jumped back. She stared at his waiting hand for several long seconds. Then she raced down the hall.

He flung himself onto his bed. He was stuck.

Still.

CHAPTER 18

Grace caught Benjamin early the next morning as he was bringing the eggs up. "Can you do me a favor?" she asked.

He dropped his eyes. "Sure, what's up?"

"Can you bring the food to the prisoner for me today?"

"Why? Didn't Isa ask you to do that?" He creased his eyebrows.

"I have some other things I have to do this morning. Can you do it? Please?" She didn't want Liam questioning her abilities. She'd never shown them to anyone before.

Benjamin set down the bucket of eggs and searched her eyes. It was something he hadn't done in years. "Are you okay? Did he do something to you?"

Grace took a step back and wrapped her arms around

herself. She didn't know how to explain her fears about Liam without incriminating herself or him. "No. He can't. He's locked up."

"Did he say something that bothered you?"

Grace swallowed. She couldn't have Benjamin acting suspicious now too. "If you must know, Isa's been more demanding lately, and I don't have time to do it all. You know how she is. Anyway, can you bring him food for a few days while I deal with Isa? Please."

Benjamin nodded, but Grace wasn't sure she'd convinced him.

She hid away for a couple of hours, worried that Liam had spilled the beans to someone. When it was time for Isa's breakfast, she couldn't hide anymore. Benjamin gave her a thumbs up and a grin when she went to the kitchens to retrieve Isa's food. He'd obviously managed to take care of Liam.

Grace grabbed Isa's breakfast and made her way to the room. Isa was already up and staring out the window. Usually, she was still fast asleep when Grace arrived. Perhaps she had things on her mind as well.

"It's freezing in here," Grace said and shoved another log into the fire. Missy danced around her ankles, and Grace slipped her a piece of bacon.

Isa stepped away from the window and flung herself onto the couch. She had dark circles under her eyes.

"Did you sleep last night?" Grace asked.

Isa shook her head and frowned. "I visited Liam."

Oh, this wasn't good at all. Isa knew Grace had healed Liam and was trying to figure out what to do with her. Grace unpacked the breakfast with shaking hands, unsure of what would happen next. But she had to say something.

"I'm surprised the guardians let you down there."

Isa bristled. "I'm queen. I can do whatever I want."

Grace wanted to argue. The guardians kept a tight hold on Isa, but she didn't want to push it. "I know. But they are protective of you."

Isa's shoulders drooped. "If you must know, Seamus was on guard again and sound asleep."

Grace hadn't put Seamus to sleep, but it was possible her spell was more potent than she thought, and he fell asleep every time he was on duty. Sometimes her spells went awry like that because she didn't fully understand her magic.

"I see."

"I'm thinking of letting him out. Do you think that would be safe? You've spent a lot more time with him than I have."

Grace sliced up Isa's sausages. "But not that much. I don't really know him." She had to lie. She couldn't risk Isa finding out what she knew about him.

Isa absentmindedly chewed on a piece of toast. "There's just something about him, and I hate that he's down there in that rat hole. How will we ever find out what he's about if we don't show some hospitality?"

"I think you're right." Grace searched Isa's face for any sign that she knew about the torture, but it looked like Liam had kept the secret. Because if he hadn't, Isa would've said something or had her tossed already.

Maybe she was safe after all.

CHAPTER 19

Ruby had no idea what time she fell asleep... if she fell asleep at all. Every time she closed her eyes, she imagined that man, Seamus, pulling the young woman into that house. The men were probably dragons working for this queen. Supposedly, Liam was with the queen now, a dragon who let her people steal from and hurt the local villagers. For the first time since he went missing, she was genuinely concerned about him.

The door banged open early the next morning.

"Get out," Cora screamed.

Ruby and Skye jumped out of bed. Cora stood at the door, her eyes red and hair wild.

"Get out," she yelled again.

"Of course we'll get our things and go. Are you okay?" Skye watched the woman with concern.

Cora collapsed on the floor in a fit of sobs. Skye went over to comfort her but whispered to Ruby. "Pack our stuff quickly."

Ruby nodded, but she couldn't take her eyes off the hysterical woman.

"Dead," Cora sobbed. "Dead, and it's all your fault."

"Who's dead?" Skye asked. Ruby rushed around the room, throwing clothes into the suitcase without bothering to fold them.

"My husband." Cora sucked in deep wet breaths. "They took him last night, and this morning, he was dead on our doorstep. All because of you." She shook out of Skye's embrace. "Get out. Now."

Ruby gathered their toiletries and zipped the suitcase. She grabbed her backpack and her mom's purse.

Skye stared at Cora, and Ruby nudged her. "Come on, Mom, we have to go."

Cora crumpled on the floor again, and Skye moved to help her, but Ruby grasped her arm. "She doesn't want our help. We need to get out of here before we bring more bad things upon these people." Guilt settled in her stomach. If they hadn't come, Cora wouldn't have lost her husband. This was all their fault.

Skye snatched her purse from Ruby and marched down the hall. Ruby took one last look at the woman and followed her mom, dragging the suitcase behind.

They stepped out into the cool morning air. Skye dug around in her purse, tears falling down her cheeks.

"Mom, it'll be okay."

Skye sniffed. "I should've kept my mouth shut. But I just wanted to help."

"I know. And we will, by telling Sid what happened here so he can take out the queen and free these people."

Skye pulled out the English pounds she had and handed half to Ruby. "Can you put those in that man's mail slot?"

Ruby took the money and shoved it into the slot on the door of the potato man, and her mom did the same at the innkeeper's door.

The door behind Ruby opened, and she jumped. The young woman who Seamus hauled into the house stepped out.

She approached Ruby. "Thank you."

Ruby gave a stiff nod. She didn't know what to say to this girl who had been violated just hours ago.

Skye looped her arm through Ruby's, still blinking back tears.

"What's the matter?" the girl asked.

"Cora's husband was killed last night because we were staying here." Skye's voice cracked a bit, and she sniffed.

The girl gave a nod. "Come with me a moment, will you?"

They followed the girl into an alleyway. "Are you with the rebels?" the girl asked.

Skye shook her head. "We're American. We came to see if the rebels were right about your queen."

The girl snorted. "Well, you got an eyeful then, didn't you?"

"Who were those men?" Ruby asked.

"They are the queen's men. Call themselves guardians. They take food from us. Another village provides linens and clothes. Another cattle and chickens. Another gives them women…" Her eyes squeezed shut, and Ruby couldn't help herself.

"But that man, Seamus, he…he…took you. Didn't he?"

"Aye, he did. But he's not so bad. I keep hoping he'll get me pregnant." Her words come out in a rush, almost as if she doesn't quite believe them herself.

Skye clutched harder at Ruby's arm. "Why?"

"Because we're not allowed to have kids, see. They take them from us when they are babies. We don't know what they do with them. Kill 'em maybe. Or maybe they raise them to love the queen. I'm the youngest one in the village, and if I get pregnant, and it's one of theirs, maybe they won't take it. Or if they do, they'll take me with it and let me raise it."

Ruby could not believe the words she was hearing. She couldn't fathom this at all. No freedom to raise your own children. To have them snatched right out of your arms. She could never live like this.

"Thank you for telling us what's going on." Skye patted the girl's arm. "We will do our best to help the rebels get rid of this queen."

The girl nodded. "Thank you. I hope we meet again."

Skye smiled wearily and dragged Ruby out of the alley and to their rental car.

Ruby still wasn't sure what this all was about, but she knew one thing for sure now. Liam would be lucky to get home alive. If he was alive at all.

CHAPTER 20

Benjamin rushed toward Grace. "Thank goodness I found you. I can't bring Liam food this morning. A cow is calving, and I'm the only one who knows how to handle it."

His face was twisted in panic. Benjamin was the only person around who had ever studied the veterinary sciences. His father had been the animal caretaker before he died.

"What about Marissa?" Grace couldn't go into the dungeons. Not yet. She wasn't ready to face Liam. Because even though he hadn't told Isa, Grace didn't know if someone else suspected. Grace had heard a few of the guardians muttering something about a wizard—because anytime anything remotely like magic showed up, everyone feared the wizards had somehow survived. Her name hadn't been brought up, and they didn't regard her suspiciously. Maybe they thought he healed himself.

"She's already down at the barns to assist me. Seriously. Isa can wait for whatever she needs. Please just bring Liam his food."

Grace nodded, nerves settling in her stomach. She could do this. She didn't have to talk to him. So far, he'd kept his mouth shut, but she didn't want to answer any questions.

She didn't even know what she'd say, and she certainly couldn't risk anyone overhearing their conversation.

She grabbed the breakfast from Olga—two large lemon poppy seed muffins and four thick slices of bacon—and slowly made her way to the dungeons. By now, all the guardians let her go by herself.

Drew opened the door, and she carefully walked down the stairs. Every cell was empty except Liam's. Grace had asked Isa why they were empty once. Surely the guardians had caught a few rebel spies and had to question them. But Isa told her they never brought the rebels to the island since they had some dungeon on the mainland. They didn't want to risk bringing such dangerous people close to her.

Grace's heart beat so hard she was certain Liam could hear it from the other end of the hall. She was being a bit ridiculous, but this was a big deal to her. Nobody could find out that she was a wizard.

She slowed as she got closer to Liam's cell, worried about his reaction to her. She didn't want him to fear her, but then again, she didn't want him being overly friendly either. She was a mess.

Grace approached the cell and found him staring at her from behind the bars. He had warm clothes and blankets again, the ones she had sent with Benjamin. Liam's face lit up, and he smiled at her. She ignored him and slid his food into the cubby. Her hands shook as she did so.

"Grace."

He reached through the bars, but she jerked away.

She swallowed. What on earth could she say?

"I've kept your secret. I haven't told anyone. If you want, I won't ask any more questions about you, but I miss your company. Please come back and just talk to me. I'll tell you any stories you want about America."

She stared at him for a few more moments and raced away. She flew up the stairs and down the hall, slowing only once she was far, far away from the dungeons.

CHAPTER 21

Isa was going stir crazy. She wanted to go outside, but there was no way they were letting her out now. They said the danger was even worse now.

She couldn't think straight. Liam showing up had her mind racing.

Missy dropped a ball in front of her, and Isa grinned. That fox knew when she needed a distraction.

She found a hall that was long and straight and threw the ball hard. Missy ran after it.

Liam.

Who was he?

There was something about him that she couldn't explain. He seemed utterly genuine. But she knew that could be faked. He'd reached for her, and she wanted that touch as much as it scared her.

He told her he was here to help her, but maybe he wasn't. Maybe he would kill her the second he got the chance. Maybe he was a rebel like her guardians said. But he told her that he was here to warn her that the Americans would help the rebels.

And Grace liked him too. She said he was always polite and friendly when she brought him food. Heck, she'd even encouraged Isa to visit him.

Missy released the ball, and Isa threw it again.

It was the opposite of what her guardians said. They said he was a liar and fought them every time they opened the door.

She wished she could know the truth for sure. Then she'd know exactly what to do.

Voices came from around the corner, from near the guardian's study. She stopped and listened.

"We should just kill him."

She crept closer but stayed out of sight from the doorway to the study.

"We can't," Pierre said.

Missy dropped the ball, but Isa ignored it.

"Why?" Seamus asked. "I'm tired of guarding the door every night. He hasn't told us anything useful. We know this is the eventual outcome. Let's get it over with."

"Seamus is right," Jude said. "He won't give us any more information. We need to end this. The longer he is in the castle, the better chance he has of attacking Isa."

"I'm telling you, we can't." Pierre slammed his hand on a table.

Missy nudged Isa's foot. "Not now," Isa hissed.

"She won't find out. She's never found out about the other rebels who've gotten close to the castle," Jude said.

Pierre snorted. "You came close with that group of American dragons yesterday. If they'd gotten any closer, and she was up in her tower, she would've seen them."

"We had no warning. We were too busy guarding the prisoner here," Seamus said defensively.

Isa's stomach fell. Liam had told her that the Americans were aligning with the rebels. He was right. He was here to warn her.

Missy nipped at Isa's foot. She had to stop herself from crying out. A shadow approached the door, and Isa slipped around the corner. Pierre's voice carried down the hall.

"She will find out if we kill him. This is the first one she's met. She'll want to see him at some point, and she's the queen. We cannot deny her that."

"But every second he's in these walls, her safety is at risk," Jude argued.

"True. But it has to be her decision. Find a way to do that, and then we can kill him."

Missy jumped up next to her, and Isa snatched the ball from the ground and threw it harder than she had before. It disappeared into the darkness, and Missy ran after it.

Her guardians were manipulating her. They didn't tell her about the American dragons because then they would have to admit that Liam was no threat and that he really was here to warn them. She now had a good reason to trust Liam over them.

They would try to convince her that he was bad and should be executed. She wondered how many times they had done this before.

To make something look like her decision when, all along, it was theirs.

CHAPTER 22

Sid arrived home after a long drive. He had been restless and didn't know what else to do. He was waiting on Baden to bring Liam home with the extraction team and Skye to arrive back from Europe with reports on the dragon village. He hated sitting around doing nothing. He parked the car, locked it, and slid out the door. He turned around, and Baden collided with him, sending them both to the floor. If Sid wasn't so concerned, he'd laugh. Runa had done the same thing multiple times when she was alive.

Sid scrambled up and helped Baden right himself. He crouched down so he could look the little dragon in his very worried eyes. Extreme fear and grief rolled off of him.

"What's wrong?" Sid asked.

"Slaughtered. All of them." Baden hunched over, his

breathing coming fast, and little puffs of multicolored smoke came out of his nostrils.

Sid's heart clenched. "Who?" He hoped against hope that Liam's name wasn't part of this, but he had to prepare himself for the worst.

"The dragons you sent to find Liam. They're dead, bodies strewn everywhere and so much blood."

Baden heaved, and rage filled Sid's chest. He stood, his jaw clenching. He turned and punched the side of his Lexus, leaving a dent. His hand felt like it was on fire, but his heart felt worse. He should've been there. Seven of his friends were now all dead, and it was his fault. And he had no way of getting Liam home.

Through tears of hate, Sid managed to ask, "Did you make it to the castle?"

Baden shook his head. "I was too upset. I would have messed up the mission. I'm sorry. I'll go back now."

"You should rest first." Those were not the words he wanted to say. He wanted to send Baden straight back. He wanted him to extract Liam from that place before his son's bloody body was hung up as a trophy. But he knew if he asked him to, Baden would go now, and he couldn't have Baden's death on his conscience too. Baden was in no position to fly back right now. He had to be exhausted.

All those dragons, those friends, his people, dead. How big of an army would they need to take over the queen's castle? He had no idea how many dragons she had loyal to her.

How could he know so little about another dragon tribe? He felt so inadequate as a leader.

They would have to attack.

That much was certain now. She'd killed seven of his dragons in cold blood, and he could not let this go. Jens was right about everything.

"Baden, rest. After that, we need to figure out how to bring Liam home."

Baden nodded, and Sid appreciated his bravery. Baden was going into a dangerous situation, and now he understood the stakes. He could camouflage himself and get into positions that other dragons couldn't. He would be the best one to extract Liam. Sid was surprised he hadn't thought of this before. He shouldn't have sent the other team at all.

"I will not fail you, Your Majesty. I will get Liam home safe."

"You will. I'm certain of it. And after that, the queen dies."

CHAPTER 23

Grace brought Liam his lunch and dinner that day, but she didn't say another word to him. Isa had asked her at least three times if she should let him out, but Grace didn't want to influence her one way or another.

She worried that if Isa let him out, he would let slip that Grace was a wizard. But so far, he hadn't said a word. In some ways, she was glad he knew. She desperately wanted someone to talk to about all this, and he didn't seem scared or bothered by her. Maybe it would be good to have someone to confide in.

Or maybe she wasn't ready for that yet.

That night, the hallways were quiet as Grace returned to her room. Isa had been incredibly chatty before bed, and Grace had been lucky to get away. Isa had asked Grace to stay with her, but Grace liked sleeping in her own bed. Plus, she had to keep some distance between her and Isa. Especially now with so many things going on.

Grace crept down the stairs to her own room and locked the door behind her—with magic. She sank onto her bed and sighed. At some point, her burden would become too great for her to carry on her own, but she never imagined it would be so soon. She thought she'd have a good twenty or thirty more years before she'd have to out herself.

She pulled out her sword and did her nightly dance. She was tired and sloppy.

She opened her drawer and stared at her other magical trinkets. The marbles that could paralyze dragons, the poison that could kill anyone instantly with no chance of revival, and the necklace that would force the wearer to do her bidding. There were other, less sinister things that she never used because she was scared of her magic being revealed. The potion that would make someone laugh at everything people said for a whole twenty-four hours, the rings that when given to a loved one would allow you to communicate from a distance, and the dress that would enchant anyone who gazed upon the wearer, making them desirable.

She sighed, put the sword away, and changed into her nightgown. She washed her hands and face and slipped into bed, her mind still reeling. Sleep would not come easily tonight as it had eluded her the past several nights.

She let out a breath. Why couldn't she let this go? Liam had kept his mouth shut about her abilities, and so she had nothing to fear. Though she supposed that as long as he was here, she'd fear him spilling the beans.

She hated carrying this secret alone. Hated not having anyone to share this with. Hated that she was a wizard. She just wanted to be a silly girl, fawning over boys like Isa.

But she'd been given a greater responsibility. One that she didn't know how she would be able to carry out. But she would have to someday, and then she would die. At least that's what the prophecy said.

But Liam knew her secret.

And he'd kept it.

Maybe he'd keep more of them.

Maybe it was time to share the burden with another. Someone who carried a burden and secrets of his own.

Grace had never trusted anyone before, but maybe tomorrow she'd trust just one person.

And if he proved unworthy of her trust.

She'd kill him.

CHAPTER 24

"**B**aden's been sleeping for three days straight." Aspen paced outside Liam's room, and Sid matched her step for step.

"I know. I've been hesitant to wake him, but we can't leave Liam any longer." He'd wanted to go back into the room after twenty-four hours, but he couldn't risk Baden being sloppy at all if he was going to rescue Liam.

Aspen rounded on him. "Why did you let him go to sleep anyway? You should've sent him straight back."

"Aspen, he just witnessed the murder of six dragons. Plus Felix. I had to let him rest."

"And you did. Go wake him up and send him on his way. I want Liam back in his own bed. Baden is small and can hide. He has a better shot at getting Liam back than anyone."

Sid nodded and cracked the door open. He approached the window and opened the blinds just a hair so sunlight came in but wasn't too bright.

He didn't see the little dragon anywhere.

Aspen flicked on the light. "Where is he?"

Sid sank onto Liam's bed. "I don't know."

Aspen gripped her hair. "I didn't think he was that cowardly. I thought he would want to protect Liam."

Sid put a hand on Aspen's shoulder. "Maybe he already left."

"But you can't know that for sure. Maybe he ran away. Now, what are we going to do?"

Sid opened the blinds all the way and pulled the window up, and then he whistled for an eagle.

One flew in and bowed deep. *What can I do for you, Your Majesty?*

Baden, the underground dragon, left some time in the last twenty-four hours. Will you find out where he went?

Of course, Your Majesty. I'll be back with a report as soon as possible.

Aspen left the room, and Sid lay down on Liam's bed, letting his eyes drift shut. Unlike Baden, he hadn't been able to sleep in days. He hated the pain in his chest over his son. He never knew being a parent would be constant worry and stress.

A FEW HOURS LATER, the eagle flew through the window again.

Sid jumped up. He must've drifted off. *Please tell me you have news.*

I do. Baden was seen flying north. I was able to check with eagles as far north as Alaska.

Sid sank down. Baden hadn't run away at all. He was going to rescue Liam.

For a moment, Sid allowed himself to hope. Maybe by this time tomorrow night, Liam would be sleeping in his own bed.

But deep down, he knew that hope was foolish.

The reality was that he would be lucky if he ever saw his son again.

And he had no good plan to get Liam back. Baden could hide.

But Liam couldn't.

The door to his room banged open, and Skye and Ruby rushed in.

"You're back," he said.

She collapsed on his bed. "That was horrible," she said.

Ruby nodded. "I never want to see anything like that again."

Sid rubbed his face. "What happened?"

"The queen's men go into the village and steal all their food and rape the women. I'm pretty sure they're all dragons, but maybe not."

Sid stood. "I need coffee, and you do too. Let's go down to the kitchens, and you can tell me the whole story."

He followed the girls out of his room, and a sinking feeling settled in his stomach.

This queen was worse than he thought.

And she had Liam.

CHAPTER 25

Isa slipped into the warm water of the baths. She wanted nothing more than to soothe her tense muscles, sore from worrying about all her problems.

She floated on her back and watched the red glow above her. Some would find the baths unsettling, but she loved the color. The water covered her ears, and utter silence enveloped her.

She closed her eyes and imagined she was far, far away from the castle. Far away from people who wanted to kill her, far away from guardians who manipulated and maybe lied to her. Far away from responsibilities of any kind.

She pictured herself on a beach with warm sun. For a while, beach books had been her favorite, and she had Grace search the library for all of them.

Today, she pretended she was at a beach in Thailand

with soft white sand and a hot, hot sun. Who would be there with her? Perhaps Liam. She wondered if he'd ever been to a beach before. Probably. Everyone on earth had been to a beach but her.

Still, she'd like to go with him.

She splashed out of her float.

Why would she want to be with him? Why not Jude or Drew? Anyone but Liam.

But no.

She thought of how he called her beautiful but in such a subtle way that she had to think about it. Her face flushed. He had reached for her too, and she wanted that touch, but she couldn't have it. He was the enemy.

Or at least that's what she was told.

Did she believe what they told her?

Not really. If she did, she would've ordered him killed already. In fact, she was almost a hundred percent sure he was on her side. Didn't her guardians confirm that when they said a group of American dragons had flown onto the island?

She swam over to the far side of the pool where the color of the gems glowed more purple than red. She liked him. Perhaps it was just because she couldn't have him. She knew that desire sometimes had to do with the forbidden.

Maybe that was it.

Maybe it wasn't.

This was the first man from the outside world who she

had met, and despite the fact she'd only known him a few days, she already trusted him more than her guardians.

How she longed to see him spread his golden wings.

He was different, and she genuinely liked him. He was kind and attractive, and every time she closed her eyes at night, his was the face she saw.

She wanted to explore this further. She had to go see him, to see how she reacted to him. To see if she really liked him or just pitied him.

She swam to the other side of her pool. She'd rarely done anything she regretted, and she hoped this would not be the first time.

Isa climbed out of the pool. She wanted to run to the dungeons, but she had to be cautious and wait until everyone was asleep. She had to wait until Seamus fell asleep.

Because he did. Every night without fail.

CHAPTER 26

It took Grace three more days to work up the courage to speak to Liam. It was lunchtime, and most of the guardians were out of the castle, and Isa was napping. Grace grabbed two sandwiches, a couple of apples, two cupcakes, another pillow, and made her way down the dungeon stairs.

She thought she'd be more nervous about this but found that she was mostly relieved. She hadn't expected to feel relieved.

Liam didn't look up from the book he was reading. She unlocked his door by magic, and his head jerked up. "You can't leave, but I thought I would join you today."

She locked the door behind her. It felt strange doing magic so openly, and suddenly she wished she didn't have to hide, that she could use her magic whenever she wanted.

But that was impossible.

Because wizards would be put to death by dragons.

And not even Isa could save her from the guardians.

Liam slowly put down his book, grabbed his own pillow, and joined her in the middle of his cell. They sat across from one another eating in silence. He was waiting for her.

"Thank you for keeping my secret. I wasn't sure you would, but I'm grateful for it. I have decided to trust you with the rest." She couldn't believe she was about to tell him everything. She'd never uttered these words before.

He took a bite of his apple, chewed, and swallowed. "Thank you. I won't betray you. I have secrets of my own, and so I understand the need for them to be kept."

Grace cocked her head at him. "Do your secrets involve harming the queen?"

He squirmed. "Only if she proves worthy to harm. I haven't seen anything to indicate that I should."

She wondered what that meant. Clearly, he hadn't been entirely honest with Isa. He could be lying now though.

Grace let out a breath. "Very well. Before I tell you this, you should know that if you betray me, I will kill you. I'm very capable of it, and I will do what is necessary to keep my secret."

He chuckled. "I don't doubt it. Now, tell me how you not only came across incredible healing powers but were also able to lock and unlock my door."

"They are different?" She took a bite of her apple. To her, magic was magic.

"I know dragons who can heal, but they can't do anything more."

"I thought you said Aspen had magic."

"She can heal because some dragons can, but I'm pretty sure she can't do anything else."

Grace let out a sigh. Maybe Aspen wasn't like her at all. Or maybe Aspen was hiding it as well. She had a dragon slayer after all.

"I am a descendant of wizards. My father was the last living one that I know of. I have a dragon slayer like your queen, and I will use it to kill someday." She shifted on her pillow, the ground cold beneath her legs. She didn't know how Liam was still alive and well down here. Not only that, he was in fairly good spirits.

"Who will you kill?"

"I...I...don't know. The prophecy that speaks of my destiny is unclear. I fear that it is Isa, but I keep hoping it's someone else. The prophecy states that I will have to defend my people and save them from certain annihilation."

Liam held his cupcake still. "And who are your people?"

Grace was surprised he asked that question. She thought it was obvious.

"The entire human race. Wizards protect humans from the dragons."

Liam took a bite of cupcake. A bit of frosting stuck on

the edge of his lip. His face didn't reveal if he believed her. Or if he did, whether he feared her.

"You know, prophecies are often misinterpreted. I know that my…I mean, the king had his fair share of deciphering prophecies in the last war. Can I read it? Maybe it means something other than what you think."

Grace shook her head. "Perhaps. But I don't have it with me now, and I won't bring the book down here."

When the time came, she'd know to act. The problem was that she'd come to love Isa as a sister, and she couldn't stand the thought of killing her. Grace's father always said she'd kill the queen, but she hoped that maybe he meant something else.

"You know, I'm a dragon. Does that mean you'll kill me?"

"No. I don't actually want to kill anyone, but I'll do what is necessary to save humanity."

And she knew she would.

Even if it meant killing her best friend.

CHAPTER 27

Isa had tried to visit Liam three nights in a row, but every night, there was a different guardian instead of Seamus. Ones who did not fall asleep. But, Friday night, she got lucky. Seamus was on duty again and snoring next to the door. Missy ran forward and waited.

She cracked the door open and slid down the stairs, excitement building in her chest. She didn't know what was coming, but she couldn't wait to talk to Liam. She hadn't felt this giddy since Jude showed up at the castle five years ago.

She'd been warned by Pierre not to seal herself to anyone, and she'd been careful. Now, she had to remind herself to be careful again. No falling in love.

Oh, don't be silly, Isa. You've just met the guy.

Missy ran ahead of her and stuck her nose through the

bars. She liked him, and Isa took that as a good sign. Isa stood closer than she had in the past, and if he reached for her again, she wouldn't back away this time.

He met her eyes as he stood and gave her a wide grin. "I didn't think I'd see you again."

"I've been trying, but the guard has been awake the last few nights. I had to wait for one to fall asleep."

"Why do you need the guard's permission? I'm beginning to think that the guardians are the ones in charge, not you." He put his hands in his pockets and leaned against the bars. He looked so cocky.

She bristled at his words. "I am queen. I do what I want. I just choose to keep the peace, and waiting for a guard to be asleep keeps the peace."

He raised an eyebrow. "You keep telling yourself that."

She didn't come here to argue with him.

"Tell me about America."

"What about it?"

"What does it look like?" She longed to travel and see the world. Books were never quite adequate at describing places. Sometimes Pierre would tell her stories about Europe, but she needed more.

"That's a complicated question. There are big cities and small towns, massive farms and giant factories. Flat valleys and large lakes and huge mountains. Where I'm from, there are geysers and fields of buffalo. But other places have palm trees and sandy beaches."

She felt her eyes widen, and her mind flashed to her fantasy the other night. "Have you been?"

"Where?"

"To the beach." She wanted to feel the sand between her toes and walk in the water under the bright sun.

"Of course. Haven't you?"

She stared at her hands. "I've never been outside the walls of this castle."

"I'm sorry." His voice held genuine concern.

"What's it like? The beach?"

He thought for a moment. "It's hot, and the sand burns your feet. The waves push you over and pull you out to sea. It's thrilling."

She tried to imagine it but couldn't. She'd wanted to go out in the waves here, but it was too cold.

"Will you take me to the beach someday? I've always wanted to see it." She couldn't believe she was asking him that question. She knew she could never leave, or her people would perish, but she could dream, right? That was allowed.

He leaned his head on the bars. "I'd love to. But I have to get out of here first."

He was right. She was the queen. If she wished for him to be let out, then he would be let out. She'd never really stood up to the guardians before, and she didn't know what would happen, but she was determined to try.

She swallowed. "Then, I will see to it that you are let out."

He reached out and gripped her hand. "Thank you."

She barely heard his words. His hand was warm and soft. Something passed through her. A thrill. And she wanted to lean into the touch and never let go.

But first.

She had to get him out.

CHAPTER 28

Dinner was a loud affair at Sid's house now. Skye usually cooked, but they had to eat in the formal dining room because the whole family couldn't fit around the kitchen table. Tonight, Ella's family joined them as well. She sat on Damon's left, her hair a bright green at the moment.

There was one very empty chair to the right of Damon.

Sid sat next to Ruby, who seemed far more willing to talk to her little brother on the other side of her than him. Aspen chatted with Ella, and so Sid felt very much alone. Aside from himself, everyone in the room was relaxed and enjoying themselves.

He was the only one missing his son.

He watched Skye wrestling Odin back into his chair and Rowan intervening when Gabe and Trinity started throwing food. Once again, he was grateful for his small family. Though it got crazy from time to time with Liam's friends, but they always went home.

The back door banged open, and Baden flew in, landing hard on the table, sending food flying everywhere.

Gabe and Trinity stopped arguing. Odin froze, and the whole room went quiet.

Aspen jumped up, her anxiety spiking. "Baden. What's going on?"

He and collapsed. "Food and water first."

"Is he alive or dead?" Aspen asked, ignoring his request.

"Alive." Baden drew in deep breaths. "But he's imprisoned. I can't get him out. I'll go back tomorrow, but I needed to come home and let you know that this will take longer than planned."

Sid didn't know what to say. Everyone in the room had gone quiet except Odin, who chattered on and banged on his plate. This was something everyone wanted to hear.

"How did you get in?" Sid asked.

Baden stood up tall. "Oh, there's a story. I watched the back door. A girl was bringing in snow for their icebox, and I followed her in. No one saw a thing. I've mastered my camouflage." The room erupted with chatter and questions. Baden snatched up a roll and ate it.

Sid chewed on his bottom lip. If Baden could get in, Liam could get out. He didn't have the skills Baden did, but he had others.

"We want to know about the castle and the queen. Surely, you explored the castle," Aspen said.

"Wait a second," Sid said. "Let's focus on what's important. How is Liam being treated?" His son was the most important aspect of this whole story.

"Good, he's being fed regularly, and he's made friends with the servant girl who brings him his food. He's in high spirits." Baden snatched up a few grapes from the fruit bowl.

"Did you talk to him?"

"Yes. He's confused."

Liam had a good head on his shoulders. If Liam was confused, then he must be hurt. Sid's stomach twisted.

"What do you mean?"

"The queen is the one who rescued him, and so he thinks she's not a bad person."

Sid clenched his fists. Liam had been hoodwinked by her. Maybe she had magic like the white witch. "But she killed our dragons."

"He didn't know about that, and when I tried to explain that to him, he seemed to think we're mistaken. That she was not the one who ordered it."

Sid moved his food around on his plate and thought for a moment. Murmurs broke out around the table, and Baden helped himself to fried chicken.

"He saw Felix die. How can he think she's good?" Sid asked.

Baden dropped a chicken leg. "I asked him about that.

He said she only killed him because she thought he was a threat."

"Has she bewitched him in some way?"

Baden bobbed his head up and down. "She's very pretty. It's possible he's just infatuated with her."

Ruby snorted. "Typical."

Sid wanted to lash out at her. That wasn't true at all.

"No way," Damon said. "That's not Liam. He likes girls, but he never lets them cloud his judgment."

"Anything else?" Sid asked. Baden had given him a lot to think about.

"I don't think so. Once I return, I will stay there until I have news to report or I bring Liam home."

"I want you to report to me once every two weeks even if there isn't news. That way I will know you are still alive, and if we don't hear from you, we'll send out someone to find you."

Baden nodded and turned to Skye. "Is there dessert?"

"Yes, pie. I will bring it out." She laughed.

Aspen gripped Sid's hand and he allowed himself to relax for the first time since Liam disappeared. "He's still alive."

LYING IN BED WAS USELESS. Even though Baden had brought good news, Sid still couldn't sleep. Yes, Liam was alive, but he was still in the dungeon of a dragon who slaughtered several of his people and somehow had convinced Liam that she's not the bad guy.

He checked his phone one more time. Two-thirty.

He got up and was surprised to find lights on in the kitchen.

Rowan and Ruby sat at the table, both with coffee cups in hand.

"Coffee's hot," Rowan said.

Sid poured himself a cup and sat with them. "What are you two doing up?"

Rowan gave Ruby a wink. "This is the only time of day when she and I can get any peace. A few times a week, we're up at the same time and we just sit and listen to the quiet."

Sid chuckled. "I guess with ten kids, quiet is hard to find."

Ruby groaned. "You have no idea. I'm not having any kids."

"What are you doing up?" Rowan asked.

Sid sighed and ran a hand down his face. "Thinking about Liam."

Rowan gripped Sid's hand. "Liam's going to be okay. I promise."

"You can't make that promise."

"I know. But Liam is resourceful, and he trained under the best. Once he realizes he's in over his head, he'll come home. Baden will make sure of that."

"And if he can't?"

"Let's not think about that."

"I want to help," Ruby blurted.

Sid stared her straight in the eyes. "No. I will not have more of you kids involved. One's enough."

Ruby let out an exasperated sigh. "Not like that. I'm great at researching. Let me see if I can find any information out on the European dragons and their queen. After what I saw in Buidseach, I can't just sit around doing nothing. You have a decent library, but if I need to I can check out the library cave as well."

"The library cave?"

Rowan chuckled. "It's what my kids call Everett's cave. They never knew him, so it became the library cave. But Ruby, you'll have to make do with Sid's library. School is here."

She sat taller. "I can go home on the weekends."

Sid didn't want this to turn into a squabble. "I think it's a good idea. But only in your spare time. You know who'd be good to help you? Damon. He's gonna need something to keep his mind off of things anyway."

"No offense, but I think Damon will just get in the way."

"He knows his way around a book and research. He and Liam were always getting into trouble. Liam was the action, but Damon was the brains."

Ruby gave a slow nod. "Well, I'm going to go get started. See you all later."

CHAPTER 29

"Should I let Liam out?" Isa asked again. She'd been mulling this over in her mind, and she couldn't decide the right thing to do.

Grace stopped lacing up her dress and came around to face her. "I thought he was dangerous."

Isa rubbed the bridge of her nose. They'd talked about this already. Never once had Grace mentioned he was dangerous. "Since when do you think that?"

"I don't." Her voice was deadpanned. "I just don't want to be responsible if he is."

"So, do you think I should let him out?"

Grace went back around and continued lacing up the dress. Isa wasn't sure why she was being evasive. She thought Grace would jump at the chance to let Liam out.

Isa had seen all the things Grace brought him. She obviously liked him.

"I think that decision lies solely with you. I wouldn't want to give you wrong advice and then wish I hadn't."

Isa was frustrated but appreciated that *she* held the role of queen, not Grace.

"Okay. Well, I'm going to let him out. Will you stand with me?"

"Of course. And I would be more than willing to continue taking care of him. I will make sure he settles in well and can find his way around."

"Thank you. That will be most helpful." Nerves danced in Isa's belly. She'd never done anything like this before, and it could go badly if things didn't work like she wanted them to.

Isa wore red today, a power color. She had Grace leave her hair down, but she put a crown on. It had a silver ring with jewels that fell across her forehead. One dripped almost to the bridge of her nose. She rarely wore a crown, but today, she was asserting herself.

Grace took her time with the makeup, creating fierce eyes and blood-red lips. Isa stood and examined herself in the mirror. "How do I look?"

"Like a queen."

"Will you fetch Drew for me? Then, meet me in my study."

Grace bowed, and Isa appreciated it. Normally she

wouldn't, but today, Isa was all queen. Grace left, and Isa settled into her chair and thought about her plan.

Jude would've been her first choice, but he was too loyal to Pierre. None of the older guardians would work, and she didn't like Seamus. Drew always seemed moldable. She'd never needed that particular skill before, but today, it would come in handy. If he did as she asked, she would have to keep him close because Pierre wouldn't trust him anymore.

She took her time getting to the study, steeling herself. She had to be on top of things. She hoped Grace and Drew would already be there, but she got there first. She sat at the desk and waited. A few moments later, Drew came in with Grace. He stumbled a bit when he saw her and then bowed. "Your Majesty, how can I help you?"

Isa stood. She was nearly the same height as Drew and could look him in the eye.

"Drew, tell me, who do you answer to? Me or Pierre?" She used her strongest, most authoritative voice.

"You, Your Majesty."

"Very well. Answer me this also. If I were to tell you to kill Pierre, would you do it?"

He swallowed. "Ye…ye…yes, Your Majesty."

"Very good. Now, go arm yourself from the weapons room. Make sure you have at least two swords on your belt as well as several additional knives. The more that are visible, the better off you will be."

He hesitated for a moment as Isa knew he would. Grace stood behind him, smirking. She knew what Isa was up to.

"Do you want me to kill Pierre, Your Majesty?" He wiped a bead of sweat off his forehead.

Isa chuckled. "No. You will not be killing anyone today. Unless that person directly defies me. I need to know that you will listen to me if I need you to. You are my backup plan. Do you understand?"

Drew nodded.

It was time to go get Liam.

To Be Continued...

CHAPTER 1

*I*sa marched down to the dungeons with Drew on one side and Grace on the other. She'd never asserted herself like this as queen before, and it felt amazing. She hoped it wouldn't create a rift too large between her and the guardians. They were her family, and she didn't like tension, but she supposed this wouldn't be the last time she disagreed with them.

And honestly, what they were doing was ridiculous.

Jude was on guard at the doors. He grinned at Isa, but his face fell when he saw Drew decked out in armor and armed to the teeth. He had no idea what was about to hit him.

"What's the matter?" He put his hand on the hilt of his sword.

Isa cocked her head. "What do you mean? Nothing is

wrong." She kept her voice sugary sweet. She had to do this right.

Jude looked past her to Drew with a furrowed brow. Isa shouldn't be enjoying this, but she was. Maybe she was just giddy about getting Liam out.

"Then, why is Drew dressed like he's going to war?"

"Because I asked him to. I would like the key to Liam's cell." She held her hand out.

A flurry of emotions crossed Jude's face as he processed what she said. His grip tightened on his sword. "I can't do that," he said through gritted teeth, finally understanding her theatrics. Good, he was smarter than she thought. Which would come in handy when she needed him to defend her.

"Am I your queen?" She spoke with all the authority she could muster.

"Yes, but I can't give you the keys." He kept his eyes on Drew.

Isa took a step forward and ran a finger down Jude's face. "Love, give me the key. That is a direct order from your queen." She decided to try a different tact. Maybe he'd respond better to his lust.

Jude gave a stiff shake of his head, and Isa sighed dramatically and stepped back.

"Fine. Drew, kill him and take the keys." This would be the moment of truth. She didn't know if Drew would really protect her or not. If he did, then she knew exactly who she'd want by her side in an altercation. She'd stop him before he actually killed Jude.

Drew whipped out his sword, and Jude's eyes widened as he stepped back. "Dragon's teeth! Isa, what are you doing?"

Drew placed the sword tip at Jude's throat. "Give Isa the key, or you die. It's simple, really."

Grace gripped Isa's arm, but Isa stayed focused on Jude. Isa hated the look of fear on his face, but she was pleased that Drew had listened to her. She wouldn't let him kill Jude, but at this moment, Jude didn't know that.

She'd sparred with all of them before, Grace included, and she'd never seen that look before. It was a look she hoped she'd never see again.

Jude swallowed hard, his Adam's apple bobbing. "Only Pierre has the key to Liam's cell."

Isa closed her eyes. This was a complication she wasn't prepared for. She could stand up to any of the guardians but Pierre. He was like a father, and she was never comfortable defying him.

But she had to do this. The way they were treating Liam wasn't right. And she was queen. It was time they all learned that.

"Lady Grace, fetch Pierre from the study. Tell him we have a situation at the dungeon. Drew, you keep your sword right where it is."

Jude sputtered but didn't say anything as Grace rushed for the study. Drew smirked, but Isa didn't find the situation funny at all. She supposed Drew was enjoying this a bit. He'd always been considered the youngest guardian and was typically just an errand boy.

She was a little nervous that this would turn ugly. She wished Seamus was on the other side of Drew's sword because she didn't like humiliating Jude like this. Plus, if push came to shove, she wasn't sure she'd stop Drew from killing Seamus. She'd bring him back to life, but that was one guardian she wished to replace. Isa hated the way Grace looked every time she saw him. As far as Isa could tell, Seamus hadn't bothered her again, but he never should've, in the first place.

The time passed excruciatingly slow, but she held her silence. She didn't want this to look anything less than serious when Pierre showed up. Footsteps rushed down the hall, and all three of them tensed.

Pierre grabbed Drew's arm and Drew turned on him, sword at his face. Pierre's eyes promised murder. Isa stepped between them and Jude so he couldn't try to help.

Then, she placed a hand on Drew's arm and lowered it. He'd more than proven his loyalty to her today.

"What is the meaning of this?" Pierre asked, eyes blazing.

"Give me the key to Liam's cell," Isa demanded, straightening so she stood tall. Not that it helped. Pierre still towered over her.

"Your Majesty," he huffed. "I won't do that. He's a threat to your safety."

"Are you questioning my judgment?" She crossed her arms and stared him down.

"Of course not. But you don't know him."

"Oh, but I do. I have been visiting him in the late nights."

Pierre's eyes flashed from Drew to Jude. "And why was I not made aware of this?"

She waited until he looked at her again. "Because I made sure to only visit when the guard fell asleep. It was quite easy with Seamus. The key, Pierre." She kept her hand out to make sure the real reason she was here was never misunderstood.

Pierre shook his head. "I have pledged to protect your safety, and I will not compromise it."

She took a step forward, knowing this was a turning point, not only in their relationship but also in her role in the castle and kingdom. "Am I your queen?"

"Yes, and that is precisely why I will not put you in danger." He was not backing down. She knew he might not, but she wasn't really prepared for it.

"I command you to let him out," she said in her most authoritative voice, making sure it didn't sound petulant and whiny.

Pierre's face had gone red. He growled. "And if I don't?"

Isa waved a hand to Drew, who still had his sword out. "Then Drew will kill you."

"Dragon's teeth! This is absurd."

Her hand was still outstretched. "It really is, isn't it? The key, Pierre?"

He hesitated a moment longer and then dug in his pocket and pulled out a set of keys. He dropped them into her hand.

"This is a bad idea. If you die, it will be my fault." He was being overdramatic, but at this point, she didn't care. She was getting Liam out.

CHAPTER 2

*I*sa rushed down the dungeon steps, thrilled that her plan worked. The other four followed, Grace and Drew holding torches. There would be consequences to face after her act of defiance, but she would deal with that later. The air cooled as she descended the stairs.

She hurried down the hall and approached Liam's cell. He came to the bars and stared at her. "Isa, you look amazing."

She glanced down at her red dress and touched the crown on her head. She'd forgotten she got dressed up. Normally, she visited him in her dressing gown and robe. He'd never seen her like this before.

She giggled, giddy with success. "I do, don't I? Let's get you out of there." She dangled the keys in front of him.

"You're letting me out?" He looked at Pierre and Jude and backed away.

She unlocked the door. As soon as he stepped out, she looped her arm through his. She worried that Pierre or Jude would hurt him.

She was surprised to find that Liam's arms were muscular and taut. She would've thought that after being stuck in a cell, he'd be weak. She had to thank Grace for feeding him well.

They entered the hall, and Liam said nothing more. She supposed he was intimidated by the whole situation, unaware that she was fully in control. But she wasn't quite done being queen-boss yet. She kept her arm through Liam's as she spun around and faced the party behind her. None of them looked happy.

"Pierre, gather the guardians in the study. We need to have a talk."

"Yes, Your Majesty." He bowed, glared at Liam, and rushed off. Jude followed.

"Drew, you may go as well. We'll be there in a few minutes."

He hesitated. "With all due respect, Your Majesty, you have pitted me against the rest of the guardians, and I fear I will not be welcome."

Isa's breath caught. She had put him in that situation and hadn't considered the consequences. "I'm sorry, Drew. I didn't mean to." She had to make this up to him.

"It will pass. But not today. So if you don't mind, I will enter the room with you."

"Of course."

Liam was still quiet, which was unusual. He normally didn't stop talking when she visited him. "Are you okay?" Isa asked.

Liam startled. "Oh, yes, I'm just tired. The cell was not built for good sleep."

"If you can wait a few minutes longer while I establish how the guardians are to treat you, we'll get you to a room, and you can sleep as long as you like."

"Thank you, Your Majesty." He gave a little bow, his face serious.

It was the first time he'd addressed her like that, and she didn't like it.

"Call me Isa, please."

"Very well. Thank you, Isa."

A thrill ran up her spine at the way he said her name. Maybe this would be more complicated than she planned.

CHAPTER 3

Damon leaned against the door of his Porsche and stared at Liam's house. He had no idea why he was even here, other than that he wanted to feel close to his friend. He was tired of the people at school constantly asking where Liam was. He knew now that Liam was in real danger, something that he had never been in before. Damon hated the possibility that he might never see his best friend again.

He pushed open the door to Liam's house because they'd never knocked at each other's homes. Of course, they'd been friends since before they could walk, so in most ways, they were nearly family. Damon's mom didn't knock when she came over either.

A couple of little kids raced by the entryway, fake

swords in hand, and Damon grinned. Once upon a time, that had been him and Liam. Now, it was Ruby's siblings.

He frowned. She still wasn't speaking to him even after she returned from her trip to Europe. He was a little miffed that she got to go help Liam, and he didn't. The other night at dinner Ruby had told his mom and dad all about her trip. Damon had listened in, but Ruby never addressed him directly.

He nearly tripped over a toy monster truck in the hall and entered the kitchen to absolute pandemonium.

Trinity and Gabe stood by the counter, yelling at the top of their lungs. It was difficult to tell what they were arguing about, but Damon gathered that it had something to do with lemons. A few of the other kids sat at the table, playing board games, and the two chasing each other with swords were now fighting in the middle of the kitchen.

This would be torture. No wonder Ruby liked peace and quiet. He didn't have siblings of his own. The only kids he'd ever really spent time with were Val's, and they were way quieter than this bunch.

Rowan sat at the table, staring at his computer, oblivious to the noise around him. Skye, toddler on her hip, was attempting to intervene with Trinity and Gabe.

Nope. This was not the place for him.

"Damon," Gabe yelled. Busted. Gabe had always liked him and was always running after him and Liam when they came to visit. There was no way he could pretend he hadn't heard him.

"What's up?" He asked.

"Wanna help me and Trinity make a lemon meringue pie?"

No, not really, but Skye gave him a pleading smile. "Sure." It might distract him from missing Liam anyway.

Gabe tossed him a lemon. "You can juice them."

Trinity glared at Gabe. "No. That's your job."

"I want to do the meringue."

She placed a hand on her hip. "No. That's my job."

Damon ignored them and sliced the lemon in half. It'd be a long afternoon, but at least he wouldn't be missing Liam.

CHAPTER 4

*I*sa let go of Liam's arm, and he fell in step with Grace. They spoke in quiet whispers. At least, Isa wasn't the only one who didn't want to kill him. She couldn't hear the whole conversation, but Grace was checking to see how he was feeling. Isa's feelings were hurt that he'd talk to Grace instead of her, but she supposed she was a little intimidating at the moment.

Drew followed behind all of them. Isa entered the somber study. Every single guardian had a frown on his face. Isa wanted to roll her eyes but refrained.

Suddenly, a white furball raced past Isa. Missy paused for a second and gave Isa a look that said, "And why did you leave me out of this?" Then, she ran for Liam and jumped at his legs, nipping at his fingers. He glanced down at her. She wouldn't settle down, so he picked her up, and she rubbed her face all over his. Isa had never seen Missy treat anyone that way, including herself.

She ripped her eyes away from them and back to her guardians. Most of them were watching Liam and Missy now. A few were even suppressing smiles. This was a good thing.

"Thank you all for joining me. I wish to address you on the treatment of my guest, Liam. He was imprisoned when he arrived, and I feel it was unjustly so. He will now stay in the castle as my guest and will have free rein to wander as he pleases. If he wishes to leave, you will not stop him. If he wishes to see me, you will not stop him. If he wishes to explore halls we haven't been to in years, you will not stop him. Do you understand?"

Murmurs of assent sounded around the room, though there was also a little grumbling. Pierre stood in the back, his arms crossed. She wondered how long it would be before he forgave her for this.

"Why don't we send him home? If he isn't a threat, then there is no reason to keep him here." Pierre focused his displeasure on Liam, but he didn't flinch. Good for him.

Isa faltered. She hadn't thought about that. Maybe he didn't want to stay. She turned to look at him and found Missy slung over Liam's shoulder, licking his ear. His face was screwed up like he was trying not to laugh.

"Do you want to go home?" she asked him.

He pushed Missy's face away, but she grabbed his hand

with her mouth. "No, I can't. Ouch." He shook his hand out of Missy's mouth.

Missy resumed her grooming of his face, and he pulled her off his shoulder and held her in his arms like a baby. Isa couldn't believe her fox was behaving this way.

"Why not?" Isa asked.

"Because I betrayed them. I came here to warn you that they were aligning with the rebels. They'll know what I did." His voice had dropped to nearly a whisper.

Relief filled her chest. She hadn't realized how much she'd wanted him to stay. Not as much as Missy, apparently, who was now struggling to get back onto his shoulder.

"He stays until it is safe for him to return home. Also, he is not to be harmed in any way. If he is, I will personally see to it that whoever harms him will die. Also, if he dies, you all die with him."

A collective gasp went out, but Isa didn't care. They went behind her back and locked him up. She wouldn't put it past them to hurt him and make it look like an accident. She knew they meant well, but she needed to make sure that Liam was protected.

She met Pierre's gaze and waited for his response. He was silent for a long few seconds.

"Very well, Your Majesty. Liam will not be harmed in any way by us. We will also make sure he has free rein of the castle. Seamus will be his guard."

"No, he won't. Liam needs no guard." And definitely not Seamus.

"How else will he remain safe?"

Liam chuckled behind her, still struggling with the excited fox. "I can take care of myself." He turned to Isa. "Why do you listen to these guys? You're the queen. Don't forget that."

She nodded, resolved. Liam set Missy down, and she raced in a circle around the room.

"The only people he needs protecting from is you, and so guarding him is pointless. Besides, he's perfectly capable of being on his own. He is not a prisoner and will not be treated as such. Do you understand? No guards."

Pierre let out a breath. "Fine. No guards. But for the record, this is a bad idea."

Liam stepped next to Isa, but she gripped his wrist. This was a power struggle between her and Pierre, and she didn't want Liam getting in the middle of it. Pierre and the other guardians had too much control over her, and she had no clue what was happening in her kingdom.

It was time for her to come into her own as queen.

CHAPTER 5

Liam had hoped Isa would stick around, but after the meeting, she told him she'd see him at dinner. He wasn't sure where to go now. He certainly wouldn't hang out with the guardians. Thanks to Isa, he had full rein of the castle, but first, he needed sleep. He wouldn't think straight until then, and he had a lot to process. He was in the enemy's lair and wasn't safe, but he didn't know who his enemy was yet.

He probably shouldn't have turned down her offer to send him home. Baden told him his parents were worried, but he felt like he was needed here. Something was going on, and he wasn't sure what it was. They killed Felix, but he didn't think Isa was behind it. Her guardians were, though. That, he knew for sure.

The guardians were clearly scared of Isa, but he didn't

know why. She'd done nothing to show that she was cruel in any way... unlike the guardians. He might not have scars from the brands they pressed into his skin, but he still remembered what it felt like.

Missy kept up with him. *Play ball?* she asked. She hadn't said a word to him until now.

Not right now. Maybe later. He had to get the lay of the land first.

Grace caught up with him, a gangly teen in tow. The boy had brought Liam food a couple of times while he'd been in the dungeon.

"Liam, this is Benjamin. He'll get you set up in your room. Then, he can take your measurements and prepare a bath. While you take a nap, we'll see if we can find some clothes that fit. Our tailor will make you a few pairs of pants and shirts, but that will take a couple days."

"Thank you." Everything here was so old-fashioned. He wondered why they couldn't fly to a town in Europe and buy clothes. The guardians were all obviously like him—a dragon shifter.

Grace scurried away, and Benjamin fell into step with him.

"I hope you enjoy it here. We never get new people." He was tall with arms that were too long and a nose that was too big for his face.

"Thanks. What do you do here?"

"I take care of the farm animals mostly. But today

Marissa is tending to them so I can take care of you. We've never had a man that needed a servant."

"What about the guardians? Don't they have servants?"

"No. They take care of themselves. Isa is the only one who gets waited on. And now you."

"Once you show me the ropes, I can take care of myself as well." Nobody had ever waited on him in his life.

Benjamin grinned. "Good, because I like animals a lot better than waiting on people."

They walked into a bedroom with dark wood furniture.

"Let's take your measurements first. Then, you can take a bath and a nap. I'll check on you every once in a while. Then, I can show you around."

Liam stood very still, studying the bedroom, while Benjamin measured every inch of his body. The large room had a comfortable looking bed, a couch, two chairs, and a fireplace with a fire already roaring inside. Sunlight filtered in through stained glass panels of dragons. There were also several clear windows high up on the wall. The room was much brighter than he would've thought, given they had no electricity.

He followed Benjamin into the bathroom. A stone tub sat on one side of the room and, on the other, a sink and toilet with a cord that could be pulled to flush.

At least they had running water. Benjamin turned the tap on the bathtub, and steaming water poured out.

"How do you heat the water?"

"It comes from the springs below. There are hot pools down there."

"That's cool. How often do you use them?"

Benjamin shook his head. "Only the queen is allowed down there. Lady Grace has seen them but has never gone in. That's the one place the queen keeps for herself."

The more information he could get out of this kid, the better. He was here to figure out the queen.

"Do you like Isa?"

Benjamin shrugged. "I guess. She's queen, so we have to, right?"

Hmm. Maybe he was wrong about Isa. He didn't want to be.

"But why wouldn't you like her? What's she done to you?"

He pinched his lips and took a step back. "I misspoke. I like her very much. Now, I'll leave you to your bath and will wake you in a few hours, if you'd like, and show you around."

Liam nodded.

He had no idea what he'd gotten himself into, but he knew one thing for sure. He was not safe here, and he was weaponless.

That needed to change.

CHAPTER 6

"Grace, wait," Liam called.

Grace froze. She wasn't ready to talk to Liam because he was bound to bring up her magic. It hadn't even been an hour since she left him with Benjamin, and Liam had already found her. She thought he was supposed to be taking a nap. Apparently, he thought sleep was overrated.

She turned slowly and gave him a fake smile. "Can I help you?"

"Yeah, actually, you can." Liam looked around. "But is there somewhere quieter we can talk? I don't want anyone to overhear."

He wanted to talk about magic. Ugh. She gripped his hand and pulled him into an empty room. She had to put a stop to his questions once and for all. She shut the door, locked it with magic, and then sealed the room from prying ears.

"Okay, listen, because I'm only saying this once. I should not have told you about who I am, and I don't want to talk about it. Okay? I was doing fine before you got here, and I don't want you making a big deal about the magic stuff."

He raised his eyebrows. "That's not what you said the other night. The other night you seemed eager to talk to me."

"It was a mistake. No one else knows, and I got excited that someone might understand. I'm sorry." She wouldn't make that mistake again.

He looked around the room. "That's okay. I don't want to talk to you about your magic anyway."

She creased her eyebrows. "You don't?"

"No."

"Then, why did you want to talk to me?"

He moved closer to her. Oh no. Did he like her? Oh, this might be worse. She wasn't looking for a romantic relationship with someone like him.

She let out a huge sigh of relief when he moved past her to the door. He ran his hand along the wood.

"It buzzes with energy. You locked it by magic, didn't you?" His voice was full of awe.

She nodded. "And I made it so no one could hear our voices." She couldn't help herself. Why did she keep running her mouth? She wondered if she could do a spell that would erase his memory. Though she tried that once with Olga when she broke a case of eggs, and it didn't work.

"That is fascinating."

"But you said you didn't want to talk about magic." Part of her enjoyed this and wanted to keep sharing, but she still didn't know if he'd reveal her secrets to anyone.

"Right." He spun around. "I need your help. Benjamin pointed out the weapons room to me on a tour of the castle, but it's locked."

There was only one reason he needed to get into the weapons room. And that was if he planned on hurting someone.

"Only the guardians and the queen have keys to that room." She chose her words carefully so she could gauge his reaction. She needed to understand what he was up to so she could warn Isa if needed. "What do you need from there?"

"A dagger. You could get me in." He rolled forward onto the balls of his feet and back again, a sneaky look on his face.

She didn't understand what was going on. "Did you not hear me? I don't have a key."

He grinned and pointed to the door. "But you have magic. They already suspect I'm magical because of my healing. They'll think I did it by myself. Besides, if we do it right, no one will even know."

She propped her hands on her waist. He was delusional.

"And why would I do that? You haven't even told me why you need a dagger."

"Because I need a weapon to defend myself. Have you seen the way the guardians look at me?" His face grew serious.

He had a point. But she didn't trust him. She should. He'd given her no reason to believe otherwise, but he was still a stranger.

"Yes, I've seen the way they look at you. But Isa won't let them hurt you. I'm not helping you."

She unlocked the door and marched from the room.

CHAPTER 7

After a couple of hours of pure torture in the kitchen, Damon finally escaped. He found Sid in the hall.

A grin formed on Sid's face. "Damon, what are you doing here?"

He shrugged. "Missing Liam, I guess."

Sid gave Damon a pat on his shoulder. "Me too." He flicked his eyes to the kitchen door. "I'm hungry as well, but I'm nervous to go in there."

Damon chuckled. "You don't want to. Trust me. You might get hit with flying lemons."

Sid dropped his shoulders. "Maybe I'll go pay your mom a visit. She'll feed me."

Damon liked Sid a lot. He treated him just like he

treated Liam, like a second son. But then again, his mom did the same for Liam.

"That she will."

Sid took another glance at the kitchen. "You're welcome to stay as long as you like. How's the research going?"

Damon cocked his head. "What research?"

"Ruby's researching European dragon royalty and what that might mean for Liam. She wanted to do something, and I suggested that she get you onboard since you are good at that stuff."

Damon ran a hand through his hair. How dare she? Liam was *his* best friend. He had every right to help her, especially if Sid asked her to involve him. He couldn't believe she'd left him out.

"She never mentioned it. But I'll go track her down." Oh, she was going to get a earful from him.

"She must've just dug right in." Sid kept his facial expression natural, but his voice betrayed his surprise.

"Any chance you might know where I can find her?"

Sid pointed down the hall. "Pretty sure she hasn't left the library since I set her on the task."

The front door slammed, and Aspen rushed toward them with Jens right behind her. Her hair was back in a short ponytail, and her face revealed the stress they'd all been feeling. She gave Sid a quick kiss.

"I'm famished. Let's eat." She held up a bag of takeout and nodded toward the kitchen.

Sid gave a slight shake of the head, and Aspen's face fell. "They're all in there again, aren't they?"

"We can eat in our room."

Aspen rolled her eyes. "I'm sick of eating in our room. Jens, would you like to join us?"

"No thanks, I already ate."

Damon left them arguing in the hall. For the first time in his life, he was grateful he was an only child.

Damon tried not to let his anger get the best of him. If he was going to convince Ruby to let him help, he couldn't get all upset.

His muscles tensed as he stood outside the library. He would have to pretend like she hadn't left him out intentionally. Though he wasn't very good at pretending.

Liam was better.

Liam was better at a lot of things.

Damon pushed open the door. Ruby stood on a stool, reaching for a book above her head. She grabbed it and spun around, a look of triumph on her face.

She met his eyes, and her face fell. She was one of the most expressive people he knew. Her face revealed everything, including how disappointed she was to see him. He wished he knew what he'd done to her. Well, before he called her a bitch at school. He shouldn't have done that.

"What are you doing here?" She frowned at him.

"Funny, I was just about to ask you the same thing." He crossed his arms and leaned against a bookshelf.

Her eyebrows drew together, and she climbed off the

stool. "I live here, for now. Last I checked, your BFF is still MIA, so I don't know why you are here." She plopped down onto a couch and cracked open the book.

She wasn't getting away with this. Damon sat on the coffee table in front of her and stared, waiting for her to acknowledge him.

But she didn't. Oh, she was good. Though she probably had to be if she ever planned on getting anything done with all her siblings around.

She flipped page after page in her book and acted like he didn't exist. He thought about what he could do to get her to let him help.

After a few minutes, when he couldn't stand it anymore, Damon snatched the book out of her hands.

"Hey!" she yelled.

The title of the book was *History of the Woodlands Dragons*. What did she need that for?

She grabbed for the book, but he held it out of her reach. "I don't know why you are here," she huffed. "But it's time for you to leave."

Damon got a whiff of something distinctly floral. She never struck him as the type to wear perfume, but he liked it on her. He couldn't afford to be distracted right now. Girls distracted him quite often. Especially ones who ignored him.

"Sid told me you were doing research that might help Liam."

She shrugged. "Yeah, so." She reached for the book again, but he jerked it away.

"He thought I was helping you." Damon kept his voice even so she didn't get more pissed at him.

She crossed her arms and slumped in her chair. "I don't need help."

"That is irrelevant. Liam is my best friend, and you won't keep me from helping him." He leaned forward, deliberately entering her space. She sucked in a breath and blinked for a second before responding.

"I'm not stopping you. But we won't be doing it together."

"Why?" He moved closer, still appreciating that floral scent.

"Because you're an asshole, and I don't work with assholes."

How dare she? He'd never done anything to deserve such an accusation. She thought she was better than him, and she'd treated him like crap.

He dropped the book on her lap. He needed to cool off before he said something stupid.

But this was far from over.

CHAPTER 8

"You're staring," Drew said, nudging Grace's arm. She dropped her eyes away from Liam and Isa.

Isa had put Drew next to Grace and Benjamin on his other side. Grace had watched Drew come in. The rest of the guardians flat-out refused to talk to him. Isa knew what she was doing when she set up the seating chart tonight.

Grace blushed and glanced at her dinner, which she had barely touched. Most nights, dinner was a lively affair with people joking and laughing, but tonight was more somber. Isa and Liam were the only ones laughing, and even that seemed forced somehow.

And now, Drew caught her staring at them.

"Do you find him attractive?" Drew's voice was quiet but devoid of emotion.

"What? Oh, no. I was just trying to figure out his motivations." That was a lie. She was just wondering what was going to unfold between Liam and Isa. She couldn't have him telling Isa her secret.

Drew snorted. "You and the rest of us."

Grace shifted her attention from Isa and Liam to Drew.

"What are the guardians saying about him?"

"What do you think? That he wants to kill the queen. None of us understand why she let him out. Do you know why? I deserve to know, considering the position she put me in." There was a hint of bitterness in his voice.

Grace sighed. Isa already asked her a gazillion questions about what other people thought. And she was certain Liam was asking her to help him break into the weapons room. Now, Drew and the guardians wanted information on Isa. She was in the middle of them all.

And they had no idea who she really was or what she was capable of.

Liam did, but he didn't understand the implications. She could kill the lot of them in their sleep if she wanted. Well, not all at once, but one by one, and no one would know it was her. She didn't know if she had the heart to do it, though, even if she had to. She hoped that when the time came for her to protect her people, she'd be able to take out only the dragons necessary. Because if she failed, then humanity would be annihilated. At least, that's what the prophecy said.

For now, though, she had to figure out how to get Drew off her back. Because she couldn't handle another "friend" needing favors from her.

"I don't. Not really. Other than she feared that he was being mistreated."

Drew watched them now more carefully than she had. "Do you think she's in love with him?"

"Oh no. She barely knows him. But she's probably attracted to him." She nudged Drew, and he dropped his gaze. "How are you doing with it all? Are the guardians treating you pretty badly?"

"Yes. But once they think about it, they'll realize that I had no choice. All of them would've done the same if she'd come to them. Our loyalty is always to her even if it seems crazy. We all fear for her life though, and none of us want to see anything happen to her. All of Europe would be exposed then."

"You all think that Liam is a threat to her life." Grace played with the chicken and new potatoes on her plate, her appetite gone. She was so confused. She wished things would go back to the way they were before Liam showed up. When all she had to worry about was who Isa would try to set her up with. She knew her quiet life would end someday when her magic would be necessary. She'd have to save humanity from whatever threat came at them then, but she wasn't ready.

"Yes, we do. But we can't keep an eye on him this way. We can't disobey her." That didn't mesh with what she'd seen so far. They disobeyed Isa all the time. Though, maybe they didn't. Maybe they just made it look like they did.

"Do you really think Pierre or Jude would've done the same thing you did?"

Drew wiped his fingers on a napkin and picked up his fork. He cut his asparagus as he spoke. "Pierre, no. Jude, absolutely. He was pretty pissed that Isa came to me instead of him. We nearly came to blows earlier. Pierre managed to talk him down though, but he's not speaking to me at the moment. Though the others aren't speaking to me either, so I guess I shouldn't be surprised."

Grace found Jude in the middle of a few of the older guardians. He voraciously attacked his food and kept his eyes down. She wondered what he was thinking.

Then, she watched Isa and Liam again. She was staring, but so what. Her loyalty might not be a hundred percent to Isa, but she had a vested interest in what happened in the castle.

And she had no idea what side Liam was on.

CHAPTER 9

Dinner was pure torture. Liam had never liked formal occasions, and thankfully his parents never made him attend fancy dinners or parties. Come to think of it, his parents rarely attended those themselves. He'd gone to the dances at school but only because his friends did. He went in a t-shirt and jeans once, but Damon gave him crap about it for weeks, so he wore a tie after that. Now he was sitting at a dinner table in an old-fashioned suit with tails. It itched and was uncomfortably warm.

"Do you like the food?" Isa asked.

The food was probably the best thing about this place. It was better than anything he'd ever had at home. "I do."

Isa was quiet, and he took a few more bites and tried to find some enjoyment in the company. But truthfully, he was dead uncomfortable. He thought things would be easier once he got out, but now he just felt like a fish out of water.

"This is my favorite dinner. Tell me your favorite foods."

This was easy. "Steak and seasoned fries. Meatlovers pizza. Tacos. Cheesecake. Moosetracks ice cream."

"That's quite a list."

"Food is something I live for." They were both quiet for a few moments. He hadn't really thought much about the food while he was in the dungeons. He was just grateful to get some.

"Thank you for getting me out," he finally said. "The castle is much better when I'm not behind bars."

Isa smiled at him warmly. He wished he'd thought this through. He had no idea what was really going on here or what he was supposed to do next, and that had his nerves on edge. He should've taken that nap earlier, but he'd wanted to get the lay of the land.

He wasn't sure what to expect from everyone. When dinner was over, would the guardians torture him again? Even though Grace had healed him right after, he couldn't forget what they'd done to him. He kept his eyes on his food or Isa because he didn't want to accidentally make eye contact with Pierre or Jude.

He didn't trust that Isa had any sway over them. Maybe they made it look like she did, but it was all a façade. He'd heard what she did to get him out, but he was positive they were already planning how to make sure she never did something like that again.

He needed something to protect himself with. Grace had been most unhelpful. He'd really thought she'd be all over helping him arm himself, but he'd misjudged her. He needed a dagger. Hell, even a kitchen knife would do.

Another course was served. He couldn't even tell what it was. Would dinner ever end?

He looked at Isa, and his stomach swooped. He could not let his feelings get in the way. He had a job to do here even if she was the most gorgeous woman he'd ever laid eyes on.

Isa caught him staring, and he flushed. She giggled and scooted her chair closer. He couldn't help his smile. He made the mistake of looking up again and found Pierre glaring at him. He shifted his eyes to his left. Jude had the same look. He dropped his eyes. Isa chattered on about Missy, and he laughed when he was supposed to, but really, he couldn't wait to get out of this room.

After dinner, Liam caught up with Benjamin. He had been the friendliest person, aside from Isa and Grace.

"Didn't you say your mom was the cook?" Liam asked.

"Yeah." Benjamin shoved his hands into his pockets and looked ahead of them to where Drew was escorting Grace through a door. Drew came back out a moment later, and Benjamin's shoulders relaxed.

"Can I meet her? I want to tell her how amazing the dinner was." And find something to defend himself with.

Benjamin beamed. "She would love that. I was heading there anyway."

Liam was surprised by how few people actually lived in the large castle. He thought there would be a slew of servants, but they didn't have many, maybe three or four. He wasn't sure he'd met them all.

He followed Benjamin into a large medieval kitchen, Missy on his heels. It had a sink and two massive stoves as well as a brick oven. A large wooden table with benches lined one wall, and shelves were filled with spices and vegetables. It smelled amazing. Like warm bread and cookies. But he didn't see any knives or other possible weapons sitting out.

A large woman stood by the sink, chatting with Grace. She had a thick accent that Liam couldn't place. Though he wasn't very good at that sort of thing.

"Mom..."

The woman turned around and dropped the dish she was washing. "Dragon's teeth! Why did you bring him here?"

Liam stepped forward and held out his hand. "I asked him too. I wanted to thank you for the wonderful dinner."

The woman gave a curt nod but didn't take his proffered hand.

"You're very welcome," she said curtly.

Grace nudged Olga, a smile dancing on the edges of her lips. "He's not going to bite."

Liam pointed to the dishes that included the knives

from dinner. "That's right. Can I help you? I have done my share of dishes before." He failed to mention they'd all gone in the dishwasher, but they might not know what that was.

Olga pointed at the sink. "We've got the dishes handled, but maybe you and Benjamin can chop apples for the turnovers for breakfast."

That was even better.

Olga gave him a puny knife with a round tip, and while sharp, it wouldn't be useful against any enemies. He needed to get his hands on a bigger one.

He met Grace's eye. He couldn't be certain, but it felt as though she knew what he was up to. She could help him if she wanted. She knew magic. But so far, she'd refused.

Missy stood patiently next to him while he peeled and cut up apples. She nudged his foot.

Can I have a bite?

Geesh. She was just like a dog but more polite. He dropped a piece on the floor, and she snatched it up. Benjamin grinned at him.

After they finished cutting up the apples and washing the dishes, they all sat around the table, chatting, including a few other servants. They gossiped about the guardians and discussed things that needed to get done the next day. Liam just listened, but he liked this conversation much better than the dinner one. They all bantered amongst each other, and there were no guardians glaring at him. He'd definitely found his place in the castle for now.

The night grew long, and Olga stood. "Time for bed."

Liam stared at the kitchen knives gleaming on the counter. There was no way he could steal one without someone noticing. He'd just let them leave first.

Marissa, one of the other servants, stood. She was pretty but very quiet. "Liam, would you walk me to my room?"

Grace wiggled her eyebrows at him. He sighed. He'd dealt with unwanted attention before, and it would be no different here. But he couldn't turn her down outright without risking her feelings.

The knife would have to wait.

He escorted Marissa to her room and slowly made his way back to his own. He pushed his door open and shut it quickly.

There was a thud. He spun around and wrenched his door open again.

"That hurt," Baden said.

Liam looked down at the little dragon who blended perfectly with the stone floor.

"Get in here," Liam hissed.

Baden flew in and landed on his bed. "This is much cushier than the dungeon."

Liam rolled his eyes. "What are you doing here?"

"Do you really think your dad was just gonna let me stay home? No way. He sent me right back to talk some sense into you. So, here I am."

Liam crossed his arms. He wouldn't be going home. Not yet, at least, but Baden might be better for other things.

"I need a dagger. Think you can sneak into the weapons room and steal one for me?"

Baden collapsed on the bed. "Sure. But first, sleep."

Liam sat next to Baden. Having him here would be a good thing. He could sneak around the castle and learn things that Liam could not.

Maybe now, Liam had a shot at figuring out what on earth was going on here.

CHAPTER 10

That evening, after Grace had left, a light knock came at Isa's door, and Missy growled. Isa slipped out of bed and tied a robe around herself. She found herself hoping it would be Liam. He'd sat next to her at dinner but had been quiet again. She chattered at him, and while he answered her, he wasn't terribly forthcoming. So different from the man she had spoken with in the dungeons. She supposed he was intimidated by all of the people, but he seemed comfortable with Grace.

Not that she was jealous or anything. Liam was new and exotic, and Grace needed a boy anyway. Liam would be good for her, and Isa would see what she could do to encourage it. Though she wasn't entirely sure she liked that idea. She sniffed. Why shouldn't she? She had Jude.

She cracked the door and found Jude there, bottle of wine in hand. She grinned and swung the door open.

"Come in, why don't you?" she said.

He slid in, wrapped an arm around her waist, and pulled her close. He kept his eyes on hers and placed a firm kiss on her lips. Her entire insides melted. She so enjoyed Jude's kisses even if Missy sat on her bed grumbling. Missy never disliked Jude before.

Jude released her, produced two glasses from out of nowhere, and poured. He handed her one, and they sat across from each other on her couch.

She placed a hand on his knee and took a sip of her wine. "Thanks for coming tonight. I needed this. It's been a long and strange day."

He swirled the wine in his glass. "You think it was a long day for you? You tried to kill me." He forced a smile.

She let out a laugh and scooted closer to him. "You know I wouldn't have let Drew kill you." She placed a hand on his chest. Jude's kisses would take her mind off of everything.

His eyebrows went up in surprise. "Do I? You threatened us. If Pierre kills Liam, will you kill us all?"

She flopped back onto the couch. "Yes. I need to make sure he's protected."

Frustration clouded Jude's face. "Why? What has he done to you? You aren't seeing reason."

She knew he didn't understand, and nothing she said

would change that. She set down her glass and leaned in to him. "Jude, I don't want to talk about this. Kiss me."

His eyes narrowed. "Is that a command, Your Majesty?" His voice was sharp and mean.

Isa's insides turned cold, and she got off the couch. "No. It's not. Thank you for coming, but it's time for you to leave."

He stood and took her hand. She tried to read his face but couldn't. "I'm sorry. I just… You told Drew to kill me, and then you were all protective and sweet with Liam. I'm hurt and a little jealous."

"I wasn't sweet with him. I needed to make sure none of you went after him. The only way I could do that was with Liam by my side. You understand, right?"

She reached up and stroked his cheek. "I only have eyes for you."

He nuzzled her neck. Phew. He was moving past the whole incident. They could forget about what happened today and focus on the here and now.

Then, he brought his lips to her ear. "You need to put him back into the dungeon."

She shoved Jude away. "You are using our relationship to manipulate me."

"What? No! I just worry about your safety. At least, let us put a guard on him. We can even use Drew if that makes you feel better." He rammed a hand through his hair and scowled.

"We? You mean the whole guardian council knows you

were coming here tonight to seduce me and turn me against Liam." She couldn't believe the nerve of him. Of them. She'd never thought they would treat her like this.

He shook his head, but she knew.

"Get out." She pointed to the door.

His voice dropped low. "Isa…"

"That *is* a command from your queen."

He grabbed the bottle of wine and stormed from the room, and Isa slammed the door behind him. She hated this. Hated the way she was now at odds with her guardians. Hated that she didn't even know if she could trust them anymore.

Everything had changed, and she didn't like it.

CHAPTER 11

Grace stalked toward Isa's rooms but wasn't looking forward to this conversation. Olga was furious. Liam had only been out a day, and already Isa was changing things. This morning she sent down a list of food she wanted Olga to make, suggestions from Liam, no doubt, and Olga was unfamiliar with all of them.

Grace thought for sure Olga would throw a pot at her head when she asked for something called "cheesecake," because what Olga thought was cheesecake and what Liam thought were probably two very different things.

She didn't know why Isa was trying to impress him. She had nothing to prove, and Liam had everything to prove. Isa insisted she was only trying to make him feel comfortable, but that was a load of dung. It wasn't Grace's place to argue with the queen though.

Grace came around the corner and ran straight into Jude. She nearly fell over, but he caught her by the waist. She was incredibly aware of his hand on her side and the way it made her heart race. Sunlight filled the upper windows, and his black hair shone bright, and his green eyes sparkled.

"I've been looking for you." His eyebrows drew together.

Grace extracted herself from him and took a deep breath. She smoothed down her hair. Jude always flustered her even when she wasn't running into him.

"How can I help?" she asked.

He ran a hand through his hair and shuffled his feet. "I'm worried about Isa."

She gave a stiff nod. It was always about Isa. For just once, she'd like someone to care about her. But that was silly. She worried about Isa as well.

"We all are."

He gripped the hilt of his sword. "I think she's in danger from Liam, and she doesn't see it at all." He ground his teeth in frustration.

Grace didn't think Isa was at risk from Liam, but she couldn't explain to Jude how or why she trusted Liam without revealing her own secrets.

"Liam isn't as big of a threat as you and the rest of the

guardians seem to think. He's not the bad guy here. He warned you about those American dragons, didn't he?"

Jude took a step closer to her. "Not you, too. He's got you all believing he's some amazing guy, but he'll wait for the right opportunity, and he'll kill her."

Jude was being unreasonable.

"He's had plenty of opportunities, and he hasn't done anything. Liam won't kill her, but Isa might take unnecessary chances with him. Things that might put her in harm's way. She's never been one to see the danger that she's in, and Liam provides a temptation for her to step out of reality."

"Do you think she's in love with him?" Jude relaxed a little bit, but he still bounced on the balls of his feet.

His words bothered Grace because Drew asked the same question. She wondered if the guardians were planning on convincing Isa to get rid of Liam.

Grace gritted her teeth. She didn't want to be a tool for them. She was Isa's lady-in-waiting. Not theirs. Besides, she liked Liam better than she liked most of them.

"No. I don't."

"Then, what do you think his motivations are if not to kill her?"

"He already told us that. He came to warn her, and now he cannot return home without being labeled a traitor."

Jude's jaw tightened. "I don't believe that for one second. But that is neither here nor there. Can you keep an eye on him and let me know if he exhibits any strange behaviors?"

Jude looked down at her earnestly. If it was anyone else asking, she would say no, but she could never resist his eyes. She shouldn't be so weak, but this was Jude.

She gave a stiff nod, and he reached out and squeezed her shoulder. "Thank you."

He moved past her and down the hall. She clenched and unclenched her fists. Did the guardians know of her infatuation with him? Is that why they used him and not Bartlby or Drew?

Grace's cheeks burned.

She had no idea she'd been that obvious.

CHAPTER 12

Pierre stared over his steepled fingers at Isa. She hated it when he did that. It made her feel like a naughty child.

Well, he was the one who'd been bad today.

She straightened in another red dress and crown, but this one was more subtle. She sat in a plush chair across from his desk and realized how backward this was. She should be sitting on a throne, and he should be sitting beneath her. *What an awful thought.* She'd never considered that before, but lately, she'd been reminded repeatedly of all the reasons she wasn't really in charge, even if everyone pretended she was.

"Did you send Jude to my room last night?" she asked.

He frowned. "Jude goes to your room often, does he not? That is no secret."

"Pierre, answer the question. Did you send him there to manipulate me?"

He shook his head and dropped his hands to his desk. "Not manipulate. Convince. You are not seeing reason."

"I'm protecting someone who shouldn't need protection. I don't know why you have it out for Liam. He's proven his loyalty to us."

Pierre let out an exasperated sigh. "Dragon's teeth! You don't find it suspicious that he showed up the day after we neutralized the threat against you?"

Isa wasn't convinced Pierre's kill-first-ask-questions-later policy made her safer in any way. In fact, it probably earned her more enemies. And they didn't even know why that dragon had come. They never gave him a chance to explain.

The fire crackled next to her as she thought about his words. "That was no threat. Liam said that dragon was his friend, and you killed him without reason."

"See, this is what I'm talking about. He's bewitching you." Pierre leaned forward across his desk, and his nostrils flared.

"You didn't answer my question. What made you think it was a threat in the first place?"

"We already knew the Americans were planning something. Plus, everyone knows not to come here without sending an eagle, or they will die. They know your life is on the line. Everyone knows."

"The Americans don't. They've never interacted with us

in any way before this. Wasn't Tavish supposed to bring us word about them? I haven't seen him since I sent him to see what was going on."

"He has not returned. But we do not need to wait for his report. I believe he is investigating the possibility that the Americans have joined forces with the rebels. Isn't that what Liam said? The Americans are out to take over. They have three kings, and their territory is too small."

Isa clutched at the folds of her dress in her lap. "Perhaps you're right. See. Liam's on our side."

Pierre's eyes pleaded with her. "At least, let us put a guard on him. From a distance. We need to watch him. Your life is at stake—you have to see this. And to be completely honest, this is very selfish of you." He leaned away and waved a hand.

Isa glared at him. "Excuse me?"

"If you were to be killed, *every dragon* in Europe would be exposed." Pierre took a deep breath and let that sink in. "The weight of this responsibility is enormous, Your Majesty. On both of us."

She knew that, but they couldn't shut her off from the world forever.

She stood and hovered over Pierre. His eyes flashed, and she wondered if he would lash out at her.

Isa steadied her voice. "Next time you have a problem with me, you come directly to me instead of using crude manipulation. I do not appreciate being treated like a fool in my own home. I like Jude a lot, and what happens between us will not be sullied by your meddling. Do you understand?"

Pierre shook his head. "I truly don't understand why you would take such a risk. But I will leave Jude out of it."

She spun and stalked from the room.

She wanted to turn back and apologize, to make things right. She didn't like being at odds with Pierre, but she couldn't let him manipulate her like that.

Sometimes, she hated being queen.

CHAPTER 13

Grace walked past a window, and a flash of red caught her eye. She stopped because red was not a color that naturally occurred outside. Someone bundled up with furs and a thick hat was throwing a ball for Missy.

At first, Grace thought it was Isa, but the person was too tall. He threw the ball again, and Missy flew after it. The ball went right through a snowbank, and so did Missy.

Grace cracked the window open—none of the windows would open more than a few inches—and heard Liam's laughter when Missy reemerged from the snow. She ran toward him and dropped the ball. With all the eyeballs on him, Grace was surprised he was able to go outside at all.

Though, maybe they didn't care if he did. Maybe they

hoped he would simply disappear into the woods and never return.

Liam asking her to help him find a weapon bothered her. He could be right about needing to protect himself, but it could be more than that as well. She was fairly certain he wasn't here to hurt Isa, but perhaps someone else was his target.

Not to mention, he knew her secret. She shouldn't have been so careless around him, but something about him oozed genuineness. Then again, those people could be the trickiest, and Grace wasn't sure she could trust her instincts. Though her instincts had served her fairly well so far.

Liam took the ball from Missy again and teased her with it. His voice rang out loud and clear in the silent field.

"I'm going to throw this so far that you'll never find it."

Missy jumped up and down in front of him.

He cocked his arm back, the ball disappeared into the woods, and Missy tore after it. Liam paced in a circle. Whatever his motivations were, he had to be lonely. He would need a friend in all this, and that friend couldn't be Isa. Grace was surprised that she wanted to be that person. She liked and trusted him. It would be nice to have someone she could talk to about magic.

She'd have to show that she trusted him, and to do that, she'd have to help him get what he wanted.

A weapon.

Her heart twisted. If she was wrong about him and he

killed Isa, that would be on her head. But he hadn't done anything to make Grace think he wanted to kill her.

As Grace watched him now, chasing Missy around the field, she decided to trust him. She might be putting her entire life on the line, but she was tired of playing it safe.

Liam brought a breath of fresh air to the castle and the promise of change. Change was something they hadn't had in a very, very long time.

And it was time.

If nothing else, things in six months or a year would look very different.

And Grace couldn't wait to see what they brought.

CHAPTER 14

Ruby walked around the library one more time before school and glared up at the shelves. She'd spent the better part of three days in here and found nothing, although a few books were promising. She'd really hoped *History of the Woodlands Dragons* would've been more helpful, but it started in the Americas and not Europe. A single line read, "They came over from Europe."

That was it. Sid's entire library focused on American dragons only. Which made sense. It'd been thousands of years since dragons flew in the skies of Europe but still. They should have at least one single book that dealt with the history there.

She needed Everett's library, but that was back home, and she doubted her mom would let her go. They had a three-day weekend coming up at school, so maybe Ruby could figure out a way to convince her to let her go.

Ruby sat on the couch and perused the books she'd read already. This was useless. Damon's annoying face flashed in her memory. She felt a little guilty for not letting him in on what she was doing, but only a little.

He'd called her some pretty rude things at school, and she had no reason to let him in, but he was Liam's best friend.

It was bad enough that she couldn't do much for Liam, and she didn't even like the guy. But Damon would only get in her way. He would ask way too many questions, and the process would take twice as long. She was a little cocky to think that, but she was good at this, and her system was solitary. Adding anyone to the mix was just a distraction.

The door flung open, and Hughie ran in. "It's time for school. Mom wants you to drive us."

She clenched her jaw. The last time she drove them all to school, she nearly had an accident when Gabe threw a Twinkie at the front window and it exploded on the dash.

When she asked him about it later, he said he just didn't want Trinity to have it. Of course, her mom didn't do anything when she told her about it that night. Ruby was expected to watch them, but they didn't listen, and she wasn't allowed to punish them.

But she planned to ask her mom about going away for the weekend, and driving her siblings to school would only make her look better. If she refused, she would absolutely not be able to go. She sighed. She hated having to suck up to her parents.

She grabbed Hughie's hands. "Have you been practicing your magic?"

He nodded eagerly. She'd been neglecting him since she started researching, but he never pushed her.

"Show me something new." She faked some enthusiasm for his benefit.

He touched her nose, but she couldn't feel anything.

"What did you do?" she asked nervously. Hughie's magic was powerful, but she hadn't seen what he did.

"I put on your pretty face." He puffed up his chest and smiled at her.

"My what?"

"Rubyyyy…" Her mother called from down the hall. A shriek came from Odin. That child would be the death of her mother. He was way harder than any of the others had been.

"Coming," Ruby called.

She rushed down the hall, wondering what Hughie meant. She hoped that he didn't change her face. She hated to think she might be walking around looking like J. Lo.

Her mom stood in the foyer, her hair a mess and flinching away from a screaming Odin.

"Don't worry, Mom. I'll take them to school."

Her mom did a double-take.

"What?" Ruby asked.

"Nothing. You don't usually wear makeup. It looks good on you. Though, I would probably not wear that much to school." The edges of her lips twitched.

Ruby rolled her eyes. That's what he meant. "Hughie," she called, but he'd already gone out to the car.

At least makeup was easy to get rid of. "Let me go wash it off."

Mom handed her a backpack. "No time. You look good. Own it."

Ruby turned and stomped toward the car. She'd just wash off the makeup when she got to school. She liked her own face, thank you very much.

Ruby dropped off the kids at both the elementary and middle school and found a spot at the back of the parking lot. She finally had time to look. She caught a glance in the rearview mirror a couple of times, but she'd been scared to check out the full effect for fear she'd try to kill Hughie. She pulled down the visor and flipped open the mirror.

She didn't recognize herself. Her already flawless skin had a touch of blush, and her cheekbones stood out. Her eyes had a dark smoky look with long lashes and dark pink lipstick. She looked pretty, but it was way too much for school. People wouldn't even recognize her. And if they did, they would think she was trying too hard.

She found a clean napkin and poured water from her water bottle. She started at her lips.

But it wouldn't come off.

It wouldn't even smear.

Neither would the eyes.

Oh, she was going to kill Hughie.

Right after she killed her mother for letting her go to school like this.

CHAPTER 15

Damon waited by Ruby's locker. He was going to try this again, but this time, he would be nicer. He felt so helpless as far as Liam was concerned, and he couldn't stand it. He would pretend to like Ruby, and then maybe she'd let him help.

Though, he'd been nice to her before, and she'd blown him off too. He just had to try harder.

Emma walked past him, and he smiled at her.

"Any word on Liam?" she asked. Of course she'd ask about him. If that guy wasn't his best friend and in real danger, he'd be incredibly irritated. Well, he was already irritated, but he was still worried about Liam.

Damon shook his head.

"Prom is right around the corner. What am I going to

do? I can't go dateless." The panic in her voice was evident, but right now, he really didn't care.

He nodded and stared at the door. Where was Ruby? She was never late.

"Damon, you promised you would help me." Emma smacked him on the shoulder.

He dropped his eyes back to hers. "With what?"

She sighed dramatically. "Prom. Liam was supposed to be my date."

"Right. Um, I'll go with you if you want."

Her face lit up, but he was still searching the halls for Ruby. He had to find her. Maybe she'd discovered something important to help them out.

Emma squeezed his arm. "Thanks. That would be awesome. And if Liam shows up before prom, you would totally understand. You're not like other guys. Thanks, Damon."

He glanced at his phone. He'd have to catch Ruby later, or else he'd be late. He spun around and rushed to class, not even sure what he'd say to her.

On the way, he played through his conversation with Emma. He was going to prom with her. Before Liam disappeared, this would've made his day. But now, he didn't care about stupid things like that. He didn't even care that Liam would steal his date if he came back.

He just wanted his friend alive.

The longer Liam was away, the more it looked like he

might not make it back. Damon's heart clenched. He didn't know what he would do without Liam.

He had to help Ruby. That research might be the very thing that brought Liam home.

AFTER SCHOOL, Damon waited by Ruby's car. Well, it was one of Sid's SUVs. Liam never drove the SUV. He always went for something flashier. Like Sid's Ferrari. Damon had tried all day to find her, and if Emma hadn't told him she'd seen her, he would've thought she was ditching.

He spotted Ruby across the parking lot with her head down. She finally looked up, and Damon's heart skipped a beat. She was gorgeous. He'd never seen her with any makeup on, and it made her look completely different. She'd always been pretty, and he was used to that, but this was different.

"Stop staring at me. I didn't ask for this." She glowered at him. Man, she was a knockout. Probably not the reaction she was looking for.

He shrugged. Maybe one of the girls at school decided she needed a makeover. She didn't, but it still looked amazing. Time to be nice and get on her good side. "It looks good on you."

"Gee, thanks." She stared at his shoes.

"I mean it."

She glanced back up and rolled her eyes. "Whatever. Can you move so I can leave?"

Damon shook his head. "Not until you let me help you with your research. If we can find good information on this queen, we can bring Liam home alive."

She shoved him out of the way. "No. I'm better on my own."

He blocked her way, and she pressed into him. "Come on, please." He tried to ignore the way she felt next to him.

"Move," She growled, and he chuckled.

"Not until you agree to let me help."

She looked up at him, her bright blue eyes shining with anger and her bright red lips pressed together. He very nearly kissed her. "Fine, you can help."

"Really?" He extracted himself from between her and the car door, not wanting to do anything that would jeopardize this.

She opened the door. "No. I lied. But thanks for moving."

She slammed the door behind her and drove away before he could even process what she was doing.

Her floral scent lingered behind.

And his heart raced.

He told himself it was because he was angry that she was leaving him out.

But even he knew that was a lie.

CHAPTER 16

Liam had never been bored before, but it had only taken him two days to feel that way here. At home, he'd always had his friends or family, homework, or video games. And for those few moments when he had nothing to occupy his attention, he had his phone.

But here. There was nothing. Grace avoided him at every turn, and Isa was friendly, but the guardians kept getting in the way. He couldn't talk to her when they were around. Benjamin, Marissa, and Olga were always working, and while he helped them sometimes, he felt like he was in the way and was slowing them down.

Benjamin had shown him the library, so he supposed he could read, but he didn't really like books. And he could only play with the fox for so long. Even wandering the castle just led him to empty bedrooms. He'd learned everything he could already.

He should be trying to understand Isa, but she eluded him. He was fairly certain she wasn't the evil queen that everyone said she was. The guardians seemed terrified of her, but he couldn't figure out why. He had to find that out. He thought maybe the guardians were the ones terrorizing Europe, but he hadn't managed to befriend any of them either. Even Drew, who was now an outcast, wouldn't say two words to him. Missy talked to him, but she wouldn't say a word against Isa.

Maybe he should go home. That's all Baden ever talked about. Liam's dad wanted him home, and he should go.

No.

That would be giving up, and he wouldn't do that. He'd figure this mystery out eventually.

He strolled down another corridor, no destination in mind. The castle was a maze of hallways and rooms, and he'd explored several of them but still got lost occasionally. He still didn't have a weapon. He'd hoped Baden would've been able to sneak into the weapons room, but he hadn't had any more luck than Liam had.

He turned a corner and saw Jude coming straight for him. He hadn't forgotten the torture, and he internally flinched every time Jude or Pierre came near him. He still didn't want to say anything to Isa either because then he'd have to out Grace for healing him, and she seemed insistent that her magic be kept secret. Plus, if he could get her to trust him, maybe she'd tell him what was really going on here.

"Hey, Jude. What's up?" He couldn't let them know they'd gotten to him. He was good at playing it cool even if he wanted to run away.

Jude ignored him and kept walking. Liam could've just accepted the slight, but he was tired of doing nothing. So he turned and matched Jude's stride. He couldn't spend the whole time here avoiding those he thought were the ones controlling Isa. His job was to figure out who the bad guys were and kill them if he could. He had to get over the torture.

"Come on, dude, why are you ignoring me?" He was surprised the words came out sounding casual. Maybe he was better at this than he thought.

Jude stared straight ahead, but to Liam's surprise, he answered. "You're going to hurt Isa. You may have her fooled, but not me, not any of the guardians."

"Are you sure about that? Drew seems pretty taken with me." He gave Jude a cheeky grin, but Jude didn't even look his way. Man, these guys were tough to crack.

"How did you do it? Did you bewitch her? You have magic, don't you?" Jude's voice was low and angry, but at least, he was talking.

"What makes you think that?"

"No one heals that fast."

He'd been waiting for this, and he could play this off. "I'm a dragon. We all heal fast."

They continued strolling down the hall like they were buddies. Liam almost snorted. That would be the day.

"That's what everyone else thinks, but not me. You couldn't turn into a dragon. Not in that cell."

"Royal dragons are different. We can heal even as humans." It was a lie but one that he was banking on Jude not knowing. Jude lashed out and grabbed his right hand. He jerked Liam's sleeve up and stared at his wrist.

Liam jerked his hand away. "Dude, what are you doing?"

Jude shook his head. "You don't have the wizard's mark, but you're hiding something. I won't let you hurt Isa. She is too important." Jude's face twisted.

Comprehension dawned on Liam. "Oh, man. You like her, don't you?"

"Isa?" Jude's voice rose three notches. Bingo. Liam had found Jude's Achilles heel, and he would use it for all it was worth.

"Yeah, Isa. Everyone calls her the queen except Grace. And now you. Guess you're just jealous that she likes me better. Maybe I'll be king instead of you." He had no idea where that came from, but he was pretty pleased with himself for thinking so quickly on his feet. Felix would be proud.

Jude spun and pinned him against the wall. He should've seen that coming, but he was having too much fun goading the guy.

"Is that your plan? You want to be king?" His voice rose.

Liam shrugged. He could work with that idea. Even if Jude told Isa he wanted to be king, he wouldn't deny it. Maybe he'd get closer to her that way.

Jude hovered over him, anger playing across his face. "You've got another thing coming. Isa is in love with me, and nothing you do will change that."

"Challenge accepted."

CHAPTER 17

As soon as they got home, Ruby grabbed Hughie and crouched in front of him. "Take it off."

"But you look so pretty." Damon had called her pretty too. She couldn't get the image of the way his eyes bore into hers when he said it. She'd always preferred her boys with blue eyes but something about the dark piercing color of Damon's eyes captivated her. She couldn't let him look at her that way again.

"Hughie."

He touched her nose and closed his eyes. He opened them again and stared at her. "It won't come off."

She let out an exasperated sigh. "Try again."

He placed a hand on her cheek and concentrated. "It won't work."

"Okay, fine. Go find Trinity and practice on her. Once you get it, come back and take off my makeup."

His head hung. "I don't want you to be mad at me."

"I'm not. But you do need to fix this. Trinity won't care if you play with her makeup. She loves this stuff."

Hughie wouldn't look Ruby in the eye, and she dropped her head until she caught his gaze and gave him a smile. "I'm not mad at you."

He shuffled his feet. "But you should be."

She reached out and tickled his ribs, and he laughed and squirmed away. He stared up at her, and she wondered how he managed to put it on but couldn't get it off.

"It's okay. Really. But I do want it gone." The makeup had attracted the attention of way too many people, including Damon. She didn't like the way he looked at her. He was a pest at the best of times, and he'd be even worse if he decided to pursue her.

Hughie nodded and ran off to the kitchen. Hopefully, he'd fix this soon.

She went in search of her mom and found her in the music room, listening to Jasper practicing the piano.

"Hey, Mom, can we chat?"

She nodded and scooted over on the couch, patting the seat next to her. "What's up?"

"I've been doing some research for Sid on the European dragons, and his library here is lacking. Can I go back to the cave next weekend and see what I can find?"

"Not by yourself." Mom flicked her eyes over to Jasper, who had missed a note.

"I was thinking of taking Gabe with me."

Skye stared at her for a moment. "He's too young. You need an adult to go with."

"Okay, how about you or Dad?"

"We can't. At this point, we can't afford to go anywhere. It would be too risky. We need to be able to act immediately."

Ruby flung herself back onto the couch. She hated how they always treated her like a child. "But I'm trying to help."

"I know. Maybe in a few weeks."

Ruby stomped her foot. "We don't have a couple weeks."

Skye glowered at her. "Are you sure you aren't just trying to go home? I know you want to."

"No."

"I just don't see how this is helpful. I don't want you to disappear too. No, you need to stay here. Sid's library is huge. You can't have exhausted it already."

"His library is rather small, actually. And yes, I have. There is nothing about the European dragons at all."

"Ruby, this conversation is over. You're not going." Mom's face was set. There was no budging.

Ruby stormed from the room. She'd find a way to get to that cave. She had to.

Liam's life depended on it.

CHAPTER 18

*G*race found Isa and Liam in the games room. Liam was teaching Isa a new card game. Missy jumped into Liam's lap, and he stroked her ears. Liam met Grace's eyes but did not address her.

Isa looked up and waved Grace toward them. "Join us. Liam is cheating, and I bet you can figure out how."

Liam chuckled and patted Isa's shoulder. "I am not cheating. I'm just better than you."

Isa stuck her tongue out like a child, and Liam laughed. Grace wasn't sure what to say. This was flirting like she'd never seen before. Sure, she'd seen Isa flirt with Jude, but that was more serious and lusty in nature. This was the stuff true romance was born from, and she worried that Liam might have ulterior motives. Grace didn't like Liam like that, and she'd been hoping for a reason for Isa to ditch Jude, but this didn't seem right. It was too much.

But that was beside the point. She would talk to Liam about it after she gained his trust. She needed to get him alone, but she wasn't sure how to pull him away from Isa.

Liam set down his cards. "After this, we should find a room big enough and show each other our dragon forms."

Oh, Grace had to put a stop to this. Isa couldn't be a dragon, and the guardians would go mad if they found out Liam was using his dragon form.

"I saw you outside earlier with Missy," Grace said. "Looks like you really enjoy the snow."

Isa gasped and set her cards down. "You went outside?"

He absentmindedly stroked Missy's fur. "Yeah. Is that a problem?"

Isa frowned. "No. I just didn't know they'd let you outside."

"I didn't think you had people watching me." He kept his voice even, but Grace could tell he was a little irritated.

"It's not that. It's just that every time I try to go outside, they stop me."

Liam leaned forward. "Haven't we had this conversation already? You are the queen, and you don't have to listen to them."

Grace nearly laughed out loud. If Liam kept encouraging Isa to defy the guardians, then they really would kill him. Isa had always been queen, but being so young, she relied on the guardians' advice and counsel for years. If she completely stopped, Grace didn't know what they would do. They were already having kittens about her newfound ability to stand up to them.

Maybe that's why Isa liked him so much. He encouraged her to defy the guardians. There were worse reasons to like someone.

"I'm going to teach you a different game," Isa exclaimed, but her voice betrayed her. Isa was bothered that Liam was allowed outside and not her, but she didn't want to talk about it. She was a master evader. But Grace had been around long enough to read her cues.

Isa jumped up and pranced to the other side of the room where the games were kept, Missy on her heels. Grace had to act fast. She hadn't caught Liam alone yet and wasn't able to tell him she had changed her mind.

She leaned closer to him. "Listen, I've decided to help you."

Liam kept his eyes on Isa, who was perusing a shelf full of games. "With what?"

"You wanted to get into the weapons room. I can get you in there."

He jerked his head toward her. "You will?"

"Yes."

He narrowed his eyes. "Why?"

"Because I think you are in danger from the guardians, and I don't think you'll hurt Isa."

He reached over and gripped her hand. "I won't. Thank you for trusting me."

Grace's eyes flicked to Isa, who was staring at the two of them, a grin playing on the edge of her lips. Grace jerked her hand away from Liam's.

She didn't need Isa thinking things about her and Liam.

The last time Isa tried to push a boy on her, things didn't end well at all.

CHAPTER 19

Grace got to dinner a few minutes late and was surprised to see her place right next to Jude. Isa had Liam next to herself again. And just like earlier today, they were the happiest people in the room. This was a disaster waiting to happen. If Isa fell for Liam, there would be hell to pay with the guardians. They would never stand for it.

"What does she see in him?" Jude hissed the second Grace sat down. Oh, man, not this again. She'd already reassured Jude that nothing was going on.

"I'm not sure what you mean. They're just friends."

Jude leveled Grace with a look and pointed toward them. "That doesn't look like just friends to me."

Isa was laughing at something Liam had said and put a hand on his arm.

"Are you jealous?" she asked.

"What? No. Isa still likes me, and even if she didn't, I know her heart is fickle. But I don't want to see her get hurt by him."

Grace cut open her potpie, and gravy and steam poured out. "He won't hurt her. I thought we had this conversation already."

"I don't mean with a weapon. I mean he could break her heart." He attacked his dinner with a little too much forcefulness.

"Isa doesn't have a heart," Grace said, and Jude snorted, a smile on his lips. She was just playing and knew that Isa's heart was actually way more tender than she allowed others to see. That was a show for the guardians. Her grandmother taught her to be that way.

"You know, Grace, I've always appreciated your ability to bring a smile to my face even when I'm grumpy."

Her chest flushed. He'd never complimented her before. She also loved how he called her just Grace. Not Lady Grace.

Grace dropped her eyes to her plate. "Thank you."

His face turned suddenly serious. "But I am worried about her. We still don't know who he really is and where he came from."

"He's from America."

"So he says. But maybe he's not. Maybe he's from the rebels, and maybe he's just a guy who wanted to see if he could infiltrate the castle. We have no idea."

"There is one way to know for sure."

"What's that?"

"Have you seen him as a dragon? If he's any color but green or purple, then you'll know for sure he's foreign because then, he couldn't be a forest or mountain dragon."

Jude creased his eyebrows, and Grace had the sudden urge to reach up and stroke his cheek. "You keep surprising me, Grace. That's incredibly smart."

She practically melted at the way he was saying her name. She couldn't look at him because, if she did, he'd see right through her. Maybe he already knew how she felt about him, and he was using it to get to Isa.

"Thank you," she muttered.

"Any more ideas in that big brain of yours?"

"No." She peeked over at him, but he was staring at Isa and Liam again. Grace was a fool if she ever thought Jude would be interested in her. She knew Isa would discard him eventually, but she wasn't sure he'd ever give up on Isa.

From across the table, Isa picked up her drink and flicked her eyes to Jude. She smiled and winked at him.

"Did you see that?" he asked with far too much excitement.

"Yes. You obviously have nothing to worry about. She's just friends with him. Told you."

Not long after, Marissa cleared the plates, and Benjamin placed dessert in front of them. Jude wrinkled his nose and stuck his fork in the dense pudding-like substance. "What is this?"

"Cheesecake," Liam exclaimed from across the table. "Oh, Isa, my favorite. I could kiss you." He dug right in and shoveled it into his mouth.

Isa blushed, and Jude scowled. He pushed the cheesecake away.

Maybe Grace had spoken too soon.

CHAPTER 20

Ruby paced in front of Sid in the theatre room, Aspen curled up next to him fast asleep. She didn't know who else to turn to, but Sid was the one who had asked her to do the research. He could help her get what she needed.

"Mom's being unreasonable."

Sid stroked Aspen's hair and watched his wife. Ruby had always loved the relationship they had and hoped she would have one like that someday.

"She's just worried. Liam disappearing has us all concerned."

Ruby threw her hands up. "But he went to Europe, chasing an evil queen. I want to go to Oregon and hole up in a cave. And just for the weekend. This could be crucial to learning more about them."

Sid looked up at her, and she saw the pain in his face. He missed his son. "Maybe. But maybe not."

His gaze fell away, and Ruby let him think. She'd learned this trick from her dad. If people were given time to think, they usually came up with solutions on their own.

She sat on the ottoman in front of him. She had to make him see.

"Are you wearing makeup?" he asked.

She rolled her eyes. "Yes. And I can't take it off. Hughie did it. I didn't ask him to."

Sid chuckled. "I've never seen you with makeup. Poor Hughie. I bet you were furious."

She couldn't help her smile. "I could never be mad at Hughie." And she couldn't. But she wished he would remove this makeup. She looked like she was on her way to a hot date at a club.

"You're a good sister. And I have an idea. Why don't you take one of the royal dragons? Harasu was good friends with Liam and would probably appreciate Everett's library. He's an adult and a trained warrior. I'll talk to him."

This was good. Then, Ruby didn't have to become a dragon. She could just ride on him. She hated putting on her dragon form, and it was why she had originally offered to take Gabe. That kid loved being a dragon.

"What about Mom?"

"I'll talk to her. You're right. This is important, and what you find could be key in helping Liam. Your mom will see that."

"Thanks, Uncle Sid. I appreciate it."

"I appreciate you being willing to help." He swallowed. "I miss him."

Ruby's heart constricted. "Me too."

It was a lie, mostly. She didn't really miss him, but she didn't want him to die over there, and she hated to see the family in pain.

"I just keep thinking we'll never see him again." His voice had gone soft.

Ruby reached out and squeezed his hand. "Knowing Liam, he sweet-talked his way into the hearts of everyone in that castle. He's good at that."

A single tear slid down Sid's cheek. "But what if that doesn't help him? What if they still kill him?"

Ruby let out a breath. She'd never seen her uncle so vulnerable before. She wondered how much of his feelings he'd been holding in. He always seemed so strong.

"Don't think about that. You'll get him back, and we'll have to listen to his stories for years. It's going to be okay."

Sid wiped his face. "Sorry. I didn't mean to get all emotional on you. It's late, and I'm tired. I'm also very worried."

"I know. Me too. That's why I want to help."

Ruby stood. She needed to leave him alone with his thoughts. She was almost to the door when she heard a sob. She considered going back but thought he probably wanted to be alone with Aspen, not comforted by his seventeen-year-old niece.

She hoped when Liam came home, he'd understand the pain he put his parents through. She would have words with him and make sure he would never do this to them again. Sid and Aspen didn't deserve this. Not by a long shot. They were the best people Ruby knew.

CHAPTER 21

"Come on, Grace, you have to give me something to work with here." Isa giggled and fell back into bed.

"I'm not interested in Liam. Or Drew." She wondered what Isa would do if she admitted her interest in Jude. Would Isa be happy or hurt? Grace suspected the first, but she didn't want to take any chances. Grace could never go after Jude. She had no idea why Isa was trying to set her up with Liam when it was so obvious that Isa had feelings for him.

Isa gripped Grace's hands. "I just want you to be happy. And discover the joy of kisses."

Grace sighed and extracted her hands from Isa. "I'm fine, and I'll figure it out on my own."

"I really think you and Liam would be good together."

Grace perched on the edge of Isa's bed. "No offense, but it looked like you and Liam were getting pretty cozy. Are you sure you don't have feelings for him?"

Isa's face fell, and Grace regretted asking.

"No. I don't. I…I…like Jude."

"But you've been ignoring Jude."

Isa rolled over. "Good night, Grace."

Grace had no idea what this was all about, but she didn't want to push it. When Isa was ready to talk, she would.

Grace doused the candles and slipped out of Isa's rooms. She wondered what Jude did to turn Isa off. Knowing Isa, it could be anything. Though truthfully, it probably had more to do with her feelings for Liam that she was trying to deny. This was like watching someone falling down the stairs and not being able to run fast enough to help. Isa would get hurt, and Grace would have to be there when her heart got broken. Liam was a mysterious stranger. Everyone knew those stories never ended well.

She came down the stairs and around the corner and found Jude pacing the hall. He raced up to her. "Did Isa ask for me?"

"No." She couldn't meet his eyes. The desperation in his voice was too much for her.

He let out an exasperated sigh. "Can you go ask her if she'll see me?"

"She went to sleep."

"You just left. She's not asleep yet."

After the conversation they had, Grace didn't want to go back in there. "I know you've gone up there uninvited before. Just do that again." She waved to the stairs, knowing it was a bad idea. Isa didn't want to see Jude tonight, and Grace didn't want to get stuck in the crosshairs. If she didn't send him up there on his own, he'd just keep bugging her.

"The last time I did that, things didn't go well." He ran a hand over his face.

Maybe that's why Isa was mad at him. Maybe this had nothing to do with her feelings for Liam.

"Please. Just go ask her." His eyes pleaded with her, and her insides went all gooey. She hated the effect he had on her.

"Fine. I'll go ask. Wait here." She just hoped Isa wouldn't be too angry with her.

Grace lit a candle and carried it into Isa's room.

Isa sat bolt upright. "What's wrong?"

"Nothing. But I ran into Jude downstairs, and he asked if he could see you."

Isa narrowed her eyes. "No. Tell him I'm tired, and I'll talk to him tomorrow."

Something was definitely up between the two of them. "Can I ask one more question?"

"Sure."

"Are things over between you two?"

Isa hesitated and let out a breath. "I don't know."

"Do you want to talk about it?"

"Yes. No. I don't know." Isa flopped onto the pillows, and Grace set the candle on a side table and climbed into bed with her.

"What's wrong?" She hated seeing Isa upset.

Isa squeezed her eyes shut. "I think Jude is using me."

Isa had to be mistaken. Jude would never use anyone.

"For what?"

"I'm not sure. Information maybe. I just don't trust him anymore. And it hurts because I like him a lot."

"What does your heart say?"

"It says that I'm a fool."

Grace's chest tightened. "You're not a fool. You're just a girl who likes a boy, and you don't want to be taken advantage of. In your position, that is a legitimate fear. I'll let Jude know you need time to think. At some point, you should talk to him."

Isa nodded. Graced placed a kiss on her forehead and slipped out the door once more.

She shut it behind her and leaned against it. She had to go and watch the one guy she really liked be disappointed because he wanted another woman.

Would he come onto her because he was lonely?

Maybe.

Did she want him to?

No. She didn't want to be second to Isa. She had too much pride for that.

But would she be able to resist him?
She didn't know.
And that scared her.
She took a deep breath and descended the stairs.

CHAPTER 22

Grace took her time going down the stairs. She hoped Jude had gone back to his room to mope there. She came around the corner, and he rushed for her.

"What did she say?" He wrung his hands.

"Not tonight."

His face fell. "Why not?"

"She's tired." It was a lie, of course, but she wasn't about to tell Jude that Isa thought he was using her. That would lead to more questions. Though Jude probably already knew why.

His shoulders slumped, and he sank to the floor. "Dragon's teeth, I've ruined the best thing I had going for me."

Grace sat next to him, knowing this was probably a mistake. She was never very coherent near him, but she couldn't let him just sit there and pout. "No, you didn't. I asked her tonight if she liked Liam, and she told me that she still likes you."

He turned to face her, his eyes shining. "Really?"

"Really."

She looked in his face and realized something she hadn't before. He was absolutely in love with Isa. This was not some passing fancy or someone he just enjoyed in his bed. He loved her.

Grace glanced at his lower leg. Had he sealed himself to Isa? She had no marking on her ankle indicating she'd sealed herself to Jude, but Grace couldn't see Jude's skin.

Grace ignored her own breaking heart. She and Jude would never be a thing even if Isa decided she no longer wanted him because Grace would always know that he loved Isa first, and she did not want to be second.

Jude would never be hers.

But he could be her friend. And tonight, he was hurting.

"Look, she'll come around. But you need to give her some space. Come for a walk with me. We can talk, and you can get things off your chest. You'll feel better. I promise."

He met her eyes. "Okay, but this walk needs to include a bottle of wine."

Grace gave him a grin, stood up, and offered him her hand. "No midnight walk is ever complete without a bottle of wine."

He took it, and Grace tried to ignore the way her stomach fluttered. She had to get over him.

But how did you tell your heart to stop breaking?

CHAPTER 23

Grace and Jude didn't bother with glasses. They just took turns drinking out of the bottle, wandering the dark halls, and exploring the vastness of the castle. Jude droned on about Isa and how much he loved her.

After a half bottle of wine, Grace's heart stopped hurting. They polished off the bottle, and Grace looped her arm through his. "I'm not ready to go to bed yet."

"Me neither. Let's grab another bottle from the kitchens and explore the gem halls."

"Oh, I haven't been down there in ages." They were the prettiest rooms in the castle. Each room was like stepping inside a geode.

In the kitchens, which were empty, thank goodness, Grace grabbed another bottle and uncorked it. Jude took the first swig and handed it to her. By now, her head was fuzzy, and she had to be careful to keep her secrets hidden.

Liam might be understanding about the magic, but Jude would not. He was a dragon who probably was trained to spot wizards and kill them. The dragons didn't talk about wizards very often, but when they did, it was always with contempt. The wizards were the reason that the queen had to hide the European dragons, in the first place.

Grace didn't even know why the wizards and dragons were enemies, to begin with. Just that it's always been that way.

Jude led the way down the stairs to the halls, and Grace followed carefully. The stairs were precarious, and she was most definitely tipsy.

Jude held onto her hand, and she loved the feel of his skin against hers. She knew she shouldn't. She needed to get over Jude, but maybe for one night, she could pretend he wasn't Isa's.

The gem halls glowed naturally. They were beneath the hot pools, so it was warmer here than the rest of the castle. The first room gleamed a bright blue from the sapphires on the walls. The crystals stuck out in massive jagged edges all over the room.

"What's your favorite room?" Jude asked.

"Amethyst." It always seemed to shine a little brighter than the rest.

Jude's face lit up. "Mine too."

He led her into the glowing purple room, his hand still

warm in hers. They sat on the rock floor, drinking the second bottle of wine and pointing out their favorite crystal shapes.

Jude handed the bottle to her. "Last bit, you can have it."

Grace swallowed the wine and set the bottle down. Jude moved in front of her and just stared. His face glowed in the purple light. Grace had never had him so close to her before, and if she wasn't drunk, she'd be terrified, but she just studied him without shame. His long dark lashes, his sparkling emerald green eyes, and his black hair, which fell across his forehead. She wanted to brush the hair away so she could see his eyes better.

He moved closer to her. "I never noticed how pretty you are. You might even be prettier than Isa."

Grace blushed and averted her eyes. "Thank you."

He stroked her cheek, and her breath caught in her throat. "I wish I would've fallen in love with you instead of her. Then I would never have to worry about my heart being broken. I bet you would stay faithful to me."

Grace held his hand against her face. "You still could."

He shook his head. "My heart is already gone."

Grace leaned forward. "It doesn't have to be. I love you, and I have for a very long time." What was she saying? It was true, all of it, but why would she say those things out loud?

"You love me?" His eyes bore into hers.

"I do." No point in denying it now.

"Isa has never told me that she loves me."

"Isa is a fool." How could she toy with this man's heart?

Jude chuckled. "Careful, Isa could have you beheaded for that." He shifted forward and stared deep into her eyes. "I think I could love you, too."

He brought his face extremely close to hers and hesitated a moment. Grace wanted this so badly, but she didn't know what to do. His breath was hot against her lips and smelled of wine.

He slowly pressed his mouth against hers, and she leaned into him. His lips moved easily against hers, and everything about it felt right.

He pulled away and smiled. "Isa's kisses don't make me feel like that."

"Like what?" Grace asked, her heart racing.

"Like the whole world stopped. I think I love you, Grace."

Grace thought her chest would explode. He stood, grabbed her hands, and led her back up the stairs, down the hall, and to the door of her room. He placed another light kiss on her lips, stroked her cheek, and whispered in her ear.

"Until tomorrow, my sweet angel."

CHAPTER 24

After school, Damon went to the training fields. Gold and silver dragons swooped around in the air. Things still went on like normal even though Felix was dead and Liam was missing. He was a little angry that things were normal, but then again, why shouldn't they be?

He stared into the sky. Actually, there were more dragons than normal. Maybe they were preparing for the worst. Damon hadn't been alive when the last war was fought, but his mom used to tell him stories at night about it. When he was a kid, he'd wanted to see a dragon war, but now, he hoped it didn't come to pass. Too many dragons died, and he didn't want to lose his friends.

He watched from the sidelines for a while, his favorite thing to do. Today, they fought more fiercely than normal. They were definitely preparing for something. He walked underneath them so he could talk to some. He was taking a bit of a risk since they could land without realizing he was underneath them, but he didn't care. He'd done it before.

A few dragons landed right in front of him and turned into humans.

"Dude, you could've died," Oro said.

"I know." He gave him a grin to show he was joking.

Harasu nudged him on the shoulder. "Too bad you're not a dragon. I bet you'd be the fiercest one up there."

Damon frowned. "If I was a dragon, I would've gone after Liam already."

The dragons dropped their eyes. Asimi put her arm around his shoulders. "We miss him too."

Damon nodded. "I know."

All of their heads suddenly jerked to the sky, and Damon turned around. Sid flew in. Damon always loved watching him, his black scales reflecting in the sunlight in a way the gold and silver ones didn't. He was the most striking of the dragons Liam had seen.

Sid dropped in front of them and turned into a human. The dragons gave small bows.

"How are you doing, Your Majesty?" Harasu asked with a slight tremor in his voice. It was odd to see people scared of Sid, but Harasu hadn't spent most of his life in Sid's house.

"As well as can be expected. Thank you for asking." Sid was more formal than Damon had ever seen him.

Oro pointed to the sky where several dragons still

fought. "We're preparing in case you need us. We'll take out that queen bitch." Oro was never tactful, one of the things Liam liked best about him.

Sid gave a small smile. "Thank you for the offer, but we're trying to extract Liam first."

Asimi crossed her arms. "You know, I trained with Felix as well. I could get him." Everyone wanted to help. Liam had to make it back alive. There were too many people counting on it.

"I appreciate your confidence, but everyone we sent out there has died except Liam. And Baden. We need to do some recon before we try again, but I will remember your offers. Today, I need Harasu's help though."

"Me?" His face paled. Harasu was brilliant, but he wasn't known for his bravery. He would not be the first one Damon would send if he were in Sid's shoes. Not that he knew what it was like to be king, but he knew the fighting dragons better than anyone. And Harasu always held back and never volunteered.

"Yes, you. Skye's daughter Ruby is doing research on the European dragons. She would like to return to Everett's cave next weekend, and Skye requires her to have an escort. I know you enjoy research. Would you be willing to accompany her?"

Relief crossed Harasu's face. "Of course, Your Majesty. When does she want to leave?"

"Next Friday after school."

"Have her meet me here."

"Okay. That's a long weekend, and she doesn't have school on Monday, but please have her home Monday evening so her mother doesn't kill me." His voice was light but still serious.

Harasu gave a small bow. "I would never want to get on Skye's bad side. Even in her human form, I'm sure she could eviscerate me."

Sid chuckled. "And if you let anything happen to Ruby, she will."

As soon as Sid was out of sight, Oro punched Harasu in the shoulder. "You're gonna get it on with Skye's daughter."

A twitch of jealousy rose in Damon's chest, and he didn't understand why.

Harasu shoved Oro away. "She's a child. Don't talk about her like that."

"Actually, she's not," Asimi said. "I know she doesn't come around very often, but I saw her at Obsidian's the other day. She's very pretty."

Harasu's cheeks flushed. "I'm just doing what Obsidian asked me to."

Damon listened to them banter. This might be his chance to actually help Ruby and not let her ditch him again. He was tired of her leaving him out.

"Can I come with?" he asked, interrupting their conversation. All three of them stared at him.

"Why?" Harasu asked.

"Because I'm supposed to be helping Ruby with the research, and I've never been out to Everett's cave."

Harasu scratched his head. "I don't know. Sid's instructions were pretty clear."

"He just wanted you to protect her. He didn't say anything about bringing others with. Come on, man, please?" Damon put on his most innocent face. "Besides, we're good friends, you know."

He hated that Ruby was leaving him out of this, but he'd prove to her that he could be an asset. Having Harasu along might complicate things, but it might be good to have a neutral party with.

But then again, he didn't want anyone else to witness their fights.

Asimi watched him with interest, her eyes dancing.

"What?" he asked, unease growing in his stomach.

"Do you like her?" A grin formed on Asimi's face.

"Who?" He knew damn well who they were talking about, but he was trying to get out of this unscathed.

"Ruby? Skye's pretty daughter. Who else?"

"What? No." His face flushed.

Asimi wiggled her eyebrows. "Look at that blush. You do. You like her."

"I don't. I just want to help." He did not like where this conversation was going at all.

"Deny it all you want." Asimi laughed. "Harasu, you can't leave him behind. The poor kid would be heartbroken."

Harasu gave a slow nod. "Okay, sure. You can go with."

Oro shook his head. "You all are fools." He put his arm

around Damon's shoulders and patted him on the chest. "I got your back, dude."

Damon had no clue what was going on, but he knew when to keep his mouth shut.

"Listen," Oro began. "My man Damon here wants a romantic weekend with his girl. Obsidian didn't specifically say Harasu had to go, only that she needed someone to go with her. She'll come here thinking she's meeting up with Harasu, and Damon will be here instead. She'll be thrilled, and Harasu doesn't have to leave Yellowstone, which we all know he doesn't want to do."

Harasu shrugged. "It's true. But I don't want to get in trouble with Obsidian."

"We'll cover for you," Oro said. "We'll tell him you were sick or something and that Damon stepped up and took your place. Didn't you say you were supposed to be helping her with research anyway?"

"Yes, Sid told me to." That was not a lie at least.

Oro flung his hands up in a shrug. "See, it's fate."

Damon wasn't sure what to make of this new development. He didn't want them thinking he was in love with Ruby, but if he tried to go along with Harasu, she might find a way to leave him behind.

If he was her only option, she'd go anyway and wouldn't ditch him.

He played along. "He's right. Please, Harasu. I promise nothing will happen to Ruby."

Harasu sighed. "Okay. But if something happens, I'm holding all of you responsible."

Oro gave Damon a big grin. "Dude, I expect to see a sealing mark when you get back, or I'll be very disappointed."

Asimi laughed. "That's a lot of pressure. But I like it. We let you go alone, but you seal the deal."

Suddenly, Oro's plan didn't look that great after all.

CHAPTER 25

Grace had never drunk that much wine. She had fuzzy memories of the night before, and she hoped she didn't say anything stupid. She'd had a chance to make a real impression on Jude, and she probably came across as a bumbling idiot. They'd gone to the gem halls, but she had zero memory of anything after that.

She sat at the table in the kitchen and held her head. Olga stomped over to her. Dragon's teeth, that woman's footsteps were loud.

"Are you the reason there are two bottles of wine missing?" Olga crossed her arms and gave Grace the evil eye.

Grace nodded, not wanting to argue with her. Moving her jaw just made her head ache more.

"Did you drink them by yourself?" Her lips twitched a bit.

She shook her head but didn't offer anything more. Olga wouldn't understand if she was hanging with the guardians.

"Here, drink this. It will help."

Grace sniffed. The concoction smelled like rotten tomatoes and cabbage. She drank it anyway, gagging, because Olga's medicine always worked.

Was Jude feeling this crappy? Probably not. He drank much more often than she did. The wine probably didn't even faze him.

She grabbed Isa's breakfast tray and made her way down the hall. Jude stepped out of a door, holding his head. She held her breath, wondering what horrors he knew about her now.

He gave her a small grin. "What happened last night?" he asked.

She giggled. At least, he didn't remember the dumb things she probably said either. "I have no idea, except you drank away your sorrows."

"Well, it must've worked. But I have a splitting headache instead."

"Go see Olga, and she'll get you fixed right up." She shouldn't have offered. Now, Olga would know who she drank the wine with, but hopefully, Olga wouldn't say anything.

He nodded, and she continued down the hall. Just before she turned the corner, she looked back, and he was staring at her. Odd, he'd never so much as looked at her before. She shook her head. She couldn't afford to think too much about it.

But for some reason, her heart didn't feel as broken.

After dinner, Grace wandered down the hall. Jude had been staring at her the whole time they were eating. Had she said something about magic? Well, if she did and he confronted her, she could blame the wine and deny it. Say she was trying to impress him or something.

A hand grabbed her elbow, and she spun around.

"Liam, you scared me."

He cocked his head. "I've been calling your name. Where are you?" He pointed to her forehead and laughed.

She let out a breath. "Sorry, I'm distracted. What's up?"

"A few of the guardians have been dogging me. You said you would help me a couple of days ago. Can you get me into the weapons room tonight? I seriously have to be able to defend myself."

She rubbed her temples. She'd forgotten about that.

"Sure. Meet me at the doors at midnight. Bring a candle, but don't light it until I get you in. I won't wait with you."

He bit his lip. "Of course. Thank you, by the way. It means a lot that you trust me and are willing to help me. I owe you big time."

She gave him a warm smile. "You do. But don't you worry. At some point, I'll make you pay up."

CHAPTER 26

Ruby knocked on Sid's office door. He'd never called her in before, and she hoped this wasn't a bad thing.

"Come in," he said, and she pushed the door open.

Sid sat in an armchair by his fire with Skye across from him on a loveseat. Her mom smiled and patted the seat next to her. It was the first time in a long time that she'd seen her mom without Odin on her hip.

Ruby sank down, and Skye took her hand.

"What's up?" she asked Sid.

"Hughie still not able to reverse the magic?" Sid grinned at her.

Ruby scowled. She would not let him experiment on her ever. "No. Now Trinity's got it as well."

Skye shook her head. "I'm okay with Ruby's makeup,

but Trinity is only thirteen, and she looks about twenty now. Hughie's working on it."

"Well, I'm sure he will get it. That kid is talented."

Ruby swelled with pride. Most people were scared of Hughie and didn't talk of him in that way.

"He is. I'm very proud of him," Skye said. She'd never said that about Ruby, but Ruby tried not to let it bother her.

Sid leaned forward. "I wanted to talk to both of you."

Ruby's stomach flip-flopped. This didn't look good. If they were in his office and he was joking about Hughie to lighten the mood, then Sid must have bad news.

Skye squeezed Ruby's hand tighter. "What's going on?"

"You know I gave Ruby a job to research the European dragons, right?"

Skye nodded. "She mentioned it. She said she wasn't having much luck."

"I haven't." Ruby sighed. "Your library doesn't have much. The books are only about the American dragons."

Sid nodded. "Right. And Everett's library will probably have a broader range of books."

Skye let go of Ruby's hand and crossed her arms, glaring at the both of them. "You two have been talking behind my back."

Sid gave a sheepish grin. "Maybe. But Ruby has a point about that library."

"She's only seventeen." Skye swallowed. "You weren't there in Scotland. You didn't see the horror those dragons are inflicting. I'm not sending my daughter on an errand by herself."

"She's been there many times before. It's Oregon. Not Europe. And I've arranged for one of the royal dragons to take her."

"Who?" Skye asked.

"Harasu."

"He's responsible." Ruby could hear the hesitation in Skye's voice. This was good. It meant she might be giving in.

"Which is why I asked him."

Skye looked back and forth between both of them. "I don't like this."

"We know. But we have to explore all possibilities. This might be key in bringing Liam home." Sid's voice cracked a bit. Liam was his only son, and he'd only lived a short life. Losing a child wasn't something a parent should have to face.

"Please, Mom. It's next weekend, and we're off Monday, so I won't miss any school, and Harasu will make sure nothing happens to me."

Skye leveled a glare at Sid. "Fine. But don't make me regret this, Sid. If something happens to her, I'll kill you."

Ruby jumped up and hugged her mom. "Thanks. I promise nothing bad will happen."

She hoped those weren't famous last words.

CHAPTER 27

At ten past midnight, Grace wondered if Liam fell asleep. She'd been waiting here for nearly twenty minutes now. But this seemed so important to him. She'd wait for another ten and then go back to bed.

A few moments later though, he came around the corner, out of breath.

"I got lost. The castle looks different at night."

She shook her head. "That it does. Now listen, I'll unlock the door, but you have to be quick. The guardians patrol the halls at night, and they'll hear you in there. Find what you need, and get out of there as fast as possible."

He nodded.

She placed her hand on the door and concentrated on the lock. It clicked, and Grace creaked open the door.

Liam squeezed her hand. "Thank you for this. I will not forget your kindness."

His words seemed odd, and she hoped she wasn't making a big mistake. If he killed Isa, she would never forgive herself. But she couldn't deny that the guardians had it out for him, and he deserved a fighting chance.

He slipped into the room, and she closed the door behind him.

She meandered the halls, thinking, not really tired anymore. In some ways, she felt like she was betraying Isa. Grace should've told her and let her decide if Liam could carry a weapon. But then, Grace would have to explain why Liam came to her in the first place and risk Liam betraying her and telling Isa about the magic. No. She couldn't have done that.

She could've just told Liam no.

But she understood his plight. In spite of Isa's threats, the guardians could still hurt him.

She came around the corner and found Jude, Seamus, and Drew heading to their rooms, and she wanted to backtrack and go anywhere but where they did.

Jude's face lit up with a smile when he saw her, and her stomach flip-flopped. Seamus and Drew pretty much ignored her and went into their own rooms.

Jude approached her. "Were you coming to see me?"

"Why would you think that?" She glanced around, all flustered now. She was in the guardian's hall, but she was trying to figure out why she'd gone here. Damn his smile for making her lose all sense.

He pointed to a door a couple of doors down. "Because that's my room."

She blushed. "Oh, no. I was just wandering the halls thinking."

His face fell, and his shoulders sagged.

She couldn't understand why he would be so excited to see her. Then, she remembered their conversation before they got drunk in the gem halls.

"Oh, I'm sorry. You must be so disappointed. I've been talking to Isa today, but she's still not ready for you to come to her rooms." Grace reached out and squeezed his hands. "Just give it time."

He let out a breath. "I will. I'm sure she'll come around."

Grace chuckled. "I would offer another walk in the gem halls with a bottle of wine, but I'm still recovering from last night."

He sighed. "I'm tired anyway."

"I'll keep working on Isa."

"Thanks, I appreciate that." He smiled, but it didn't reach his eyes.

She continued her walk down the hall, but as she turned the corner, he was still standing there.

Staring at her.

CHAPTER 28

The weapons rooms had walls full of every kind of sword, dagger, and mace that Liam could want. Spears and bows had their own room. Some of the weapons were probably older than any of the American dragons.

He studied the swords. They would be pointless since he couldn't hide them. He pulled down a few long blades and tried them out. He could have so much fun in this room if he had longer, but he had a mission to fulfill, so he made his way into the dagger room, which was smaller than the sword room but still filled to the brim.

He found one with a thin blade but longer than most. Its tip was deadly sharp, the handle was easy to grip, and it was pitch black and would be easy to conceal. He hoped he'd never have to use it. He didn't know how he would explain to Isa that he killed one of her guardians, but he was here to root out an enemy, and he wouldn't let anything stop him.

He stepped back and examined a few more. Just to see if he could find anything better.

"Don't move," Isa hissed.

A tip of a sword pressed into the small of his back.

To Be Continued...

CHAPTER 1

*L*iam dropped the dagger and put his hands up. The tip of Isa's sword bit into his back. "This is not what it looks like."

He tried to keep his breathing even. She could put the sword through him if she was as deadly as her people claimed. He swallowed. He had to play this right.

"It looks like my guardians were correct about you." Her voice was low and deadly. Maybe he was wrong about her. He'd really thought she was a good person.

"Can I explain?"

"You better, quickly."

He shifted forward and turned around to face her. This wasn't much better as the sword pointed straight at his heart. She stood tall and confidently. He had no doubt that if she chose, she'd run that sword right through him. Her angry eyes penetrated him, made more visible with her hair pulled away from her face. His breath caught. He'd always found her beautiful, but this was different. This woman was a warrior, not a queen.

"I got into a fight with one of your guardians. I need to be able to protect myself. I know you threatened them, but they aren't afraid of you."

"You have no marks on you. You're lying." She did not move the sword at all. He thought about pushing it away, but he was afraid he might lose his arms. He spotted Missy behind Isa but kept his focus on the woman with the sword.

"It wasn't a long fight, and they got me in the gut, not the face." He hoped she wouldn't go asking the guardians about the fight because this was a lie, and he needed her to believe him.

Liam watched her eyes. He could see her thinking. He could try to convince her that he wasn't lying, but it might be better to let her think it through. She threatened her guards, which meant she didn't trust them completely either.

"Who did you fight with?" she finally asked.

"I can't remember his name. But it doesn't matter. What matters is that I'm not comfortable wandering your castle unarmed. I want to carry a dagger. Just in case."

She lowered her sword a little. "I don't want you carrying a weapon no one can see, but perhaps you are right about being armed. Do you know your way around a sword?"

"Yes, very well."

"Fine. Put the dagger away and choose a sword instead. If you are to be armed, everyone will know it. Nothing hidden."

He let out a breath of relief. He preferred the dagger, but he'd take the sword and live to see another day.

"Thank you."

She gave a stiff nod. "Know this. If you plan on hurting me, I am a master at swordplay. You won't win."

He felt a grin forming on his face. "Yeah, perhaps we should spar and see who's better because I'm pretty skilled myself."

"Pick your sword, pretty boy, and then you can walk me to my room. We'll see about sparring. I think you will be sorely disappointed." She smirked at him.

He perused the room, still fully aware that Isa had not put her weapon away. He selected a long sword he could wield with one hand if he wanted. He much preferred short swords, but if he would be carrying it in the open, the long sword looked more threatening. It had a blue hilt and glimmered in the light coming in from the upper windows. He still found it odd that it was light in the middle of the night.

He sheathed the sword and strapped the belt around his waist. He'd never carried one like this before, and it would take some getting used to.

He followed Isa out the door, and they walked quietly to her room. Missy trotted next to him.

Told you she was one of the good guys.

You didn't say much when she had a sword to my back.

I knew she wouldn't hurt you.

Liam didn't though. He wanted to say something to Isa, anything, but he felt like he should wait for her to speak. He was a guest in her home, and she was the queen. Sure, his dad was a king, but here in this castle, things felt different. The people here revered her, and they treated her like royalty. His dad liked things informal.

He'd never been up to Isa's room, and he wondered why she brought him here. She stopped just before she opened the door. He glimpsed Baden hovering above her head. Liam shook his head. Baden should be out spying on the guardians, but instead, he was following Liam. They would have to have a talk about that later.

"Thank you for walking me back. I don't like wandering the halls late at night on my own."

He wanted to bring up that she had been on her own when she found him in the weapons room, but he kept that to himself.

"You're very welcome. I will see you tomorrow at breakfast." He gave a small bow and turned to go. She opened the door, and Liam heard the unmistakable click of a crossbow, a sound he'd been trained to hear by Felix.

He dove at Isa.

They landed hard, and Isa's head cracked on the floor. "Dragon's Teeth!" she yelled.

Liam was more concerned about the crossbow than her head. He jumped up and put a hand on his sword, ready to fight the one who wielded it. But no one was there.

A gleaming black crossbow perched on a stand. Liam stepped toward it and glanced at where it shot. A bolt was lodged between two stones in the hallway.

Isa stood, rubbing the back of her head.

"Are you okay?" he asked.

She nodded and came to where he stood examining the crossbow.

Isa circled it, concern etched on her face. Then she snatched the crossbow off the stand and threw it into the fire. She marched into the hall, wrenched the bolt out of the wall, and tossed it into the flames as well. Her eyes blazed.

"Should I go get Pierre?" he asked her. He had no idea what to make of this. If he hadn't been here, she'd be dead.

She shook her head violently. "Don't tell anyone about this. Swear on the queen's name that you will keep my secret."

"Why?" How could he keep this to himself? She was in danger. The guardians were supposed to be her protectors. They couldn't do that if they didn't know about this.

"Because they'll assume it's you, for one thing. And for another, I don't want to get locked back up. Whoever is after me can get into my room, so there is nothing the guardians can do that will protect me. I'm grateful you were here with me. I will be more cautious on my own. I swear."

"Isa, I worry for your safety." There was no way he could keep this a secret.

"I can protect myself. Promise me you won't say anything." Her eyes pleaded with him.

He didn't like this. Sure, he'd saved her life now, but he was just one person. "I won't tell your guardians." But he would be telling someone. Someone was trying to kill the queen and make it look like it was him.

He stared at the crossbow in the fire. "What does this mean?" he asked.

"It means there is an assassin in the castle."

He was the only new person here, so whoever the assassin was, they'd been here for a very long time, just biding their time.

Isa might not feel a need to do anything, but she hadn't been trained as an assassin. He had.

And he knew that the assassin wouldn't stop until his mission was complete.

CHAPTER 2

*L*iam kept his mouth shut, and at breakfast, Isa didn't say a word about the attempt on her life. Then, she escaped back to her room, and he hadn't seen her since. He tried to find Grace as well, but she was also MIA. He wanted to talk to her about what had happened. After searching for both of them, he went to his room to examine his sword and make sure he knew how to wield it properly.

A few minutes later, someone knocked on the door, and Grace poked her head in. "Isa wants to see you."

"Finally," he muttered and followed her down the hall. He would tell Grace about the attempt on Isa's life, but not here.

"I don't know how you managed to get Isa to let you carry a sword," she said.

He chuckled. "Neither do I, quite frankly."

Grace pushed the door open. "At least, everyone knows not to mess with you."

He followed her into a room he'd never seen before. "Except that I had kinda hoped to keep it quiet. I don't want everyone knowing I have a weapon."

"Shh," Grace said and pointed to the opposite side of the room. Isa stood there, wearing all black with a tight fitted shirt and pants. It was the first time he'd seen her in something other than a dress.

She looked stunning.

He forced his eyes away. The enormous room was tall and wide enough for several dragons to fly comfortably. Light filtered in through windows at the top of the room.

"What is this place?" he asked Grace. He kept his eyes on Isa, who stood next to a barrel of weapons. It looked like she was trying to decide what she wanted.

"It's where Isa trains with the guardians. She learns how to fight dragons. And men." Her lips twitched.

He supposed it made sense. No one would want to fight outside in this weather.

Isa beckoned to him, her eyes dancing. "Time to see if you know how to use that thing." She pointed to his sword.

"I've been thinking. It might not be a good idea to spar." He tried to keep his face serious, but he was having trouble.

She narrowed her eyes. "Why not?"

"Because I don't want to accidentally kill you." He winked at her, and Grace laughed.

"Ah, but if you really know how to use that, then you'll have enough control to make sure that doesn't happen."

He was having trouble concentrating now. Her looks kept throwing him off.

He took his sword out and swiveled it in his hand, not looking at her. "How do I know you won't kill me?"

She approached him and whispered in his ear. "Because if I wanted to kill you, I would've done it last night."

He shivered though he wasn't sure if that was out of fear or desire. She brushed past him and strode about ten feet away, sword raised. "Come, let's see what you're capable of."

Well. She asked for it.

He approached quickly and attacked, hoping to take her off guard, but she dodged, and his sword didn't even make contact with hers.

She came back, sword swinging, and he only just got his up to block it. They spun in circles, swords clanging against one another. He'd fought with Felix on numerous occasions, and he got to the point where he could beat Felix the majority of the time, but Isa was a different force altogether.

She moved with grace and ease. Her sword was lighter than his, and she whipped it around with lightning speed. Even if he were trying, he wouldn't be able to kill her.

But he might be able to beat her.

He ducked and thrust his sword up with enough force that it should've knocked hers out of her hand, but she twisted around and managed to lock their swords together.

He tried to retreat, but she swiveled, causing his wrist to bend until he couldn't stand it anymore.

He dropped his sword, knowing he could duck and catch it, but Isa thrust the tip of her sword into his face.

He looked into her smiling eyes.

"Gotcha." She grinned.

His cheeks burned. He'd been beaten.

By a girl.

CHAPTER 3

"Dragon's teeth! What do you mean someone tried to kill Isa?" Grace picked up another egg and stared at Liam. He perched against the barn door with his arms crossed.

"I just told you. They rigged a crossbow to kill her when she entered her room. She was lucky I was there, or she would've died." A muscle ticked in his jaw.

Grace ignored him for a few moments and continued collecting eggs. She had to think about the ramifications here. Isa's life had always been under threat, but no one had actually tried to kill her before. Was this the betrayal the prophecy spoke of? Was someone she loved trying to kill Isa?

"It's more important than ever that Isa not find out I

can do magic. She'll think it was me. But why are you telling me this? You should be telling the guardians."

"Isa doesn't want me to. Technically, I shouldn't even be telling you, but I need someone to help me find out who's trying to kill her."

"I'm not sure we should hide it from the others." She didn't like all this secrecy. If someone was trying to kill Isa, everyone should know. That would be the only way to keep her safe. She and Liam alone wouldn't be able to protect her.

He glowered at her. "Why?"

"This is a job for the guardians, not me." She thrust a basket at him and pointed to the chickens. "Look, since you are here, you can help."

"This smells awful." He wrinkled up his nose.

"Chickens stink, but their eggs taste good."

He took the basket from her. "Isn't this a little beneath you? I mean, you're Isa's lady-in-waiting."

"I try to help out wherever I can. Isa doesn't keep me all that busy, but the cook and maids do." She stared into a cubby that was covered in chicken poop. It was just her and Liam down here. She waved her hand, using a spell to clear out the poop, but instead, all she got was a face full of hay. She sputtered. She hated it when her spells went wrong. She wanted to ask Liam more about Aspen, to see if she ever had any trouble with her magic, but she didn't.

He snatched an egg out of the hay. "That's good of you. But why won't you help me? It's likely one of the guardians is behind this. I can see where Isa would want to keep this quiet, but surely you don't want to see Isa die."

Grace's insides burned. "Of course I don't want her to die." She'd always looked after Isa, and she'd always known someone could potentially threaten Isa's life, but she'd never thought that person—or dragon—was in the castle. She always assumed it would come from an outside source.

"This isn't just about the threat to her life. Out there, all kinds of rumors circle about her being an evil witch, which we both know she's not. We need to figure out who's really in charge. I'd bet anything they're behind the attack on Isa."

A hen pecked at Grace's hand, and she jerked it back to find a red mark forming on the stinging skin. She spun on Liam. "What rumors? What do you mean?"

Liam let out a sigh and set down his basket. "I know. I haven't talked about this much. The rebels want to kill her. You knew this already. But have you ever thought about why? It's not because they want her job. It's because they think she's killing them and stealing their babies."

That's ridiculous. Isa wasn't killing babies. The rebels were just out for her throne. "You're lying."

"I'm not."

She marched up to him. Something wasn't adding up. Liam would never be here helping Isa if he thought those things about her. "So why, in the queen's name, are you here? Tell me the truth."

He ran a hand through his hair. "Why? That's a good question." He slumped on a wooden crate. "Nothing is as I expected it to be. You want the truth. I was sent to find out what was going on and kill Isa if she was evil.

"But you know what? That's not even the whole truth. I wasn't supposed to come. Just my mentor, but the guardians killed him, and I couldn't leave without avenging his death. I want to help Isa, and I don't feel right leaving without figuring out why everyone thinks she's evil. And now, I have to protect her from whoever wants to kill her."

Grace mulled those words over. She should be grateful he confided in her, but she felt burdened. Now, she would have to help him. Her mission was to protect the humans, and if someone was trying to overthrow Isa, then perhaps they were the evil ones, and she wouldn't have to kill Isa in the end.

Because she always feared killing Isa would be the end game. But now, Liam was giving her an opportunity to find a different end game.

"Okay, I'll help you."

He jumped up and gave her a hug. "Thank you. I wasn't sure I could do this on my own."

She extracted herself. "First, though, you have to help me find all the eggs."

He grabbed his basket, a smile on his face, and went hunting for eggs.

CHAPTER 4

Nearly three weeks had gone by, and there was still no word on how Liam was doing. Sid had to be patient, but patience wasn't exactly his forte. He felt like all they'd been doing was spinning their wheels. Jens had been on his case to do more, but he wasn't about to send more dragons over there until he had more information.

Which meant waiting for Baden to come back.

Sid jerked open the door to the Purple Dragon. He needed to talk to Ella. She was someone who hadn't been in the middle of everything, and he just wanted a new perspective. His entire world had gone belly up, and he didn't even know what to do anymore. Liam was deep in the lair of the enemy and could die at any moment.

And Sid wouldn't even know it.

The thought haunted his every step.

It was mid-afternoon and quiet in the shop. Ella waved him over to a table where she and Freddie sat, chatting with Jens. Sid gritted his teeth. If not for Jens, Liam wouldn't be in the position he's in because they never would've known about the European dragons at all. He gave Jens a room at his house, but Jens had basically stayed out of his way. He knew Aspen talked with him occasionally though.

Jens gave him a nod as he sat.

"Any word?" Ella asked.

Sid shook his head, and Jens took a sip of his coffee. "She's going to kill him." He stated the words like it was just polite conversation.

Sid clenched his fists and scowled at Jens. "Liam is resourceful and smart. He'll figure it out."

Ella gripped his hand. "But he's still a kid. If Damon was over there, I'd be a wreck."

Sid didn't want to think about what could be happening with Liam. "I am. Damon's been spending a lot of time at our house."

"At least he's not going after Liam. I thought he might try." Her face relaxed a little.

"I would be more worried if he was a dragon, but as a human, he wouldn't get anywhere near the castle where Liam is held," Jens said.

Ella let out a sigh. "I wouldn't put it past him to try. Liam is his best friend, and those two always found a way to work around his limitations. Though, if he ever found a way to become a dragon, he'd sacrifice everything for it. I guarantee it."

Jens leaned back and stroked his chin. "Interesting. I didn't realize any humans were so eager to join us."

"Just those who are closest to us. I'm sure if Aspen thought there was a way, she'd sign up, too," Sid said.

"Well, since it's impossible, we'll just have to utilize the dragons we have. When are you attacking the castle?"

And lose more people? Sid gripped his cup. They needed to have a solid plan before that happened. Plus, he needed to get Liam out of there before they attacked the queen or her people could kill him. "I haven't decided to attack the castle."

Jens let out an exasperated sigh. "That's the only way to take her out."

"She's killed everyone I've sent except Liam and Baden. I'm not risking any more lives. Plus, as long as Liam is still alive, we aren't doing anything but finding a way to get him out of there alive."

Jens pounded a fist on the table. "You have to. Every day we put it off is one more day that my people have to live in oppression. You sent your people over there. You know what it's like. You are the king of the free world, and no one else can help us."

"I will. But for now, we need to think about more stealth strategies."

Jens stood, his chair clattering to the ground. "Stealth

didn't work for you the first time, and it certainly won't the second. You want to see more people die, keep doing it this way. You want to win? Send an army."

Jens turned and stormed from the shop.

Ella waited until the door slammed behind him. "He's right, you know."

Sid dropped his head into his hands. "I know. But I can't risk Liam's life."

CHAPTER 5

Grace led Liam to her room. This discussion required privacy. "You know this could potentially start all kinds of rumors." She pushed the door open and waved him in. Then, she locked it and sealed it with magic.

"Then, why did you bring me here?" He examined the humble surroundings. She never thought much about her room, but now it gave her pause. Her small bed, low to the floor, her scratched-up armoire and dresser, and the rough stone walls. It wasn't much, but it was hers. She loved it all, actually.

"Because this is the only room in the castle that I truly believe will keep our secrets. And if someone is trying to kill Isa, then we need to keep everything close to us. You already know I can keep a secret, and I know you can."

He sat in a small chair next to the fireplace, and she on her bed, crossing her legs. "So, what do you think we should do?" she asked.

"That depends on who we think is pulling the strings. My money is on Pierre."

Grace frowned. She'd never liked Pierre much, but she didn't think he'd want to hurt Isa.

Graced fiddled with the edge of her pillowcase. "And what do you think we should do about him?"

He creased his eyebrows. "Nothing yet. We need to find out if he is the bad guy or not."

"But how?" At least Liam wasn't about to go after a man he didn't know was guilty or not. She knew there was a reason she liked him.

He shrugged and frowned at her. "I don't know. That's why I came to you."

"Didn't you say you were training to be a spy? Shouldn't you have ideas?"

He should be better at this. She didn't even know why he needed her help.

"My training was far from complete. My mentor trained me first on how to kill. Though Isa did kick my butt sparring, so I'm not sure I'm as good as I thought I was."

Grace chuckled. "Isa could kick anyone's butt. I bet you're better than you think."

"That still doesn't help us. How will we know if Pierre is doing it or not?"

A knock sounded on Grace's door, and her eyes widened. "Quick, hide," she hissed. She pointed to the armoire, and he stood behind it where he wasn't visible.

She cracked open the door. Benjamin stood there, holding a basket of strawberries. His face flushed. "We had a few extras, so I brought you some."

"Thank you." She took them from him.

"No problem. What are you up to?"

"Just resting. Isa kept me up late last night." She faked a yawn.

Benjamin frowned and craned his neck to look past her. He or Olga saw Liam come down here, and now he was snooping. She clenched her jaw and bit back a snarky comment.

"Do you want to go for a walk or something?"

"No. I really just want a nap. Thank you for the strawberries." She held them up and then shut the door, locking it. She sealed it with magic again and leaned against it.

Liam poked his head out. "Is it safe?" he whispered.

"It is." She set the strawberries on her table. "He must have seen you. He and Marissa are probably already gossiping about it."

Liam popped a strawberry into his mouth. "Does gossip move fast around here?"

"Like lightning." She hated that nothing was ever a secret in the castle for very long.

"Then, that's what we'll do."

"What?"

"We'll start a bunch of rumors and see if we can smoke out the traitor."

Grace gaped at him. "That's a brilliant idea." This way, no one would get hurt, and they could still find out what was going on.

But what kind of rumors were they going to start?

CHAPTER 6

Grace stared at Liam as he sprawled on her bed, his hands behind his head. Good thing he wasn't lying there when Benjamin poked his head in or the rumors would really fly. She didn't want that. They had to concentrate on rumors to out the person trying to kill Isa.

"Any ideas what rumors to start?" Grace asked.

"Yeah, the obvious one. Isa is going to kill Pierre."

"That's horrible." She didn't want anyone thinking bad things about Isa. Grace threw another log on the fire.

"It is. But if Pierre is in charge, and he thinks she'll kill him, nothing will out him faster." Liam took out a small kitchen knife and threw it in the air. Grace watched him. He caught it every time, but she hoped he wasn't counting on her magic to save him if he stabbed himself.

She shook her head and concentrated on the issue at hand. "But if he's not, then he'll be terrified she'll hurt him."

"Except it will just be a rumor, like you and me sleeping together. Pierre might not even believe that Isa wants to kill him, but in case it's not him, we should plant rumors about others too."

Grace tapped a finger on her nose while she thought. The knife went in the air again, and he caught it by the handle. "Maybe we should say that you are going to kill the queen."

He chuckled. "That one is already out there."

"Sure, but you've quashed it at every turn. Now you won't. Let people accuse you of it. Then whoever is trying to hurt her might try to team up with you."

He caught the knife again and sat up. "That's a good point. I'll deny it in certain company and leave it ambiguous with others."

Grace chewed on her lip. "We should do one more. It's a rumor that's already starting, but I think we should encourage it." She hesitated a few moments.

Liam turned his head. "Out with it already."

She didn't want to accuse him of anything, but she was curious. Plus, it was a good rumor, thanks to Jude.

"That you want to marry her."

He gave a crooked smile. "That's floating around already, is it?"

She creased her eyebrows. "Yeah. You don't seem bothered by it."

"I'm not. Jude got all pissy with me one night, and I was just messing with him. So, I'm the one that started it. But why do you think it's a good rumor to feed?"

"Well, if Isa plans to marry you, whoever is doing the ruling will be threatened by it. They might not be able to control you, and they might try to end her or you before you can seal the deal."

"Okay then. Three rumors to out the bastard. Time to get to work."

He pocketed his knife and sauntered out of the room.

Grace stood at the door and watched him ascend the steps. She wasn't sure this was a good idea because it could all come back to her. But she was involved, and they couldn't turn back now.

CHAPTER 7

"Lady Grace, wait up," Jude called from behind her.

She spun, her heart racing. Though she wasn't sure if that was because she liked him or because she was about to feed him lies. She'd been having second thoughts about the plan ever since Liam left her room, but she'd committed to it, so it was now or never.

Jude smiled as he approached.

"What's up?" she asked. She found herself fiddling with the edge of her hair, and she clasped her hands. She didn't know she'd become such a girl.

His brow furrowed, and she had to resist touching the adorable crease it made on his forehead.

"Nothing, I just wanted to talk to you. I saw you with Liam earlier."

She suppressed a smile. "Oh, yeah. He was asking me things about Isa."

Jude frowned. "Like what?"

"Like her favorite foods and things that would make her feel special."

"He did? That bastard." Jude glowered.

Grace cocked her head. "What's wrong with that? It just sounds like he's being nice."

Jude gave an angry shake of his head. "Dragon's Teeth! He's just using her. Excuse me, I have an American dragon ass to kick." He started walking away, but she put a hand on his arm.

"Jude. Don't. I think he's genuine."

"I don't. I think he wants her position. The power. And that will never happen on my watch. He's working for the rebels." His face twisted in anger.

Grace shook her head. "Speaking of power... I heard Pierre is overstepping his."

Jude's mouth dropped open. "Where did you hear that? The prick Liam again?"

"No, Isa. But I probably shouldn't have said anything. Sorry, I should go." She raced away from Jude before he could ask any more questions.

Let him come up with his own conclusions.

"Where, in the queen's name, did all these strawberries come from?" Olga asked. "I'm making strawberry shortcake tonight, strawberry pie tomorrow, and strawberry cake the night after that. And everyone gets strawberries in their cereal in the morning."

Grace giggled at the mounds of strawberries in the kitchens. She didn't mind. Next to cherries, they were her favorite fruit.

Marissa pushed a bowl toward her. "Here, help de-stem these."

"Sure." Grace rolled her eyes.

Marissa wanted something from her. Again. Marissa never asked her for help or acknowledged her most days. She'd just have to wait and see what Marissa said. The room was silent for a few moments. "I heard you and Liam are getting mighty cozy."

That rumor again. Ah, well, she could fix this. "No. I'm just helping him with Isa. He's totally smitten."

"She'll just use him and spit him out like all the other boys," Olga said. Grace didn't know where she was coming up with that. As far as Grace knew, Jude was the only boy Isa had been with.

"I don't know. She seems to really like him." Grace hesitated for dramatic effect. "If I tell you something, do you promise not to tell anyone?"

Both Olga and Marissa stopped what they were doing and stared at her. "You know I can keep a secret. Out with it, girl," Olga said.

"Well, Isa and I were chatting, and Olga, you might be making a wedding cake sooner rather than later."

Olga dropped her bowl of strawberries, and Marissa let out a squeak. "No way. I don't believe it."

"Believe it," Grace said.

"Maybe he'll tame her after all." Olga picked up a few of the strawberries that fell out of the bowl.

"Or he'll kill her," Marissa said matter-of-factly.

"Where did you hear that?" Grace wasn't sure what to think about this.

"Oh, come on, everyone knows he might kill her." She shook her head.

"I guess that's possible. He's awfully secretive." Grace pretended to ponder. "You don't think he wants to marry her just to become king and then do away with her?" Guilt settled in Grace's stomach. She hated doing this.

Marissa continued to de-stem her strawberries. "That's a likely scenario."

Grace tried to hide her grin. So far, the rumor mills were churning.

They were going to out the traitor.

CHAPTER 8

Sid entered the kitchen and found Aspen nursing a cup of coffee. She much preferred going to the Purple Dragon and getting various mochas and lattes, but these days, she stayed home most mornings.

Sid grabbed a mug out of the cupboard and poured his own cup. Aspen looked up at him when he sat down.

"I've been talking to Jens," she said.

He raised his eyebrows. "Really?"

She sighed. "He's our guest."

"I'm beginning to not trust the guy."

Aspen fiddled with her cup. She wouldn't meet his eyes. "I don't see why not. He's just passionate about saving his people. Anyway, I talk to him more about everyday life and things, and I lay awake last night thinking about something."

Sid held his breath for a moment. Whenever she used those words, it meant he probably wouldn't approve of what came out next. That hadn't changed in the twenty-two years she'd been queen. She always had some crazy idea.

"What's that?" he finally asked because he knew he couldn't stop her.

"We should tell Jens about the babies."

The babies had been a secret from even his own people. Aside from the dragons taking care of them and the council, no one knew about them. They were dragons thought to be extinct, and until they were older and they knew their powers and abilities, Sid wanted them kept hidden from all prying eyes.

"Why?" He couldn't figure out why she'd be so flippant with their identity.

"Because they are his people. The purple and green dragons came from Europe. He deserves to know about them."

Sid sighed and rubbed his forehead. "I don't think this is a good idea. We don't know anything about him except what he told us about the queen. We don't even know if he is genuine."

"Correction. You don't know anything about him. I do. And I trust him, and I think we should tell him. Maybe even take him to meet them. If the tables were turned, I'd want to know."

He shook his head, and Aspen let out a breath of exasperation. "Why don't we show him around Yellowstone today, and you can get to know him better. Maybe then, you'll understand why we should tell him."

Sid met her defiant eyes. He had to indulge this, or she'd go off and tell him on her own. "Fine. But I'm not making any promises." He didn't see how this would possibly change his mind.

Sɪᴅ, Aspen, and Jens stood outside Sid's house. "I would like to show you around the park if that's okay," Sid said.

Jens scratched his chin. "No offense, but I'm not here on a sightseeing trip. Plus, I've been here for a few weeks now. I've shown myself around."

Aspen chuckled. "We know. But we want to talk to you, and we figured you would enjoy a drive around Yellowstone while we are talking. There's no place on Earth like it."

Jens hesitated but then climbed into the Jeep. Sid wasn't sure why he was wary of a drive, but the man's nerves were on edge. Jens was staying at his house, but Sid hadn't really tried to befriend the man. He'd gotten the feeling it was mutual. Sid was too distracted by Liam, which he still felt was Jens' fault. But, Aspen had the right idea. He should get to know Jens a little better.

The spring thaw was well underway. The roads were

fairly clear, and the animals were beginning to come out of hibernation. The floor of Yellowstone looked much different than it had twenty-two years ago.

The royal dragons now lived openly, and so it was common to see them sleeping in a field or capturing a buffalo for dinner. People were allowed to approach the dragons, so often, dragons would have a crowd of tourists around them taking pictures.

They turned onto the loop, and Jens spotted a dragon in a field with a human scrambling off his back. He did a double-take. Sid supposed it would look strange to see how easily humans and dragons interacted now.

"Why have you brought me on this drive? Have you come to your senses? Are you ready to attack?"

Sid gripped the steering wheel. "My son is trapped at the castle with the queen."

"You need to realize that he will die," Jens spat out. "How many times do I have to say that?"

Sid clenched his jaw. "He is resourceful. We have an underground dragon there with him, trying to help him escape."

Jens swiveled in his seat. "She is a monster. If you had any prayer of bringing your son home, you would've sent an army."

This was not how Sid had envisioned the conversation going. "I've been king for a long time. I trust my own decisions."

"You do not understand. She enslaved us. Most of my friends and family are trapped as humans. She would have us all die."

Sid frowned. "I know that. But I'm trying to figure out her motives. We'll be better prepared to take her on if we understand why she does what she does."

"Why did the white witch fight you?" Jens voice was earnest.

"Because she wanted to control the human and dragon race. It sounds like your queen doesn't even leave her castle."

"She controls us through her guards, and I dare say if she thought she could, she'd try to control you as well. She fears us. But we don't have the numbers to overtake her. Too many of us died in the rebellion, and those who do not wish to risk their lives will not help us. Before she forced us to live as humans, she stole all of our eggs and now keeps them in the castle. If someone manages to mate, and the child is born as a human, they take him away the day he is born. I don't know how she knows or what she does with them."

This was more than Jens had said in all the weeks he'd been there.

They drove around a bend, and Sid tried to process all that he said, but it still made no sense. Sid didn't understand why the queen was behaving the way she was, and he felt blind. There seemed to be no purpose to her cruelty.

Aspen poked her head between the seats. "Why does she want to control your lives?"

Maybe now she saw the wisdom in keeping her mouth shut about the eggs. They couldn't add that into the mix right now.

"I don't know. I do know she is the third generation queen. Her mother died when she was young, and her grandmother passed away a few years ago. Things got infinitely worse when her grandmother took over as queen. We hoped things would get better when she died, but the new queen seems to be just as brutal."

"How did her grandmother die?"

"The rebels. I wasn't with them on that trip, but they all died. It's why the rest of the European dragons won't help us anymore. Once we killed her grandmother, things didn't get better, and we did not gain control. You have to send an army in. I've watched the videos of the war here. One that big cannot fail."

Sid shook his head. "Not as long as she has my son hostage. I don't even know if you're telling me the truth. If she's so vicious and cruel, why is Liam still alive?" Something wasn't adding up.

Jens gripped his hair. "I don't know what else I can say. Donohue's daughter was slaughtered because he spoke to some Americans about us. They murdered my mate because she refused to give up our eggs."

Tears streamed down the poor man's face.

Aspen squeezed his shoulder and met Sid's eyes defiantly in the rearview mirror. "Well, we have some good news for you. The queen is not the only one with a stash of eggs. We have some green and purple eggs too."

CHAPTER 9

Sid was going to kill Aspen. He had to bite his tongue so he didn't snap at her in front of Jens. He gripped the steering wheel and tried to calm the rage. She thought she was doing the right thing, but she trusted way too easily.

Jens craned his neck back, his tears suddenly disappearing. "What do you mean?"

Sid gave a slight shake of his head in the rearview mirror, and Aspen visibly swallowed. "Well, after the first dragon wars, several of your people populated the west coast of America, but as a mixed-race of purple and green. But the white witch and the canyon dragons annihilated them. Once the war was over, we went hunting for eggs and found a stash of pure purple and pure green."

At least she didn't tell him they'd hatched them. Thank goodness for small miracles.

Jens gripped Sid's arm, his eyes flashing. "And what did you do with the eggs?"

The car jerked slightly, and Sid grasped the wheel tighter. "Nothing," he lied. "We have them in a vault."

Aspen sat back and glared at Sid.

Jens snorted. "That is a lie. If you found the eggs, you hatched them. Where are they?"

Sid parked at Old Faithful Lodge. He needed to talk to Jens without worrying he might crash the car. He got out and walked toward Old Faithful without a word. He didn't know how to dig himself out of this hole.

Doors slammed behind him, and Jens rushed to his side. "What are we doing here?"

"I'm showing you Yellowstone's most famous attraction."

Jens threw his hands up in the air. "I don't care about attractions. I want to know what happened to the eggs."

Aspen grabbed Sid's hand, and it took most of his willpower to not pull away. She meant well, but he needed some time to fix this.

"The eggs are safe and protected. That's all that matters. At least until we figure out what to do about your queen."

"No. That is not okay. Those eggs belong to my people. I demand that you give them to me." Jens stomped his foot, glaring at him. Old Faithful erupted, but Jens didn't even give it a glance.

"And what will you do with them? Take them back to Europe and have them all confiscated by the queen? They are fine here. Safe. Let them be," Sid said.

Jens was quiet for a moment. "You are right. They are safe here. But I must see them. Take me there. Now."

Sid took a deep breath. There were too many other things going on for him to worry about the babies as well.

"I will. But not today. It's too late. We will go first thing in the morning." It was a lie, but he had to tell it to get Jens off his back.

CHAPTER 10

*G*race wasn't sure why Isa put Jude right next to her at dinner again, but she was glad. She'd been so caught up in all the drama with Liam that it was nice to just be a girl for a few moments. The rumors were floating around nicely at this point, and so now they were just waiting to see if the enemy would present himself.

Jude speared one of his carrots. "So. You've been spending an awful lot of time with Liam."

She wondered why he even cared about that. "I know. Isa wants me to keep an eye on him." Not completely true, but it was a good excuse and one that Jude wouldn't check on.

Jude snorted. "I thought Isa trusted him completely. She doesn't want anyone keeping an eye on him."

"Says you. How do you know she's not trying to be sneaky about it?"

"Because I know Isa. She's just trying to help you. You like him, don't you?"

Grace swallowed. She hadn't thought Jude would think that.

He flashed his eyes to Liam, who was laughing at something Isa said.

"No. But even if I did, why would you care? You want back in Isa's bed. If I liked him, and he liked me, then maybe she'll call for you again." That came out a little more bitter than she had intended.

Jude gripped his knife and fork harder, and his plate shook as he cut up his roast.

"I do not want to be back in her bed."

She'd hit a nerve, but at this point, she didn't care. Grace knew she and Liam spending so much time together looked bad. That was a sacrifice she'd make to help Isa. Besides, she didn't want Liam. She wanted Jude, but she couldn't very well tell him that. This was a mistake though because she could very well be the one who had to kill him. She wished, not for the first time, that the prophecy had been clearer.

He was silent for several moments, and she ate her carrots and roast. After they finished, Marissa took her plate and set a slice of cherry pie in front of her. Her mouth started watering before she could even get her fork into it.

Jude slid his own plate toward her. "Go on, I know it's your favorite."

She always grabbed the leftovers in the kitchens on cherry pie night. But it was a lot of other people's favorites as well, so she rarely got any extra.

"How did you know it was my favorite?" She couldn't recall ever mentioning it to him before.

He studied her for a long moment. "You really don't remember anything from the night in the gem halls?"

"I don't. What happened?" She was suddenly worried she'd told him she was in love with him, but if all she did was tell him about cherry pie, then she was fine.

He chuckled. "Relax. Nothing happened, but we did talk about our favorite foods, and you went on for about an hour about cherry pie."

She dropped her eyes to the pie. What a silly girl she must've been. "Oh. Sorry."

"It was kinda funny, actually. I couldn't possibly eat mine when I know how much you love it."

Oh, he was so sweet. How did she not realize this about him? "Did you tell me about your favorite dessert?"

"I did. You don't remember?"

She shook her head. "The wine. It made me forget everything."

"Perhaps we should take another late-night stroll down there, and I can tell you again." His voice had gone low and sexy.

Sweat formed on her palms. She wasn't ready for this,

but oh, did she want it. "No wine this time though. I want to remember your favorite dessert."

"No wine. Just me and you." He grinned.

"Sounds like a plan. But I don't think I can wait that long for this particular piece of information."

"Well then, I'll tell you. It's chocolate cake, and I fully expect you to reciprocate when Olga makes that delicious thing next time."

She slid his pie in front of her, having already devoured hers. "You've got yourself a deal."

CHAPTER 11

*L*iam wandered the halls of the castle as he so often did after everyone else went to sleep. They were lit with soft lights and dancing shadows. Some people would be scared of what lurked in the dark, but not Liam. He loved it. He always had.

At home, he'd wander the quiet streets at night. No one ever messed with him, and if they did, he could turn into a dragon.

Here, that was a little more difficult, but he had his sword. He was grateful he had Grace on his side. Maybe, between the two of them, they'd be able to figure out what was really going on in Europe. Because it was fairly clear Isa was not the one controlling everybody. She didn't even seem to know what was going on with her own people.

Or did she?

She might be putting on a show. If she was, it was a good one, fooling even Grace.

He turned the corner and entered a hall with windows high on the wall, light still streaming in even though it was the middle of the night. He wondered what winters were like when it was dark all the time. He'd have to ask Isa.

He liked her, but he wasn't sure why. Liam thought back to the things Felix had taught him.

Never trust anyone.

If they seem too good to be true, they probably are.

Always suspect.

Felix was a little paranoid though, and he never even trusted Liam. Or Sid for that matter. In fact, Felix had once told him that if he discovered that the king was not honorable, he would kill him.

What would Felix have done in this situation?

He certainly wouldn't have killed Isa. He would have befriended and watched her as well as everyone else in the castle. Which was what Liam was doing.

But Liam wasn't dumb. He knew his heart was starting to get in the way, and that might cloud his judgment. He'd never been put off-kilter by a girl before. Even with the ones he liked, he had complete control over the relationship.

This was disconcerting because she made his heart do things it had never done before. And most of his nighttime walks were to try to get her off his mind.

But it never worked. She consumed nearly all his

thoughts. Some of which involved his concern over whether she was killing European dragons in cold blood. But most of them were focused on the way her eyes danced when she looked at him or the graceful way in which her body moved.

He wondered what she thought of him. Grace had warned him that she kept lovers in the castle, but they were playthings and disposable.

It didn't matter. He was here on a mission, and if he let her into his heart, he'd never be able to think clearly about what to do.

Felix had taught him many things: How to watch a room and find men who were lying. How to fight with a sword—though, apparently, not as good as Isa. How to kill a man without him even knowing you were there.

But he never taught Liam what to do if he fell in love with his target.

CHAPTER 12

The next day, Drew led Liam past the large room where he'd fought with Isa. Baden flew above them, and Missy trotted next to him. She was unusually quiet today. Baden had spent the better part of the morning trying to convince Liam to go home, but Liam wasn't ready to do that yet.

"Why aren't we going in there?" He pointed to the large space. When he asked if he could spar with a few guardians, he figured they'd be in there.

"Because only Isa trains in there."

Drew opened the door and led Liam inside. This room was smaller with mirrors along the walls. Barrels were scattered about with long sticks and sparring swords.

To his disappointment, only Benjamin was there.

"Where is everyone?" Liam asked.

Drew chuckled. "No one trusts you not to run a sword straight through their heart, so it's just me and Benjamin."

Liam crossed his arms and scowled. He'd never get good enough to beat Isa, fighting with the cook's son. Benjamin was scrawny and looked like he'd never picked up a sword in his life. He knew he was being a bit judgmental, but really, look at the kid.

"Benjamin," Drew said with a smirk.

"Yeah?" Benjamin jogged up to them. He couldn't weigh more than 130 pounds, dripping wet. Liam would slaughter him.

"Why don't you show our guest here what you can do?"

Benjamin furrowed his eyebrows. "Are you sure?"

Drew nodded.

Benjamin grabbed a few wooden sticks and handed two to Liam. "I like fighting with the sticks so I don't have to hold back."

This kid had to be joking.

"You fight with two?"

Benjamin spun the long sticks in circles, showing skill that Liam immediately envied. "Yeah, don't you?"

Liam rolled his shoulders. "Sure."

He'd never fought with two in his life.

THE DRAGON KINGS BOOK TEN

BENJAMIN KICKED LIAM'S ASS. He'd never seen someone move as this guy did. It was like watching old Jackie Chan movies.

Liam was screwed. Here, he thought that Felix had trained him well, but Felix hadn't taught him anything.

Benjamin held his hand out. "You okay?"

Liam took it. "Yeah, though my pride is hurt. Who trains you all?"

"Pierre," Drew said from the other side of the room. "Benjamin isn't a dragon, but we're all trained to protect the queen. Even Grace. Though she trains on her own. She doesn't like Pierre much. She and Isa spar sometimes."

Grace was becoming more interesting by the moment. She'd never mentioned not liking Pierre.

"Well, I pity the fool who would try to come in and hurt the queen."

Benjamin dumped the sticks into a bucket. "We all thought that was you."

Liam grabbed a cloth from a shelf and wiped the sweat off his face. "Ah, come on. You know that's not true. I wanted to help her."

Drew leaned against the door. "That's not what I heard."

"What did you hear?"

"I heard you want to marry her."

Liam scoffed, but he was pleased with how well the rumors flew. Grace had definitely done her thing well.

"Really? I mean, she's gorgeous and all, but she's dangerous." Drew narrowed his eyes, and Liam backtracked. "Not dangerous enough to kill. But she's got a temper; you can't deny that. Look, I don't mean to start things, but I heard that she was fed up with the way the guardians are trying to control her and wants to get rid of them."

Drew snorted. "Where did you hear that?"

Liam smirked. "Where did you hear that I wanted to marry her?"

"Point taken. You ready to spar with me? I won't be as nice to you as Benjamin."

"Bring it." Liam grinned.

They both unsheathed their swords. This was how Liam wanted to practice. Not with sticks. Though he could learn a thing or two from Benjamin.

Rumors were being planted and were spreading. Hopefully, they'd out the traitor in no time.

CHAPTER 13

"Close the door, would you?" Pierre asked Isa, looking worried.

Isa shut the door behind her after Missy followed her in. It was strange meeting Pierre, one on one. He usually had other guardians with him, but today, he was alone in the guardians' study.

Pierre sat by the fire, holding a glass of whiskey, and he pointed to the chair across from him.

"I know you prefer wine." He motioned to the decanter and glass on the table.

"I do." Isa sat, and Missy jumped onto her lap. This was odd. She hadn't met with him like this since the day her grandmother had been killed. Maybe that's why she didn't like this room. It's where he broke the news.

He poured her a glass of wine and sat back in his chair, sighing. "I'm concerned."

"About?"

"You gave Liam a sword."

"To protect himself from the guardians who want to kill him."

"He'll use it to kill you."

Isa rolled her eyes and nearly stood back up and left. "Is that what this is all about?" She was tired of everyone accusing him of nefarious plots. She liked Liam a lot. Probably more than she should.

"You mock, but I take your safety very seriously." He sighed in exasperation.

She shouldn't have to set this record straight again, but she would. As often as she needed to. "He won't hurt me."

Pierre scowled. "How do you know?"

"Because he's had plenty of opportunities, and he's never done anything to me. I believe he is who he says he is, and he wants to help me. Help us."

Pierre scowled and stared into the fire. "We don't know anything about him. There is no way to know if we can trust him or not. I don't."

"And I do. My opinion is the one that matters, isn't it?" She didn't like using the queen card, but it was the only one that worked as of late. Besides, she was nearly of age, and then they would have to listen to her. She had to make sure they saw her as a leader and not a puppet.

"Dragon's Teeth Isa. You aren't seeing sense. Maybe he's

a good guy, and maybe he's not, but that's no reason to arm him."

Isa didn't know what other argument to make. Her guardians had been exhibiting strange behaviors, and so she clung to what she knew. They'd been overprotective and secretive. If something were to happen, she'd trust Liam and Grace by her side before most of her guardians. Pierre was blind to it all.

"Look, you didn't disagree when I said he needed to protect himself from the guardians. That means you know they were threatening him. A sword, openly carried, will protect him. I didn't give him a dagger or anything he could conceal."

"But he could kill you."

She chuckled. "He couldn't actually. I sparred with him the other day."

Pierre dropped his glass. It shattered into a thousand pieces, and Isa shrieked. Pierre stood up, eyes blazing. "You did what?"

Missy nudged Isa's hand, and Isa started petting her. "We sparred. And he's not very good. He's obviously not been training for more than a couple of years. I destroyed him."

Pierre paced the room in front of her. "Of all the idiotic things you have done in your years, that one tops them. You know what's at stake. You cannot put yourself at such risk. What, in the queen's name, were you thinking?"

"I knew what I was doing, and I was not at risk. I could

run him through with my sword if he even showed an inkling of a desire to hurt me, but he never has. You need to back off, or I will replace you." Oops. She didn't mean to say that last part.

He glowered at her. She hated making threats against him, but he was being completely unreasonable.

But then he gave a quick bow of the head. "Yes, Your Majesty."

Pierre picked up another glass and poured whiskey into it. He sat down and stared at her, his eyes softening. She had to find something else they could speak about so this meeting wouldn't end on a sour note.

"Now, tell me the affairs of my kingdom. We haven't spoken of those in some time."

CHAPTER 14

*L*iam couldn't find Isa anywhere. He checked with Grace, but she hadn't seen Isa since breakfast. He went to her room, the sparring rooms, the library, and her tower.

And now, Grace was checking the baths. She pushed open the door to the hall where he had been pacing.

"She's not there either. Just relax. She's fine. Isa likes her privacy, and so she'll often take Missy and hide in a random room. This is not that unusual."

"Right. That was before we knew someone was trying to kill her." He rubbed at his chest. Worrying over others was new for him. Ugh. He hated being compromised, but he totally was. At this point, he should pack it up and go home, but he couldn't leave her now.

Grace put a hand on his arm. "She's fine. I promise. Go read a book or something, and I'll send her to you as soon as I find her."

He nodded but knew that would never happen. He hadn't talked to any of the guardians other than Drew, but he had a feeling one would know where she was. They didn't guard her like that just to let her disappear randomly in the castle. They probably wouldn't tell him, but he was good at spotting liars.

He went up three flights of stairs and down another long hallway toward the guardians' study. He'd only been in there once.

Seamus stood outside the room. If Liam could find a way to blame everything on him, he would. But Liam couldn't let his grudges get in the way either. He steeled himself and approached the poor excuse of a man.

He reached around for the door handle, but Seamus hit him away. "What do you think you are doing?"

"Going to talk to Pierre. Do you protect him too?"

Seamus stood there, all cocky-like. "You can't go in there."

Like hell he couldn't.

"Last I checked, Isa said I could go everywhere. Who are you to stop me?"

Seamus pushed him. "Look, you little bastard, I said you can't go in there, and so you can't."

"Oh yeah? Stop me." He shoved Seamus aside and reached for the door, but Seamus tackled him. He hit the ground hard, his head cracking on the stone. For a second, his vision blurred, but then he saw an opening. He punched Seamus in the nose.

Seamus howled with pain but pummeled him in the stomach.

CHAPTER 15

Grace stopped and pretended to polish a vase so she could eavesdrop on a conversation.

"Do you think we should tell him?" Bartlby asked. He was an older guardian who Grace had never really known, but he was always polite when she served him.

Drew rubbed a hand along his face. "That rumors are flying about Isa wanting to kill him?"

They had to be talking about Pierre. Grace wasn't sure how Liam got that particular rumor going because Grace just alluded to it.

"Yes. You don't think she does? Do you?" Bartlby rubbed his hands together nervously.

"Well, she did threaten him. She's been all out of sorts

since Liam showed up. I have no idea what Isa wants anymore."

"We should tell him."

Drew rubbed his chin. "But what if it's not true?"

"Well, we should tell him it's just a rumor. Let him figure out what to do with it."

They walked away from Grace, and she couldn't follow them, or it would look suspicious. She went down the hall and found Jude pacing in an empty room.

She debated passing him but decided to see what he'd heard. She slipped into the room, and he stopped, his face full of worry.

"Hey, stranger. Just wondering when we are going on that walk in the gem halls." She kept her voice light. Something was obviously bothering him.

He gave her a tight smile. "Sorry, I've been distracted."

"What's on your mind?"

"Should I tell Isa about Liam?"

"What about Liam?"

"That he wants to be king."

Grace let out a breath. She wasn't sure what the right answer was for this one. They'd wanted to smoke out the bad guy, but she didn't know how telling Isa would be helpful. Isa was the victim here. Plus, it might hurt Liam and Isa's relationship, and Grace didn't want that.

"I don't know. Do you think she'll believe you?"

"Maybe. Maybe not. But either way, she deserves to know.

I just don't want her to shoot the messenger." Jude clenched and unclenched his fists. "Overall though, I don't think Liam wants to hurt her. But she should know what he's up to?"

Grace creased her eyebrows. "Since when do you trust Liam?"

"I don't. But maybe I've been overreacting."

Grace didn't know what to think. It was odd, Jude confiding in her. She liked it. "I thought you were in love with Isa."

"Me too. But I realized I'm not. If Liam is on the up and up, then who am I to stand in their way? But if he's not. I owe it to Isa."

Indeed he did.

But Grace still wasn't convinced he should tell her.

It would upset the balance in the castle.

Again.

CHAPTER 16

Something hit the door hard. "What was that?" Pierre asked, standing abruptly.

"I don't know." Isa's heart thumped.

She set Missy down and followed him to the door of the study, and Pierre put a hand out. "Stay back, in case it's dangerous."

Isa rolled her eyes but stood back while Pierre cracked the door open. The noises got infinitely louder, and Isa peered around him.

Liam and Seamus were rolling around on the ground, punching each other. Dragon's teeth! She shoved past Pierre, and he rushed out after her.

"Stop," she shouted, but neither of them acknowledged her. She grabbed at Liam's shoulders, and Pierre yanked

Seamus back. The fighting pair stood, both red-faced and breathing hard.

"Explain yourselves," Isa demanded, not letting go of Liam.

"He was trying to get into the study. I stopped him." Seamus wiped a hand along his nose, smearing blood everywhere.

"He threatened me. I was just protecting myself." Liam's face and hair were completely messed up. Missy sat next to him, her beady eyes on Seamus.

"Liar," Seamus growled.

Isa actually bet on Seamus telling the truth, but she was certain Liam had a good reason for wanting to get in, which he would tell her later. She knew he didn't trust any of the guardians, not after the crossbow incident.

She looked at both Seamus and Liam. At least swords weren't drawn.

Jude and a few of the older guardians turned the corner and approached them. "What's going on?" Jude said.

"This prick tried to break into the study." Seamus held his nose with his hand, and blood seeped past it.

"Why were you guarding it anyway?" Liam asked, shaking off Isa.

Yep. He was definitely lying about the self-defense.

"Because Pierre wanted to talk to Isa without being interrupted."

Jude scowled at Pierre, and Isa wondered what that was

all about. But now was not the time. She had to diffuse this situation and fast.

"See, Pierre, this is why I allow Liam to carry a sword." She waved at Seamus. "The guardians are bullying him."

Pierre leveled a look at her. "Your Majesty, you don't really believe his story. He obviously provoked Seamus."

"I did not. I was just walking past, and Seamus goaded me." Liam folded his arms and stood tall.

Oh, he was good. She had to give him that.

"That's not what happened," Seamus yelled.

"If Liam says you goaded him, then that is exactly what happened." Isa enjoyed taking Liam's side over Seamus.

Pierre sighed and ran a hand through his hair. "Isa, you've got to stop thinking with your heart and start thinking with your mind."

All eyes turned to her, and her cheeks flamed. She wanted to look at Liam and see his reaction, but she was too embarrassed. Instead, she kept her eyes on Pierre.

"Keep your guardians in check, Pierre. Jude, will you help Seamus clean up? I'm taking Liam. It was a pleasure speaking with you, Pierre. I hope we can do it more often."

She grabbed Liam's hand and pulled him away from the rest. She tried not to think about how much she enjoyed his hand in hers. Maybe Pierre was right. Maybe she was thinking too much with her heart.

Isa waited until they turned the corner so no guardians could hear them.

"Missy, go get Lady Grace and bring her to my room." The bottle brush tail disappeared around a corner.

Isa stopped and examined Liam's face. It didn't look too worse for the wear though his eye would bruise, and he had a small cut on his chin. He didn't say anything. But his eyes never left hers. She could get lost in those eyes.

"Come on, let's get you cleaned up." She found herself wanting to take his hand again, but that might be a little awkward. She loved the way it felt in hers... like it belonged there.

He followed her to her room, and they'd barely crossed the threshold when Grace raced up the stairs.

"What happened to you?" she blurted when she saw Liam.

"I got into a fight with Seamus," he said with pride.

Grace chuckled. "Of course you did."

Isa wasn't sure she was comfortable with the easiness Liam and Grace had. She was a tad jealous and didn't like it.

"Grace, can you bring warm water and bandages?" Isa asked.

Grace nodded, winked at Liam, and rushed from the room.

"Do you like her?" Isa asked as soon as Grace was out of earshot.

"Grace? She's fantastic. She's been the one person, aside from you, who treats me like a human being. But if you're asking if I like her in a romantic sense, no. She's not my type. But I do consider her a good friend."

Isa let out a breath of relief, quietly. She didn't want Liam thinking she had feelings for him.

"That's a shame. She's quite a catch, and she's had trouble with a few of the guardians. She could use a good man."

Liam didn't respond, and Isa helped him take off his sword. He winced.

"Looks like your face didn't get all the injuries." Isa never understood a guy's need to punch each other when they got mad.

He grimaced. "No. My ribs certainly took a pummeling."

"Let's see it then."

"What? My ribcage?"

"Yes."

He gripped the edge of his shirt, but when he tried to pull it over his head, he dropped it, his face contorting in pain.

"What's the matter?" Isa asked.

"It hurts. Can you help me?"

Isa's fingers brushed the edge of his back when she grabbed the shirt, and he hissed.

"I'm sorry. Did that hurt?"

He shook his head. "I just wasn't expecting it."

She tried to hold back her grin, but she wasn't sure she'd accomplished that.

She pushed his shirt up and over his head, and he shook it down his arms. She stared at his chest. She had an excuse, looking for injuries, but she very much appreciated what she saw. Dragon's teeth that man was beautiful. In spite of him not being all that good at sword fighting, he was all muscle. But bright purple bruises were forming along his ribs.

Grace came into the room, sloshing water everywhere. "Seamus did a number on you."

Isa wasn't all that surprised. The boys had been gunning for each other for a while now.

"Pretty sure Seamus got it worse." Liam smirked, and Grace giggled.

"Lady Grace, leave us, please. I'll attend to his injuries myself." She had to figure out what was really going on here.

Grace met Liam's eyes but left the room quickly, shutting the door behind her.

"I didn't realize you were that eager to get me half-naked and alone in your room." He gave her a cheeky grin, his pretty blue eyes mesmerizing her.

Isa's cheeks blazed.

"That's not why I sent her out." She couldn't let him distract her now.

"Are you sure? Pierre did accuse you of thinking with your heart instead of your mind."

She glowered at him, and he smiled again. She dipped a rag into the warm water and set to cleaning his wounds.

"No, I wanted you alone because I need you to tell me why you were trying to get into the study. I don't, for one minute, believe you were defending yourself. Seamus may be hotheaded, but he wouldn't leave the door unprovoked."

Liam winced when she pressed against a scrape. "I wondered if you really believed my story or not. Thanks for sticking up for me anyway."

"So why were you trying to get in?"

He sighed. "Because I was worried about you. I'd looked everywhere and couldn't find you. Grace said you were probably fine, but when I realized Seamus was guarding the door, I thought they were doing something to you. I know you think that crossbow thing was nothing, but I don't. And when I couldn't find you, panic set in."

"What makes you think it was one of them?" She had the same suspicions, but she wanted to hear his reasoning.

"I don't know. Who else could it be? I don't trust them, and I care about you."

She didn't know how to respond to that. She knew the guardians cared about her safety, but she always felt like that was because she was the queen, not because of her, personally. But he seemed to be genuinely concerned about her.

Her chest tightened at the thought.

She liked that he cared about her.

But that made things infinitely more complicated.

CHAPTER 17

Grace knew it looked creepy that she was standing at the bottom of Isa's stairs, but she had to talk to Liam and find out what was going on. She didn't even bother to try to look busy. She just waited and tried not to make eye contact with the portrait of Isa's great-grandmother. It always felt like that picture followed her with its eyes.

After about thirty minutes, she got concerned that he might never come down, and if he did, Isa would be with him, and then it would look really bad. Though she could say she was on her way up to tell Isa something.

Footsteps sounded on the stairs. Just one set, she thought. Liam came around the corner, whistling. Though he moved rather slower than normal.

He met her eyes. "Waiting for me?"

She nodded and got right to the point. "Why did you get into a fight with Seamus?"

"Because he's a prick. I was worried Pierre had Isa in there and was going to kill her. But he didn't. Though that might be because I interrupted them."

Grace moved closer to Liam and dropped her voice. "So, you think the rumors are doing their job?"

"I do. Lots of people are worried about stuff, and I'm surprised more fights haven't broken out. People are tense."

He and Grace walked on down the hall. "Yet, no one seems to be flushing out," she said.

"Not yet. I wish it would hurry up. I hope they can't trace the rumors to us."

Grace had the same thought. If they ever did, she would have a lot of explaining to do.

They rounded the corner and found Jude and Drew chatting. The guardians stopped talking as Grace and Liam passed. Jude glared at Liam.

As soon as they were out of earshot, Grace grabbed Liam's arm. "You don't think they heard us, do you?" she hissed.

He shook his head. "Doubtful."

"From now on, we only talk about this in my room. I'll see you later."

She raced away from him, anxiety building in her chest. If they discovered she'd been involved with the rumors, she'd be in a world of trouble. Not just with Isa but with Pierre and the guardians. She wasn't sure what would happen to her. They might kick her out. They might kill her.

She was a fool for agreeing to this plan. She should've just kept her head down and let Liam do his thing.

Grace turned three more corners, slipped into the library, and collapsed into one of the chairs. The smell of books always comforted her. She knew that stress would eventually come and that she would be thrust into the thick of things—the prophecy said so—but she had hoped she'd be a little older when it happened.

Missy jumped onto her lap, and Grace stroked the soft fur. She hadn't even seen the fox following her. If she couldn't notice a white fox stalking her in the hallways, how would she notice someone sneaking around?

She was not built to be a spy.

CHAPTER 18

"How are you going to stall Jens today?" Aspen asked the next day. Sid had announced to Aspen before bed that he had no intentions of showing Jens the eggs. He tried to explain his reluctance to share with Jens, but he wasn't sure why. He just didn't trust the guy.

Aspen didn't agree with him, but she promised not to go behind his back and bring Jens to the babies. At least, he didn't have to worry about that. Or at least, he hoped he didn't.

"I don't know." Sid rubbed his eyes. He'd been up most of the night thinking, and it had done him no good. He needed to fly and clear his head. Worry was his constant companion these days, and he wanted things to go back to normal. And they might not for a very long time, even if—when—Liam came home safely.

Sid crept downstairs and out into the cool air. He drew in a deep breath and changed, his scales sparkling in the sunlight. He wasn't sure where he would go, just that he would fly until his mind settled.

He flew south into the canyonlands territory. There were no dragons there anymore though sometimes the river dragons flew through. Sid settled on the edge of the Grand Canyon and stared out into the vast space, one of his favorite places to bring Liam when he was younger.

He'd thought for sure he'd seen the worst of it when he watched the canyon, woodlands, arctic, and fire dragons essentially go extinct. He thought that had earned him a life of peace and quiet.

But here he was, twenty years later, potentially on the brink of war once again. And there would be a war. He could feel it in his bones. He just hoped that the war wouldn't involve him avenging his son's death. He wasn't sure he or Aspen could handle that.

Sid shook his head and spotted a pair of yellow wings in the distance, an underground-river dragon.

Something interesting had happened in the aftermath of Runa's death. Turned out Runa wasn't the only underground-river mix. Stella, Runa's mother, led Sid and Aspen to a cave in Arizona where the underground and river dragons had been interbreeding for years and had nearly enough to create a new race. The council had debated for the last five years whether to recognize them or not and still hadn't decided. Sid figured that, as a whole, they just didn't want to share the power. He'd chatted with Pearl about it from time to time, but she was never very forthcoming.

Runa had been the first of her kind to leave the cave because the sun did not blind her as it did the underground dragons. After Runa died, words of her heroism spread amongst the dragon kingdom. And so, the new mixed race of dragons knew it was safe to leave their caves. Most could only camouflage their bodies, not their wings, but a few could do their whole selves like the underground dragons. Baden was one of those and took to Liam when he was a small child, following him around like Runa used to do with the rest of them.

But Baden was an old man at heart and didn't have the light Runa did. Liam loved him though. And now, he was in danger too.

Sid let out a long breath, and smoke flew from his nostrils. How many of his loved ones would die before this was over?

Too many, that was for sure.

He stretched his neck high and spotted a speck of green approaching from a distance. What the...?

Jens landed hard next to him. *You can't hide from me, Your Majesty.*

CHAPTER 19

Isa brushed Grace's hand away from her dress and scowled. "Dragon's teeth! Be careful, would you?" She held her arm out and showed the angry red mark.

"I'm sorry. I don't know what happened." Grace's face flamed.

"You scratched me." Isa huffed away and sat down at her mirror.

Isa had been snappy with her all morning, and Grace couldn't do anything right. She let out Isa's braid and began with gentle, long strokes, and then she moved the brush under Isa's hair, at the base of her neck, and brought the brush back. It got stuck on a tangle, and Isa jerked away. She grabbed the brush out of Grace's hand and threw it across the room.

Grace took two deep breaths and sat on the chair next to Isa. She had to tread carefully. Isa had never treated her this way before, and Grace hoped it wasn't her fault. "What's going on?"

Isa looked at her, lips trembling. "I...I...heard some things, and I don't want to believe them."

Grace took Isa's hands in hers. Oh no. The rumors. She hadn't thought about what she would do if they got back to Isa. "What did you hear?"

"That Pierre wants to kill me. That I want to kill Pierre. That Liam is just trying to get close to me so he can kill me and make it look like an accident. That Drew, Jude, and Seamus were going to mutiny on Pierre. That Olga is going to poison me and...and..." Isa took three more deep breaths. "And that you are in love with Liam and jealous that he likes me, and so you started the rumors about people killing each other."

Damn that boy. Grace really would kill him. But first, she had to make good with Isa. She wondered where all the other rumors came from. Liam must've been sharing far more than they discussed.

"First of all, and let me address this off the bat, I am certainly not in love with Liam. Not even close. He has become a good friend. One like I've never had before except with you. But I assure you, I have no feelings for him. In fact, I've been rather encouraging of him pursuing you. If I am guilty of anything, then it's that. I promise you that I have not started any rumors." If Isa found out Grace was behind them, she'd be so angry.

"He likes me?" She clutched at a hand mirror on her desk, her jaw tense.

"A lot. Maybe even more than Jude, and goodness knows I've heard Jude go on about you."

Isa's fists clenched, and she exhaled.

"What about the other rumors? Do you think they are true?"

Grace hesitated. "Well, I don't think Olga is out to poison you though you know she doesn't like you."

Isa ground her teeth. "I know. I've tried to get the guardians to agree to a few more servants so her workload isn't so much, but they've refused."

Grace fetched the hairbrush again. "Can I continue to brush your hair?" Isa was talking to her, but Grace sensed she was still angry. A vein twitched in her neck.

Isa turned around, and Grace brushed softly, working through tangles as she came to them. "As for the rest of them. Well, only you know if you want to kill Pierre, and I don't follow enough of the guardian's drama to know if they are doing any of those things."

Isa nodded but didn't say anything. Finally, Grace finished and set the brush on the dressing table.

Isa wouldn't look Grace directly in the eye. "I can get ready for bed on my own tonight, and I can dress myself in the morning. I'll call for you when I'm ready."

Guilt settled in Grace's stomach. She had lied to Isa.

And Isa knew it.

GRACE STORMED down the castle halls, looking for Liam to give him a piece of her mind. Isa obviously thought Grace was behind the rumors. Sure, she started a few on her own, but it had been all Liam's fault. She never should've listened to him. If Isa never forgave her, then she just threw years of friendship away.

She found Liam in the billiards room with Drew and Jude.

They were laughing and joking like old friends. When did this happen?

No. He didn't get to be friends with them while Isa accused Grace of starting rumors. She didn't know when Isa would trust her again. Not anytime soon. That was for sure.

The guys didn't even notice her enter. She grabbed for Liam's pool stick just as he was about to hit the white ball, and it went wildly off target.

"Hey," he yelled at her. "What was that for?"

Jude smirked. "Looks like someone is in trouble…"

Liam looked down at her. "What's the matter?"

She set the pool stick on the table. "We need to talk."

He reached for the stick. "After I finish my game."

She got to it first and tossed it across the room. "No.

We're talking now." She turned to the others. "Sorry, boys, you'll have to beat him later."

She grabbed his hand and dragged him from the room but didn't stop there. She opened the door to the stairs to her room and pointed. He went down them and didn't look back. Once in her room, and after having it sealed with magic, she rounded on him.

"Isa found out it was me starting the rumors, and she's pissed. This is all your fault."

Liam smirked. "If she was still pissed, you wouldn't be down here with me. I'm sure you denied it, and she believed you."

Grace faltered. "I did deny it, and she didn't believe me. She asked me not to come back until she calls for me."

"It will pass. She probably has to mull things over. I'm sure you're fine, and once she thinks about it, she'll believe you. But it's good that things got back to her, don't you think?"

Grace crossed her arms and glared at him. She couldn't believe he was so blasé about this. Isa was her best friend, and Grace betrayed her.

Grace busied herself, straightening the things she had sitting on her dresser. Not that they needed straightening. "No, it's not. It was a dumb idea. We still don't know who is doing this, and all we've done is sown seeds of suspicion where they shouldn't be. I'm done with this, and I don't want to talk to you anymore."

He furrowed his brow. "Why not? We're friends."

"Because I value my friendship with Isa more. Get out."

She opened the door and pointed up the stairs. He gave her a strange look as he walked out, but Isa had never accused her of being disloyal, and she wasn't about to let some stranger change that.

CHAPTER 20

What are you doing here? I thought you couldn't be a dragon. Sid stared at Jens. This was what the babies would look like when they got older. Sid shook a little with Jens' anger and he put a shield up in his mind so he couldn't feel his emotions.

Turns out the queen's spell doesn't reach your borders. Jens paced back and forth in front of him. *I'm tired of being put off. I want to see the eggs, and I want to see them now.* His insistence bothered Sid a little.

A warm breeze blew around them, and Sid debated what to do. Finally, he decided to be honest with him. *I don't trust you. Not yet.*

Jens let out a jet of green flame. *Excuse me? Why not?*

Put yourself in my shoes. You show up on our doorstep with a dying dragon, and you expect us to send an army to Europe. We know that something is going on, but we hardly have enough proof to wage a war.

Jens shuffled his wings. *Your people saw what she was doing in Scotland. That's not enough proof?* He huffed, and two poofs of green smoke came out of his nose. *You'll have proof soon enough when she kills your son.*

Sid shuffled his wings. In a lot of ways, he knew Jens was right, but as long as Liam was alive, he wasn't about to risk anything. *I hope you're wrong. I need you to be wrong. My son isn't dead yet.*

I want the eggs. He stood tall, meeting Sid at eye level, his green eyes narrowed.

I cannot show them to you yet. Once we've taken care of the problem at hand, then we can discuss it again. Sid was not about to be moved on this.

Jens glowered at him and scratched at the red rock. *Discuss it? So even if I'm right, you won't give them to me? I should've known to never trust a royal dragon. You're all the same. I bet you have your people under a spell as well, and they don't even know it.*

Sid resisted the urge to roll his eyes. *I am a fair king, and my people love me. Ask any of them. Please understand that you have put me in a precarious position, and it is not just my choice what to do with those eggs. I answer to a council of dragons from all tribes. Once the issue with the queen is dealt with, we will discuss it with them and make a decision.*

That's not good enough. Forgive me, Your Majesty, but I think we're done. America is not as big as you think it is. I'll find the eggs myself. I'm sure there is someone who knows about them that is far more generous with words than you are.

Up until now, Jens had never been threatening. Maybe Sid's gut was right about Jens being fishy. Or maybe he just wanted the eggs. Either way, Sid didn't trust him.

Jens took off in a flurry of green wings and red dust. Sid sunk down to the ground. Just one more thing he had to worry about. He needed to warn Sequoia and Murdoch, but he didn't know how. If he flew out there, Jens would surely see where he went.

No, Sid would have to be far more discreet, which meant no visiting the babies for some time. He flew home, and as he approached the house, he heaved a sigh of relief. Pearl was still there.

He had time to head off the danger.

CHAPTER 21

Grace stayed in her room for most of the day, trying to calm her anger. Once she felt like she could be trusted not to lose it on anyone, she slipped out the door and made her way to the kitchens. She hoped Liam wouldn't be there, but that's where her friends were, so she went anyway.

Isa slipped out of the kitchens' door and marched down the hall away from her. Grace doubted Isa even saw her. What in the queen's name was Isa doing down here?

Grace stood there for a moment, unsure of what to do. Olga would not take kindly to Isa in the kitchens.

Grace waited for Isa to turn the corner then steeled herself before she went through the door, and she was glad she had. Olga stood at the counter, barking orders. Fruit and potatoes were flying across the room as well as a few utensils. Grace ducked and missed being struck in the head by a spoon.

Olga stopped her rant. "You." She pointed a finger at Grace.

"What about me?" Grace mocked innocence, but she had a pretty good idea what this was about. Somehow, Isa's visit to the kitchens was her fault.

"You told Isa I didn't like her."

"That's not a secret."

Olga pounded on the counter. "But she never thought much about that until you said something to her. Now she wants to come down here and help me in the kitchens for lunch every day. Do you have any idea how much work that will be? The kitchens will have to be spotless, and I will have to think carefully about what kind of jobs I give her. It will be so much harder than just making lunch myself."

Grace let out a breath. "I'm sorry. I could convince her to not come and help."

"No. You stay out of this. You've done enough damage as it is. For now, you are not welcome here. Leave." Olga grimaced at her.

Grace tried to ignore the sting as she left, but her chest felt heavy. This whole thing with Liam was spiraling out of control, and if she wasn't careful, she'd end up with no friends at all.

Marissa barged into the kitchen and flung herself down

in a chair. "Isa wants you to attend to her. Apparently, I'm not good enough."

A weight lifted off of Grace's chest, and she left the kitchens. She contemplated her fate as she walked down the hall. At least Isa didn't hate her anymore, and Olga would get over it. Isa would eventually tire of helping Olga, or Olga would learn to relax around Isa. This might not be a bad thing, really.

She turned the corner and plowed into Jude. He glared down at her.

"Thanks a lot," he said.

"For what?" Now, what had she done?

"Don't play dumb. You know." He brushed past her and stormed down the hall.

Great. It was *I hate Grace day.*

She let out a sigh. She'd had some pretty bad days, but aside from the day her father died, this one might be the worst.

CHAPTER 22

Sid walked into the kitchen and found Aspen, Pearl, and Jens chatting at the kitchen table. Sid was surprised to see him there. He thought Jens had gone searching for the eggs on his own, but there he was, chatting up the two most important women in Sid's life. He wasn't sure how he'd beat him home.

He thought about kicking Jens out, but he wasn't ready to do that. He wanted to keep Jens close. Especially after the threat he'd made. As long as Jens was here, he wasn't anywhere near those babies.

Aspen jumped up and gave Sid a kiss on the cheek. "Val wants to meet us all at the Purple Dragon."

"Why?"

"Ella wants updates."

There were none, but he wanted to get away from Jens.

Sid gave a stiff nod and flashed Jens a grin that he didn't mean. "We will see you later."

Jens glowered at him. "I like the Purple Dragon. Perhaps I can join you."

Sid gritted his teeth. He needed time away from that man. "Pearl, you should come too."

"I really should be getting back." She yawned and rubbed her eyes.

"No, I insist. You come with us. Ella hasn't seen you in ages."

Pearl gave him a strange look, and he raised his eyebrows at her. She nodded. "Okay. But just for a little bit."

They piled into Aspen's Jeep, and Aspen kept Jens talking about Europe. Right before they left, Sid told her about the threat Jens made, so at least, she wouldn't be spilling any more beans.

They found everyone at the Purple Dragon, sitting around a large table. Ella stood next to Rowan, waving her arms in the air and spinning a tale, Sid was sure. He poked her in the ribs, and she squealed and spun on him.

"Sid, I'm too old for that. I'm liable to fall down and break a hip." She gave him a smile.

"Ella, you're only fifty-eight. Not that old."

"Shhh. Most people don't know that. I tell everyone I'm forty."

He grinned at her. "Well, I expect they believe it. Where's Freddie?"

"At home, working. He's supposed to be retired, but last week, the government came to him and asked him to do some programming thing. He was a little too excited about the project, so I might as well put in some hours here."

They settled around the table, and a server brought Sid a latte. Pearl sat next to him, and Jens sat on the other side of the table, thank goodness. When Jens was distracted by Ella, Sid leaned over and whispered in Pearl's ear.

"Jens is on the warpath. He wants the green and purple eggs. Feels like he's owed them since they are European dragons. He doesn't know we've hatched them."

Pearl took a sip of her drink and giggled like he'd said something funny.

"Understand. I'll be careful."

"Warn Sequoia and Murdoch as well."

Pearl nodded.

Sid knew this wasn't over, not by a long shot, but at least he could breathe a little easier.

For now.

CHAPTER 23

Grace spent a lot of time in the library over the next few days. Olga was still screaming about her kitchens, and from what Benjamin told her, Isa in the kitchens was a disaster. She didn't know how to do anything and just basically made a mess.

Isa, on the other hand, loved it. She was crowing to Grace just this morning that she learned how to toast bread. The kitchens were becoming the highlight of her day. She was making friends with servants she'd never really spoken to.

Jude still wasn't talking to Grace, and she had no idea why, but she guessed it was because of the rumors.

A boot kicked her chair, and she looked up from her book, the light from the sun streaming in through the window blinding her momentarily. She glowered when her vision cleared.

"Please go away." At least she could control one relationship in her life.

Liam set a plate with a steaming slice of cherry pie in front of her and sat down.

"How did you get Olga to make that?" She put a bookmark in her place and picked up the pie. She wasn't about to turn the dessert down, and he knew that too.

"I didn't. Well, I sort of did. I told Isa it was my favorite, and she dragged me down to the kitchens and demanded to be taught how to make it. I've never seen Olga turn that many shades of red. Anyway, I hung around after Isa left and helped Olga clean up. I told her this was for me, not you, or she would've never let it go. I'm not sure she's going to let you back into the kitchens anytime soon."

"Thank you."

He met her eyes. "I do owe you an apology. I'm sorry this turned out to be a mess. I know you took the brunt of the fallout. We'll find another way if you still want to work with me."

Grace sighed. "Isa's life is at stake, and far more rumors were started than the ones you and I did. Now, I'm wondering if there is some truth to any of them."

Liam frowned. "Like what?"

"Jude and a few others mutinying. Olga poisoning Isa. Pierre wanting to kill her." Grace waved her fork around as she talked. The pie was really good. Either Isa was a better cook than Grace thought, or Olga did all the work.

Liam leaned back. "The last one is my fault, but the others I hadn't heard. Let me do some investigating, and I'll let you know what I find out."

Grace had hoped Liam had started all the rumors, but he hadn't. That meant there might be some truth to the others. Liam showing up seemed to start everything, so maybe they were threatened by his presence.

"We'll need another plan," Liam finally said.

"That, we will." She was tired of this already, but they did have to keep Isa safe.

"Let me see what I can find out about these other rumors, and then I'll meet you in your room later."

That rumor mill—the one about her and Liam—wouldn't die for a long time if she kept bringing him to her room, but as long as Isa didn't believe it, she didn't care.

She needed to keep Isa safe, and Liam was her best shot.

CHAPTER 24

*L*ater that afternoon, Aspen rubbed the back of Sid's neck. "Why don't we go flying for a bit? I haven't been in ages, and that always clears your mind."

He nodded and stood, stretching his arms above his head.

"I think you're right. Flying will clear my head."

They went outside into the warm afternoon air, and he inhaled the smell of pine and grass. Summer was on its way. He was just about to change when an eagle landed in front of him. His stomach sank. It was never good when they came to him unbidden.

Your Majesty, a few river dragons have been killed.

His insides went cold.

"By who?"

A small band of green dragons.

Aspen gripped his hand. "Do you know where they are now?"

No, they disappeared after that. We have no idea where they went. We have not seen them since.

"Thank you for that. Will you gather the council and let them know we need to talk. I'll meet them in the chambers in an hour."

They were going to call for war. He knew that now, but he still feared for Liam's life. But the green dragons had come onto his territory and attacked his people. He couldn't ignore this anymore. The eagle flew off into the distance.

"I still need to clear my head," he said.

"Sid, we need to talk about this."

"We'll talk about it in the air."

He changed, and Aspen clambered onto his back.

He took off. He could fly north or west, but he always loved the park with its steaming hot pools and mountains. It was early morning, and not many people were around. He flew over a stand of pines, inhaling their scent. He did not want to think about this new development. He wondered if Jens could possibly be involved but then dismissed the idea. This had to be the work of that queen. What was she doing?

Sid, what are we going to do?

I don't know that we have any choice. The council will want to declare war. I won't let them. Not yet.

Why? They attacked us.

A small band of them did. We have no idea who they are or why they are here. They might not even be associated with the queen.

I want Liam back safe and sound as well, but I think you might be in denial.

Sid flew over a prairie and followed a group of stampeding buffalo. They were probably the most dangerous animals in the park, killing more people than bears or dragons, but Sid loved to watch the way they moved as one, racing across the grass. This was a rare sight. Normally, they moved slowly.

Aspen grew quiet, and Sid knew she was watching them too.

They came out of the field and into the canyon where cliffs rose high, and the river raged below. He knew she was right, but he couldn't count Liam out just yet.

I won't take any action that will risk Liam's life.

Of course you wouldn't, but if he were to return today and you decided to send an army, what's the fastest you could have them there?

It took time to gather an army and train them for what they would be facing.

A week, minimum, maybe longer. A month would have us better prepared.

Get a few dragons to patrol the immediate area so that we can protect those on our own land. Then, prepare for war to appease the council, but stall. Gather the dragons together and begin training. Drag it out for a month or two. It will look like you are doing something, but at the same time, we'll be giving Liam time to escape.

Aspen, you are a genius.

She patted his neck. *I know. Whatever would you do without me?*

I'd be a mess. But you already knew that. Okay, then it's decided. We'll prepare but won't go over there until Liam is back with us.

Sid turned and flew toward the cavern, now eager to meet with the council and let them know his decision.

CHAPTER 25

Isa had hoped Liam would have pursued her a little more after his fight with Seamus, but he seemed to withdraw, and she didn't know why. He was friendly with her, and they did have a ball making pie, but he kept his distance emotionally.

Each night, she'd contemplated having Grace send him to her room, but each night, she chickened out. If he didn't want her like that, she didn't know if she would be able to handle the rejection.

Tonight was no different. She lay in bed for a long time, remembering all the lines on his abdomen and the way his chest rose and fell as she doctored it. A knock sounded, and she leapt out of bed. The curtains were closed, so the only source of light was the glow of the fire. It was enough.

Missy growled as Isa raced for the door, hoping that it

was Liam. She cracked the door open, and disappointment flooded her chest.

"Jude. What are you doing here?"

He rushed past her. "I have to talk to you."

That was rude. He wasn't usually so pushy. She shut the door behind her.

He sat on one side of the couch and she on the other. "I thought I made it clear that I didn't want you in my room anymore."

"I know. But I have to tell you something, and I'm afraid you won't believe me." He ran a hand through his hair and frowned.

"Why?"

"Because it's about Liam."

She crossed her arms. "If you're here to tell me that he wants to hurt me or kill me, then leave."

He scooted closer. "That's not it. I swear. But he is deceiving you."

She chuckled. "Oh, you mean about the Seamus fight. I knew that wasn't self-defense, but he did tell me why he was trying to get into the room." She let out a breath of relief. Maybe she and Jude could be friends. She liked him better than most of the other guardians, even if he was a little too loyal to Pierre.

Jude faltered. "Um, no, that's not what I'm talking about. But why did he want in?"

She narrowed her eyes at him. "That is none of your business. If that's not what you came to tell me, then out with it."

Jude hesitated for a moment. "He's here to make you fall in love with him. He wants to be king."

Dragon's teeth! Isa's heart stopped for a moment. "How do you know this?"

"Because he told me."

"Why would he tell you?" She didn't know what to think. If that were true, then he'd been lying to her.

"I was goading him. I don't think he meant to say it." Jude stared at her with pleading eyes.

Isa stood. "Thank you for that information. You may leave now."

"Do you believe me?" he asked with earnest.

"I don't know. But you've certainly given me something to think about."

He reached out and squeezed her hand and then left. She shut the door behind him.

She didn't know if she could trust Liam, and she didn't know if she could trust Jude. If he was telling the truth, that meant Liam came here to marry her. Her insides buzzed with anxiety and excitement. Though she wondered if that was something she really wanted.

Maybe.

But not if he was here under false pretenses.

CHAPTER 26

Sid spent very little time in King's cave. It was used only for council meetings and special occasions. He hadn't planned on being back here so soon after the last time.

The council stared at Sid, the room silent. This was the first time dragons had been attacked on his land since the war. This changed everything.

He knew what the council would say, and he wasn't ready for it.

Well then, we know what to do now. We have to attack even though Liam is still there, Kairi said. Her eyes bore sympathy, but she never was very caring. She always saw the big picture but rarely understood the small ones.

"We need time to prepare an army, and we will but right now, we need to protect our own borders," Sid said.

The best way to do that is to attack. You're stalling because you are thinking like a father, not a king. All you want to do is protect Liam. If she's sending dragons over here, he's not going to survive much longer anyway.

Sid was so tired of people assuming Liam was as good as dead. Baden said he was still alive, and until Sid heard otherwise, he wasn't taking any chances.

"You don't know that." Sid grasped Aspen's hand. She'd been staying quiet, but he was afraid she agreed with them.

The longer we wait, the more might she'll have. We have to attack now. Kairi puffed up her chest.

Sid looked at all of them, glad there were no canyon or arctic dragons. If there were, they'd be at war right now.

Not for the first time, Sid thought the council was too large. Too many voices. Sure, they were there to advise him, but they also bore a great deal of influence. He appreciated their guidance, but he hated the fact that he had to run all his major decisions by them.

Kairi's right, Pearl said. *You know I love Liam, and I wouldn't do anything to put him in harm's way, but we cannot risk her trying to defeat us here. We're still recovering from our last war. We need to be proactive.*

Sid glanced around at the other dragons murmuring their agreement. Was he the only one who thought sending an army was a bad idea? He thought about what he would do if Liam wasn't there now.

He'd send an army. Of course, he would. He couldn't let her come over and kill his own people.

But Liam *was* there. He couldn't separate those ideas. There had to be a way to appease both.

He needed time to think, but nobody wanted to give him any more. He and Aspen had talked about what they should do, but he wanted to stall them.

He glanced around his council. *I've heard your words. I will consider them all.*

Kairi snorted, blue smoke coming out of her nostrils. *Sid, the time for consideration is over. You need to act.*

"We cannot send an army yet," Sid said. The council encircled him, and he scowled at each of them. He had no idea why everyone was agreeing with Kairi. He had to protect Liam.

"Why not?" asked Xanthous. "I thought the only reason we didn't before was because we were not sure what we were facing. My people were the first ones killed. I'm with Kairi."

Sid clenched his fists. He wanted to turn into a dragon, but he'd brought Aspen with him, and he never spoke to the council in his dragon form if she was around, out of respect for her.

"We still don't know what we are facing."

"Yes, we do. She killed Felix and the delegation of dragons sent to fetch your irresponsible son. Then, she sent warriors over here."

Rage filled Sid's head, but he quickly quashed it. He needed to keep his cool.

"Now, wait just a minute…" Aspen began, but Sid

gripped her hand hard. She stopped talking and glared at him.

Sid cleared his throat. "Yes, it's true she killed them. But now she has Liam held captive, and if we send in an army, we risk her killing him and Baden as well."

That is a risk we have to take. We cannot allow her to so openly kill our dragons. Not only that, but we know for sure that she has enslaved and tortured her own people. She must be stopped. Kairi's voice filled Sid's head.

"I don't disagree with you, but I will not risk my son's life. We can start mobilizing, but we need more information before attacking."

The council went quiet for a moment. From the way Kairi cocked her head, he was certain they were talking but intentionally leaving him out. He didn't even know why he still had to listen to his council. He was king, wasn't he?

Pearl stared at him with worried eyes. He hoped she was at least sticking up for him.

"We can't let them walk all over us," Aspen hissed in his ear. He was surprised she was on his side. During their flight, she'd made it seem like she knew they'd have to attack.

"It's a delicate balance. Let's see what they have to say. But we won't let them put Liam in more danger."

Aspen crossed her arms and huffed. Let her be angry. Better her than the council.

After what seemed like forever, Xanthous met his eyes once again. "We have come to a decision."

"You mean your advice, right? Am I not king? Isn't the decision mine?" He trod carefully, but he didn't want them to forget who he was.

"If you want the support of your people, you will listen to us."

Sid took a deep breath and refrained from telling them where they could shove that support.

"What is your recommendation?"

Xanthous sent a puff of yellow smoke into the air. "You have three weeks to extract your son. Then, an army led by the sea dragons will attack. This is not up for negotiation."

"Three weeks is not long enough. Give me six, at least."

Kairi pushed Xanthous out of the way. *I wanted one week. You have your sister to thank for the additional two weeks. If you do not like our terms, then I will take my dragons, and we will attack tomorrow. We know how to fight. We will not lose. Tell me your answer—tomorrow or three weeks?*

Trapped, once again. And now he had few choices. "Fine, three weeks."

"What? Sid? No." Aspen tugged on his arm.

Kairi took off down the hall. No one else said a word.

He leaned down and whispered to Aspen. "If we want their support, we have to oblige. Let's just trust Baden can work his own magic in three weeks."

CHAPTER 27

A knock jarred Grace out of a very deep sleep, and she threw on a robe, debating whether to get the sword out of her drawer.

"Who is it?" she called.

"Liam."

She let out a breath of relief. She'd expected him earlier, and when he didn't show, she fell asleep. She released all the magic on the door and opened it. Liam shoved past her and collapsed onto her tiny bed. His eyes were bloodshot, and his hair was messed up. She closed the door and locked it with magic again.

"You okay?" she asked.

"No. I couldn't sleep. I'm scared for Isa. For you. For me. We have to figure out what to do. I can't stop thinking about how that crossbow almost got her. If I hadn't been there, she'd be dead."

Grace tried not to think about that. Isa never told her about it, which meant that Isa wasn't taking it seriously. "We tried something, and it didn't work."

"Maybe not, but it did tell us that treachery runs deep in this castle. I know what I'm going to do to help Isa, and I had a thought for you as well, but I'm afraid you won't like it."

He sat up, and she studied him. His face betrayed his fear. She wondered what he was planning on doing to help Isa, but she was more curious about what he wanted from her.

"Probably not, but out with it anyway."

"Can you use magic to figure it out?"

Dragon's teeth, she couldn't use magic.

But why not? Surely a magic spell could reveal who was behind this all, and it didn't mean they would know she was the one using the magic. A spell would make their jobs so much easier. Why didn't she think of that before?

"That's a brilliant idea, actually, but I have no idea how. I'll have to do some research, and I might need some help."

He leapt up and pulled her into a hug. He smelled woodsy. "Thank you. I was so worried you would be upset that I wanted you to use your gifts."

"It's smart, really. No guesswork if I get the spell right."

He let out a sigh. "Maybe I'll be able to sleep now."

She gave him a small grin. "I hope so."

She let him out and locked the door behind her. Maybe he'd sleep, but she wouldn't. She'd spend the rest of the night thinking of the possibilities.

CHAPTER 28

After the war with the white witch, the council had requested more power. They argued that having one dragon in charge would lead to more power plays from those vying for power, and it opened up the possibility for a potentially unstable dictator.

At the time, a more powerful council seemed like a good idea. If they disagreed with the king, they could override him, but only if their vote was unanimous. Sid was surprised Pearl had taken their side, but he didn't have time to think about that right now.

Now, he had to form his own plan to bring home Liam alive. He had three weeks.

That wasn't enough, but drastic times called for drastic measures.

He heaved his bag onto the table at the Purple Dragon,

and Ella approached him with a drink in hand. He looked around but didn't spot Jens anywhere. Sid had told him to meet him here.

"Thanks," he said.

"Any word on Liam?"

"No, not yet, but we're hopeful." Sid ignored the anxiety in his throat. He had hoped to have heard from Baden by now.

Ella patted his shoulder. "Damon really misses him."

"We do too." He squeezed his eyes shut for a moment and pushed away the pain.

"Whatcha got there?" She asked.

"Leverage."

Ella narrowed her eyes. "What?"

"Don't worry about it. I'm just hoping it works to get me more help."

"If you need anything, let me know." Ella eyed the bag.

"I will."

The door opened, and Jens entered, looking wary, and took the seat across from Sid.

"You should get something to drink," Sid said.

"No, I'm good, thank you. What is it you wanted to discuss?"

"I need to figure out how to extract Liam. Do you have any idea why the queen might not have killed him yet?"

Jens raised his eyebrows. "I've never heard of her taking one alive before. Perhaps she found him attractive and has decided to play with him first."

Sid clenched his fists under the table. He would not let Jens get to him.

"In any case, we would like your expertise on how to get him back."

Jens crossed his arms and smirked. "And why would I do that? You have refused to help me in any way."

"We have sent dragons, and my son was captured. All because we have tried to help you."

"And yet, you hold our children hostage."

Sid rolled his eyes. "That is not what we are doing, but as a gesture of goodwill..." Sid pushed the bag toward Jens. "Four eggs, two green and two purple. Once the queen is defeated, we will give you the remaining eggs that we have." Sid was very careful with his language. He would give him the eggs but not the children.

Jens opened the bag, and his eyes lit up.

"Now, we will talk. I will tell you everything you need to know about this queen. I don't think we can save your son, but I will help you."

Sid heaved a sigh of relief. He was now a little more hopeful that he would be able to get Liam back before the sea dragons attacked.

CHAPTER 29

The next morning, Isa had a plan. She searched everywhere for Liam before she found him in the conservatory, sitting in the sun. This room was always a little too humid for her, but it had several tropical plants and pretty flowers.

He grinned when she walked in. "I miss the warmth of the sun." He closed his eyes and faced up.

"Is it true?" she asked, not bothering to sit down. She was already sweating through her dress, but she did enjoy the scent of jasmine that permeated the room.

His eyes flashed open, and he stared at her. "Is what true?" He wiped his hands on his pants.

"Why are you here, Liam? And don't lie to me."

He studied her for a moment, and she wondered what he was about to say.

"Who told you? Jude?"

"So it's true? How could you do this to me?"

"Isa, sit down please, and I'll explain everything. Including why I had to deceive you. I didn't lie completely. I just didn't tell you the whole truth."

She didn't sit. She was too angry. He'd really deceived her. She'd thought Jude was lying to her.

"First of all, I should start with who I am." He stared up at her, but his voice was soft.

"You're not Liam?" Dragon's teeth! Was *everything* he told her a lie?

"No, my name is really Liam, but I'm not just some random dragon from America."

She paced in front of him, the smell of the flowering trees distracting her. "Fine, who are you?"

"My father is the king of America. Up until we discovered you, we thought he was king of the whole world."

She narrowed her eyes at him. He was a prince in an enemy land. She thought for a moment about what he was saying. "So you want my kingdom too?"

"No," he said a little too quickly.

"But Jude told me you want to be king."

He let out a breath. "I do. But that's because I want you, not because I want your kingdom. Look, the thought didn't even occur to me until after I was here."

"Then, why did you come?"

"To warn you. That was the truth. But my dad didn't want me to go, so I came on my own. I couldn't let my people come over here and attack without even knowing if the rebels were telling the truth. But after I arrived, and I met you, I...I..." He approached her and gripped her hands in his.

She reveled in the way they felt in hers as he stared deep into her eyes. The electricity coursing between them was undeniable.

She had no idea what was happening, and she didn't trust him, but she wanted him.

"I fell in love with you, Isa. So hard, I didn't even know what happened."

Isa felt her knees go weak.

Liam *loved* her.

To Be Continued . . .

Dear Reader,

Awww, Squee!!! I love romance and Liam and Isa. Sigh. Though Liam is going to be in a world of trouble when Isa realizes he's been less than honest with her.

I hope you've enjoyed The Dragon Kings so far. This is one of my favorite stories and I can't seem to stop writing in this world. Continue the story here.

Also, if you loved this book or even if you hated it, please leave a review.

Love you guys! Thanks for taking this journey with me.

XOXO

PS Stay in touch!

PS Want to stay in touch?

We're going to spend the rest of the year having one big party to celebrate all my upcoming releases. Come join us: Kimberly Loth Release Party

Be the first to know about all my upcoming releases, events, and giveaways by becoming a FB fan! Or even better (and more reliable)join my newsletter :).

If you want to see adorable pictures of my family, puppy and my travels, follow me on Instagram.

Want More from Kimberly Loth?

Kimberly Loth has published several series. Read on for sneak peaks from each one.

- The Dragon Kings: Obsidian
Circus of the Dead Book 1
The Thorn Chronicles: Midnight Angel
Stella and Sol: God of the Sun
Sons of the Sand: The Smoking Lamp

-

"May I see your tattoo?" Sid asked, startling Aspen.

"My what?"

"Your tattoo, the one on your ankle."

"Oh, sure." Until tonight, she'd been super careful about keeping the tat covered. Sid was the first person to see it, and she wanted to show it off a bit.

He slid onto the floor and pulled her foot into his lap.

Shivers ran up her spine. He slowly traced the words with his finger and whispered under his breath.

Aspen's first instinct was to pull her foot away, but she enjoyed it as much as it tortured her. She bit her lip and waited for him let go. Instead, he adjusted so that he could see her, but he continued to hold her foot in his lap.

"When did you get this?" he asked.

"Um, about a month ago. It's not really a tattoo."

He raised his eyebrows.

"It's gonna sound crazy, but it's a dragon marking. It appeared when I touched that black dragon."

He let go of her foot, moved onto the couch, and pressed the play button on the remote.

About halfway through the movie, her eyes refused to stay open. After fighting with them for fifteen minutes, she gave in, allowed them to close, and settled her head into a soft warm pillow.

Ella shook her awake. "Aspen," she whispered. "We need to go."

"No," Aspen said and closed her eyes.

Ella shook Aspen again. "Come on, we've got to leave. You can't stay here."

"Yes, she can," Aspen's pillow said.

"I was trying not to wake you up, Sid," Ella said. "I'm sorry."

"No worries." He brushed hair out of Aspen's face.

Aspen shot up, embarrassed. She stumbled around the couch looking for her boots. Ella handed them to her.

"Here ya go."

"Thanks," Aspen mumbled.

Aspen fumed. His lap was not where her head should have been.

Download now: https://www.kimberlyloth.com/products/obsidian

Want the whole box set?

https://www.kimberlyloth.com/products/copy-of-dragon-kings-book-bundle

"A price for a night off would be a kiss. That's all."

"A kiss."

I've fiercely protected my heart, and I want it to be special. I'm not kissing anyone until I know he's worth it. Samuel is definitely not worth it.

He chuckles. "What's the matter? You don't want to give me your first kiss? I underestimated your need to get out of here."

"How did you know?"

He closes the distance and runs a finger along my jaw.

"Obeah man. I know more than you think?"

"Then you know what a kiss means for me."

"Of course. If I didn't, I wouldn't have asked you for it. It has to mean something."

A night in New Orleans meant freedom.

He drops his lips and whispers in my ear. "Surely you can see the loophole. Get off the island, ditch Juliette, and hop on a plane. What are you waiting for?"

I jerk away. "Why would you…"

His eyes are deadly serious as he puts a finger to his lips. A sign to keep quiet.

He's helping me.

Download now:

Circus of the Dead Book One

Want the whole box set?

Circus of the Dead Book Bundle

I cleared my throat. Dwayne smiled a wide toothy smile and my father glowered like I'd done something wrong. Which, of course I had, but it would be worth the punishment if I got the answers I needed.

"Could someone please explain?" There. I asked the question. So out of character for me and yet satisfying in a strange way, like the way I felt when a teacher praised me for a good job. I bit my bottom lip and tasted butterscotch, which was weird because the cake we had, contained nothing of the sort. While I knew asking questions was not an act of disobedience, I also recognized the power in the asking. As if I was taking control, even if that control was small. I took a sip of my water. Father hesitated for a moment and then frowned. He looked up and saw my mother standing in the kitchen, her eyes boring into his. He didn't look away from her when he answered me.

"You'll be marrying Dwayne."

Download now: Midnight Angel

Want the whole box set? The Thorn Chronicles Book Bundle

The prince entered and sauntered up the path to the thrones. He didn't seem awed or nervous of my guards. A little too cocky for my taste.

He wore white billowy shirts that opened at the neck with a necklace that rested on the hollow of their neckline. It was a simple necklace, with no jewels.

Just before he reached the stairs to the thrones, he stopped and bowed. The prince rose from his bow and looked at my father.

"I am High Prince Leo, the fifth son of High King Ajax of Stella. I have come to see if it would be possible to join our kingdoms."

His voice was rich and lilting. He had a devastating smile, rich caramel skin, and dark piercing eyes.

Father glared down at him. That was a bold statement for a prince in foreign territory. "How exactly would we join our kingdoms?"

His eyes met mine. "Through marriage of course. I have no kingdom of my own. Marriage would create a partnership that I think we have both longed for."

I always knew I would have to marry a prince.

Never had I imagined a barbarian prince would seek my hand.

Download now: God of the Sun

Want the whole box set? Stella and Sol Book Bundle

I wrapped a towel around my hair and stomped out to my closet. A light breeze blew across my back. That was odd. I spun around and froze.

Standing in front of me was the most gorgeous man I'd ever seen. And I'd seen a lot. The man in front of me was exotic. His shaggy black hair fell into his dark eyes with lashes even Nora would envy. A five o'clock shadow covered his jaw. He looked like a rock god.

My mouth dropped open. Then I remembered I was standing there in nothing but a bra and underwear. I ripped the towel off my head and attempted to cover myself.

"I'm not wearing any clothes," I said stupidly.

He grinned, showing adorable dimples. Then he tugged at the hem of his linen shirt and pulled it over his head, holding it out for me.

Download now: The Smoking Lamp

Want the whole box set? Sons of the Sand Book Bundle

ALSO BY KIMBERLY LOTH

All Books can be found at www.kimberlyloth.com

The Dragon Kings (Young Adult Paranormal)

Obsidian

Aspen

Valentine

Skye

The Kings

The Dragon Kings Books 6-30

Circus of the Dead (Young Adult Romantic Thriller)

Circus of the Dead Book 1

Circus of the Dead Book 2

Circus of the Dead Book 3

Circus of the Dead Book 4

Circus of the Dead Chronicles Books 1-10

The Thorn Chronicles (Young Adult Paranormal)

-

Midnight Angel

Destroyer Angel

Fallen Angel

Guardian Angel

-

Stella and Sol (Young Adult Fantasy)

God of the Sun

Prince of the Moon

King of the Stars

Queen of the Dawn

-

Sons of the Sand (Young Adult Paranormal)

The Smoking Lamp

The Blazing Glass

The Glowing Sands

The Exploding Sky

ABOUT THE AUTHOR

Kimberly Loth has lived all over the world. From the isolated woods of the Ozarks to exotic city of Cairo. She currently resides in the beautiful Sugar Creek in southern Missouri, with her husband and her adorable dog Maisy.

She's been writing for twelve years and is the author of the Amazon bestselling series The Dragon Kings. In her free time she volunteers at church, reads, and travels as often as possible.

She loves talking to school groups and book clubs. For more information about having her come speak at your school or event contact her at kimberlylothteam@gmail.com.

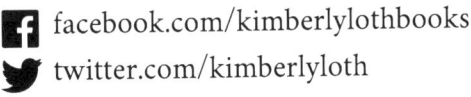

facebook.com/kimberlylothbooks
twitter.com/kimberlyloth

Made in the USA
Columbia, SC
07 June 2024

36809441R00347